The Wraiths Of Raglan Wood

The Wraiths Of Raglan Wood

W. B. Baker

Copyright © 2010 by W. B. Baker.

Library of Congress Control Number: 2010905408
ISBN: Hardcover   978-1-4500-7751-4
        Softcover   978-1-4500-7750-7
        Ebook   978-1-4500-7752-1

All rights reserved. No part of this book may be reproduced or transmitted in any form or by any means, electronic or mechanical, including photocopying, recording, or by any information storage and retrieval system, without permission in writing from the copyright owner.

This is a work of fiction. Names, characters, places and incidents either are the product of the author's imagination or are used fictitiously, and any resemblance to any actual persons, living or dead, events, or locales is entirely coincidental.

Wolfhounds incorporated in cover art were provided courtesy of Kevin Peuhkurinen at Big Sky Photography (www.bigskyphotography.ca). Irish Wolfhounds courtesy of Arahu Irish Wolfhound (www.arahu-iw.com).

This book was printed in the United States of America.

To order additional copies of this book, contact:
Xlibris Corporation
1-888-795-4274
www.Xlibris.com
Orders@Xlibris.com

BY THE SAME AUTHOR

The Lion and The Falcon
Random House/Xlibris
Philadelphia, PA; USA
2009

The Ravenous
Random House/Xlibris
Philadelphia, PA; USA
2007

Ordeal Of The Dragon
Random House/Xlibris
Philadelphia, PA; USA.
2006

Vault Of The Griffin
Random House/Xlibris
Philadelphia, PA; USA.
2004

The Orphans of Carmarthen
Random House/Xlibris
Philadelphia, PA; USA.
2001

A Solitary Frost
Random House/Xlibris
Philadelphia, PA; USA.
2000

A Solitary Frost
New Millennium Publishers
(First Edition)
London, England; UK.
1998

The Director's Handbook
A Survival Guide for the Theatre Director
(Private Printing)
Kansas City, Missouri; USA
1995

Celtic Mythological Influences on American Theatre 1750-1875
(Chwedioniaeth Geltaidd Dylanwad Ar Chwaraedy Americanaidd)
University Press of America
London; New York.
1994

About The Author

William Baker **(PgD, PhD, DLitt, ThD, DPhil)** conducted his graduate studies at **The University of Hawaii** at Manoa in Honolulu and at **Coleg Y Brifysgol Caerdydd/University Of Wales** (United Kingdom). A Rotary Foundation International Graduate Fellow, he later studied at the prestigious **Royal Academy of Dramatic Art** in London, and holds earned Doctorates in Theatre History **(PhD)**, a Doctor of Letters **(DLitt)**, a Doctorate in Theology **(ThD)**, and a Doctorate of Philosophy in Comparative Religions **(DPhil)**.

Stage and film credits include performances in England, France, and Wales; with affiliations featuring **BBC Radio Wales**, **The National Theatre of Wales**, **The International Festival of University Theatre**, along with numerous appearances on **ABC**, the **BBC**, **CBS**, **NBC**, **20th Century FOX**, and films produced by **Miramax Pictures**, **Orion Films**, and **Universal Pictures**.

Previously a university professor and Departmental Chairman, Dr. Baker's publications include: **Celtic Mythological Influences on American Theatre** (London/New York), **The Director's Handbook**, **A Solitary Frost** (London), **A Solitary Frost** (Second Edition/Philadelphia), **The Orphans Of Carmarthen**, **Vault Of The Griffin**, **Ordeal Of The Dragon** (Philadelphia), **The Ravenous**, and **The Lion and The Falcon**. His poetry, texts, and novels are currently available from bookstores around the world and at Amazon.co.uk, Biblio (United Kingdom), from Books.MusicaBona.Cz (Ceske Republice), Bundesministerium fur Wirtschaft und Arbeit, (DE) Buch,de: die ganze medienwelt (Germany), Kinokuniya BookWeb (Japan), as well as throughout the United States, Australia, Canada, India, and South Africa. Many of his publications are available from the prestigious Foyles of London, Blackwells Bookshop of Oxford, Waterstones, The Lawyer Book Store, and History Bookshop.com.

William Baker's extensive academic and professional biography is catalogued in **The Cambridge Blue Book**, **The Worldwide Honours List**, **Who's Who in the World** (Marquis), and **Contemporary Authors** (Thomson Gale). The author has been awarded numerous honours and citations, including: **The International Peace Prize**

(United Cultural Convention), **Top 100 Writers** (Author Laureate), **Man Of The Year** (USA), **Men of Achievement** (Cambridge), **Outstanding Intellectuals of the 21st Century** (UK), **Great Minds of the Twenty-First Century** (ABI), **The Royal Edition of The Dictionary of International Biography** (Melrose Press), and an Investiture of Knighthood from **The International Order of St. George (KtOBE).**

The author has been nominated for such prestigious awards as **The American Medal of Honour, The International Medal Of Freedom, International Writer of the Year** (England), and **The International Authors and Writers Who's Who.**

W. B. Baker was bestowed **The Queens Golden Jubilee Medal** at the command of **Her Majesty Queen Elizabeth II,** upon receiving the commendation of His Grace, The Most Reverend and Right Honourable Dr. Rowan Williams, Archbishop Of Canterbury, in recognition for outstanding contributions to the Monarchy of the United Kingdom. Additionally, he received vestment as **Companion of the Order** and **Knight Grand Cross** of the International Chivalric Order of St. George (Great Britain), and serves as **Diplomatic Attaché** for The Peers Of The Black Raven (England).

Recent accolades include a **State Senate Resolution** in his honour and a **Congressional Tribute** from The House of Representatives of the Congress of the United States in Washington, DC.

* * * * *

WITH APPRECIATION

Many individuals and organisations should, by rights, entertain particular recognition and special mention for their important contributions with respect to the historical exploration and investigation required for the production of this fictional work set in the county of Gwent (now Monmouthshire) and, specifically, within the villages of Raglan and Abergavenny in south-east Wales.

W. B. Baker

* * * * *

Once again, my appreciation and greatest respect is humbly offered to

Lady Marion Veronica Brett

and

The Right Reverend Michael Greene-Butler

of

Southampton, England

Whose friendship and encouragement over the many years have inspired this author's attempt to capture something of both their honour and innate nobility.

* * * * *

Interior Illustrations, including all medieval woodcuts, various line illustrations, and historical engravings of the period were acquired through painstaking research within the Public Domain.

The magnificent Irish Wolfhounds incorporated in cover art were provided courtesy of Kevin Peuhkurinen at Big Sky Photography (www.bigskyphotography.ca).

Irish Wolfhounds courtesy of Arahu Irish Wolfhound (www.arahu-iw.com).

The author would like to extend his personal thanks to Kevin Peuhkurinen for not only his photographic skill in capturing this singular representation but for the photographer's kind permission to adapt and redistribute his original image.

* * * * *

W. B. Baker

Noteworthy appreciation is, likewise, extended to the following individuals and organisations for their invaluable contributions of time, information, and expertise:

CADW
Welsh Historic Monuments
Cathays Park, Cardiff
Wales, Great Britain

Rick Turner
Inspector of Ancient Monuments
Arolgydd Henebion
Cadw Inspectorate / Arolygiaeth Cadw
Welsh Assembly Government

Lorraine Griffiths
Cynorthwyydd Personol i'r Cyfarwyddwr
Llywodraeth Cynulliad Cymru

Frank Olding
Heritage Officer
Blaenau Gwent
Wales

Julian Thomas
Brenda Cook
Caerphilly Castle
Caerphilly, Mid Glamorgan
Wales

Cyngor Bwrdeistref Sirol Caerffili
Pecadlys Llyfrgelloedd
Pontllanfraith, Coed Duon
Wales

Caerphilly Local Studies Collection
English & Cymraeg
Caerphilly, Blackwood, Rhymney, and Bargoed
Glamorgan, Wales

W. B. Baker

Nic Pitman
Community Librarian
Caerphilly, Wales

Helen Lerry
Julie Lancaster
Daniel Morgan
Library Assistants
Caerphilly, Wales

Maureen Bowler
Janice Pratten
Supply Library Assistants
Caerphilly, Wales

The Library of Bargoed
The Square
Bargoed, Wales

Steve Kings
Senior Library Assistant
Bargoed, Wales

THE WRAITHS OF RAGLAN WOOD

Leighton James
Library Assistant
Bargoed

And

Llyfrgell Genedlaethol Cymru
The National Library of Wales
Aberstwyth, Wales

The author would like to especially acknowledge the significant contributions of Frank Olding, Heritage Officer for Blaenau Gwent who was instrumental in procuring the necessary historical references utilised within this work of fiction.

* * * * *

Shelly, Allison, and Rebecca Mitchell all warrant noteworthy gratitude and commendation. When the author found himself in desperate need of encouragement and prayer, these three young women found the strength to believe when, much as I hate to admit it, my faith had almost succumbed to the night.

Appreciation is also extended to Ruth Beamer, Harry Hiestand, and Marty Beamer for their continued support and encouragement.

Great indebtedness is due David and Teresa McAlister, for watching over both the physical and spiritual interests of the author through a particularly difficult season of my life. Without their continual prayers and unfailing encouragement this publication would never have seen completion.

Thanks is extended to Donald Cohron—for hours of laughter, friendship, and encouragement offered so willingly over literally hundreds of cups of tea; and for the inspiration on the back cover.

To the beautiful, enchanting Linda Cohron goes my heartfelt gratitude; for refusing to give up when, quite frankly, hope was almost gone—and for her great sacrifice of letting her husband, who suffers so terribly in being married to a fantastic French-Indian woman, postpone his long list of neglected projects long enough to give her the heaven-sent solitude of few hours alone in peace and quiet.

In a world that seems so often callous and cold, it is my great fortune to have found such fine and devoted friends.

*****

Gary Scott Mitchell.

Where does one begin to praise a friend who has been closer than a brother: whose unrelenting pragmatism and common sense may be only surpassed by the gentleman's steadfast denial to concede he might ever be considered as "that guy."

A thoughtful, compassionate, and considerate human being who has spent a lifetime cultivating the sometimes preposterous and often improbable disguise of pirate and brigand.

A rogue.

A scoundrel.

A misbegotten knave.

Who, in real life, is one of the finest men I have ever known. As he has often proclaimed, a demigod should possess the finest of camouflage to secret his identity from the rest of us mere mortals.

Candour and withering honesty being virtually impossible to maroon from a ready, uncanny wit; Mr. Mitchell has proven to be one of those most rare acquaintances. So uncommon indeed that, over the years, I count myself a better man largely due to the benefit of his friendship.

Throughout a lifetime of travel around the world, it may be quite confidently stated that the author has found this gentle man to be invaluable as both colleague and confidant—the most exceptional and extraordinary of associates.

For the best part of thirty years, I has been my privilege to know Gary Scott Mitchell.

Distinguished adversary, spurious blackguard, mongrel and scamp—for whom I would gladly throw away my life without a second thought.

No man could ever claim a finer friend.

* * * * *

Illustrations

(As They Appear With Chapter Headings)

Il. 4   King Henry V
            At the Battle of Agincourt 58

Il. 5   The Morning of Agincourt 68
            25 October 1415

Il. 6   The Wraiths of Raglan Wood 82

Il. 7   Morning Service on the Field of Agincourt 86

Il. 8   Du Guesclin and Troussell 96

Il. 9   Blazon of Sir William ap Thomas 102

Il. 10   Windsor Castle 112

Il. 11   An Old Drawing of Raglan Castle 120

Il. 12   The Siege of Jerusalem.................................. 126

Il. 13   Stone Stairs of the Vault
         At Raglan Castle.................................. 136

Il. 14   The Battle of Poitiers 148

Il. 15   An Ivy Covered Doorway............................... 156

Il. 16   Dirt Track through a
         Lonely Forest in Wales....................... 164

Il. 17   The Forest of Dean 178

Il. 18   *Joao sem terra assina carta Magna*
         King John of England signing
         The Magna Carta................................. 190

Il. 19   A Hollow Log along the track of
         Welsh Forest... 208

Il. 20   A Lightning Storm in the Forest.................... 218

Il. 21   The Castle Kitchen.. 234

Il. 22   The Exterior of Raglan Castle 248

Il. 23   Geoffrey of Bouillon 258
         (Medieval Woodcut)

Il. 24   The Wolfhound in the Clouds 266

Il. 25   Illuminated Alphabet..................................... 274

Il. 26   The Battle of Fang and Tooth 284

Il. 27   A British Wolf Hunt 290
         (Medieval Woodcut)

Il. 28   Moonlit View of Eton College 308
         By Edward Williams

Il. 29   Illuminated Text 320

Il. 30   The Graveyard at Eton College Chapel 328

Il. 31   Exterior of Raglan Castle 336

Il. 32   Margaret of Anjou 348
         From World Noted Women.
         New York; D. Appleton & Co., 1883

Il. 33   Eton College Chapel 356
         Painted by Canaletto; 1754
         The National Gallery, London

Il. 34   King Henry VI of England 364

Il. 35   Eton College Chapel by John Ruskin 374
         Works, "The Library Edition."
         Eds. E. T. Cook & A. Wedderburn

Il. 36   The Tower of Raglan Castle 384

Il. 37   The Fields of Wales 392

Il. 38   The Effigy of William ap Thomas 404
         St. Mary's Priory Church, Abergavenny,
         Wales

Il. 39   Exterior of Raglan Castle 412

Il. 40   Return of The Hound of Annwn 420

Interior Illustrations, including all medieval woodcuts, line illustrations, and period engravings have been thoroughly researched and proven to be taken from Public Domain.

Photographs adapted by the author from freely available sources and domain.

* * * * *

CONTENTS

By The Same Author 5
About The Author 9
Acknowledgments 13
Illustrations 23
Contents 27
Preface 31
Maps 37
Dedication 42
Author's Introduction 43
Prologue 49
Chapter One 59
Chapter Two 69

Chapter Three 83
Chapter Four.. 87
Chapter Five.. 97
Chapter Six 103
Chapter Seven... 113
Chapter Eight... 121
Chapter Nine 127
Chapter Ten... 137
Chapter Eleven 149
Chapter Twelve... 157
Chapter Thirteen 165
Chapter Fourteen.. 179
Chapter Fifteen 191
Chapter Sixteen... 209
Chapter Seventeen.. 219
Chapter Eighteen.. 235
Chapter Nineteen 249
Chapter Twenty 259
Chapter Twenty-one 267
Chapter Twenty-two... 275
Chapter Twenty-three... 285
Chapter Twenty-four.. 291
Chapter Twenty-five... 309

Chapter Twenty-six 321

Chapter Twenty-seven 329

Chapter Twenty-eight 337

Chapter Twenty-nine 349

Chapter Thirty 357

Chapter Thirty-one 365

Chapter Thirty-two 375

Chapter Thirty-three 385

Chapter Thirty-four 393

Chapter Thirty-five 405

Chapter Thirty-six 413

Epilogue 421

Dénouement 427

Castles Cited In The Text 433

Selected Bibliography and Contributors 487

Preface

When presenting his or her latest novel, it has become entirely anticipated that the author should take a few pages to provide readers with some brief account of its objective or intent. In the past, with extremely few exceptions, this writer has discovered that the Author's Introduction strained creativity to much greater lengths than actually writing the book itself.

For the first time in my life that is, in this one particular instance, entirely not the case.

Rather than offer some pretentious justification about the value of research and publication about people long dead and locations half-forgotten, I thought it wise to simply clear the air and offer some honest reflections.

First and foremost, apologies should be made with regard to the characters portrayed within this work of historical fiction. Most authors would spend some time at this point to state how great liberties were taken with regard to situations and personalities; that, basically, they should not be held accountable for liberality with the truth taken in the name of artistic licence. To that, I say bollocks.

The whole point of historical fiction is to express some point or idea that the author wishes to make—that may or may not have actually played a role in how history might be told or recounted by those who took a part. Histories, one must remember, have always been written by the victors; by those who have a particular axe to grind or perspective on what actually happened. They are, as a consequence, quite often no more accurate than the fanciful ranting of writers several generations removed.

I would, however, have to offer very many apologies for any misrepresentation of actual fact: it being my foremost intent to base fictionalised accounts of relationships upon the solid base of recorded history. The work I found was one which I could not take up and write off hand and, should I have known the emotional cost, I should hardly have ventured to undertake the task. One wonders if, at some future date in some other existence, the author might be held accountable by those portrayed. If that be the case, then I at least will be able to defend the nature of the individuals portrayed within this work; for I, by default, am a direct consequence of their character and personalities.

Dealing with so rich a period of British history, it became clear from the outset that there was simply no way one might be true to all that was occurring in England, Wales, Scotland, and France during the years in question. One simply was forced to draw from practical experience in dramatic production and modify the premise slightly to state that: if it is not in the book, then it doesn't exist. Otherwise, this novel would simply become another dry account of events long past and often better off forgotten.

* * * * *

As in any work of historical fiction, the writer initiates the plot with extensive research into the period and specific geographic locations in question. Such was the case in this instance, with great care being given to the accuracy of what was actually happening in the region of Monmouthshire, and around the village of Raglan specifically.

With regard to characterisation, it should be made quite clear that many of the personages portrayed within the novel were actual people and, in many cases, distant relatives. I must confess that certain of the characters are shamelessly based upon actual family members it has been my fortune and, in certain instances, displeasure to claim as family. What can I say, other than most families, as I understand, have an equal number of heroes and unsavoury characters with which they must contend.

The maps and illustrations dispersed at regular intervals throughout the book are actual medieval woodcuts, engravings from the period between the thirteenth and eighteenth centuries, and line drawings that currently exist within the public domain. Some of the rather crude representations are solely the personal responsibility of the author.

For my authorities, I refer the reader to the bibliography and contributors portion of the text at the close of this publication. While many, many more references are available on the subject matter, this author thought it prudent to simply list a representative selection of what is currently available for examination and trust the intrepid researcher to sort them out as best as possible to suit his or her needs and individual interests.

One of the most difficult challenges which presented itself in the creative process was that of remaining objective to the intents of characters. Any failure to present the historical characters as they actually were, I can assure you that it has not arisen from any wilful neglect, carelessness, or idleness on my part. It was done completely deliberately. I must trust to their kind indulgence for forgiveness should ever we meet.

Finally, the novel was dedicated to

Sir Dafydd Gam
Personal Bodyguard of
King Henry V
Killed at Agincourt
1415

only after serious contemplation.

While there are any number of Kings of France and later Queens and Kings of England to which the writer can claim relation, I thought it best to remove them as far as possible on the genealogical ladder. Some records pronounce Dafydd Gam as a hero, others portray the man as a bloodthirsty mercenary who only sold his sword, or in this case a spiked war hammer, to the highest bidder. Drawing upon my own family as inspiration, he and the rest of my ancestors are portrayed as incarnations of those whom I have known during my lifetime.

For that, they will have to defend themselves as best they can should the need ever arise.

All this being said, it remains this writer's great privilege to proudly claim a genealogy rife with ancestors with great accomplishments and even greater disappointments: a spurious heritage that, after much thought, will probably be better off to end with the author. Still, I would proudly stand beside a parentage which bears the odd stain rather than stand with those who have deliberately elected to unceremoniously cast their ancestry away.

Though the one single goal of my entire life is to be acknowledged by the nation of my birth; and by all accounts, it appears that I shall fall far short of my forefathers who were accounted Kings, Earls, and received their knighthoods for, seemingly, far less than I have ever done—nevertheless, at all times and in every season, it is with great delight and honour that I am and will forever be proud to call myself a son of Britain.

—W. B. BAKER

MAPS

English, Welsh, and Scottish readers may be quite familiar with the geography of England and Wales, however, it would be sensible to include illustrations of the region of Monmouthshire and its castles for those poor individuals who had the misfortune to be born outside Britain.

These should allow readers an opportunity to recognise the importance of the territory during the period of the Welsh Revolts and its comparative location within the United Kingdom. For this very reason, customized illustrations have been included to reveal not only the boundaries of the counties of Wales, but the locations of the castles and historic sites throughout England, Wales, and Ireland that are specifically mentioned within the text.

W. B. BAKER

Map One

Map of County Gwent Monmouthshire

Map Two

Map of Medieval Wales

Illustrating Boundaries Of
Later Welsh Kingdoms

Map Three

Map of Medieval Wales

Illustrating English and Welsh Counties
And Castles Cited Within
The Text

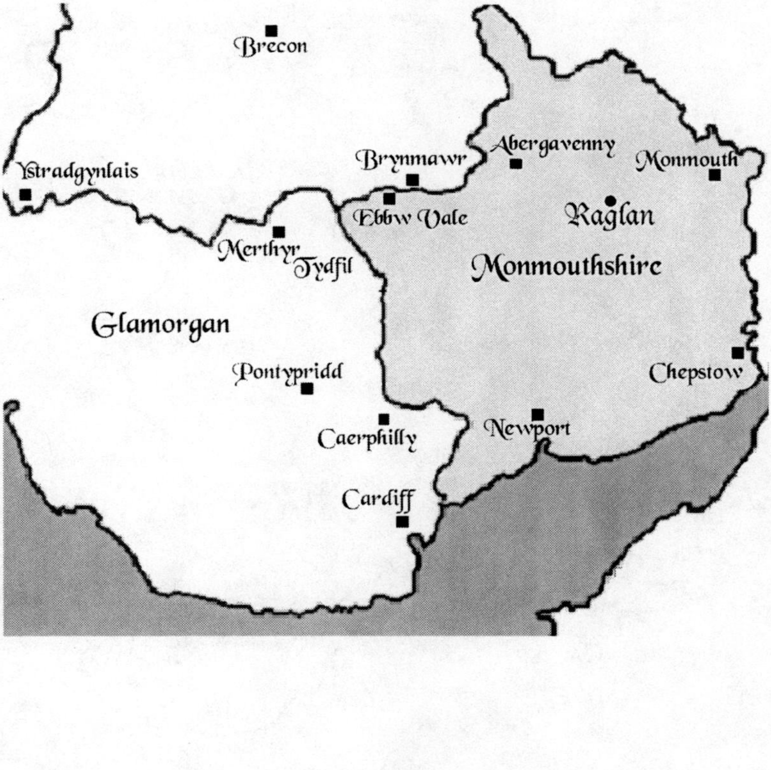
Brecon
Ystradgynlais
Brynmawr
Abergavenny
Monmouth
Ebbw Vale
Raglan
Merthyr
Tydfil
Monmouthshire
Glamorgan
Pontypridd
Chepstow
Caerphilly
Newport
Cardiff

CLWYD

GWYNEDD

BASINGWERK
CASTLE

CAERLEON
CASTLE

POWYS

DYFED

DINEFWR
CASTLE

WEST
GLAMORGAN   ABERGAVENNY   GWENT
              MID
MANORBIER   GLAMORGAN   DINGESTOW
CASTLE   CASTLE
              SOUTH
              GLAMORGAN

- Harbottle Castle
- Wark Castle
- Carrickfergus Castle
- Bowes Castle
- Trim Castle
- Conisbrough Castle
- Basingwerk
- Caerleon
- Kenilworth
- Orford Castle
- Warwick
- Dinefwr
- Abergavenny
- Wallingford
- Rochester
- Manorbier Castle
- Dingestow
- Windsor
- Dover
- Corfe Castle
- Arundel
- Bramber Castle

For

Sir Dafydd Gam
Personal Bodyguard

of

Henry V
King Of England

Killed On The Field
at
The Battle Of Agincourt
25 October 1415

My 20th Great Grandfather

Author's Introduction

The Hounds of Hell
Churchyard Beasts
The Skriker
Padfoot
The Hounds of Annwn
Cu Sith
The Capelthwaite
Mauthe Doog
Gwyllgi, the Dog of Darkness
Black Shuck

Swooning Shadow
The Yeth Hound
Bogey Beast
The Gurt Dog
Bargheust

Recognized and feared by these and many other names, ghost dogs have haunted the lanes and lives of countless generations. To be sure, phantom hounds have shared the gloom of night with humankind since nightmares of antiquity gave them form.

Nocturnal spectres, no one can really know their origin; whether conceived in myth or imagination. Cwn Annwn, Gram, and Cerberus all appear as guardians of the underworld and their progeny likewise strike something of the malevolent in us all. Larger than a wolf, many are reported to exhibit glowing crimson eyes and haunt the ancient pathways, graveyards, crossroads, or ancient scenes of execution to this very day. Some traditions even contend that the calf sized creature strides out of the sea by night to wander along the lonely lanes.

Ghostly apparitions of shadow hounds continue to the twenty-first century as portents of death throughout the British Isles: from Yorkshire to East Anglia, Middlesex and Rutland all the way to Dartmoor and Lancashire. In Hertfordshire, fierce black hounds with crimson eyes still haunt the centre of the road where the hangman's noose once swung on its gibbet. In Devonshire, the Yeth

Hound is a headless dog, reported to be the spirit of an unbaptised child, which rambles through the forest and wails until the dawn.

Most often seen as portents of death, the spirits have been recorded in thousands of anecdotes over the past eight hundred years. Some have herded farm animals across the distant and desolate fields, while still others appear to quite brazenly wait for men and women to dare to venture out from behind their heavily bolted doors.

* * * * *

Britain, more than any other nation present or past, confirms this notion through the millennia and, while certainly not the oldest civilization mankind has seen, the indiscretions of thousands of years seem to have indelibly tattooed themselves upon its hills and heaths.

Druids perceived a supposed relationship between the acts of man and the forces of nature. Influence to control the unknown was practiced through the worship of deities and through specific behaviour that, it was presumed, would placate unseen forces they simply could not understand. In our attempts to recognize the role of superstition in early Celtic society, it becomes important to note that many rituals practiced by pre-Christian clans were later incorporated into Christianity as a method of conversion. For example, the birds announcing the birth of the goddess, Rhiannon, later became the angels announcing the birth of Christ.

The ancient Celtic concept of the migration of souls and entire mystery of death and rebirth did not simply disappear with the introduction of the Roman assembly of deities, nor the later incursion of roaming Christian monks. The superstitions and rites of the ancient creeds had held men's imaginations for more than a thousand years, and those of the Banfáith for perhaps two thousand years earlier—revered by the Picts, Juts, and Huns just as ferociously and fervently as the dogma of any later Christian denomination. So ingrained and fundamental to the elemental fears of men were their beliefs that even the well-worn track of history has not been able to completely scuff them off the road.

An extremely superstitious lot, the Druids played into the dark mind's eye of the population. Old stories of the walking dead, supernatural hounds, and gruesome sacrifice all bubbled together in the communal subconscious of the laity. Ancient sacrificial ceremonies, stripped of their more macabre elements for more manageable consumption by a sensitive public, reared their long buried heads whenever opportunity arose.

The tenacity of Britain's savage past emerged any time the walls of a public meetinghouse or private dwelling were erected: ancient superstitions holding that the skulls of unlucky captives were to be dispersed at regular intervals amidst the foundation stones to keep migrant evil spirits from taking up residence inside the structure. The introduction of Roman law had abruptly halted the grisly practice and hurriedly substituted coins, ornaments, and the skulls of domesticated animals provided by the local butchers. Christians, quick to pick up on the metaphor of Christ being the cornerstone of their religion, insisted that all symbolic offerings be limited to the inscribed markings on the largest sandstone piece. That being publicly agreed, it did not lessen the unabated flow of mysterious additions of various animal bones into the wet mortar most every night.

England, Scotland, Wales, and Ireland were not going to give up their ancient gods without a struggle, no matter how loud the voice of public opinion might decry them during the day. As has always been the way of humankind, the orthodox rules the day, while those clinging to the fringes of the unknown will ever command the night.

This pattern of religious rites had, in truth, metamorphosed from the Cult of the Severed Head—an early ideology distinguished by the grisly and macabre practise from which they derived their name. In addition to hacking free and collecting the horrific trophies from their captives, the practitioners of this ancient cult believed that drinking from human skulls imparted the strength, valour, and magical powers of their victims. In order to prevent the spirits of their victims from returning to haunt them after death, the cult would bury some of their skulls within the foundations of buildings or in the stanchions of bridges. Shrines were often deliberately constructed in the niches of prehistoric holy wells and sacred springs; no doubt as much as to procure a steady supply of sacrifices as to pay homage to the ancient water goddesses.

One would like to believe that god or gods set particular worth upon its heirs: affording those consigned to wander the opportunity to prowl the countryside in the hope that the living may take notice of eternity. The other, rather obvious conclusion is far more frightening—in that the dead actively seek to persecute and haunt the footsteps of any individual unlucky enough to stray across their nightly paths.

It was for this very reason and belief that the ancient practitioners in Anglia and Wales attempted to protect themselves from retribution: their children being regularly sacrificed to appease the famished thirst of spirits roaming within their midst. Quite commonly, infants were ceremoniously and ritualistically dispatched when laying new foundations for communal buildings or bridges: the idea being that innocent blood might slack the appetites of the unseen.

Ancient rites entombed the bodies of countless innocents within the walls or cornerstones though, as was stated earlier, with the unexpected migration of Romanised Christianity, *civilised* society replaced the pagan practice by advocating the substitution of human sacrifice with that of animals.

Skulls and bones of thousands of hastily slaughtered dogs were buried in and along now fallen walls in the firm belief that their ghosts would protect the occupants from roaming apparitions of evil.

The builders could have no suspicion that the spirits of the loyal beasts might ever rise again and turn against them in vengeance.

—W. B. Baker

* * * * *

Prologue

Histories of conflict are inevitably penned by conquerors and certainly not the subjugated: the premise being that the side with the most survivors is, in fact, probably most capable of spreading the exact and accurate rendition of events as they actually occurred.

Whether or not those accounts may be anything near factual.

Succeeding generations rarely take the time to pause and consider whether or not the truths of history might have been neatly tailored to snugly fit the aspirations or ideals of those left alive to tell the tale. Like idiots we, as contemporary heirs, simply accept what we have been told: convinced only that the views of the defeated are, in some respect, less valid or unworthy of regard. Opinions and objectives have tempered more tales than we may ever know: the victors always counting upon the dead to keep their estimations to themselves.

Long before the muddy boots of King Henry V staggered back from France to trudge out of the foam to England's shore, entire companies of his troops had been working hard to authenticate the recent events at Agincourt. Who better to verify the bravery and courage of Henry and his conscripts than they who were actually there—whether those actually doing the writing had any evidence or, in point of fact, had witnessed anything at all. In reality, the truth was far less important than the wealth of propaganda King Henry might reap from a triumphant return: the authors, as well, remaining convinced that their immediate futures might be poised in the precarious balance of public opinion back in England.

All things considered, it might have well been the worst century since mankind had been summarily expelled from Eden. Or, for those who insist on being far more pragmatic: at least the worst since the century before—as noted earlier, we as a species are nothing if not pragmatic. It is exactly this hard-headedness that tends to force us into repeating the identical mistakes of untold centuries preceding.

The Black Death had swept across the countryside like an indiscriminate blanket of noxious fog: starting far to the east in central Asia and quickly reaching the Crimea; where ships and their stowaway rats spread the plague throughout the whole of Europe and the Mediterranean.

Soldiers and merchants introduced the "Great Pestilence" or "Great Mortality" to Britain and the continent, where the death rate in certain areas was near half the population. As a result, those already suffering from malnutrition from harsher winters and reduced harvests now found themselves battling the unseen ailment with empty bellies.

Heavy rains began to fall in the autumn of 1314 and continued virtually for years: which only primed a one hundred year struggle for survival between Britain and the continent.

From the onset of hostilities, English forces had accounted themselves quite well—with decisive victories at Poitiers and Crecy; though the past forty years had predominantly been awarded to the French. In 1413, Henry the Fifth inherited the throne of England and immediately claimed legal rights to lands in France. More than economics or politics, his decision to invade France and finally conquer Normandy might well have been a matter of simple survival. One must remember that English kings had long been struggling to unite the country through continued warfare with the clans of Scotland and tribal chieftains of Wales. Similarly, the lords of France were locked in violent battles for influence and territory across the channel. Rumours of the deteriorating sanity of Charles VI spread to England and made Henry give an invasion real consideration.

There was no way the Court could hide it: King Charles VI of France was quickly going mad. People who step back and forth across the bright line of sanity tend to do so whenever and wherever they happen to feel like it—which makes it bugger all difficult for anyone to explain away their actions to passersby.

The latest heir to the crown suffered from periodic bouts of insanity, during which, he completely believed the unlikely prospect that he was made entirely of glass—a malady that made his throne and nation quite attractive not only to France's immediate neighbours, but to those who vied for power and possessions from within his borders as well. So intense had the man's madness become that Charles VI had even commanded that slender steel rods be inserted and sewn into the seams of every piece of his clothing—to prevent his body from accidentally shattering in case he stumbled or someone deliberately tapped him with the edge of their sword.

With their king completely incapable of governing, France's noble houses quickly slipped into a bitter struggle for power. Though medieval France comprised a populace of well over fifteen million and was, in fact, at least five times more populated than Henry's England, it was partitioned into rival fiefdoms, with each feudal lord responsible for mustering his own private militia to protect their sovereign's territory.

While the princes and lords of France vied with each other for power in ongoing civil violence, the twenty-eight year old king of England saw his chance to end the Hundred Years War and take back some British honour.

All Henry needed was an army with which to sweep the old feudal world aside.

England's king attacked the problem with a fervour that showed not only creativity, but an even ruthless efficiency. Every ship in the entire country was commandeered by Henry's military in order to raise a fleet to cross the Channel. Each town and village was called upon for provisions and supplies. Indeed, though it might be difficult for some people to accept, every goose in the entire monarchy had to sacrifice exactly six of his or her wing feathers to be used for arrow flights. Britain, without even noticing what was happening right before its eyes, was witnessing the beginnings of its first professional military.

What with the economic state of the country, Henry raided the treasury and was even forced to pawn the crown jewels to subsidize his expeditionary force. Though relatively inexperienced as a king, Henry V did correctly recognise that what ultimately mattered most at the end of the day were his troops: insuring that his force was well paid, supplied, and adequately fed and watered would very likely ultimately determine victory. To accomplish this, the young king made it a point to make certain that absolutely everything was organised down to the last detail. His captains drew up local muster rolls to secure knights and local bowmen and, when that did not provide adequate manpower, his ministers actually emptied the gaols and prisons; offering complete amnesty to absolutely anyone, regardless of the foulness of their crimes, who would personally accompany King Henry V across the channel to France.

Companies of archers from Gwent in Wales and from Lancashire under the Duke of Manchester were ultimately lured to the docks of Southampton by profit and the tasty prospect of adventure.

It would also be relatively fair to say that a great majority of the ragtag crowds who found their way out of the public houses and to the wharfs were essentially extremely well-armed convicts, felons, and thieves. Had the expeditionary force not embarked for France in relative haste, most of southern England might have paid dearly for Henry's desperation. Even with so short a military bivouac on England's southern shore, the conscripts were having a great deal of trouble staying sober and out of trouble with local magistrates. The growing number of rapes and assaults by idle combatants who, essentially, had carte blanche until ferried to France to direct their antisocial behaviour against Henry's enemies meant that locals would not put up with such impiety and injustice for very long.

Not exactly the cream of England's shores to be sure; however, the skilled professional archers had proved themselves time and time again during the Welsh revolts: having fought together as units, side by side, for years. Experts with the longbow, the men from Gwent had a fearsome reputation. Neither were the Lancashire bowmen to be dismissed as merely run of the mill archers. What the longbow lacked in accuracy, it more than made up for with firepower; in that an experienced archer could nock and fire up to ten arrows every single minute—making the weapon approximately four times faster in the field than the standard issue French crossbow.

Utilizing so many archers when compared to the number of heavily armoured knights and men-at-arms might have appeared a rather questionable decision to most of Henry's captains. More than any strategic advantage, it turned out to be purely a matter of simple economics. The strapped English paymasters were finding it necessary to compensate knights at the going rate of four shillings per day. Men-at-arms earned the standard rate of twelve pence a day but, when one considered that they had no horses to feed and quarter, the heavily armoured infantry was well worth the price. Still, archers only commanded a mere pittance of six pence per day in salary: which meant that, if deployed correctly by his captains, the lowly bowmen were definitely the king's best value for the money.

France suffered from no such economic considerations.

While Henry's army were paid conscripts from every social class, the forces they would meet across the channel were, without exception, members of the aristocratic nobility. Adhering to the ancient code of chivalry and honour, the Lords of France, possibly more than any other military force of its time in Europe, were religiously committed to a code of personal honour.

Counts and marquises accounted themselves to the King Charles VI as true feudal lords: their knighthood obligating them to appear and fight as need may rise for personal honour more than any affairs of state. They were the burnished elite of a completely military society: defining their rank and mere existence by a code of behaviour that made them superior within the European feudal system. Battle was, to them, the only ultimate test of one's mettle and family credentials: personal glory and victory believed to be awarded judiciously by Heaven for attempting to live and perfect a virtuous way of life.

A concept that, in the eyes of many, might well have outlived its time.

As the wealthiest class of society, each noble was expected to provide for himself the finest, most modern and expensive armour he could afford. While many English knights were forced to wear outdated armour made of iron that had been passed down from father to son for generations, the French nobility possessed armour and accoutrements made from the finest steel. State of the art chainmail, shields, and body armour meant that the iron bodkins of English arrows had, in reality, little or no chance of ever penetrating high quality steel or actually inflicting any damage: a fact that Henry's nobles might have considered a bit more carefully before venturing over to the fields of France to deliberately pick a fight.

The events at Agincourt would determine whether their king returned in victory or the latest monarch of England had pulled an unbelievable gaffe.

* * * * *

My Lord, the simplest truth may miss man's groans
When he, in conquest of mere piece of land,
Forgets he fights above his father's bones,
And only briefly in the sun may stand.
Despite the gains of life, his finite hand
　May only once caress the timeless stone,
　　That stands forever, top the Dark Unknown.

—Warin of Llanhennock

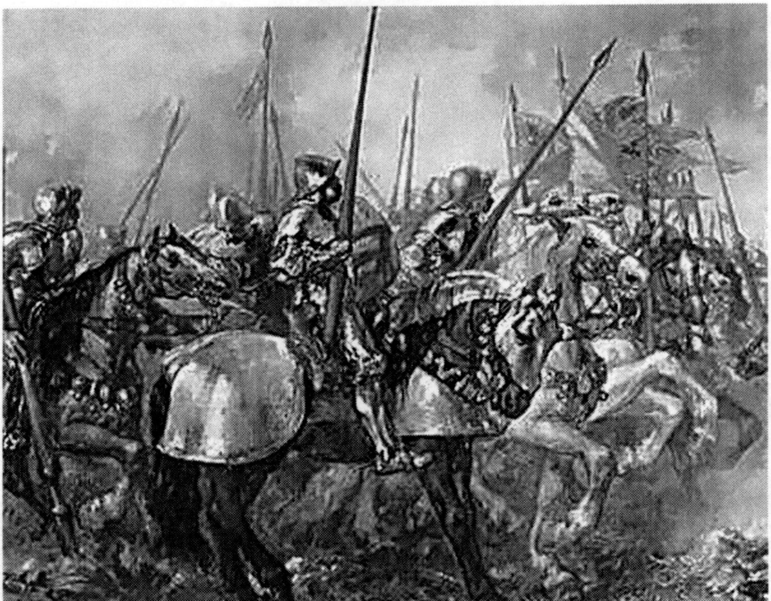

Chapter One

On the 14th of August, 1415, Henry set out for Normandy and led the assault against the French port of Harfleur.

Though the English had originally planned for the siege to last, at the very most, a fortnight; the resilient garrison held out for five long weeks. By mid-September, the meagre English supplies were running desperately low and, though many historians neglect to divulge the facts, several thousands of Henry's men were either already dead or had quietly worked their way back to the rear and unceremoniously deserted back home across the channel. As a result, the original force of approximately eleven thousand soldiers had dwindled down to little over eight thousand. However, as luck and fate would have it, just when the English were about to pack it in and head back to Britain, the fortified gates of the town were unexpectedly thrown open in surrender.

One of the first men into the town was the Welsh mercenary, Dafydd Gam; a former dissident and genuinely vicious enemy of the English during the Welsh Revolts.

Fighting the crown from Gwent since the tender age of sixteen, Dafydd's reputation for brutality on the battlefield had served him rather well—even after Gam had eventually defected to join the English. The man's fervour and natural talent for killing quickly propelled the hardy Welshman up through the ranks; with the gruff, stocky warrior actually becoming one of Henry V's most trusted men-at-arms and, eventually, the King of England's personal bodyguard.

As fortune had it, Gam's very first prisoner at Harfleur turned out to be the commander of the French garrison; whom he promptly delivered to Henry's emissaries. One must bear in mind that, contrary to contemporary practice, there were implicit directives governing medieval warfare. Prisoners were not usually slaughtered on sight but, rather, delivered back to each respective side after the conflict ceased to be exchanged for rather hefty ransoms. Indeed, that was one of the primary reasons the nobility would bother to involve themselves at all to appear on the battlefield: one might capture one or two individuals of significant personage and be able to live quite comfortably upon their ransom for decades. Accordingly, knights fully anticipated to be ransomed back upon cessation of hostilities. Strange as it might seem to modern sensibilities, as the captains of Harfleur had agreed to surrender—and in accordance with the chivalric code—each was released under his own recognisance with the implicit understanding that he would turn up to be taken into custody once the English returned to cross the channel at the end of the campaigning season.

"Let's finish this now."

Dafydd drew his short sword and stepped up beside his hostage. Having spent a lifetime in the Monmouth Valley of Wales dispatching Englishmen at his personal discretion, the old dog was having real difficulty with Henry's concept of chivalry.

"Put it away."

The short bark of a command came from the opposite side of the room; behind the long plank table and next to the front window of the commandeered public house. Noticing that there was hesitation on the part of Gam to comply, a tall figure stepped half-way into the slivered light and repeated his order.

"I said, put it away, Taff."

Dafydd flinched in indignation and shifted his attention to the voice in the shadows. If a dog, then Dafydd Gam was most assuredly a terrier and not a retriever: much more likely to gnaw at any arm that came within reach than to subserviently obey commands from an Englishman. The offensive slur of 'Taff' rudely slapped the Welshman's sense of pride and instantly infuriated the old soldier. He had contended with the insult for the better part of his life and, true to his rancorous reputation, had carved a bit of revenge out of any who dared to use the derogatory term in his presence.

While the river Taff ran almost the entire length of Wales, a fact that anyone from the region would immediately know; it was reference to an increasingly popular English rhyme that summed up the longstanding hatred between Welsh and English:

>   Taffy was a Welshman, Taffy was a cheat
>   Taffy came to my house, and stole a piece of meat
>
>   Taffy was a Welshman, Taffy was a thief,
>   Taffy came to my house and stole a piece of beef.
>
>   Taffy was a Welshman, Taffy was a sham;
>   Taffy came to my house and stole a piece of lamb

There were far more vulgar and tasteless rhymes, to any of which the Englishman might be referring and, of all the infantry pillaging the streets of Harfleur that day, Dafydd was probably the very last one any might want to deliberately aggravate.

The sound of a longsword being slid free from its scabbard forced both the scribe at the table and the French captain to drop to the floor and well out of range. When Dafydd took a step toward his shadowy adversary, the man's voice rose to a defiant bellow.

"Hold your hand, you Welsh bastard!"

Gam's chin raised up as his body shuddered to a halt. It was not the words but the timbre that forced the scarred soldier to hesitate. He had recognised the voice.

Stepping forward more fully into the light, the features of Sir Roger Vaughn were profiled against the light. The tip of the man's weapon dropped down to thud against the table as a broad grin slid across his adversary's expression. To the amazement of clerk and Captain alike, the two men stepped face to face and continued to exchange insults.

"You English son-of-a-bitch."

Dafydd now smiled broadly himself and, likewise, drove the point of his dagger into the surface of the table.

Pivoting around the naked point of his weapon, Sir Roger carefully removed his basinet with one hand and kept the blade between him and the much older Welshman. Noticing the two men still crouching at either edge of the table, Vaughn addressed them without ever taking his eyes off Dafydd.

"My apologies for the untimely intrusion of this Welsh clout."

Roger grinned and nodded to Gam at the opposite end of the roughly hewn boards. "Devilish awkward to have a man of such limited intelligence stumble into affairs of state."

Dafydd took his cue and mockingly genuflected in response. "My regrets, *old boy*." The king's bodyguard emphasised the last two words with a condescending colour as he stepped to his left and splintered a crack across the table top with his weapon.

"Not in the least, you inbred mongrel."

Sir Roger Vaughn countered his enemy's movement precisely: keeping the distance between them exact while each stepped over the outstretched legs of the men still crouched upon the floor. Never taking his eyes off the old soldier, Roger made his explanations to the unwilling witnesses.

"You see, this bastard was fathered by a black ram by the dark of the moon," he went on with even greater abuse. "He has always had a particularly bad influence—on his enemies and friends alike," he paused to shoot a quick glance at the onlookers. "With the singular exception of myself."

Vaughn took a congratulatory bow.

The Welshman inched a bit closer to the table to keep Roger in range. "What is that stench?" he taunted. "Can either of you smell it? That sick-sweet smell of brownnosing that screams sophistication."

Dafydd had likewise begun to include the French captain and English notary. He raised the point of his blade and threatened the man across the table. "Keep talking and I'll peel you like an onion: layer by layer; until there is nothing left of you but an evil odour and their watering eyes." Gam nodded toward the unenthusiastic spectators.

Roger took the challenge and stepped in a bit as well.

"Keep knocking on the gates of Hell and, sooner or later, someone is bound to answer." The knight raised his blade flatly to meet Dafydd halfway over the now scattered pile of papers.

Knocking the French captive rudely aside with his knee, Gam re-sheathed his dagger. "I'm afraid you have always underestimated me."

Sir Roger followed suit and neatly withdrew his sword. He leaned in to drive his point home instead. "On the contrary, I have always held you in the highest esteem," he paused, "but only as a Taff."

Gam grinned and backed toward the doorway. "I would like to say how very much I will miss your company, but we both know that would be an out-and-out lie."

Vaughn leaned on the table with both hands and shot the retreating king's bodyguard a smile.

Now silhouetted against the door frame, the Welshman waved with a flourish. "I will, for that reason, confine myself to simply saying . . . sod off."

Now laughing, the knight called after Gam, "Tell that voluptuous daughter of yours to keep her heaving bosom warm for me."

A two-fingered salute shot back through the doorway as Sir Roger Vaughn collapsed in a fit of laughter.

The two bystanders slowly rose to their feet and, after staring blankly at each other, turned to the knight for some explanation.

Still trying to compose himself, Roger shot a glance toward the doorway to make sure Dafydd was not coming back.

"Without question; the biggest bastard I have ever met."

Vaughn had had enough of the afternoon and crossed to glance outside before daring to poke his head out in the street. With one hand upon the lintel of the rather squat doorframe, he checked the safety of the lane one last time before making an exit.

Popping his head back inside for an instant, he clarified.

"Without a doubt, the fiercest man I have ever had the great displeasure of knowing." Sir Roger Vaughn paused. "My father-in-law," he glanced outside again to make certain no one on the street might hear.

"My friend."

* * * * *

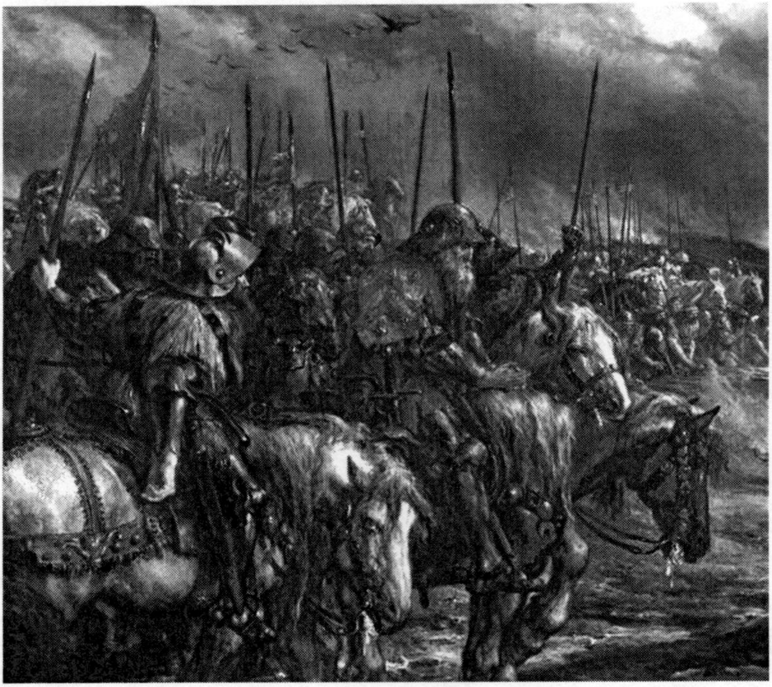

Chapter Two

What with the unexpected tenacity of the French garrison, the English troops, who had consumed all their meagre supplies during the interim and had not actually eaten a decent meal in weeks, descended upon the French harbour of Harfleur like a cloud of starving locusts.

Ransacking not only the garrison but most of the town as well, Henry's men abandoned all restraint and looted homes, businesses, and churches alike and made off with whatever valuables they could carry. Indeed, such was the very reason many had agreed to embark on such a questionable venture in the first place: glory and honour might be well and good—but gold was far more tangible.

To the dismay of Britain's high command, the English troops discarded any self-discipline or principle and began to wreak vengeance upon the unarmed citizenry. So terrible was the abuse that John Stephens, one of the English chaplains in attendance, penned his personal disgust in a later account of the raid:

> "Amid much lamentation, tears, and grief, two thousand townsfolk were escorted beyond the limits of the army lest they should be molested by the thieves amongst us . . . who are more given to pillage than to pity.
>
> And thus, by the judgement of God, they became travellers where they had thought themselves inhabitants."

Quite predictably, the assault on Harfleur triggered a backlash of hatred and indignation that instantly rippled across the countryside: causing King Charles' government to unfurl France's blood-red war banner and immediately declare open season on the English. A chivalric crusade against the invaders was then decreed; with members of the French aristocracy quickly honing in from every direction upon Henry's expeditionary force.

Contrary to their original strategy of taking Harfleur and retreating directly back across to Southampton, the English now marched north from Harfleur toward the safe haven of Calais; one of the few harbours Henry's forces still held on the continent. Despite the lack of supplies and his men's exhaustion, he remained confident they would be able to march the two hundred and sixty miles north and take further action against the French before being forced to make a strategic departure. Though scouts and spies reported that a massive counter-strike was being organised by the French authorities, Henry V was convinced that he and his men could reach Calais in time. His intention was to pillage, burn, and loot every home and village along the way: which would go far in undermining the authority of Charles VI and, as a bonus, give his conscripted army the opportunity to further line their pockets before sailing home. More captured treasure would not only help the English king personally but make it all that more easy to raise another army should he find it necessary in the months or years to come.

Gold, without fail, can always be counted on to make a great incentive.

Across the provinces of Normandy, the glaring absence of the wildly unpredictable and mad King Charles VI had thrown France's defences into an uproar. By default, fate had conferred command of the French nobles and defence of their borders to one of the king's most devoted generals: Marshall Jean Ean le Maingre "le Boucicault."

Certainly no novice with regard to strategy, Marshall Boucicault remembered well how small contingents of English had regularly inflicted heavy defeats dozens of times during the Hundred Years War. Memorably at Crecy and Poitiers, the English had benefited from strategic errors and French overconfidence and their commanding general was determined not to make the same mistakes again.

France's leading tactician realised that their heavily armoured cavalry had been decimated by employing direct frontal charges against English archers and infantry. As a result, against the insistence of his impatient captains, the Marshall was perfectly prepared to wait until fortune might favour the French. Instead of rushing headlong into some misguided assault, Boucicault carefully drove the retreating force of English raiders inland: away from the coastline and reinforcements. Without any hope of being resupplied, Henry's expeditionary force would inevitably grow weaker with each day's march; while the ever-growing numbers of French nobles from across the northern provinces would soon join the mounting resistance in Normandy.

Marshall Boucicault's plan was actually rather shrewd in its simplicity.

Henry's prolonged five week siege of Harfleur had cost the English far more than time. Their supplies were running dreadfully low: so much so that troops, being continually driven by the advance guard, had no opportunity to rest and were, in fact, close to starvation. So desperate had the situation become that Henry's army was reduced to gathering berries, nuts, and even eating leaves just to stay alive. Scavenging for raw shellfish from polluted waterways had resulted in a devastating epidemic of "the bloody flux" or dysentery.

With no time to stop, those who died were either simply left beside the road or buried in shallow, makeshift graves thinly scraped into the mud. It had been raining off and on for over a fortnight; which made the now regrettable trek to the north even more miserable. The French vanguard watched from nearby hilltops as over two thousand Englishmen wretched, vomited, and eventually succumbed; only to be buried anonymously in unnamed fields or simply rolled into muddy ditches and abandoned to the animals.

Just as desperation began to strangle the survivors of Henry's army, the retreating legion discovered a shortcut across the River Somme and appeared to have outlasted Boucicault: the refuge of the English-held port of Calais now being well within marching distance.

The waiting Frenchmen were not going to let that happen, as Chaplin Stephens noted in his diary:

> "Just as we reached the top of the hill—on the other side we saw emerging about a half a mile away from us—the grim looking ranks of the French . . . filling the broad field like a countless swarm of locusts— and a forest of spears—with the great helmets gleaming in between . . . was truly terrifying.
>
> And there was only a valley, and not so wide at that, between us and them."

True to his reputation, Boucicault had assessed the terrain and cleverly predicted precisely where the English would, more likely than not, attempt to ford the river Somme. The

French defenders had simply positioned themselves on the east bank of the river and kept pace with the English until the nobles were able to jump ahead of Henry's force and interrupt their retreat where the Somme looped between the villages of Fouilly and Nesle. In a brilliant manoeuvre, the French general deployed the bulk of his forces ahead of Henry in a classic pincer movement: effectively cutting off England's escape route to its ships; waiting a mere forty miles away at the port at Calais.

The obvious result was that the English were now trapped quite some distance inland and removed from any hope of reinforcements.

24 October found the contingent of English on the main road that bisected the little villages of Maisoncelle, Tramcourt, and Agincourt. With French forces to the north of Agincourt, Henry set up his camp adjacent to Maisoncelle. It had become immediately apparent that the crude maps the English brought with them had not taken into account the contours of the fields. Indeed, the supposedly flat terrain dropped off rather steeply on either side toward Agincourt and Tramcourt; which gave little room for a company of men to manoeuvre, depending upon how the skirmish might play out. King Henry positioned his men across the narrowest point of the field: a line that would force the French to consider long how to best charge without fighting the lay of the land themselves.

After losing so many men at Harfleur and to dysentery over the past month, the original English army of eleven thousand had been drastically reduced to slightly less than seven thousand. Of these, there were about five thousand five hundred archers and roughly fifteen hundred armoured men-at-arms.

The poet Drayton later placed William ap Thomas of Gwent and his contingent of two thousand Welsh bowmen first in the order of battle—under the armorial ensigns of each county; *Adar Morganwg* followed by *Gwaed gwn Gwent*:

> Glamorgan men, a castle great and high
> From which, out of the battlement above,
> A flame shot up itself into the sky;
> The men of Monmouth (for the ancient love
> Of that dear country neighbouring them so nigh)
> Next after them in equipage that move,
> Three crown imperial, which supported were
> With three armed arms, in their prone ensign
>   bear.

Facing them across the narrow valley were approximately twenty-eight thousand well-rested, heavily armed members of the French aristocracy: each more than eager to prove themselves upon the field of battle. The situation looked quite bleak for England—battle was now unavoidable and the following day would pit them against the finest army the whole of Europe had to offer.

Upon completion of his duties as chaplain, John Stephens took a moment to comment in his journal by the light of a meagre fire.

"When, at last, the light failed and darkness had fallen between us and them, every man who had not previously cleansed his conscience by confession put on the armour of penitence—and the only shortage that night was one of priests."

Less than half a mile away atop the opposite hill, a very different mood prevailed amongst the lords of France. Throughout the night, the French nobles mocked King Henry and drank to their impending victory—the sounds of laughter and smells of roasting meat only torturing the English further.

The French were hugely confident: not simply because they outnumbered the English by at least three to one; and possibly five or six to one. Marshall Boucicault, however, did not take the ragged English army lightly and he worked out a strategy to outwit them.

In his battle plan, Boucicault had ruled out the traditional cavalry charge—they had failed before against the English bowmen. The bulk of his army would advance carefully toward Henry's army on foot; supported by a secret weapon the English would never expect: a company of crossbowmen that had been hired from Italy. At the same time, his cavalry would outflank the English and annihilate his archers with a surprise attack from the sides and rear. Without the protection of his bowmen, King Henry and his knights would be completely helpless.

All in all, a brilliant strategy—had the French nobility only opted to follow his instructions.

Dawn of 25 October, St Crispin's Day, found the French army of twenty-eight thousand divided into three imposing battalions. Facing them at the distant boundary of the field stood the bedraggled remnant Henry's dilapidated invasion force.

Each side was attempting to assess their opponent; captains discussing amongst themselves how best to engage the enemy. Indeed, the combatants stood there on the rain-soaked heath in the glow of dawn for nearly three full hours without either side committing their forces. At 11:00, King Henry V ordered his archers to advance to range; where they hammered pointed stakes into the mud to dissuade the French from a headlong cavalry charge.

Though the pennons flapped in the breeze and concealed the English, Marshall Boucicault immediately realised that Henry's archers had deliberately taken up a line directly across the narrowest point. As the ground dropped off rather steeply on each side to impenetrable thickets and forest, his plan to outflank the English with his armoured knights was now impossible. The French commander was desperately trying to come up with another plan when the English archers stepped out from behind their stakes and began to taunt the French nobles.

The aristocracy had threatened to cut off the first two fingers of any archer they managed to capture to prevent them from ever being capable of firing a bow again—which now prompted over five thousand archers to stab two fingers in the air at the nobility. With the Englishmen shouting insults about their questionable parentage and cursing at the top of their lungs, the French nobility, enraged at being abused by simple commoners, abandoned all restraint and, against direct orders from their commander, launched a headlong charge against the English line.

Exactly as Marshall Boucicault had feared.

Though the iron bodkins of the archers had little effect on the heavily armoured French, sadly, such was not the case with their unprotected chargers. Thousands of arrows screamed down upon the galloping beasts: knocking the horses out from under riders in merciless screams. With their opponent's cavalry cut to pieces and now entirely on foot, the English dropped their bows and stepped up to take on the Frenchmen with daggers and heavy lead hammers. Ignoring any quaint ideas about chivalry or fair play, the rabble simply stabbed their aristocratic opponents in the neck under their helmets or rammed their blades through the eye slits of their steel visors. Others pounded any who had fallen with the great hammers: shattering extended arms and legs as their victims lay sprawled out helpless in the mud.

After two weeks of heavy rain, the clay under the thin layer of grass had been quickly carved free by thundering hooves and plated steel. The gooey muck immediately adhered like glue to the heavy armour of the French knights and made it impossible for them to advance, or even to get back up once they had fallen. The English archers, clad only in cloth, moved easily through the quagmire. Unencumbered by any lofty ideals of mercy, the mercenaries from England's gaols hacked and butchered any unlucky French aristocrat misfortunate enough to have fallen within range.

With their honour on the line, the remaining armoured men-at-arms threw themselves toward the English line; realising too late that the terrified horses that survived the initial hail of arrows had spun around in wild and frantic attempts to escape: while the thousands of French infantry in the ranks collapsed in on them from behind.

The natural bottleneck of the field made it impossible for the French to hold ranks; as they had to funnel to the centre to advance to avoid sliding down the slopes of either side. Whenever a knight or horse fell, he became hopelessly stuck in the boggy ground and was immediately crushed by all the knights advancing from behind. In point of fact, more Frenchmen died from collapsed lungs and being trampled by their own kinsmen than ever made it to the front line to succumb in battle.

By ignoring their commander, the French nobility had played right to the strength of the English.

Panic spread through the ranks of Frenchmen; who could not look up for fear of being hit through their visors by still more showers of arrows. Too many soldiers, attempting to shoulder their way to the front, simply knocked their fellow countrymen down into the quagmire. Instead of a glorious battle of skill and experience, Agincourt degraded into a dirty, savage bloodbath. Many had their arms, hands, and heads hacked off and collapsed under the swelling ranks: ground to death beneath the heavy armour of those still attempting to get past them and join the fray.

It was utter carnage; with almost eight thousand French knights slaughtered in the first hour alone.

The ill-advised charge of the French cavalry had pushed through the ranks of crossbowmen, forcing them out of range and to the back of the field; and that single eventuality sounded the death knell of Boucicault's knights. The Marshall's carefully orchestrated strategy to defeat the English invaders had been reversed: an unintentional casualty of his captains' zeal to quickly exterminate the English.

By ignoring their commander's instructions and blindly throwing themselves at Henry's archers, senior nobles of the invincible French army had, in point of fact, blindly thrown themselves over the hedges—like a flock of sheep to the waiting wolves.

* * * * *

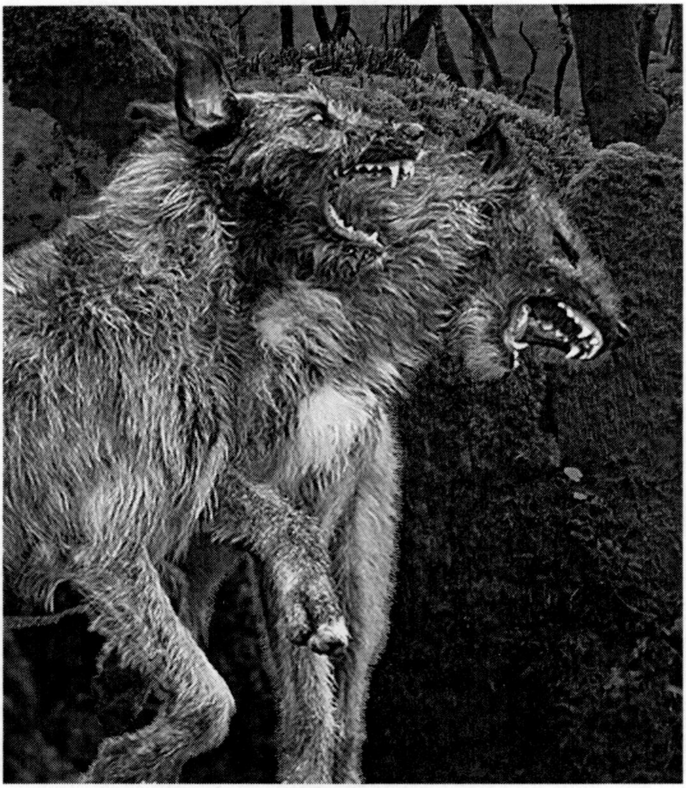

Chapter Three

Eternity: the curse of Deities and the Damned alike.

Thirst holds no terror in a realm laden with streams. As poverty poses little dread when all people round share a similar caste: so, too, to those whom time may never gnash upon with savage measured days—infinity inflicts its universal plague of customary sameness upon any who might share their eternal perpetuity. Small wonder, to many who have considered the attitudes of gods, countless immortals appear to have gone quite insane over the centuries. Likewise, the departed, faced with the brutal tedium of an existence beyond the constraints of time; must share an imposed restraint of persisting in a plane where lifetimes of experience and understanding have lost all familiarity.

Without a doubt, any spirit of man or beast must surely wile away the years considering the possibilities of retribution.

Accordingly, legions of angels and demons have always appeared to envy and eagerly entwine themselves with the restlessness and exhilaration of the living. So, too, the spirits of those who have trodden the earth in eons past seem, at times, terribly reluctant to leave the finite world behind. To glimpse what one might perceive as the wanderings of restless spirits, though disconcerting at the very least, speaks nothing to the terror of being engaged deliberately by spectres who give the impression that their sole purpose is to interact once more with vengeance against the living.

Rather than being consigned by the Creator or His opposition to afflict the mortal, it well may be that souls of innocent and persecuted inhabit still the lonely lanes and glens; where now abandoned stones stand in silent testament of the past and its many hideous crimes.

There, the innocent continue to ever walk familiar paths alongside the culpable—intent upon visiting retribution or reward upon the oblivious heirs of humankind.

After a thousand years of patient waiting, the hounds of Raglan Wood were about to be rewarded for their persistence.

Centuries of tedium had honed both their hunger and their rage.

* * * * *

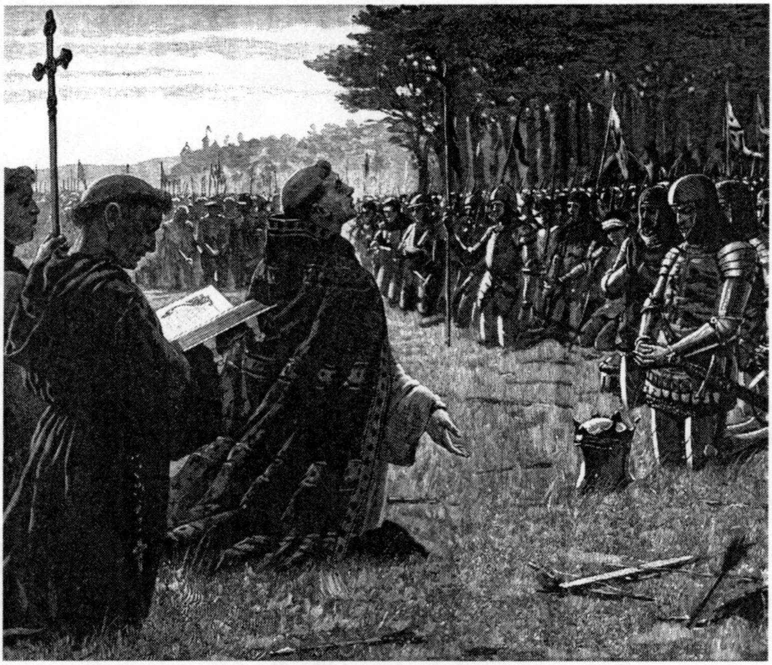

Chapter Four

Two hours after the first, disastrous decision to storm the longbows, the duke of Brabant, Antoine of Burgundy, arrived quite late to Agincourt. Immediately assessing the gravity of the situation, the duke rallied the remaining French for a counter attack and threw themselves at King Henry's personal entourage: men who had been held in check for just such a contingency—personally commanded by the former Welsh mercenary, Dafydd Gam.

Surely, if necessity is the mother of invention then, quite probably, desperation might well be the father of madness.

Nothing less than reckless abandon might ever make the nobles from Paris hurl themselves into the face of such grave jeopardy. Having faced extermination for the past two hours, perhaps the Duke's suicidal charge toward King Henry was no less foolhardy than standing stationary and waiting to be butchered.

In less than an hour since Boucicault's first charge, some one thousand French nobles had been captured by Henry's men, with thousands more unceremoniously slaughtered in the quagmire that had opened up adjacent to the English lines. Still, Brabant's surprise attack from the flank managed to disrupt those standing closest to the King of England; who immediately fanned out in a thin skirmish line to protect their liege.

While one squad of knights feigned assault from the right to draw the attention of the bowmen, the main body clambered and clanked up the slight grade on Henry's left flank. As fortune would have it, that particular parcel of ground was slightly more stable than most of the battlefield: there not being horses to tear through the thin grass and expose the mud lying underneath. Solid footing gave the initial advantage to Antoine's desperate assault. French armour was virtually impervious to arrow fire even at the closest range and, without exposed horses to fire upon, the Welsh archers that defended England's exposed left flank were forced to battle hand to hand. Unprotected archers, caught by surprise on solid ground, were relatively defenceless against the burnished steel plate of the French heavy infantry.

Dafydd Gam was the first to recognise the threat and literally shoved King Henry in the chest to push him back into the lines and out of range. With a dagger in one hand and his spiked war hammer clenched tightly in the other, the Welshman shouted above the clamour and tumult for any help he could find.

William ap Thomas and his contingent of Welsh bowmen had been the first to engage the clattering charge of French horsemen, but had been withdrawn after half an hour and replaced with longbow men from Lancashire under the command of the Duke of Manchester. This put the archers from Gwent directly between the duke of Brabant's desperate charge and the Royal Entourage.

The course of history is a fickle thing; changing its track through time for concrete actions, not subtle human sentiment. Thousands who died that day at Agincourt did so for intangible ideals such as Honour, Duty, and Brotherhood. The Gwent commander had no intention of doing the same. Instead, he rallied his men to intercept the French advance: with the sole intention of being seen by Henry and his Lords. He postured with a flourish as he waved his bowmen into position.

"For God and King Henry!"

Pushing past Dafydd Gam and the remainder of the king's bodyguard, William bravely brought up the rear of the assault: leaving himself a clear avenue of escape back across the English lines. As the archers slammed into the razored fury of the French nobility, William turned, raised his sword above his head and tried to catch King Henry's attention.

"For England and the King!"

Having been forced back to avoid being knocked down, Dafydd looked to his right and found himself standing next to his son-in-law, Sir Roger Vaughn. The sight of William ap Thomas prancing around and shouting while his archers were being straightforwardly butchered only feet away made Gam's stomach turn.

Elbowing Roger as the king's personal entourage quickly formed a second column, Dafydd drew Roger's attention to the peacock parading between them and the French.

Having completely assured himself that King Henry V was certainly now watching, William sprang into a speech that he must have, no doubt, memorised for just such an occasion.

"Crown our efforts with Victory and the inevitable power of light over darkness, of justice over Evil and Brutal Force."

All expression drained from the faces of Roger Vaughn and Gam. Gobsmacked, they stood there amidst the unholy screams and carnage with their mouths open in amazement.

"Bugger me." Roger spoke without emotion.

Only being jostled in the side by still others of Henry's men attempting to get in position brought Dafydd back into the reality of what was still happening around them.

"If the French don't stick that pig, I'm going to gut him myself."

"You'll have to get in line," his son-in-law quipped back.

Just then, the last of William's archers fell and the duke of Brabant's force broke through the gap. Dafydd stepped up and delivered a savage, hammering blow to the chinstrap of the nearest Frenchman; cleaving off his entire lower jaw. Bathed in blood, Gam then stepped up as the knight fell forward and smashed through the back of his unprotected skull.

Sensing imminent death, William ap Thomas dropped his sword, wheeled around, and darted down the grade like a faint-hearted fox: using the king's own personal guard as a human shield to safeguard his spineless retreat.

As fortune would have it, King Henry V of England clearly saw that as well.

Sir Roger Vaughn stepped up beside his father-in-law and slashed through the nearest Frenchman's chainmail at the knee. Severing the limb, the noble squealed like a rabbit in a snare and fell straight into the mud. Vaughn did not have time to end his misery; as still more Frenchmen stomped over the body of their comrade and mashed him entirely out of sight into the now oozing muck as they tried to reach the English.

With his king now in very real danger of being killed, Dafydd turned and screamed.

"Get the King back up to the wagons!"

As he waved frantically up the grade, Antoine, duke of Brabant, stepped through the writhing mass of bleeding, dismembered men and cleft Gam's skull wide open from behind with a savage two-handed blow. The Welshman collapsed to his knees like a wet sack of grain and toppled sideways to the ground.

At long last, the Lancashire bowmen swarmed from the right and circled behind the men from Monmouthshire. Without hope of being reinforced themselves, the Frenchmen found themselves cut off on all sides by furious serfs and commoners who began to pound and batter them with huge lead hammers fashioned for just such occasion. King Henry and his men managed to clamber back from the line and save themselves: but at a terrible cost to the courageous men from Gwent.

The craven William ap Thomas was last seen scampering across the fields—off in the general direction of Calais.

* * * * *

By mid-afternoon, the English stood relatively confident of carrying the day. What with the aristocracy of Boucicault's forces assuming that, while defeat was dishonour, they would simply surrender and be ransomed by their kinsmen once back in England; in a very real sense, Henry V had the problem of taking far too many prisoners.

The code of chivalry demanded ransom, but the English now had literally thousands of captives—far, far more than his men could adequately handle. There was no way so small a force could shuttle them all the way to Calais; not with the French perfectly capable of rising up against the Englishmen at the very first opportunity. Not willing or able to simply release their enemy with a sound thrashing and allow the French to regroup and attack again, King Henry reluctantly gave the order for his knights to murder the captured Frenchmen in cold blood.

They refused.

While visions of indignant priests and English knights appalled by the blatant disregard for the rules of war might spring to mind, the basis of their righteous anger may have been more firmly grounded in economics than in morality. Prisoners meant ransom. Certainly, one could receive enough ransom for any of the well-heeled aristocrats to live quite comfortably for the rest of one's life. Many of the British realised they might never live to seize upon such an opportunity again and steadfastly refused to let the prospect of such wealth slip through their fingers.

Unwilling to accept the inherent danger of his prisoners breaking free and attacking the English from the rear, young King Henry then turned to his archers to carry out the grisly task.

As nobles on both sides stood in abject horror, the bowmen of the duke of Manchester and those from Gwent massacred over two thousand prisoners where they stood—hacking their way through the unarmed, huddled throng with knives and swords as threshers might wade through a field of wheat.

Bodies of butchered Frenchmen were piled up to six feet high: a scene of almost unbelievable slaughter that the English chaplain, John Stephens attempted to later relate in his account:

> "When the strength of the enemy had been utterly wasted and the rigours of battle ended, we who had gained the victory came back through the heaps of the slain. And I truly believe, there is not a man with a heart of flesh or even stone who, had he seen and pondered the bitter wounds of so many Christian men, would not have dissolved into tears time and again for grief."

25 October 1415 marked a turning point, not just for the Hundred Year's War but for the entire of western civilisation. The unbridled carnage of that single afternoon abruptly inked a bloody epitaph upon the golden ideals of an Age of Chivalry.

* * * * *

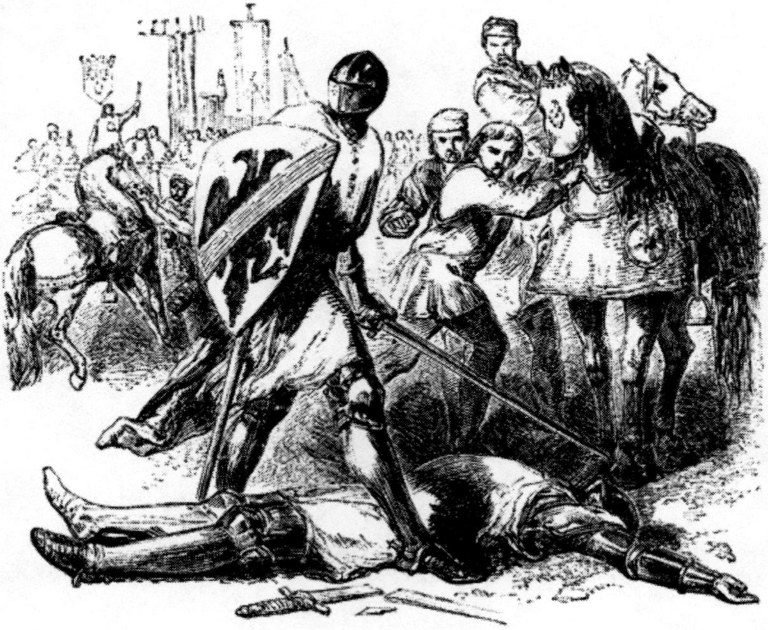

Chapter Five

"Compliments of the season."

Dafydd's weak jest was one of a whisper made through gritting teeth. He held out a cup of anaesthetic to his son-in-law on the adjacent blood-soaked cot. A mixture of hemlock, opium, and boar's gall bladder; the noxious concoction was about all the English physicians had to offer the wounded to help control the pain.

Remarkably, the duke of Brabant's men had been able to close the distance and were only, at their nearest, perhaps two strides from dispatching England's king. To do so would have meant immediate victory for the French and, as it happened, one of the nobles actually managed to get close enough to sever a jewelled portion off Henry's circlet crown. Again, destiny and history deferred their fortunes to the serendipities of simple chance.

With the coincidental arrival of the duke of Manchester, the French counterattack immediately dispersed and put to flight, while any left alive from either side were bustled back to the medical wagons. Forcefully dragged through the mire and muck away from the last of the fighting, the king's personal bodyguard had been heaved upon one of the many muddy cots next to the mortally wounded Sir Roger Vaughn.

So brutal were the injuries of most that doctors could do very little other than attempt to slow the flow of blood and try to ease their pain. Shaved rabbit fur moistened with raw egg whites was packed tightly into the most grievous gashes and cavities: the hope being that the poultice might prevent men from bleeding to death before muscles and skin might be stitched back together like so many sections of torn cloth. To sedate their screams, the vile anaesthetic was forced down between breaths to haply numb the unlucky before they went into shock. The air within the tents quickly grew thick with the stench of burning flesh as red hot irons seared down against naked skin to cauterise those lucky enough to survive.

Vaughn's condition was little better.

The tip of a French sword had glanced off his shield and caught the femoral artery in his thigh. It was only a matter of minutes before the man bled to death. And he knew it.

"Hmmm." Roger sniffed the disgusting concoction of bile and hemlock.

"A bitter, yellowish-blue blend with bright high notes of salt and stringy green—an invigorating banquet of refreshment."

Dafydd managed a weak smile as Roger raised the cup and offered a toast.

"In retribution for some Horrendous Sin . . . I, sadly, have absolutely no recollection of committing."

His best attempt at levity, Roger's face wrenched up as he forced the slippery mixture past the point of gagging and tried his best to swallow. Not at all convinced at his ability to keep it down, the knight collapsed back on the canvas cot and listened to the sound of his own blood spattering upon the ground beneath him in heavy drops.

"You tell that voluptuous daughter of yours to keep her heaving bosom warm."

"Are you trying to tell me that you aren't going to make it back to Abergavenny?" Dafydd whispered with blood continuing to trickle down his face.

"No." His son-in-law was losing consciousness. "That's what I'm trying desperately not to tell you."

Both lay there in the late October shade and listened to the distant shouting that now, to both, strangely seemed even farther away.

"Clever fellow, Death is . . . to snatch me away in the flower of my manhood . . ."

Sir Roger Vaughn never finished his sentence. He died beside his father-in-law; thinking of his wife waiting back home in Wales.

Sensing the same, Dafydd closed his eyes and sucked in a laboured breath.

"So here we die . . . in an open field—like waifs and strays."

Minutes later, two attending physicians happened to make their way down the aisle of staggered cots and found the two men dead. Without ceremony, their bodies were quickly thrown upon the pile outside to make room for still others on the way.

Knighthood suddenly seemed far cheaper than any at Agincourt had expected. Who, likewise, never dreamed a muddy field in France might ever cost so much.

* * * * *

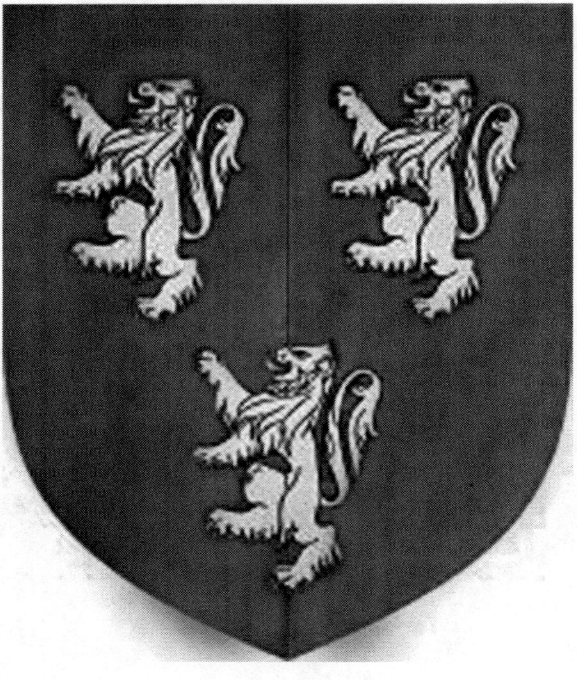

Chapter Six

"These are my sons."

The setup of the pathetic joke was always the same; regardless if whomever chanced to be standing nearby had happened to have heard the jest a thousand times. William ap Thomas would position himself next to his oldest son, Thomas, and pat him affectionately upon the head. Named for his Grandfather, Thomas ap Gwilym, the lad gritted his teeth and prepared to bear the same lame witticism that seemed to have no welcome end.

"Give this one a penny and he will be good."

Resigning himself to the inevitable, the lad smiled faintly—as his father expected.

Glancing over the two youngest with an inclusive nod, William raised his eyebrow and delivered the excruciating quip.

"The other two are good for nothing."

His siblings were still too young to get the play on words and took the insult with far more aplomb than it deserved: though they never seemed to understand the hilarious response of friends and passersby. The oldest son did not have the heart to explain it to them. From what he had seen, this was about as close as they might ever get to being praised or appreciated.

Their father would most certainly see to that.

* * * * *

For many Welshmen, William ap Thomas had literally become the archetype of success.

The man had, completely ignoring the impracticality of the rhetorical expression, bootstrapped himself out of the mire of anonymity. Never mind that the boots were not, in fact, his own: that they had been purposely selected and then stolen specifically for that reason alone. While the use of cunning and deceitful tactics for personal gain might be praised by some and equally abhorred by others, all who had occasion to make his acquaintance agreed that, when it came to expediency, there was no individual better suited or apt to promote William ap Thomas than the man himself.

Sired from one of the more prominent houses of minor Welsh gentry, William's father, Thomas ap Gwilym of Perth-hir, had led by example: marrying Maud Morley, daughter of Sir John Morley, who held an estate in the parish of Llansantffraed in county Monmouthshire. As the fourth son of Gwilym ap Jenkin of nearby Wern-ddu, Thomas realised that a strategic marriage would be the only hope of social advancement or recognition.

His son, William, was certainly no idiot and took the lesson to heart.

Accordingly, he took a wife from a prominent family—one Elizabeth Bluet, the daughter of Sir John Bluet of Daglingworth and widow of Sir James Berkeley. Making the most of the alliance, William ap Thomas parlayed his new position as husband to great advantage and success: assuming the position of Steward of the Lordship of Abergavenny. When Elizabeth died in 1420, he retained Bluet Manor of Raglan as a tenant of his stepson, James Berkeley, 1st Baron Berkeley, and in 1425 Lord Berkeley agreed that William could continue to hold the property for the duration of his life.

Keeping with his meteoric rise, William saw no advantage to be gained from the role of widower and determined to marry a second time. Choosing another heiress, he set his eye on Gwladus ferch Dafydd, the widow of Sir Roger Vaughan and daughter of Sir Dafydd Gam—both of whom had served alongside him and died on the field at Agincourt five years earlier. It was tragic that neither could have lived: in that she would not be in this situation if her husband had survived, and that her father would have killed William ap Thomas without qualm for even thinking of touching his daughter.

Political affairs aside, Gwladus was worth pursuing on her own account. Strikingly beautiful: a feature which William, after being intimately acquainted with her father, fully attributed to her late mother; the hand of Gwladus was a prize sought by more than a few who returned from Agincourt. Later described as *Y seren o Efenni* or "the Star of Abergavenny" by renowned poet Lewys Glyn Cothi, her substantial possessions and pedigree made Gwladus all the more desirable.

To someone with such aspirations as William ap Thomas, there could be no hesitation. He hurriedly tied the marriage knot at Bredwardine, Herefordshire, in 1421—only months after burying his first wife.

Destiny, after all, could not be expected to wait around for long.

The Wraiths of Raglan Wood

* * * * *

William ap Thomas was a bastard.

Though sired from a notable lineage and the darling of Richard, duke of York, his friends and political associates often found it strange that none of his own immediate family had much to do with their notable kinsman. To them, William was invariably the life of any party; witty to a fault, shrewd in turning a phrase or any opportunity to his advantage: the one man to count on whenever something needed to be done. Sensing that popularity in many situations quite often led to power; he seldom failed to steal at least a modicum of attention from any room he chose to enter.

After receiving his knighthood and amidst great speculation, he had heralds in London create a spectacular blazon of three lions rampant on a split field of cerulean and crimson for his shield.

Many rumours from his friends at court as to the symbolism of the three lions led William to tell them it was for the Holy Trinity. Though, when his friends in Wales asked the identical question, he explained it was the three houses: of Bluet, his first wife; Vaughn, his second wife; and, of course that of Thomas ap Gwilym, his father. His children sided with the first explanation; in that, as far as they could tell, their father considered himself a minor deity and expected to be treated as such. His cronies admired the artwork more than any hidden meaning but, then again, his associates did not have to live with the man—and friends could always excuse themselves and leave any time they wished.

To prove his absolute authority at home, William would deliberately berate and beat his children in front of company: demanding that each run and fetch whatever object he desired; and then strike them for not being quicker: no matter how hurriedly they returned. Children, to him, were the inevitable consequence of marriage; unavoidable aspects of wedlock and trophies of his own virility to be used as he saw fit.

As a result, his offspring were never held or hugged, never told that they were good—for, in their father's eyes, they were never good enough. William drove them like animals; to better their cousins: not so they might accomplish more with their lives, but that he might appear a better parent than his siblings. He offhandedly called them bastards, claimed them beetle-brained, then derided them as fat whenever any might unwittingly eat more for dinner than their father thought they should.

Their mother, Gwladus, fared little better.

Whenever guests might compliment her table and turn to William to affirm the lady's capabilities in the kitchen, he would regularly jam his jaws to capacity and try to talk over and through a mouthful of food.

"Well, I'm doing my very best to choke it down."

More than simply rural and certainly not representative of his kinfolk, William ap Thomas was, in a word, base. Any conversation without the presence of someone the man needed to placate could be counted on to be punctuated with foul jokes and dirty limericks. Disregarded from the company of his relatives as intentionally profane, blasphemy seemed the perfect way for the man to make his point: so the latest knight of Raglan deliberately and quite regularly inserted the name of the Lord as adjective to illustrate his frustrations.

Fury defiantly lurked on a deceptively tight bowstring of indignation; ready to strike out at any instant in uncontrollable rage. To make matters all the worse, when guests had politely excused themselves and made a run for the door and safety, William would regularly, and quite rightfully, bemoan their hurried departure as a reflection on his behaviour. At least, until he began to ease his pain with drink. Alcohol reliably reassigned blame to someone in the household staff or member of the family who obviously had not addressed the evening or his company with the respect either deserved.

When possessed by alcoholic rage, the new master of Bluet Manor would head for the thick leather strop he set aside on a nail behind the pantry door. Realising that, even when inebriated, he would find it difficult to hide his wife from public scrutiny—he called his children to him in the kitchen and shut the door so servants might find it difficult to hear their screams. Fortunately for his offspring, his allegiance to the duties of the duke of York severely limited the time and opportunity their father had to travel back to Raglan.

So many progeny have endured an illegitimate birth; each spending a lifetime in attempts to regain some self-esteem. Being denounced as a "son of a bitch" for accidents of genealogy or events well out of one's control often proves to be one of life's greatest tragedies. Each of us, however righteous, has to respect someone for overcoming undeserved slander and prejudice for actually being a bastard—with, of course, the distinct exception of William ap Thomas.

Decidedly not.

When it came to being a undeniable bastard, William ap Thomas was, without question, a self-made man.

* * * * *

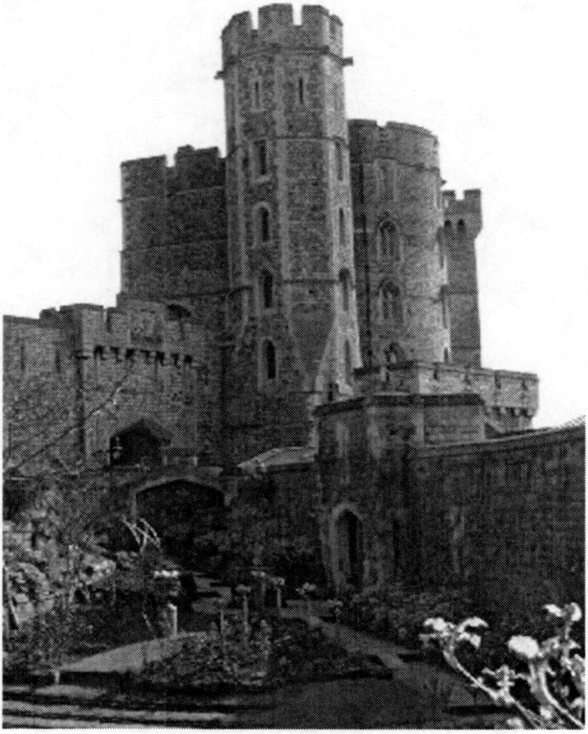

CHAPTER SEVEN

If true—that God is really no respecter of persons; then Fate, from all appearances, might prove to be even less pernickety: randomly selecting whose star will rise and whose curtain will fall.

Ignoring convention and often what might appear as common sense, Fortune seems apt to favour some rather than others: indiscriminately choosing to bless the least worthy amongst us. For unknown reasons, Destiny or Chance glanced over better men and, for some inexplicable cause, chose the son of Thomas ap Gwilym of Perth-hir—not that William ap Thomas was likely to ever voice any objection.

Such was the case when Henry VI assumed the throne in 1422. As the only child and heir of Henry V, he was King of England at the age of only nine months when his father died—and King of France at the unbelievable age of twelve months with the death of his maternal Grandfather, Charles VI. The infant king's mother, Catherine of Valois, was a mere twenty years of age herself and, what with the prolonged hundred years of hostility with France, was publicly sequestered from having much to do with the boy king's thoroughly brief childhood.

The British nobility sprang into immediate action with the sudden, unexpected death of their Monarch on 31 August, 1422.

Apparently succumbing to dysentery contracted during the siege of Meaux, the thirty-five-year-old King of England passed away at the Château de Vincennes near Paris. Fully aware of the predicament his impending death would have on England, Henry quickly named his brother, John, Duke of Bedford, as regent of France in the name of his two-month-old son. After the King's death, his widow returned Henry's body back to London; where he was interred at Westminster Abbey.

Parliament hurriedly met and established a Regency Council to rule until the new heir came of age:

mainly comprised of the immediate family. John of Lancaster, duke of Bedford, and the boy king's uncle, was immediately appointed as senior regent, though Henry V's other surviving brother, Humphrey, duke of Gloucester, ruled while John secured England's claims in France. In matters of state, the late king's half-uncle, Bishop Henry Beaufort, protected the interests of their infant monarch and made certain the regent government did not lose control of the duel monarchy and Lancastrian dynasty.

Under this makeshift administration, William ap Thomas found himself being awarded a knighthood in 1426 from Henry VI, even though the child king of England was not even officially crowned until November 1429—a full month before the young boy's eighth birthday.

Graciously accepting the moniker of "Y marchog glas o Went" or "the blue knight of Gwent," William went on to establish himself as a person of consequence throughout south Wales. By 1432, what with the additional assets and property acquired from his second marriage to Gwladus, William finally had the funds to purchase Bluet Manor at Raglan outright from his stepson, James Berkeley, and began to build a castle of his own.

Good things might actually come to those who wait and the world truly be inherited by the meek at some distant point in human history but, as far as William ap Thomas was concerned, someone might as well step up and claim it until a better candidate happened to come along.

* * * * *

All the while, Gwladus kept her tongue and raised their children in as much obscurity as her husband's all too public career might allow.

Thomas, the eldest son, had been born in 1422; with William born in 1423 and Richard in 1425. Elizabeth, the only daughter of the union, made her appearance in 1427. If their father had little time to spare for his offspring, Gwladus resolved from the outset that her children would not suffer from his absence. If truth be told, all—including the household staff and servants—relished the weeks of William's absence from Bluet Manor. With the master of the house not in attendance, a sense of peace and joy seemed to settle upon the hearth and gables; revitalising a mood of cheer and exhilaration that seemed to deliberately avoid the man.

Small, demure, and rather quite beautiful; any who had met Gwladus ferch Dafydd could not help but speculate about what accident of destiny ever might have brought the two together. While William ap Thomas was off in hot pursuit of fame and recognition, Gwladus was perfectly content to play with the children out on the lawn. After heavy rains, mother and four children would hurry down to the pond like a hen with her ducklings and cavort in the mud for hours. When exhausted from their games, the Lady of Bluet Manor would call her children round her on the bank; where contests would be held to see who might make the perfect mud bowl or most life-like animal from clay.

Bluet Manor, absent its tyrannical Lord, was very near idyllic.

Huge flocks of woodpigeons, rooks, and songbirds regularly swept the sky with their preened and tapered wings. Each crisp November night, woodcock would arrive from the far north by moonlight to join the native birds and roost in the nearby trees. Morning rain across the valley often blurred the scenery a bit but could not disguise the sound of foxes scuffing through the fallen leaves or the footsteps of herds of deer browsing along the forest paths.

After washing up, mother and children would often spread sheets out upon the rolling lawn and watch the whirling clouds pass overhead: pointing out ships, or cows, or dragons that swirled into shape and then silently dissolved to form something altogether new. Exhausted, their mother would sense the time and, in the context of yet another game, cause all to scamper back to the house to bathe and have a nap before beginning their lessons.

The daughter of Sir Dafydd Gam and former widow of Sir Roger Vaughan, Gwladus was rather well educated for a woman of her position. As a result, their mother took every absence of William ap Thomas as an opportunity to school the children with stories of their ancestors and, much to their distaste, mathematics and writing.

Particularly her daughter, Elizabeth.

Perhaps it was an act of simple self-preservation: understanding the way of the world might protect the girl from enduring the sorrow it seemed her mother had to bear.

Thomas and William could well have been twins: only a year apart and much the same of temperament.

Their mother had noticed it as well; that the boys appeared to be mirror images of the other. Thomas was right-handed, brushed his hair to the left, could see far better with his right eye and threw right-handed. William countered by being left-handed, forcing his hair to the right, could see better on his left and threw left-handed. It seemed as if one person had been cut precisely down the middle and then the two halves set to face the other. Personality wise, the two oldest boys were much the same—in that they were identical yet completely opposite. Thomas was outgoing and assertive like his father; William, sensitive and intuitive like his mother. Still, they seemed to compliment each other perfectly and set off on their own adventures whenever possible; leaving the two youngest, Richard and Elizabeth, to entertain and occupy their mother.

Richard, while far from effeminate, much preferred playing with his baby sister and mother. He had a singular fear of getting dirty and tried to stay inside as much as possible—a trait that made the third son a perfect playmate for little Elizabeth. Only two years apart, they enjoyed playing together under Gwladus' watchful eye. While the two older boys were out sword fighting with dead sticks and branches, Gwladus would set Richard and Elizabeth on her lap and read slowly from the scriptures; pointing to every word and trying to teach her precious children to read.

Bluet Manor in the moonlight was even more enchanting.

Long, dreary evenings were spent with each child taking turns poking the coals of massive, crackling logs nestled in the oversized fireplace. Their mother would join them there—all kneeling tightly together to stay warm in the draughty hall. The children then took turns telling stories of scary beasts that lived in make-believe distant lands; of princes and princesses and witches with steaming brews; or of what each wanted to become when grown.

How very sad it is that time can never seem to embrace contentment for very long; that innocence must ever appear so tenuous and delicate. Equally, how tragic: that the fairest of dreams are regularly quite easily blown apart by even the slightest breeze.

* * * * *

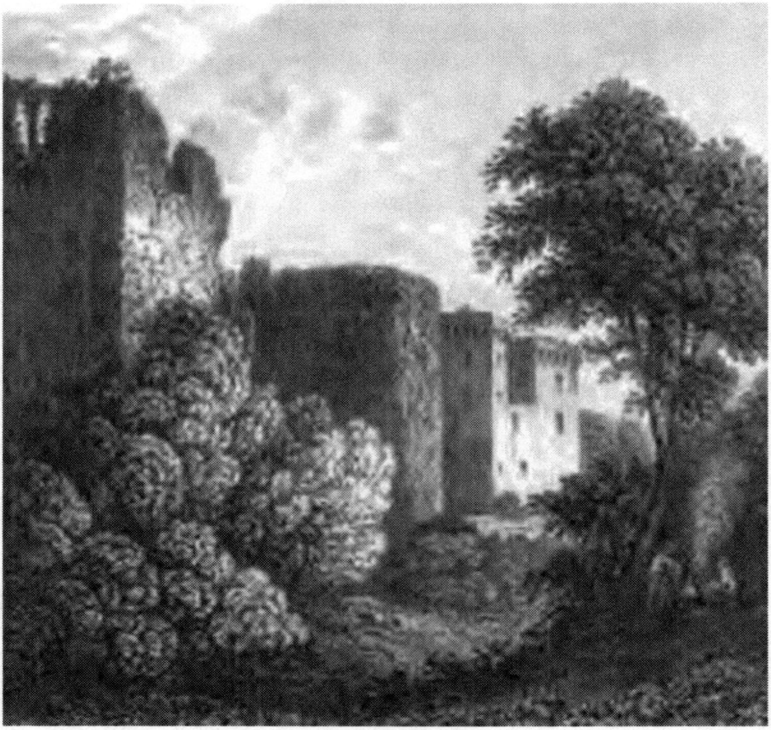

Chapter Eight

William stood alone at the end of the lane that led off to the stables.

His father and mother had had another contest of wills that morning: violent clashes of personality that appeared to be more and more common of late. Gwladus was terribly upset at his father's insistence upon teaching the two oldest boys to ride. At eight and nine, their mother did not mind too much if each sat in the saddle one at a time while the mount was walked by halter for short distances around the grounds. William ap Thomas considered the practise juvenile; demanding that Gwladus keep her opinions to herself and leave him to teach Thomas and eight year old William how to ride.

Watching as his father reached down from the saddle and yanked the terrified older Thomas up by his arm and positioned him directly behind the pommel, William noticed a look from his mother's eyes that the boy had never seen before. A glare of such fierce resentment had never dared to cross her face in all the lad's memory: a defiant stare that instantly and forever changed not only each parent but William as well. Thomas did not catch its glower; as he was doing his utmost to wriggle free from his father's grasp and slide down the stirrup to the safety of the ground.

Just as Gwladus stepped forward past her second son to speak her mind, her husband seized the reins and whipped his mount to the right; deliberately forcing the tail of the beast to slap across her face. Looking back over his shoulder with a smile to show that it had been intentional, he forced the imitation of an even wider grin and leaned down with venom in his eyes to whisper softly under his breath so his children might not easily hear.

"Don't even start your bitching."

To eight year old William, it seemed the entire event had been slowed down a hundred times. Each word and movement being recorded in slow motion in his mind. And, strange as it seems to say so, the boy instantly knew he had watched his family die right before his eyes.

His father whipped the flanks of the gelding with the reins, while Thomas tried desperately to hold on to the pommel.

"Let's go back inside."

Their mother had much to say but, true to her nature, would wait until the children were asleep that evening before she spoke her mind. Responsibility for her children was the woman's highest priority; even if it meant keeping them safe from hearing what she truly thought of their father's behaviour.

William ap Thomas' raucous counterfeit laughter echoed back across the field as Gwladus turned to take Richard and Elizabeth each by the hand and usher them back up the steps into the house.

Not knowing exactly what to do, William walked down the lane away from the house and watched the horse gallop away down to the edge of Raglan Wood. For the first time in his life, the boy honestly felt that ugliness had somehow, and quite intentionally, rubbed off his father and stained his mother's world.

Perhaps it was the events that followed that only made him feel that way.

Life has the tendency to cauterize the unforeseen with emotion and unexpectedly scar one's memories. The lad had been left alone between mother and father upon the track: an unfortunate vantage point that unwittingly forced young William to somehow make some sense of what the eight-year-old never should have seen.

* * * * *

That the accident could certainly have been prevented was obvious: that his father was, to a large part, to blame—unquestionable: and that William ap Thomas, given his nature and temperament, would adeptly shift the focus of guilt away from himself—completely predictable.

Jousting down the meadow at full gallop so near the broken timber would have normally been quite challenging for even the best of riders; doing so in a pique of temper while attempting to use one arm to hold a child balanced against his waist was tantamount to impossible. Time after time, the gelding would check his stride to clear the protruding trunks of fallen elms and firs; only to be whipped back up to speed while still scanning the uncut hay for yet more obstacles ahead. That the steed was bound to stumble sooner or later seemed obvious to everyone but its master.

Catching his right front hoof on an angled branch jutting waist high from the grass, the horse might well have righted himself in time had not the entire trunk of the fallen tree rolled with the contact and twisted the still sturdy limb in an unwieldy arc that followed the animal's chest. The thick obstruction smacked the galloping missile in the brisket just between its rider's outstretched stirrups and the tightly cinched girth. Unable to plant its hind legs, being held aloft, the animal could brace neither of its front hooves as the shanks and thighs scraped down against the still spinning branch and log.

For an instant that to young William seemed eternity, the threesome rolled in mid-air above the grass; then plummeted like stones knocked from a rocky ledge. His father leapt still further to his left to avoid the gelding's weight, while the poor horse could do nothing but tag the turf with his crest and withers as the animal's back and hocks followed its shoulder to the ground. Abandoned by his father and still clinging desperately to the swell of the skirt and pommel, young Thomas sat helpless as the cantle of the seat caught him in the middle of the back and drove him headfirst into the ground.

Eight-year-old William screamed.

He screamed with all his might; over and over: knowing that he should run, but unsure as to direction. In the end, he sprinted madly back up the lane toward his bewildered mother, brother, and sister; glancing back only long enough to watch the horse manage to struggle to its feet: to see his father take hold of the reins and stare blankly down into the crumpled underbrush.

None of their lives would ever be the same.

* * * * *

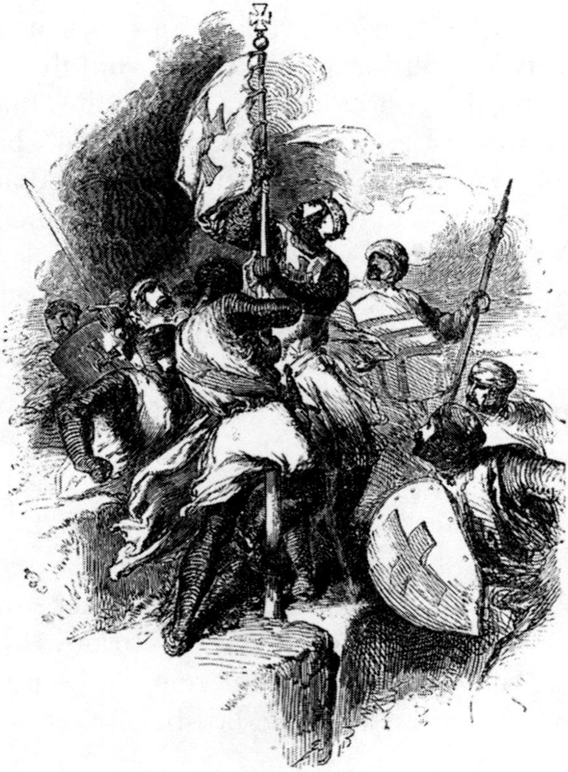

Chapter Nine

The Third War of Welsh Independence had begun in 1400 under the charismatic leadership of Owain Glyndwr and, for a time, seemed to almost guarantee sovereignty west of the river Severn.

Glyndwr was heir to Powys, the northern region of Wales, and a descendant of Deheubarth on his mother's side of the family. His ancestors having fought for Llywelyn ap Gruffydd during the last rebellion, Owain's conflict with Reginald de Grey, Lord of Ruthin and close friend of Henry IV of England, over common land that Grey had appropriated without legal right, blossomed almost overnight into a dramatic revolt against the English. Victories in the Plynlimmon area of the Cambrian Mountains of northern Ceredigion established the region as a basis of operations against the forces of King Henry.

The legendary source of the "five streams:" the river Severn, the Wye, Llyfnant, Clywedog, and Rheidol; the boggy terrain was the scene of battles since Hywel ab Cadogan met Owen Cyfeilog almost five hundred years earlier. It was from Plynlimmon that Glyndwr marched to attack towns near Ruthin: to sack Montgomery, scorch Welshpool, and raze Cwm Hir: and where the Welsh-born Dafydd Gam had once attempted to assassinate Owain Glyndwr for the king of England.

Though the portent of a comet in 1402 seemed to herald Welsh independence, the English Parliament were far less superstitious and introduced Penal Laws against the Welsh, prohibiting any public assembly in Wales. More importantly, the legislation denied Welshmen from bearing arms or residing within the settlements: attempting to force the dissidents back into the hills.

In response, Owain Glyndwr held Parliaments of his own in Machynlleth, declaring himself Prince of Wales: a defiance of the monarchy that pleased William Wallace and the clans of Scotland, not to mention France. Indeed, a number of Frenchmen did cross the channel to throw their support to Glyndwr but a succession of defeats at Pwllmelyn, Anglesey, Aberystwyth, and Harlech Castle resulted in The Charter of Brecon, which severely restricted the rights of any natural born citizen of Wales. When Prince Henry (later King Henry V) retook most of the territory that had been captured by the dissidents, Owain Glyndwr went into hiding and, for all practical purposes, the last of the Welsh Revolts fizzled to an inglorious end.

If truth be told, as the end grew near, many Welshmen saw the writing on the wall and switched allegiance in hope of title and reward; notably Dafydd Gam, who became with time, the king of England's bodyguard and personal friend.

With the end of the rebellion and Battle of Agincourt in 1415, great numbers of Welsh quickly attempted to ingratiate or marry their way into English acceptance. To the humiliation of many in Wales and amusement of still others, Owain ap Maredudd defected to London and married the widow of Henry V, Catherine de Valois, daughter of Charles VI, king of France: taking his grandfather's name of Tudor. Which meant that, only years after the great revolts and Agincourt, Henry Tudor, Owain's son born of Catherine was, in fact, half-brother of Henry VI: a heritage that would prove of great interest to Parliament and London when Henry VI and Edward, his heir, would later be murdered in 1471.

Chasing the irresistible wagging tail of encroaching Anglisation, William ap Thomas abandoned the position of Steward of the Lordship of Abergavenny and shrewdly manoeuvred through the political backwash of Gwent to become Steward of the Lordships of Usk and Caerleon under Richard, duke of York. Demonstrating his keen and sharp-witted insight time and time again, the son of Thomas ap Gwilym eventually served on the duke's military council and found himself elevated to the station of Sheriff of Cardiganshire and Carmarthenshire.

The perfect position from which to launch his political career.

* * * * *

"These are my sons."

It must have been the attendance of a new courier from the court that sparked the all too familiar attempt at levity. Either that or the fact that William had walked close enough to remind his father of his favourite allegory. In either case, by the time William the elder had stood and positioned his boy beside him in the customary position previously occupied by Thomas, the full impact of the irony hit the man.

The onlookers caught the heartbreak of the calamity as well; having each heard the joke dozens of times. The boy looked up to his father's face; presuming to bask in the tyrant's pain and watch him, just for once, twist in the wind. When he saw the semblance of a 'pity me' expression lightly tattooed across the patriarch's brow, young William's mood instantly turned to loathing. Even now, his father was playing the situation to his own personal advantage; manipulating the spectators into commiseration or compassion that the old man fully intended to make the most of the very first time an opportunity arose.

The tears that all standing in the room there saw well up in the small child's eyes were far more the result of the acid of his heart than any consequence of grief. The fact that that somehow made him more like his father proved simply too horrible for the boy to contemplate.

* * * * *

Eternity, for good or ill, hangs upon every instant—the future constantly being transformed by each fleeting sensation or sentiment: whether dismally bleak or sublimely brilliant.

Emotion may well be the defining characteristic that transcends the soul and elevates humankind above all other creatures; the singular imprint that infuses each man, woman, and child with something of the character of the Divine. That said, the sense of awareness or heart's impressions reach far beyond the clutching scope of man's audacity.

Fear does nothing to frame the human mind.

A rabbit caught in a snare knows as much of fear as may any man. Scents on the wind strike panic in the hearts of stag and sheep alike: terror and fright are common afflictions to every farm and field. Equally, melancholy haunts the hearts of countless beasts; forlorn at being separated from their mates or masters. So, too, do loneliness, delight, assuredness, and shame. The falcon or swan may pine itself to death when faced with life without its mate; fawn and lamb alike bound with glee each morning at the simple prospect of being alive. Similarly, every boar and buck proudly defend their territory with bravery few men may ever know; while even dogs will cower in humiliation when reprimanded for behaviour they, upon rejection, recognise as wrong.

Creatures of sea and air select their mates by beauty; ignoring suitors or potential partners who appear too plain or common. Further, those too shy or timid to contest their claims, not graced with superior strength or excellence, frequently abandon the company of the herd or flock: withdrawing in desolation as worthless or ignored.

Hatred and Affection are two horns on the head of the self-same beast: clearly evident and observable in every species. Jealousy the same, palpable in the hollow of desolate and miserable hearts, just as Grief can not be alleged as entirely human in its attributes.

Of all passion and sentiment, it would seem that only Guilt remains as sole province of the human heart.

Only women and men find themselves damned for their convictions—constantly weighing their worth against their shame: holding their hearts in contempt, sentenced by feelings of remorse; judged and condemned for their disgrace or villainy. How an individual confronts and copes with Guilt ultimately determines a person's worth: to oneself and, likewise, to one's company.

William ap Thomas parsimoniously spread any instinct of guilt over the death of his firstborn son on everything and everyone but himself. Shattered by the loss, his father reprimanded the child's own mother for instigating the course of events by starting the argument and, not surprisingly, blamed the horse for not reacting in time to see and then clear the fallen tree. More than anyone, though; William ap Thomas pointed the finger of culpability at God.

Gwladus, quite rightfully, held her husband personally responsible for his sins and immediately shrank from the horror of her loss by snatching the two youngest children solely to herself; refusing to allow their father to be left alone with either for a moment. Her maternal instinct flared into an all-consuming fire—threatening to mutilate her second husband in his sleep if he even dared to touch them. While Gwladus' fury was nothing to be trifled with; the fact that she had related the details of Thomas' death to her siblings and friends gave the latest Lord of Raglan far more pause for concern. Sad: that the man gave more thought to how the tragedy might affect his political aspirations than how his lapse in judgement might ultimately end up affecting his family.

As a result, the entire household of Bluet Manor instantly and irrevocably dissolved.

William ap Thomas immersed himself in his sense of duty to the duke of York: a decision which kept him, for the most part, away from the estate. Not that his wife objected in the slightest. Not having her husband around to constantly remind her of Thomas; she dedicated every waking moment to six-year-old Richard and the four-year-old Elizabeth.

Preferences on both of his grieving parents' parts which, regrettably, left their eight-year-old boy alone to cope as best he could.

A pitiable set of circumstances which unseen forces zealously decided to resolve for themselves.

* * * * *

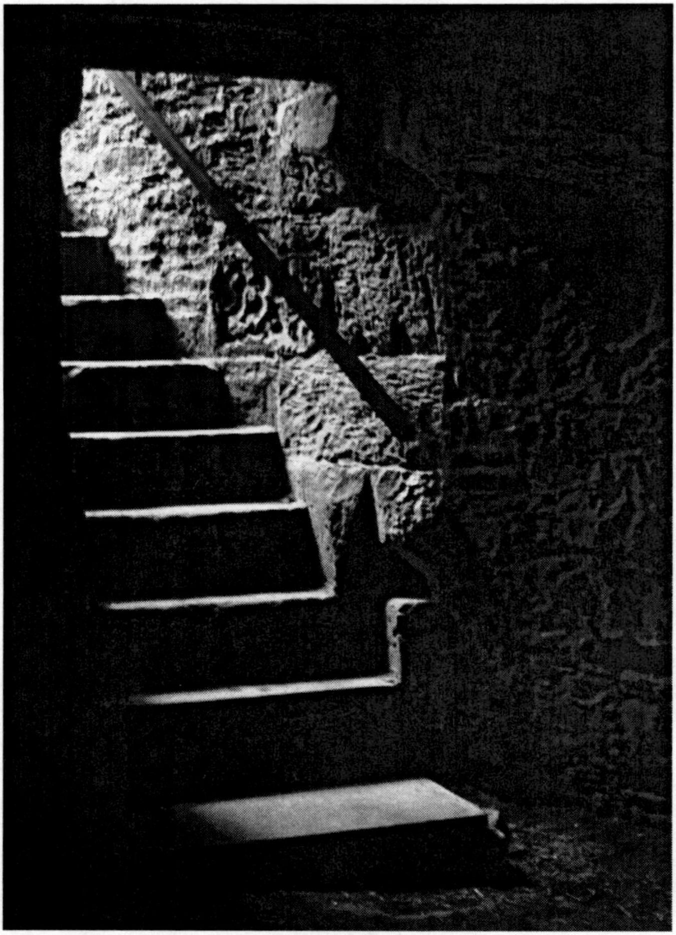

Chapter Ten

The baby's cries woke everyone within earshot.

Little Richard was having another nightmare and screamed even before he had awakened. Elizabeth, being the only girl, had the great privilege of a room of her very own in the centre of the hall: a detail that only made her less appealing to her older brothers. Girls were delicate, scented and frilly creatures who had apparently no function other than to annoy boys and steal their things when William wasn't looking.

The somewhat dilapidated state of Bluet Manor had forced the two boys to room together in the first bedroom at the top of the stairs. Though after Thomas' death there was substantially more room to sleep, the boys tried to spend as little time there as possible.

Which meant that their father and mother had the largest room at the far end of the hall. William supposed that it must be fair, what with them being so much bigger, but its position on the first floor meant that every time William ap Thomas stormed in after a night of heavy drinking, he would wake up all the children as he stomped up the stairs and slowly staggered past their doors.

Young William was beginning to really dislike the man.

He tried to calm his little brother down as quickly as possible. If things went to form, a shout would echo from the hall any second; which it did.

"If you don't shut up that crying, I'm going to come down there and give you something to really cry about!"

There it was. Their father's superb parenting skills displayed yet again for the family and servants to hear.

The older son rolled out of bed and felt his way through the darkness to hug his crying little brother. Richard had been having the same nightmare on and off again since Thomas died and was suffering from terrible dreams at least once a week.

The door kicked open; it swung back and hammered on its hinges. There, illuminated by the light of a single candle was the figure of their father. William would later swear he could see the rage in the old man's eyes even in the candlelight.

"What the Hell is going on?"

William ap Thomas, for all his practised diplomacy in matters of state, felt that none was ever due his own family and household. He ruled the manor like a demigod; completely convinced of his infallibility, if not his immortality. He stepped up to the cot of his youngest son and pushed young William off the edge onto the floor. Not bothering to even lean over and offer the semblance of compassion or concern, the man kicked the bed frame with the side of his foot and yelled at the child yet again.

"Shut up, you little bastard!"

The older of the boys got to his knees and reached out in an attempt to comfort the other: shushing the youngest as best he could. Which proved to be a big mistake.

Their father turned, shoved the candle right into young William's face and screamed.

"Get back in bed or I'll slap the piss out of you!"

Concerned now with his own survival, the oldest darted back into the shelter of the darkness and pulled his blanket up to his chin. Having awakened completely and realised what was going on by now, Richard choked back his bawls in favour of avoiding the threat of being hit and blubbered into his covers.

"Any more of this and I'm going to get the belt."

The door rammed shut upon its latch as all could hear their father screaming down the hall.

"Damn it all. I wish I'd never had any children."

Gwladus lay weeping in her own bed; Elizabeth in hers; Richard as well, under the covers. Only young William lay there frozen silent in the dark, having firmly made up his mind.

Dislike, hell.

William truly hated his father.

* * * * *

Remarkable: how death seems to bring out the very finest and most corruptible of those forced into making its acquaintance.

Some immediately rise to comfort, help, and hold; others look straight away for profit or gain within the confines of its shadow. A limited few legitimately pause to appraise their fears and feeble contribution to the world. Of these, a small number withdraw from their family and friends entirely and, for reasons they themselves may not entirely understand, resolve to disappear within the safety of their minds—relatively confident that pain may not reach them as easily behind the veil of solitude.

That William, at only eight years old, opted for the latter might have struck his family as strange; had not each been consumed with attempts to disguise their own sense of loss over Thomas' death. With so dysfunctional a family, no one really missed the second son at all: loneliness being a terrible price to pay for his independence.

While the mist silvered the spiders' webs each morning and goldfinches postured atop the heads of prickly thistles to chirp out defiant claims to their territory, the lad withdrew to his favourite hiding place to barricade himself behind sadness and tears.

An abandoned vault or root cellar, the dilapidated doorway had succumbed to decades of negligence and screened its weathered planks behind a curtain of ivy that very nearly reached the ground. Ten narrow steps of stone led down from ground level to a room barely eight feet square; so small, in fact, that the boy could not even hazard a guess at its original purpose. On the exterior, the stable embraced the western wall; while a small tack-room linked against the eastern side. Its creation seemed to be one of those integral design decisions that appear to be so necessary during construction: and immediately prove to be entirely impractical upon completion.

Wedged in as it was between the two other buildings and shielded from the weather, there was no time or season when its temperature varied more than a few degrees.

During the brightest of days, the sun shone through the gaps made from missing planks and lit the stairs so perfectly that a candle was not even necessary to navigate the stairs.

In short, it was an ideal fortress for the young William's privacy: the perfect garrison for the child to shelter his loneliness. Provided he made certain that no one ever saw him sidestep and bob through its ivy curtain, the boy could spend the entire day nestled safely away from unwelcome hugs and prying eyes.

Not that Bluet Manor had been witness to very much affection or many hugs of late.

* * * * *

Those who visited Bluet Manor outside Raglan did so at their own risk.

As Steward of the Lordship of Abergavenny, Caerleon, and Usk, in-laws and William ap Thomas' own family could never be certain whether or not the Lord might be at home. Surprising the family with an unexpected visit might, more often than not, meet with the optimistic outcome of timing one's appearance to when William was away on business. As a consequence, stopovers to see the nephews, niece, or Gwladus were carefully and conscientiously planned around other appointments or trips to the area: so visitors might respectfully excuse themselves in a blinding hurry should they actually find the Lord of the Manor at home.

Some men are terribly adept at differentiating and detaching work from personal affairs.

William ap Thomas was not.

Should his anger be evoked from some perceived injustice, humiliation, or sense of betrayal while executing his duties under Richard, duke of York, one could be quite certain that the Lord of Bluet Manor would bring his fury back to roost at home. Far too savvy to inadvertently slit his own political neck, William sheathed any sense of bitterness or loathing until far from any who might report his resentment to his employer. Which meant that any within earshot of home became ready targets of the man's hostility. Kernels of aggravation and contempt, when propitiously fuelled by drink, quickly ripened from silent sulking into open contempt and overt physical aggression.

Though often astonished and amazed at the man's irrational rage, at least the occasional guests found themselves able to escape. Sadly, Gwladus and her children had no such alternative.

As a result, it came as no surprise when William caught his namesake by the hair and threw him into the kitchen where the leather belt lay waiting. From years of abuse and watching his father whip the hell out of Thomas, little William knew better than to scream or try to get away. He stood there in the middle of the room and was whipped until his father either quit in exhaustion or until the cries of the boy's younger brother and sister from the other room obliged a merciful end. Though tears streamed down the child's cheeks, he never made a sound: although cut and bleeding from his neck down to his ankles, the lad stood still and shuddered silently under every lash. He knew all too well that, should he make a break for the door, the alcoholic would simply turn his fury upon one of the younger children or his mother: and that was a prospect the boy considered even more horrible.

William waited for the customary phrase that signalled the tirade of abuse was nearing an end.

"I wish I had never had any children."

As sure as the sunrise, and just as eagerly anticipated, William ap Thomas would then re-hang the belt upon its special nail. As his hand gripped the latch of the door and without ever revealing the slightest twinge of emotion, he would hesitate in some semblance of recognition of what he had done.

"I'm sorry."

That, for him was the end of it. Not that he really meant it; nor that father or son believed for a second that the half-hearted penance would keep the man from whipping his now-eldest son to the point of unconsciousness the very next time he was drunk.

William ap Thomas would then stride out, grab his bottle, and head upstairs to drink himself to sleep; leaving the boy's mother to bathe the lad's open wounds and hold him as the child trembled quietly in pain.

Only eight years old and incapable of doing anything but cry, William ap Thomas' son loathed the man with all his heart and prayed to God that he would simply die.

*****

It was six months after Thomas' death, after enduring another of his father's brutal beatings, that William picked up his shirt and left his helpless mother alone to quiet the screams of Elizabeth and Richard. Not knowing exactly where to go or what to do, the lad closed the door behind him as he walked outside to be alone. So distraught that he didn't even pause to hide his objective, little William made his way by the angled rays of sunset down the stairs of his hiding place. He collapsed in the dust and then crawled on his hands and knees into the darkest corner, curled up as small as he could and cried himself to sleep.

The late October moon had begun to rise when the lad woke up and realised that he was not alone.

Perhaps it was a faint yelp that brought him out of dreamless sleep. It might have been the weight of little paws against the cloth of his blood-smeared trousers. Though the boy blinked hard and strained his eyes, the oblique light of the harvest moon cascading down the cellar stairs offered no real assistance in making out his visitors.

Two tiny tongues licked softly against the tracks of lashes that had dried upon his cheeks.

William slowly raised his arms and could feel the fuzzy hair of a pair of puppies leaning against him on either side. There, in absolute darkness, they stood on their hind legs and whimpered as they tenderly bathed his face and neck. Indifferent as to how they managed to get down the stairs or the possibility that their mother might return at any time, the boy loosely hugged them close and felt them try to climb up in his lap and wriggle up against his ribs.

Mercifully, he drifted off to sleep: the child's back wedged into the corner and his newfound friends nuzzled tightly against his sides.

* * * * *

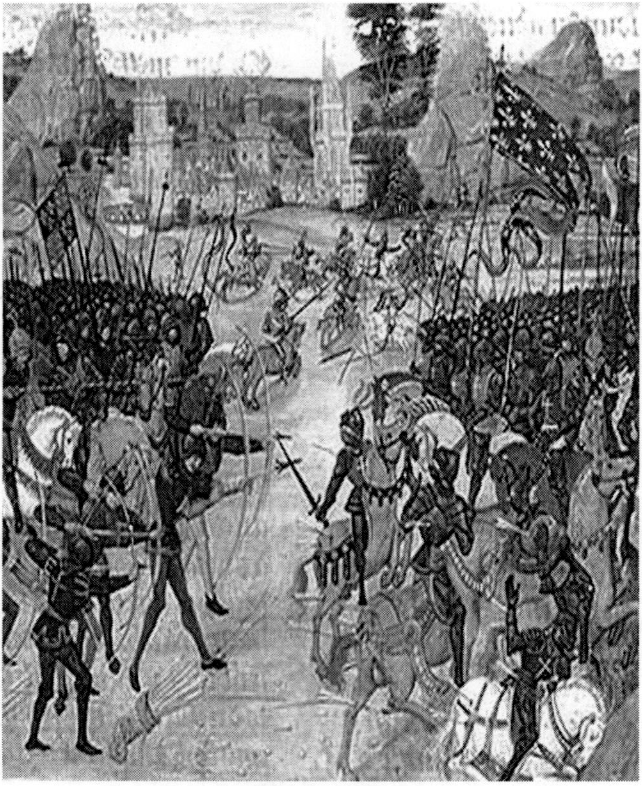

Chapter Eleven

Gwladus ferch Dafydd had slowly spiralled into a state of deep depression.

Though once vital and spirited, the devastation of losing both her husband and father on the field at Agincourt only ten years earlier had ravaged the woman's faith. The widow of Sir Roger Vaughan and daughter of Sir Dafydd Gam, without ever really realising, had withdrawn from life in an act of pure self-preservation. Then, when Thomas had been ripped from her life by the actions and seemingly callous indifference of his own father, Gwladus went into a perpetual state of shock.

Far more devastating than simple depression or unhappiness, the agony of life began to take a physical toll on her appearance.

Her shoulders had started to slope down ever so slightly and misery began to etch a sense of alienation and dejection in her eyes. Still, for all the young woman had been through, Gwladus took encouragement from the scriptures, set her face like flint, and determined to save her two youngest from misfortune or further catastrophe. Though she loved William no less, she trusted that, being older, he might be better able to cope with the intolerable situation life had seemingly so heartlessly thrust upon them.

Even at eight, his mother saw something undefeatable in the child's character. Perhaps something of herself: not a 'poor soul,' but something of a survivor that basically refused to abandon hope—who, with encouragement if not physical support, might find the strength of will to make it through the darkest of days. All mothers hope the same for their children: most are disappointed. A few, like Gwladus, are actually surprised; that, against all likelihood and to her astonishment, an extraordinary strength of spirit emerges from tribulation and trial on rare occasions and defines the very finest of a family's pedigree.

The Wraiths of Raglan Wood

* * * * *

William woke to find himself alone.

The reflection of the morning sun upon the whitened stone mirrored against the southern wall of the vault. Rain had collected upon the topmost steps through the breaches made by missing boards and intensified the glare of dawn.

Perhaps it was that peculiarity that stirred him from his sleep. Since the onset of the rainy season in September, which seemed to last most of the winter, actually seeing the sun in the morning was something of a rarity. Some years in Gwent the winter seemed to bypass the valleys altogether; simply leaving them under the cold, driving rain until spring happened to consider it time to wander back round.

The lad winced against the ricochet of radiance and then rolled to his knees in the half-lit shadows and called out softly for the pups. In case their mother had returned to their man-made den in the middle of the night, William didn't want to startle her into an attack. From his best guess by touch alone, the pair could not have been more than four to six weeks old, so he knew that they could not manage the steep staircase to wander out into the world on their own. Accordingly, unless carried out in the quiet of the night: either through a hole in the wall that lay hidden in perpetual darkness or up the stairs in the mouth of a protective mother; they were, more than likely, still quite close by.

When, after several whispered calls of encouragement, the puppies did not respond; the lad decided it might be best to creep back out as carefully and quietly as possible. As the sun was rising almost directly to his right, the broken door and its shawl of vines opened directly north and made plotting a course across the floor practically impossible if one were attempting to avoid little obstacles that could be almost anywhere. The last thing he wanted was to step on them and accidentally injure one.

William crawled as quickly as he could toward the bottom step. His father, if experience was any teacher, would not be up for hours; but his mother would be terribly upset if she happened to check his brother's room and find one of her boys missing.

And his mother had enough problems of her own to deal with without him making her life any more difficult.

* * * * *

As the second child of Richard of Conisburgh, 3rd Earl of Cambridge, Richard Plantagenet, 3rd Duke of York could hardly have been born into greater privilege. His mother, Anne Mortimer was the heiress of Lionel of Antwerp, the second surviving son of Edward III; an accident of genealogy that gave the family claim to the throne over that of the House of Lancaster. Sadly, she died while giving him life and his father was executed in 1415 for his participation in the Southampton Plot against

Henry V. As a result, Richard Plantagenet found himself in the unwelcome state of 'attainder' under the English criminal law.

Under the auspices of Westminster, Parliament quickly pronounced a 'corruption of blood' or stain upon the family name for their act of treason; which meant that the Plantagenets of Conisburgh's progeny were stripped of their lands and heredity titles. Luckily, the boy Richard happened to be the closest male heir of Edward of Norwich, 2nd Duke of York who had, likewise, been killed at the Battle of Agincourt. As his nephew, Henry V allowed the boy to inherit the title and lands of the Duchy of York and he further inherited the estates of the Earldom of March when his maternal uncle, Edmund Mortimer, 5th Earl of March, died later that same year. Such ponderous inheritances not only meant that the King of England took particular notice, as the Plantagenet Edmund Mortimer had previously been proclaimed on several occasions to have stronger claim to the throne. All of which meant that, when he reached the age of majority, Richard of York became one of the most powerful and wealthiest nobles in the entire of England.

At the end of the Hundred Year's War, the 3rd Duke of York controlled vast tracts of property in Gloucestershire, Lincolnshire, Northamptonshire, Wiltshire, and Yorkshire; not to mention the Mortimer estates around Ludlow and in Wales. Richard was knighted in 1426, as was William ap Thomas, but by John of Lancaster, 1st Duke of Bedford; the younger brother of Henry V. When Richard followed Henry V to Paris to be present at his coronation as King of France in 1431, William ap

Thomas was left to manage his interests in Wales and north in England.

It had been three years from the date when Henry VI had begun his siege of Orleans and fully two years since Joan of Arc had led her celebrated counterattack against the English usurpers and her fame had risen to perpetual immortality. Her capture by the Burgundians in 1430 resulted in the young woman's eventual purchase and extradition to Henry's forces from Duke Philip of Burgundy. After she attempted to escape on several occasions, the lengthy trial for her alleged heresy finally began at Rouen.

With the triumphant Henry being crowned that very year in Paris, it says much of the transient grandeur of humankind that one nation may crumble in humiliation under the muddy boot of conquest—just as its conquerors, in mid-celebration, discover they are not victors but merely survivors. Still, the day, for however brief, belonged to England and her nobles and Richard, duke of York, was expected to take his place at the right hand of his king.

Such was the sequence of events that, equally, affected the residents of Bluet Manor outside Raglan. Opportune for William ap Thomas, in that such authority and power propelled him out of the anonymity of county Gwent; fortunate for Gwladus and her children, in that their lives were far more serene with his absence; but most lucky of all for his second son, William; who was nothing short of ecstatic to be free, even for a matter of months, from his father's cruel and often brutal attentions.

The Wraiths of Raglan Wood

In 1432, William had just celebrated his ninth birthday and was in high spirits. Each morning after breakfast, the boy would be left pretty much to his own devices to entertain himself throughout the day: idyllic afternoons that the young lad spent romping through the fields and shadowed glens of Raglan Wood.

Though he had returned each morning for several days to search for the missing puppies, his efforts rummaging around were futile. The lad had secretly nicked a candle from the kitchen when no one was around and made an extensive search through the abandoned clutter of the stone cellar. Not only were there no crevices or passageways through the thick stone walls, there was no sign that any animals had dared to take refuge so close to the company of humans. What perplexed him most of all was the absence of footprints amidst the layers of filth. To be sure, William could easily make out the imprints of his boots; but there was no sign of tiny paws or toenails to be seen.

A realisation that might have just as easily dismissed the animals as only characters of a forgotten fantasy or wishful dream—had it not been for the succession of events that were to follow and haunt the young lad's imagination.

* * * * *

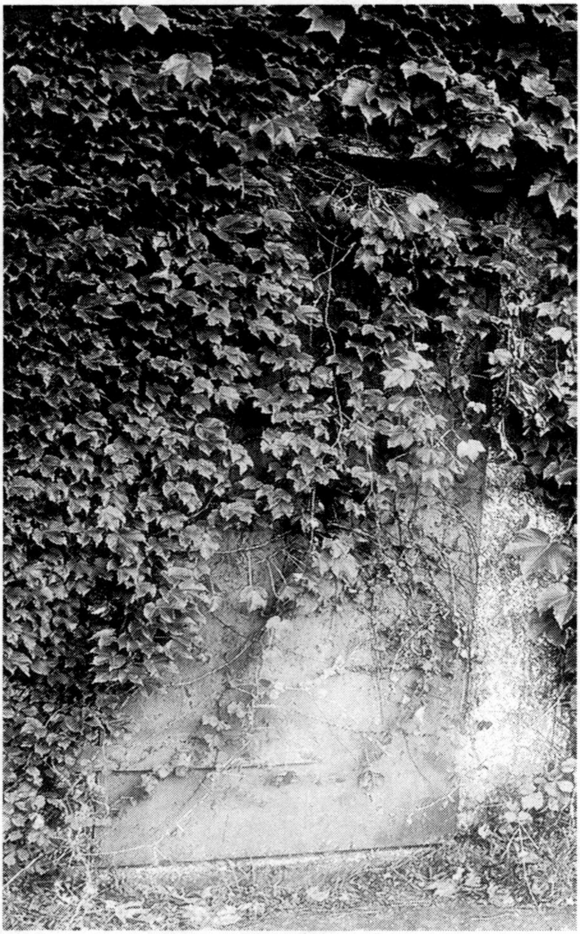

Chapter Twelve

Having purchased Bluet Manor outright only months earlier from James Berkeley, 1st Baron Berkeley, the oldest stepson from his first marriage, William ap Thomas decided to dismantle the walls of the ancestral home and build a castle of his own. Realising that his duties would now occupy even more time and attention, the Lord decided to make a last minute assessment of the outbuildings before taking his leave: his plan being to save the manor itself last for demolition so that the family might not be forced to leave until most of the new construction had been completed. It was this appraisal of outbuildings, cottages, and walls that brought William ap Thomas around eventually to his son's secret hiding place.

As luck would have it, the boy had just come up from the empty vault and was heading back toward the main house after having another look around the back kitchen door to see if the pups might have been out scavenging for scraps during the night. He chanced to see his father and his foreman, Gareth, exiting out of the stable next door. Were either to have taken time to notice, they would have seen the boy's very hope and joy drain from his face.

A short andiron of a man, Gareth ap Hywel had brought his crew of workmen from nearby Abergavenny to look over the plans and get an idea of exactly how to undertake the massive building project. The heat of the day already beginning to show on the squat Welshman, he took off his cap to mop his brow.

"Who cuts your hair?"

William ap Thomas pointed to the squashed, matted curls of his new employee.

"And why are they so angry at you?"

Gareth forced a thin smile of amusement that strained itself only slightly higher than a sneer. He was beginning to understand why his colleagues and friends back in Abergavenny had seriously warned him about taking the job.

For all his abilities, William ap Thomas was not at home with other people. His insecurities, combined with the need to always be in authority, regularly came across as rudeness and aggression. As a result, the man had very few real friends. In his mind, friendship was expensive; what with the occasional need for gifts, the time involved to socialize, and having to pretend to be concerned about problems or situations that did not involve himself personally.

After all, who needed the price of friendship when a little indifference or open, unbridled hatred never cost a thing?

Completely oblivious that he might have offended, the Lord of Bluet continued walking and crossed toward the splintered door of the abandoned cellar. William clearly saw that his wit was not going to be appreciated. "You'd meet cleverer people at a guildhall meeting of village idiots," he murmured under his breath.

As Gareth moved up on his father's left side, the boy immediately stepped further to his own right and slipped quickly out of sight behind the easternmost exterior wall of the tack room.

Something stopped William ap Thomas dead in the doorway.

Swinging back the suspended ivy curtain out of the way to force the door, a sound rose from the shadows at the bottom of the stairs: a noise that seem to resonate from the walls themselves. Its pulsing, guttural rasp unexpectedly grated against something in William's mind: forcing the hairs on his arms and neck to spring to attention. The man's shoulders pulled up involuntarily on their own.

"Did you hear that?" He shot a glance to Gareth who now stood inches away.

"Hear what?"

The contractor countered to his right and tried to push his shoulders past William for a better look.

Just then, a low, rumbling growl rolled up from the inky blackness; the sound of some creature that seemed to echo from the halls of Hell itself: a snarl from the throat of a gigantic beast that lay in wait and lurked just out of sight.

"What is it?"

The expression on Gareth's face revealed nothing but simple curiosity; just as the one on William's could not conceal his fright and apprehension.

Pulling back from the entrance, William ap Thomas promptly composed himself as best he could; realising that the demonic voice had been meant for his ears alone. Gareth stepped over the threshold, peered down the flight of stairs, and strained his ears for any sound. Confused, he turned and pulled the door closed behind him.

Having regained his self-control, the Lord of the Manor gestured to Gareth and to the detailed drawings the workman still held. "See that you start the demolition with that cellar. Throw all the rubbish from the other buildings in and level it with earth." William ap Thomas then gruffly turned and hurriedly crossed the lawn to say goodbye to his family in the main house.

"As you wish," Gareth shouted in the direction of his retreating employer.

Several of his labourers crossed up the grade to meet him and discover what was happening.

Gareth scratched the back of his ear. "What a queer man."

"They say that, now with his wife's inheritance, the man considers himself the tool of God," one of them offered as they watched their employer step back outside and meet the groom.

"Oh, he's a tool all right," Gareth snapped back, watching his new employer mount his horse and ride away.

"Falling face first into all this wealth, and he doesn't even have the decency to hate himself."

Sharing a chuckle amongst themselves, the quartet then strolled off to fetch their hammers and pry bars and left young William alone; leaning against the tack room wall. Once they had walked some distance down the hill, the young lad came around the corner of the building and slowly crossed up to the doorway to the cellar.

The boy William glanced around for a moment to make certain he was completely alone, then opened the rickety wooden door to the abandoned vault and listened carefully for himself. Having personally just ventured down the stairs only a few minutes earlier, he knew for certain there could be nothing there.

Which made it all the more difficult for the boy to explain how he had heard the demonic growls as well.

* * * * *

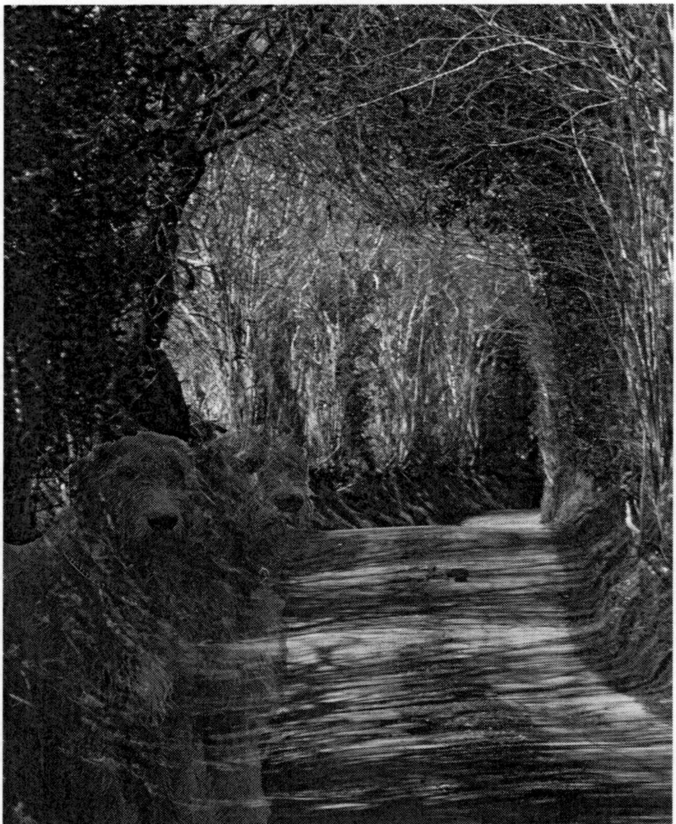

Chapter Thirteen

Great quantities of pale, almost yellow sandstone blocks began to be delivered daily; stacked in impressive manmade sculptures across the lawns of Bluet Manor. Transported by oxcarts and wagons from Redbrook on the river Wye along the Monmouth Road, the mooing procession made its way almost seven miles, passed through the tiny village of Raglan itself, and then up the rising ground about three-quarters of a mile north northeast to the building site.

As per the absent Lord's wishes, Gareth and his ever increasing work force were making preparations to begin on the Great Tower. The mason stood alone at a makeshift table that had been hastily and somewhat unreliably constructed by resting a few planks across two uneven stumps. His labourers had spent quite some time over the preceding weeks clearing back the trees and were now engaged in the laborious process of digging out the scattered roots before starting on the foundations. Recognising that William ap Thomas had quite specific dimensions and angles in mind, the master craftsman was meticulously studying the plans and drawings to avoid running afoul of his employer's well known temper.

To his immediate right stood a much taller man, then a third that seemed to have understood poverty far better than the pair with him. The third's clothing was on the state of complete collapse; a fact that his two friends took great care not to notice or mention.

Happening to glance up from the complicated sketches and doodled illustrations, Gareth caught sight of young William watching from the tree line. He motioned for the lad to join them as he took a break and rested his straining eyes.

The other two men continued their conversation while young William trotted in their direction.

"So, what did he say?" The shorter man asked the tall one in the middle.

"Get this," the centre of the three responded. "He started quoting scripture to me. Said something like,

'I shortly pour out my fury upon thee, and accomplish mine anger upon thee: and I will judge thee according to thy ways, and will recompense thee for all thine abominations. Mine eye shall not spare, neither will I have pity.'

"At least I thought it was scripture, from all the thee's."

"I think it's from Ezekiel," Gareth answered with a bit of authority, still watching young William coming up the grade from their left.

"So what did you tell him?" the crewman on the far right asked the one in the centre.

"I told him he could blow it out his . . ."

Just then, Gareth ap Hywel rammed his right elbow into the taller man's ribs quite forcefully and nodded toward the boy.

"Nose." he answered hurriedly, "I said he could blow it out his nose." The man in the middle clutched his side and moved a bit further to his right away from Gareth.

"Good morning."

Their foreman obviously taking time to make the lad feel far less ostracised, the two other men decided to take a break themselves and walked over to the well to get a drink.

"You make out what this says?" Gareth pointed to the sketched outline of the tower wall.

The nine-year-old was rather introverted and often shy around people, so it took a moment for him to overcome his bashfulness and close the distance. William leaned in to look where the man had placed his calloused, rough finger.

"Stately and," he paused. The boy had to turn the piece of paper slightly to avoid the glare of the morning sun. "Handsome." He looked up at Gareth with a sense of accomplishment.

"Stately and handsome."

"What in the name of the devil's hairy black . . ."

The old man caught himself before the curse managed to make it off his tongue. Glancing down sideways at William as he leaned even closer to the drawing and tried to make out the words himself, Gareth shook his head ever so slightly.

"We can build it, but how the . . . ," he caught himself again.

"Stately and handsome?"

William smiled.

It was refreshing for someone to actually express an honest opinion about anything that concerned his father; whether blasphemous or not. The servants and household staff valued their positions and employment and regularly bowed their heads and took their master's reproach without comment. The frank sincerity of the stranger was an open window of candour that the boy truly appreciated.

Not entirely sure as to the child's intent, Gareth took time to protect himself; even if they both knew full well he didn't mean it.

"Never was too good with reading words," he pointed at the drawing. "Numbers and measurements I understand, but never really learned to crack real writing." He turned to William and leaned in ever so slightly; slowly repeating the words as if they were a foreign tongue.

"Stately and handsome?"

Both laughed aloud together at the absurdity: that a group of men from the hills of Wales who were, for the most part illiterate, would know how to magically understand such an obtuse instruction when erecting walls of stone.

William noticed another scroll of paper held down by a flat rock next to the edge.

"What's that?"

Gareth relaxed a bit and loosened up to let his natural good nature show. "This," he spread out the diagram directly over the castle plans, "This is a map of this area of county Gwent."

William now crowded close against the builder's side to have a better look.

The old man knew, living so isolated in the country, that the boy must never have much opportunity to interact with anyone other than his immediate family. With grandchildren much the same age, he softened the tone of his voice to try to let the boy know he could be a friend.

"Well now, let's see."

He took a twig and, with his right hand, tapped where he wanted the lad to look. "This is Abergavenny," he pointed to the west. "and this is Monmouth. And there is Cardiff and, over here, Caerphilly."

"Where is London?"

"Oh, London is . . . ," Gareth stooped down to retrieve a stone and tossed it about twenty feet to the right of the table. "London is about there."

Obviously disappointed, William studied the map very carefully.

Raglan itself lay on a small branch of the river Usk, almost directly centre and slightly south of an imaginary line between Abergavenny and Monmouth. Similarly, if one connected the tiny village in an supposed triangle with Bristol on the border of England for its right corner and Cardiff on the river Severn for its left, Raglan lay at the top; again, almost exactly in the centre and bordering the vast emptiness marked on the map as simply 'Forest of Dean.'

The lad cocked his head as he thought for a moment and came to a conclusion. He put the tip of his left index finger on the small mark that indicated where they were.

"So we are . . . here." William took in the entire countryside that lay under his arm. "In the middle of nowhere."

Gareth grinned.

"Right smack in the middle of bleeding . . . ," Watching his profanity was going to take more effort than he had originally thought. The old man cleared his throat.

"Right."

William slowly lifted his finger and then took in the expanse of forest and fields that lay between the distant villages and towns.

"Damn near the naked ass of the back of beyond."

Gareth's eyes cocked open; taken completely by surprise. Perhaps he needn't be as careful as he had originally supposed.

* * * * *

William took particular notice of the workers walking from their rooms in Raglan every morning to come to work.

He found it strange how, when they came to a distinct point along the track, all circled wide to their left and crossed themselves. While many would often pause along the way to talk or relieve themselves after a hearty breakfast, none would break their stride at that particular point in the caravan of men from town. The second son of the manor found it all the more unusual; since he recognised the location to be exactly where his father's horse had stumbled: precisely where his brother, Thomas, had been crushed to death that fateful morning all those years ago. The gnarled branch still protruded up from the fallen tree-trunk like a mummified elbowed arm; as if to wave a sordid, obscene gesture of defiance to any members of the outside world that chanced to wander by.

Gareth ap Hywel came up the road with the same two men that had been with him at the table.

Edward Ruddel and Charles Gardiner were obviously English, but not the least bit typical. Even Gareth found them out of place within the crew of labourers that came and went from the nearby village. Both appeared to suffer from lamentable retrospection: in that, after their finest days of health appeared to have passed them by without distinction, each now wished to have had the courage to have taken part in the wars with France.

Rather, Ruddel and Gardiner had taken the path of least resistance; preferring to stay at home and warm in bed instead of gambling with their lives on some grassy foreign field. Too late they realised that those who made it home did so to great aplomb; but, even more importantly, with rather a large load of expensive trinkets and souvenirs. While their mates who joined the lists and fought with Henry in France now held lands and property, these two had to face the prospect of spending the remainder of their lives as common labourers: a likelihood that, now, forced each to nightly drown their youthful cowardice with drink.

"I don't care what either of you say," Edward could be overheard defending himself as the three came up the grade.

"Those were the best eggs and sausage I ever flapped my lips over."

The two men with him stared at each other in disbelief.

Edward Ruddel had a distinct interpretation of the English language. Without intent or even realising, the newly adopted Welshman constantly fractured words and expressions in interesting if not highly provocative ways. Either he substituted words that sounded similar to what he meant but implied something totally different or combined strange and obtuse phrases together to make his point. Regardless, there were more than a few occasions during the day when the expressions that managed to escape his lips actually proved painful to the listener.

Upon realising that he was not intentionally having them on, his friends tried to accept him despite the slaughter of convoluted euphemisms and confusing metaphors. Though some of the resulting conversations might appear as utter nonsense to anyone passing by, at heart, Edward Ruddel was a decent man. A bit peculiar at times, but entirely decent.

The lad motioned for Gareth to cross over for a moment, so the mason excused himself from his companions and stopped just long enough for a brief chat.

"Good morning, lad."

"Sorry to disturb," the boy began. He rose as he spoke and met the grizzled man halfway. Pointing to the arch of workers trudging up from town, the boy drew Gareth's attention to the silent spectacle.

"Can you tell me the meaning of the detour off the road just there? Pray tell, why do each cross completely off the track into the weeds down by that fallen tree?"

Staring back along the grade to where his master's son was pointing, the man crossed himself again quite slowly and stared.

"That is the spot where the old caretaker's cottage once stood." Gareth's booming voice had involuntarily dropped to a hushed level half its normal volume. "The base of that fallen trunk, off in the undergrowth, once marked the gate of the front stone wall."

He reached over and put his hand on the child's shoulder, then leaned over and whispered in the boy's ear. "When you happen to walk past; don't loiter."

The heavy stump of a stone mason looked directly into William's eyes. "The living are not welcome there."

The boy turned to watch as the last of the local workmen stepped wide around the spot: as his older friend took a knee to keep their conversation private from passing ears.

"Some swear they have seen candlelight bob up and down around the old foundation and heard the wailing of lost souls or dying animals rising up from amongst the trees." He paused to wave casually at a group that made their way up the road to the construction site; then leaned back to whisper to the lad.

"You want no part of it; nor did the Morleys either. Something cruel yet lies and lives there amidst the fallen stones. Something unholy, God help us. For any who venture off the trail and through its cursed plot will surely need His pity."

"Why is it cursed?" William turned to face his teacher.

Gareth broke from gazing at the bend in the road and tried to dismiss the sense of foreboding that now seemed to weigh the morning air. Completely ignoring the question, he tousled the boy's hair with his right hand and forced a laugh.

"Now be off with you. Run and play."

Without further explanation, the old man stood and started on up the hill to the still-waiting Charles and Edward, pausing only two steps later to glare back toward the rotting trunk. He deliberately spat in its direction then hurried along the grade to rejoin the members of his crew.

Now more curious than ever, William sat back down beside the track and stared at the gnarled branch that seemed to beckon to him above the weeds.

* * * * *

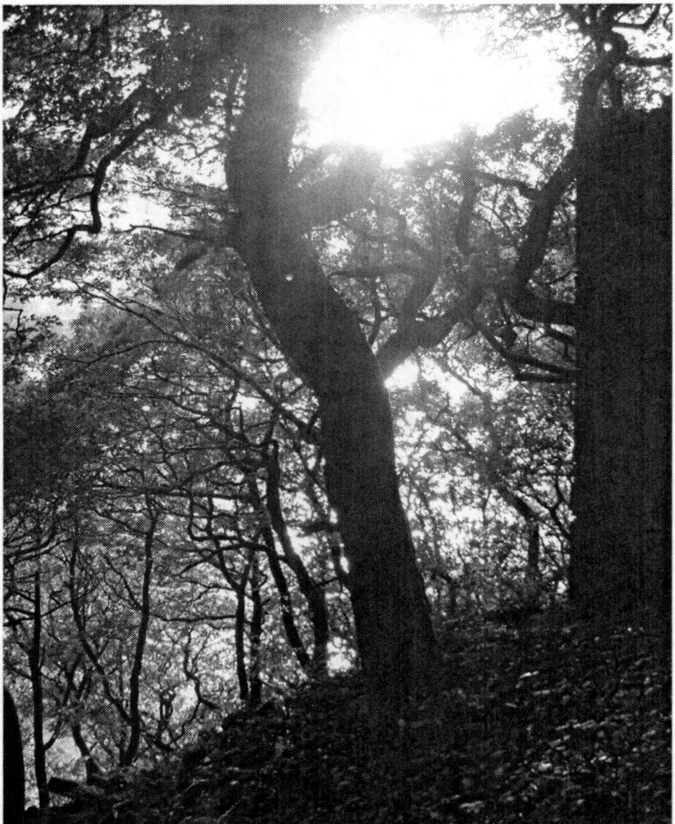

Chapter Fourteen

Raglan Wood during the winter and early spring was a cold and cheerless place.

In actual fact, Raglan Wood did not legitimately exist. The little village lay in an ambiguous area of the county Gwent in Monmouthshire; where the ancient claims and boundaries of authority were often unclear and frequently disputed. The hamlet occupied an unfortunate position between two opposing territories and, though claimed by each in ancient rights was, in point of fact, held by neither side.

To the east lay the Royal Demesne of the Forest of Dean.

Nestled between the Rivers Wye and Severn, the Forest of Dean, for all its size, appeared to have been misplaced by time.

Essentially, the woodland ran unbroken over a huge expanse of some two hundred square miles of virgin timber. Before the Normans had even dreamt of Dover, the Saxons had set aside its groves of birch and holly, beech, ash, and oak. Then, after Harold and William had danced at Hastings, the vast regions of the Forest of Dean were specifically reserved for the pursuit of boar and stag. Though restricted entitlements had been granted to quarry out tiny portions in the search for iron and coal, even the clatter of hammers could not consume the great glen's overwhelming stillness. In a nation renown for tranquil beauty, the Forest of Dean, for all of man's designs, remained the Eden of England's crown.

The Forest of Dean, using the designations applied in Britain to territories constrained to forest law, embraced two completely different types of property: that awarded or purchased by nobility and that held by the Crown. To the extent of warrant, the former was under its owner's discretion; in that the property might be subdivided into local parishes or communities and inherited or sold according to the designs of the nobles. The considerable bulk, however, remained as the King's Wood and, as such, was considered the Monarch's private hunting grounds. Miles of standing forest remained intermixed with impenetrable thickets: uninhabited and completely the province of the Crown.

At the time of the Battle of Hastings, truth is, no one was entirely confident of its boundaries. The Forest of Dean was, for the most part, a god-forsaken plot left over from the earlier Saxon dynasty. In essence, it was a wild and untamed parcel of primeval forest: which ran from Gloucester and Minsterworth along the west bank of the river Severn south past Tidenham to Chepstow Castle. Its western border followed the river Wye: from Ross-on-Wye north of Walford and then meandered past Monmouth, by Redbrook and Hewelsfield, and ended to the east of Chepstow where the river Wye emptied into the Severn northwest of Bristol and both went on to meet the sea.

Almost from the Norman Conquest, debate began over the extensions of The Forest's boundaries; particularly between the representatives of the king and the local nobles who, in the absence of justifiable authority, often adjusted their claims to better suit their needs. Only the poor truly suffered from the contention; in that fines for poaching, theft of wood, and waste were unnecessarily severe and, what with great, private tracts regularly expanding in the absence of the king's officers, it was often difficult to really determine exactly where the true property lines might actually lie.

To the west of Raglan and Bluet Manor lay the Brecons and the equally imposing Fforest Fawr, or Great Forest. A range of mountains, moors, and forested woodland that ran from Llandovery, Brecon, and Hay-on-Wye on the north to Brynamman, Ystradgynlais, Merthyr Tydfil, and Pontypool on the south. Ranging in width from Llandeilo and Amman Ford on the west to Capel Y Ffin, Llanellen, and past Abergavenny to the east, the wilderness featured great ridges of limestone, fantastic caverns, and magnificent waterfalls.

Having been inhabited since the Stone Ages, portions of the original woodland had been regularly set to the torch for thousands of years; leaving clearings in the forest that, on the outset, proved quite attractive to advancing Norman lords. That said, the plague of the Black Death, along with constant raids by the local Welsh chieftains, made the area far less than idyllic. What the region lacked in impenetrable glens, it more than made up for with rugged terrain and moors. The Black Mountains on the east north-east of Abergavenny stumbled down the ancient landscapes and buried the eastern expanse with acres of thick timber to the north of Usk and just to the west of Raglan.

William's observation that Bluet Manor and the tiny village of Raglan itself both lay on the ass side of the back of nowhere, though slightly crude and earthy, was remarkably spot on. Removed from the sophistication, civility, and grace of London and its outlying suburbs, the initial object of anyone wishing to make a name for themselves in Britain was to first find a way to escape the remote and distant borders. Not that the Black Mountains and Forest of Dean had ever encouraged or invited the company of man.

Pagan beliefs and Christian superstitions do not appear from nowhere.

In a region where humankind had only recently dared to loose the latch and brave a glimpse inside, the unknown might well rule supreme. Tales of demons, portals to the underworld, and ghouls sired from the forest spirits themselves to thwart the hand of man regularly resonated around the lonely hearths of Monmouthshire and echoed down the dimly lighted passageways of the scattered, isolated manors.

Only the foolhardy naively dismiss the unknown as harmless: only the completely ignorant dare assume the darkness lingering on light's periphery might ever remain entirely void of malevolence and malice.

* * * * *

Gwladus daubed at the bloody slashes in her husband's shirt.

"They look like claw marks, either that or a mouth of incredibly large teeth." She leaned in to take a closer look. "Are you sure you didn't snag it on some rusty metal gate?"

The fabric had been cut clear through in two parallel lines; neatly slicing the flesh on the back of William ap Thomas' right arm with identical incisions. The gashes, though not terribly deep, must have hurt horribly: as if a pair of blades had caught the man just above the elbow.

Wincing a bit from the sting of the alcohol, her spouse snapped back at his better half. "Keep your comments to yourself, woman."

Doing her level best to avoid another argument, his wife tried to gently lift the still-sticky cloth free from his skin. "I don't think you are being quite reasonable, my dear."

"I assure you I have," he flinched upright slightly, "no intention of being reasonable."

His wife inserted her fingers into the now-free fabric and tore it slightly more open to have more room to work. The incident apparently having occurred near the hour of midnight, Gwladus had been roused from her sleep by the man's commotion and her normally sweet disposition was a bit more satiric.

"You're a grumpy old bastard tonight, aren't you?"

Currently at a distinct disadvantage, William suffered her facetious remarks with a patience only intense pain might have provided.

"I have no intention of being a grumpy old bastard. I have no wish to be but what I am . . . the target of some thoughtless, unprovoked assault."

His wife wrapped her husband's upper arm with a bandage made from a section torn from a clean kitchen cloth and tried to show a bit more compassion.

"What happened?"

Checking the quality of her ministrations, William picked up the bottle and crossed over to the wall cabinet to retrieve a good-sized cup; leaving his wife to clean up the jumbled table on her own.

"I hardly know," he started; trying to put the events of the evening in some semblance of progression in his mind. The fact that he had been drinking did not help, of course.

"It was on the track just now. I was coming up from some business in the village."

Couples that have been married for very long often create a code to conceal certain matters from their children. 'Business,' in this instance, meant that her husband had been visiting his cronies and spent the evening in the indiscriminate company of single men, their female companions, and any number of foaming flagons. Gwladus took the inference in stride; knowing that any further comment would only result in further unwelcome hostility.

An unexpected shudder made him gulp a swallow down and then quickly pour himself another.

"I remember distinctly." her husband went on. "We had been talking about the Black Hour."

Noting that his children, who had also been roused by the commotion and wandered down to the kitchen to see what was going on, had no idea what he was referring to, William took the briefest of pauses to explain.

"On the 17th of June last year there was, at three o'clock in the afternoon, an eclipse that completely blocked out the sun. We were talking about how, in August 1133, the sun hid his face at the death of King Henry I. Seven years later, during Lent, the same thing happened again; but last year the sky went so completely dark that, according to everyone who witnessed it, no one could see anything at all."

William glanced over at Gwladus, almost as if to see if she was buying into his latest alibi. She was not.

"So," he turned back to address his more trusting children, "we were debating if it was sign that someone in the Royal Family might die."

Gwladus conspicuously knocked over the bowl of water that she had been using to daub the towel. It was, again, his wife's way of deflating his elaborate excuse for being drunk again without having to involve the children.

Undeterred, he poured the last contents of the bottle into his glass and continued with his seemingly rehearsed account.

"I was approaching the ruins of the old caretaker's cottage. A blast of wind seemed to come from nowhere; hitting me from behind and quite literally knocking me to my knees." William pointed to the visible stains on his trousers as he then took a seat in the nearest kitchen chair.

"In the moonlight, there suddenly appeared two huge red eyes. Like coals from the fires of Hell: and the stench of an open grave rose round to scent the air."

William discarded the now empty cup and stepped over to the closest cupboard for another bottle.

"Suddenly, I heard the growl of another terrible beast and felt it strike me from behind. I turned to see another set of unblinking crimson eyes only a few feet away."

Truly concerned, but only due to the physical evidence of the attack, his wife looked again to the dressing covering the rather nasty gashes on the back of her husband's arm.

"And?"

He thought for a second to himself. "I can't explain it. But the head of a gigantic hound hung there with its mouth agape. A head," he emphasized, "and a head alone: for I could clearly see the white stones of the walk just where the body should have been."

Gwladus gasped involuntarily.

"Just then, the chapel bell in Raglan began to chime midnight and the monster dissolved right before my eyes back into the fog. I'm not at all certain whether it went back into the woods or straight down to Hell, but I wasn't waiting around to find out."

The man tried to twist his arm to get a better look at the wound. "Then, I kicked at the door until one of the servants let me in the kitchen—and the rest you know."

"There is something positively ghoulish about that grim old pile."

Gwladus looked off in the direction of the caretaker's cottage and proceeded to finish wiping any residue of water from the table.

"I was told no Morley would hazard near it. Even my father made a point to keep us out of the vicinity when coming back from Monmouth to Abergavenny: said none of the Morleys would venture near the ruins on the grounds for generations . . ." she stopped in mid-swipe, obviously attempting to remember, "Something about it being built on an old Roman shrine or pagan holy place; that dark powers wait there for the end of time."

She carefully dried her hands and folded the cloth again slowly. "I remember one autumn when I was a little girl; seeing the wind whip cross the fields and fling the fallen leaves against the sky. Until it reached *that place*. Not a single leaf moved inside the dark outline of stones; and not one cast into the air fell to the ground inside its walls. Standing as near as I braved, I could clearly see that nothing lurked inside but shadows. Still," the daughter of Sir Dafydd Gam paused for a second, "something was standing there all the same: something terribly real."

Challenging her remarks as superstition in spite of what he had just witnessed, William ap Thomas attempted to rationalise the evenings' events somehow in his mind.

"Blithering nonsense."

His reason regained control over his imagination. "And, don't forget, I was married to a Morley—so dumb a dynasty you had to pin their names on their coats so strangers could tell them how to get home."

Both stood there in the candlelight and listened to the wind whine and whistle through the ancient cracks of Bluet Manor. Just as their moods had lightened, the devilishly awkward sound of a dog barking in the distance came riding in upon the wind.

Without another word, William ap Thomas stepped quickly to the door, bolted the latch securely, and stared out the kitchen window and down the winding, darkened lane.

Something was standing outside—patiently waiting for the sceptic to step back out into the far from empty darkness.

* * * * *

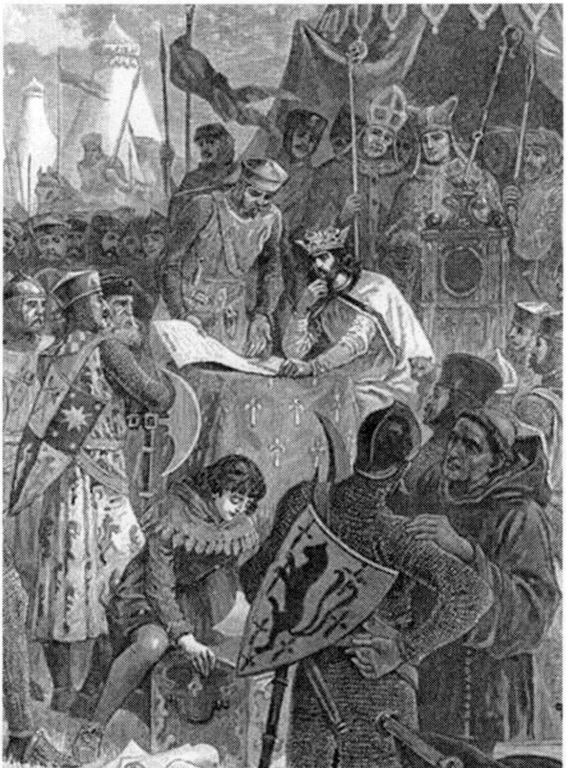

Chapter Fifteen

Llanddewi Rhydderch lay nearly five miles from Abergavenny. Bryngwyn was only two miles west of Raglan; while Llanfair Kilgeddin was situated a mere six miles south-east in the opposite direction. Llandenny lay three miles south of Raglan and three miles north of the little village of Usk.

The road from Carmarthen to Gloucester ran very close to one hundred twenty-four miles and from Shrewsbury down to Bristol another one hundred twenty-eight. It is important to recognise the boundaries of this irregular plot of Welsh territory; for, while Raglan Castle was being constructed, the roughly sixteen thousand square miles surrounding William ap Thomas' new sandstone creation saw an unbelievable, almost incomprehensible induction of whores.

There were prostitutes on the corner of every lane in Raglan.

There were ladies of the evening spaced evenly along the Monmouth Road. Practitioners of the world's oldest profession even camped out along the nearby banks of the river Wye. There simply was nowhere anyone wished to walk, ride, or run that did not offer the work crews distraction; and that did not battle for their patronage.

They appeared almost as if by magic; as if somehow, almost overnight, some silent signal rang out across the Head of the Valleys Road, from mountains to the sea, that hundreds of men were in desperate need and would pay well for the company of a woman.

Their presence tried the true of heart; challenging faithful husbands and lovers to beat back the temptation to stray. Their attendance at every function instantly raised the ire of not only local girls of identical vocation; but that of wives and girlfriends who, in their Christian duty, found it more straightforward to forgive them than to let their loved ones walk the streets unaccompanied and unprotected. Local shopkeepers were deluged with business, their trade easily tripling from the sudden introduction of women of 'industry.' It seemed that no one had bothered to consider how introducing a famished work force of lonely men in the middle of nowhere might result in a veritable feast of available harlots ready and eager to slack their yearning and desire.

For the first time in most of the workman's lives, it was wholly a buyer's market.

Any man from the work crew, after being paid for the day, and venturing back to home or rented room—any: regardless of height, weight, or physical appearance, could rest in the confidence that, should he desire to pay for the company, he might not be forced to spend the evening alone. If one didn't see exactly what he wanted, he only had to turn the corner and keep walking until he did. All any had to do was pick the height, weight, age, and size and keep strolling until his perfect woman fell into his lap—quite literally.

The erection of Raglan Castle was heaven to men like Charles Gardiner. Regardless of how hard the work, how long the hours, how thick their accents, how slick the roads after the rains; there was always warm and willing female companionship available. Ready to service their lust; eager to thrust their feigned familiarity upon any passing client for the mere price of a coin.

His friend, Edward, did not seem to share Gardiner's enthusiasm at the unexpected bounty of willing flesh.

Temptation, more than assertions and convictions, weighs the principles of humankind. Particularly for men who daily lived in the shadow of doubt and death; character was far easier calculated from one's diversions or leisure pursuits than from hollow pronouncements about one's integrity. Not willing to get involved in what might well turn out to be a festering, infectious relationship, Edward Ruddel tried to excuse himself as politely as possible to avoid offending Charles or the man's latest whore.

Too drunk to really make much sense or defend his sudden, overwhelming lust for the rather plain but definitely well-endowed prostitute, Charles tried to get his friend to join them for a spontaneous *ménage à trois*.

"Come on. She is probably more green than she is cabbage looking."

Gardiner tugged at Edward's shoulder. "It will be on me."

Taking another hard look at the well-worn, equally inebriated woman that Charles was desperately trying to hold up on his own, Edward smiled and shook his head. "Aren't you afraid of what you might contract from the bargain?" The state of Gardiner's new love left little doubt about her mileage and the very real possibility of infection.

"Fear keeps men alive, my friend."

Charles took another swig from his bottle and shoved it between the fat woman's sagging breasts where she managed to wedge it with ham-fisted hands. Though the years and mileage had transformed her cleavage from a thirty-six short into a forty long, there appeared to be years of service left in the old gal.

"I've always preferred women over principles," he turned and laughingly rammed his stubbled chin into the woman's once well-upholstered chest. Raising his mouth to hers, he grinned. "And women without any principles most of all."

Edward saw that there was nothing he could do to make Charles change his mind.

With one last attempt to share his evening's rather questionable prize, Gardiner slapped his friend Ruddel on the shoulder. "Come on, love conquers all!"

Edward nodded with a broad smile and then turned to free himself from the situation before it turned violent.

"Maybe where you live."

His friend would not take 'no' for an answer. Stewed to the gills, he decided that Ruddel could wait for him to finish his business and then make sure that he made it home.

"Tell you what," Gardiner made one last suggestion. "You will stand right here and wait for me to come back round."

Edward, not nearly drunk enough to agree, nodded. "All right. But don't bet on it unless you get really good odds."

Oblivious, Charles stammered on through his slurred directions.

"If I'm not back in an hour, then search the woods."

"Right." Edward nodded obligingly.

"If you can't find me there, then search the pubs."

"Right."

"And, if not there, then search this wench's house."

"Where's that?"

"Search me." Gardiner giggled into the equally inebriated woman's face.

"Hold on."

A stout shape stepped from the mounting fog and deliberately interrupted the trio. It was Gareth ap Hywel. Returning from the butcher, the old man had turned up his collar and shoved his hands deeply into his pockets; wedging the neatly tied chop of cheap meat under his armpit to make it home for dinner. The briefest of glances made it clear exactly what was going on.

Without breaking stride, their foreman caught Edward by the shoulder and spun him around to pull him away. "You two have a spectacular evening," he barked over his shoulder at the now groping lovers.

Twenty or so feet down the lane, Ruddel glanced back over his shoulder to see if Charles had managed to make it off the street. "I'll wager he lives to regret that decision," Edward snickered to himself.

"So much for his dignity."

Gareth snugged the package of meat up a bit tighter under his armpit.

"What's dignity? More often than not, men wrap themselves inside it: a clever cloak from which each darts out to indulge the hungers of their heart."

Ruddel had never seen this side of Gareth. He held his peace as the two men navigated the swirling fog of the road together.

"More often than not, dignity is nothing more than a symbol of the cruelty, greed, and lust for power that have set men at each others' throats down through time." Gareth shot a glance back over his shoulder as well.

"The struggle will go on—for a whore, or a castle," he nodded toward Raglan. "Perhaps even for a kingdom. None of us will ever be truly dignified until the last vestiges of cruelty and greed have been ripped from the very last of us."

The old man paused.

"When that time comes, maybe the centuries of soot and tarnish will finally be buffed away and Wales might gleam again."

W. B. BAKER

* * * * *

William ap Thomas journeyed alone from Sandal Castle back for a brief visit at Raglan.

Overlooking the river Calder on the southern edge of the city of Wakefield in West Yorkshire, Sandal Castle passed from the Crown to William de Warrenne, 2nd Earl of Surrey, in the early years of the twelfth century. Based in Lewes Castle in Sussex, which had been erected by his father, the Warrenne family built additional castles in Surrey at Reigate, and Conisbrough Castle near Doncaster. When John de Warrenne died, the family's estates in Yorkshire passed back to the Monarchy and King Edward II granted the manor of Sandal to Lord d'Amory in 1317 as a reward for his service in the Scottish Revolts, specifically at the Battle of Bannockburn.

Edward d'Amory, in turn, granted Sandal to Edmund of Langley, his fifth son. Alongside his more vigorous elder brother, John of Gaunt; who built Pontefract Castle and Knaresborough Castle in Yorkshire, Edward was granted Wark Castle near Coldstream in the Scottish Borders and Fotheringhay Castle in Northamptonshire. Edmund was made the 1st Duke of York in 1385 as compensation for support of his nephew, King Richard II of England and, as heir and 3rd Duke of York, Richard Plantagenet unexpectedly woke up one morning and found himself as one of the wealthiest men in the whole of England.

John of Lancaster, 1st Duke of Bedford, and younger brother of Henry V, who had knighted Richard, Duke of York in 1426, died in May 1436. Only a few months later, Richard was appointed to succeed John as the crown's Lieutenant in France.

The duke of York faced a particularly tough situation when he arrived from across the channel.

England was confronted with the prospect of either conceding most of the territories taken earlier to achieve an acceptable negotiation with the French nobles; that or be forced to capture even more provinces to guarantee permanent control of their claims over on the continent. To make matters even more challenging for Richard of York, the political environment was shifting right underneath his feet. The Regency Council established by Parliament to preserve the Monarchy until Henry VI came of age, though still boasting Humphrey, duke of Gloucester, and Bishop Henry Beaufort of the House of Lancaster, had lost the support of the French nobles in Burgundy. Following the Treaty of Arras in 1435, the provinces in Burgundy stopped supporting Henry's claim to the throne of France.

Richard Plantagenet, 3rd Duke of York was no man's fool.

He fully appreciated that his appointment to the duke of Bedford's position was simply a makeshift and temporary solution to England's problems with France. Richard was to lead only until the child king, Henry VI, reached his majority. In spite of this, until then, his new duties kept him far from his private interests in England and Wales.

Under this provisional administration in south Wales made necessary by the Hundred Years War with France, William ap Thomas touted himself as the perfect man in the ideal place at the best possible of times. Stewardship of the affairs of Richard made him personally responsible for both lands and property; which proved wonderful for William. His need to be officious, combined with an undefeatable sense of superiority, meant that the duke of York would be regularly kept informed of sloth and waste in his absence. So, by arrangement with his absent landlord, William ap Thomas made these regular unannounced inspections to gauge the goings on at the Duke's manor homes and castles.

Socrates once said that men should 'rule worthy of their might;' pronouncing that great influence is regularly accompanied by even greater accountability. Sadly, tagging along with influence can be great pride, self-indulgence, and a greatly inflated sense of self-esteem.

It was precisely for these reasons that the Scottish barons cautioned Robert the Bruce in the Declaration of Arbroath in 1320: that, should he refuse to lead them into battle, his nobles would simply give the crown to someone they deemed more worthy.

Likewise, King Henry I of England acknowledged that his authority over the kingdom was under the warrant of the law with the Charter of Liberties of 1100, though it was not until 1215 that the early barons actually forced the then King John to proclaim specific rights were guaranteed to freemen in the Great Charter of Freedoms or Magna Carta. For the first time in history, a monarchy was duly forced by its subjects to be bound by law and legal procedures.

Divine Right had to be duly recognised by law.

Now, what with the strain of the Regency Council, the continued conflict in France, and the absence of the duly appointed Richard Plantagenet, 3rd Duke of York; William ap Thomas had to seriously watch that he did not overstep his delegated authority in Wales. That said, the Lord of Abergavenny would regularly push his sense of entitlement right to the breaking point.

Having travelled for an entire day from Sandal Castle in Sussex, Richard's duly appointed Steward found it necessary to call on the castle at Chepstow before swinging back north to pay a visit to his wife and family. Two hundred miles in the saddle had taken quite the toll on William's backside, so he decided to spend a few days on the Severn before making the thirty mile ride up the river Wye and through the Forest of Dean. One of the first strongholds in Wales after crossing the Severn, many agents and representatives would drop in unexpectedly to trade stories and information at Chepstow before heading back to Bristol, the east, and the trappings of civilisation.

Atop its rocky precipice over the eddies of the River Wye, Chepstow Castle was the first of literally hundreds of English outposts across the mountainous wilderness.

Without a doubt, it was certainly one of the oldest. William Fitz Osbern, close friend of William the Conqueror, had laid the foundation stones in 1067. The Battle of Hastings only having settled the squabble over invasion a few months earlier, Fitz Osbern scarcely lived long enough to call the castle his home; succumbing to pneumonia only four short years later in the summer of 1071.

His son, Roger, rebelled against the Crown almost immediately afterwards and, as a result of the failed uprising, Chepstow passed into the hands of the king.

When William Marshal married Isabel, the heiress of Earl Richard de Clare, all of her castles passed to William and their heirs and in 1245, the last matriarch of the Marshal line died and Chepstow Castle was passed to her son, Roger Bigod II, the then earl of Norfolk. His son, also named Roger, later expanded and remodelled Chepstow to become one of the centres of entertaining nobility in Monmouthshire.

Improvements included an impressive new hall block on the north side of the lower bailey; while the range included a fabulous, vaulted cellar, a kitchen, domestic accommodation, several magnificent service rooms, and, obviously, the hall itself. A huge tower was subsequently erected on the south-east corner to provide accommodation worthy of noblemen of high rank or visiting royalty.

Roger Bigod III had no heirs, so his magnificent castle at Chepstow was destined to be passed on to his brother, John Fitz Osbern. Seeing that the heir was heavily in debt and, what with the king rather anxious to obtain ownership, the Monarchy and successor came to an agreement whereby, in return for an annuity during the earl's life, his lands were thereafter to pass to the Crown.

When John died in 1306, the king immediately took possession and discovered that, despite what he had seen in Chepstow's glory, the earl had left the castle in a state of major disrepair.

The once magnificent fortification served briefly as a prison, was severely looted, and eventually passed to Thomas de Brotherton, the king's brother. It was sold to Despenser for the term of his life; but when he was put to death for his own indiscretions, the castle conveniently reverted right back to Thomas de Brotherton. Chepstow then passed through his second wife and daughter to the great-great-grandson, Thomas Mowbray, duke of Norfolk. He himself was executed for treason in 1405 and Chepstow Castle remained in the king's hands until granted to Thomas's younger brother, John, in 1413.

William ap Thomas, ever the opportunist, saw its potential and made a point to express interest whenever his duties brought him down the Wye.

Indeed, after his death, Chepstow would pass in an exchange of lands to his second son William: so, even if out of reach during his lifetime; a few decades of subservience would happen to pay off rather nicely for the heir of Raglan Castle.

W. B. Baker

* * * * *

The river Wye cut a swathe through Britain like a long, keen, rippling blade; forming a natural boundary between a good portion of the parishes ruled by England and Wales.

With headwaters in the Welsh mountains at Plynlimon, it gently sauntered past Hereford, Monmouth, and Tintern before joining the mighty Severn just below Chepstow Castle. The river Wye seemed to have been waiting for the Steward of Richard Plantagenet all along; as if, somehow upon reaching its banks, the winding waterway might signal the gnarled and knotted fingers of Raglan Wood that their Lord had made his way back home.

Ever the social butterfly, William stopped and spent the night in Gloucester. On the river Severn, the ancient market town was also one of the duke of York's interests; being that most of the wool gathered from flocks across the Cotswolds was processed exclusively in Gloucester. For a man like William, there was only so much time to be spent investigating the intrigue of marketing sheep. Originally intending to kill the remainder of an uneventful afternoon before continuing his journey, the duly appointed envoy of York opted to carry on rather than deal with the overpowering smell another day.

His initiative was to prove completely worthless.

William ap Thomas made the same mistake as many diplomats: in making the harebrained assumption that their hosts might extend similar courtesies to custodians of nobles that they do to aristocracy. So, when William rode proudly up to the gates of Chepstow Castle; confident of being well-fed and sumptuously entertained for the evening in luxury, he was more than annoyed and piqued to be brusquely turned away without so much as a 'by your leave' or an introduction.

Forced to spend the night in rather questionable accommodation over a public house, he was all the more surprised to find a folio on the washstand in his room. He supposed it to have been forgotten by a previous occupant who had, like he, been obliged to lower his or her expectations for the evening.

Originally penned by one Robert Traverner almost two hundred years before, the envoy had stumbled across a copy purloined from the shelves of Oxford University; or at least that was what he gathered from glancing at the stained annotation penned boldly upon the frontispiece.

Bored beyond belief by days of drudgery, of sheep and bales of wool, of questioning how in the name of Hell everything he was doing was ever going to amount to anything; William flipped open the vellum pages and began to read aloud.

W. B. Baker

Midst sultry breeze, suffused with scent of graves,
Down darkened ways, do these corrupted walk;
To pass the tombs of sovereigns and knaves,
Their open vaults, whose whiffs at which souls balk:
    And though quite blind, they wrench and shrink to shy
    From reeking stench of evil all pass by.

There, looming in the gloom, a brackish lace
Of crimsoned-edged briars wait to rend;
Enfolding men within razored embrace,
Against whose slashing kiss arms flail and fend—
    While souls, though torn, quite still attempt to stand:
    Lest air of cold despair their motion fan.

If they smell, scents must surely shroud the air,
When fear and terror veil with acrid smell,
To cloak its breezes pungent with despair.
Yes, bain doth blanket black the mists of Hell:
    Where souls must surely know they endless grope
    And tireless strain, beyond the reach of hope.

"Damn," he commented to aloud. "This is certainly a barren source of amusement."

He tossed the creased manuscript upon the rickety table that leaned against the wall next to the bed.

"Wedged somewhere right between ominous and foreboding."

As he drifted off to sleep, a delicate breeze appeared to wait for the man to take his dreams, then brushed lightly over the warped sill of the open window and quietly caressed the cover of the folio back open. Without any sound, the puffs of air seemed to exhale across the room and gently flipped over each sheet of verse until it found the exact page where William had been reading.

The Steward of the duke of York could never have suspected just how dead on his observation might prove.

* * * * *

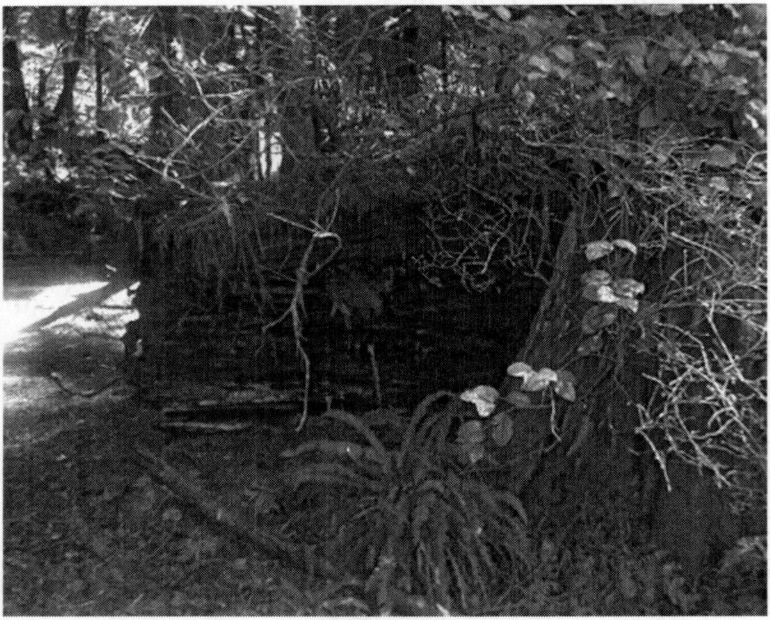

Chapter Sixteen

The duke of York's emissary sensed something lurking at the edge of the undergrowth: a malevolent presence or entity that crouched just out of sight and seemed to glare at him each and every time he passed its leafy lair.

The ancient stand of forest had originally only been hewn back a short distance from Bluet Manor. With the bulk of the fields and pastures being deforested as necessary over the generations for firewood and building materials, even hundreds of years had only laid bare the flattest parcels of land. As a result, the ancestral home of the

House of Morley resembled a patchwork quilt of green; with buildings of stone isolated on sections of farmland that were incorporated into a chessboard of dense glens and woodland. With the forests of Brecon to one side and the Forest of Dean on the other, even on the clearest of days there was a very real sense that the trees were basically biding their time: waiting for men to disappear so they might simply stride across the heath and reclaim their stolen territory.

Had it not been for Gwladus, William ap Thomas would have gladly left them to it.

Unfortunately, his decision to marry into one of the finest families of Abergavenny made a timely abdication almost impossible. His political aspirations depended upon the perception of wealth and influence; and, even with all his associates scattered across England, abandoning his heritage and his wife's substantial inheritance would be tantamount to cutting off his nose to save his face. Still, there was nothing to force him to spend any more time than necessary at Raglan; so he saw to it that he was absent whenever possible. London, the Court at Windsor, and Westminster were tantalising titbits of glory and recognition that he saw no reason whatsoever to refuse.

Yet, each time the Steward of the Lordship of Abergavenny returned to Raglan, he felt certain that ominous eyes watched his progress through the trees. It was for that very reason that he had instructed his workmen to clear away even more timber from the expansive building site of his castle. Though under the pretence of creating a better line of site and open ground to counter attack and improve Raglan's defence, the real reason was to distance his home from the ever-menacing thickets and glens that seemed to stalk the shallow glades and dells. Thoroughly convinced, after his frightening encounter, that spirits of the supernatural haunted the nearby forest, William made it a point to never, under any circumstances, travel the track from Raglan to Bluet Manor in the dark. Even in broad daylight, he would not venture into the woods without being accompanied by at least three or four men.

Perhaps a completely irrational fear of the unknown, but one that perfectly suited the purposes of his young son. His father's terror and superstition made the surrounding forest all the more inviting: a welcome refuge from the beatings and abuse that seemed to plague Bluet Manor with the man's return.

For that very reason, the young boy spent most every waking moment playing alone in Raglan Wood.

* * * * *

Young William never dreamed at night.

Though the central manor remained as yet untouched by his father's colossal building project, Bluet Manor seemed very little like a home. Perhaps that was because he knew it would not be left standing very much longer: maybe it was because the halls, bedrooms, and even the kitchen housed so very few good memories. Though his mother and younger brother and sister seemed quite content to spend their days inside, even the constant drizzle could not keep young William within its walls for very long.

As soon as he finished breakfast, the boy would exit through the kitchen and poke his pockets full of food. Pieces of bread, the odd chunk of cheese, meat left over from dinner the night before: anything that might tide him over till his mother called him back for the evening meal. Anything remotely edible regularly found its way into his pockets.

He bolted out the door and into the welcoming woods; spinning around as soon as he lost sight of the clearing to deliberately lose his way. William intentionally ran from the bleating calls of sheep: away from the sound of chisels and the clumsy hands of humankind.

Alone in the forest, the little boy found sanctuary.

Sunbeams showered through the rain-kissed leaves that fluttered like miniature fairy wings far above his head, splitting through the gnarled, clustered branches into broad waterfalls of light. The topmost leaves fluttered back and forth against the morning breeze to catch the yellowed spray, then swivelled in the wind to send still smaller rays of light to yet other leaves that patiently waited underneath the canopy. Down, down the sunlight streamed through serene layers of emerald green: where every leaf, branch, and trunk seemed to gently sway to catch the fractured light until the entire stand of trees was filled with slender shafts of gold.

Here was a pristine world unstained by grubby men.

Within this cathedral of foliage, young William left behind the very grey people he knew. Constant contact with the earth and stone had smeared everyone he came across each day with the odour of dank despair; as if the earth itself were anxious to reclaim their flesh into the loam. Where the forest had been hacked back next to Bluet Manor, the muddy earth and muck sucked at the feet of the labourers working on the castle. It tugged at the hooves of their draught horses and clung to the wheels of their wagons and carts. To make it even worse, the stench of sweat and dung from the open latrines seemed to attract every flying insect from miles around. Constant buzzing became a percussive accompaniment to the endless clang of hammers. Constant rain only seemed to make the scene even more depressing. The trickles of weeping overflow fled off the high ground across the rutted earth; seeming to carry off the surplus sins of the lurching gangs that continued to labour amidst the sporadic downpours.

Serene and silent, William's kingdom contradicted everything mankind had come to represent. Elms, oaks, firs, and yews spread out their massive arms to embrace the rolling sky and, when it rained upon the forest, they gently draped their limbs down around him to offer shelter from the storm. Spring and summer hosted the constant songs of robins; then rested during autumn and winter so that the thrushes could flap in between the branches to take the rowan berries.

Few had ever known so perfect and peaceful a refuge.

It was after a particularly stirring re-enactment of Agincourt that the boy decided to put aside his wooden sword and have a bite to eat. As his grandfather, Sir Dafydd Gam, had died there in France seventeen years ago and eight full years before he had been born, William made up scenarios in his imagination where he would gallantly fight by his grandfather's side. He was incredibly proud of his mother's father, even though the two had never met: pleased to think that someone in his family had actually died a hero. Whether anyone over in England bothered to remember made no difference to his grandson; just as whatever his father did for a living made no difference to him.

It was on these occasions that William desperately wished he had only been born before; when men were known for their deeds and values rather than simply politics and money.

Climbing up on the same hollow log that had claimed his brother's life, the lad bathed in the splintered brilliance of morning. He pulled out a piece of crusty bread and hunk of homemade cheese. It was here that the boy daydreamed of the world and of what he might become.

Daydreams were young William's friends.

Some fair, some often fickle; they teased his mind with hope, with transparent aspirations of life the lad realised he might never live to see; with the promise of a thousand bright tomorrows no one might ever chance to steal. They taunted and tortured him with wishes of what he hoped would be: completely ignoring the cruel realities of life the lad had learned to neatly lock up within his mind. No different, he supposed, than any other boy from any other time: the truths of life we often find in our imagination. Sleep might offer simple dreams, but one's inspired imagination often teemed with exquisite hope: a faith that, somehow, life might become infinitely more bearable than it all too frequently seems—particularly when one is trapped between the hollow night and empty dreams.

Crunching on a particularly tough crust, young William felt something brush against the back of his right ankle.

So lost in his own world, the lad had not even thought that some wild animal might have taken refuge from the earlier rain inside the hollow trunk. He stopped swinging his legs; sure that, whatever it was, he was far less likely to be bitten if he held quite still.

Something unexpectedly licked the back of the boy's bare calf.

Afraid that some starving, wild animal was going to pull him straight off his perch and rip him apart inside the hollow log, William decided to take the initiative and slowly lowered a piece of bread down between his knees. Gently, a mouth clamped down and closed over the morsel; waiting for him to let go before pulling away. At the same time, the boy could feel another muzzle nuzzle against the back of his hand looking for a fragment of its own. Without hesitation, he leaned forward over the rotting maw of the hollow log and relinquished the remainder; which instantly disappeared back into the darkness of the trunk.

Carefully climbing off his saddle of crumbling bark, William took two steps away before peering back into the cavity. Four little eyes stared at him from some five feet back, letting the lad know that he had stumbled upon their nursery. Quite slowly, he broke off bite-sized pieces of all the food he had left and offered it compassionately to the tiny animals.

For the very first time in William's life, he felt he might have helped someone in a worse predicament than himself. He held his hands up, extended his fingers, and showed the backs and fronts.

"All gone."

Sensing that the creatures might not have eaten for some time and might truly be starving, the boy backed away slowly and scampered back up to the pantry to steal some extra food.

* * * * *

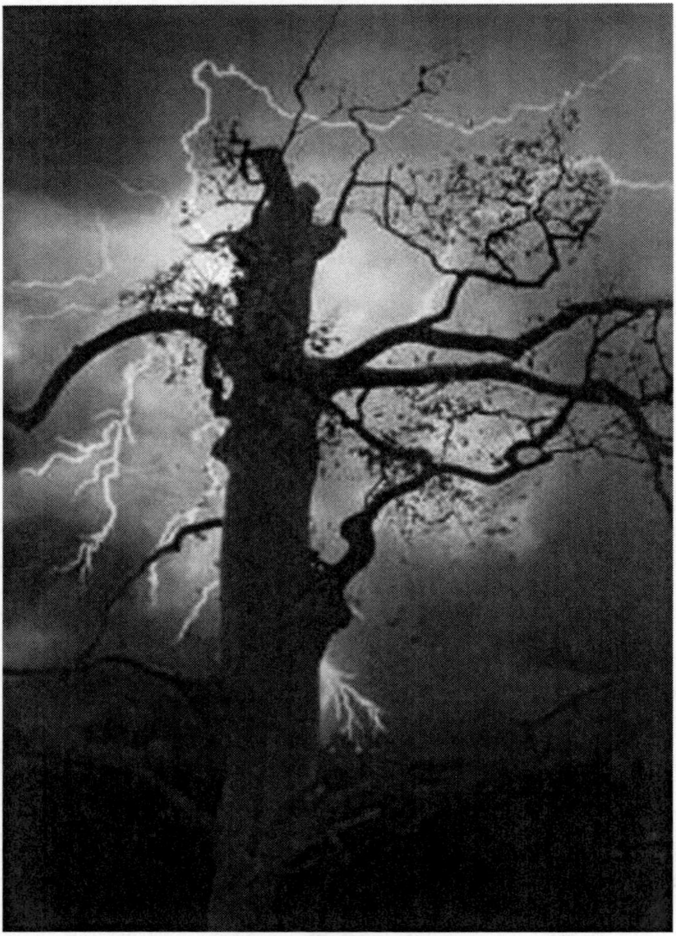

Chapter Seventeen

His horse had come to know the roads by heart. So well, as a matter of fact, that William could literally drop the reins across the pommel and the animal would keep right on plodding along without encouragement.

The rhythmic clopping started the Steward to wondering how many hundreds of times they had slogged this self-same track since coming back from France and Agincourt. Though his work took him all across south-eastern Wales and a great deal of England, William ap Thomas always considered this part of county Gwent as home.

East from Abergavenny all the way to Monmouth Castle, then south in an almost perfect square down to the fortifications at Newport and Chepstow, this region of Wales had been such a thorn in the western flank of England for so many centuries that dozens of castles had been hurriedly constructed across Gloucester, Shropshire, Staffordshire, and Leicestershire in the attempt to keep the wild Celtic tribes at bay. So, though not particularly vast, the region of Gwent became of strategic importance in holding the territory around the Severn and Hertfordshire. In addition to castles at Abergavenny, Monmouth, Caerphilly, Cardiff, and Chepstow, generations of English kings had barricaded their reigns behind massive fortifications at Arnallt, Bronllys, Grosmont, and Newcastle, at Skenfrith, Caerleon, Newport, Usk, Dixton, and dozens of other strategic positions across county Gwent alone.

Having been called to matters that needed his immediate attention down in Newport, the duke of York's Steward returned to check on the progress of his own castle by way of the Vale of Usk.

Rising from the Fan Brycheiniog or the Carmarthen Fans mountains in mid-Wales, the river Usk traced its track back from the heart of Newport town, up past Caerleon Castle, and the village of Usk itself before reaching its origin north-west of Abergavenny and Brecon. It was not a particularly difficult ride, in that most of its bogs and marshes could be easily avoided if one made a point to stay on the main road. The real difficulty arose when one passed the lagoons and grassland and ran across the fingers of forest that constantly seemed to surround and swallow up travellers upon the Usk Road to Raglan. The Brecons stabbed out to the east from Rhiwlas and Bryngwyn; while the Forest of Dean knifed out into the rolling meadows to the west from Llandenny and Penyclawdd.

Utterly bored and in a desperate attempt to distract himself from increasingly painful saddle sores, William ap Thomas decided to have another go at reading. He unfolded the folio open to his bookmark and began to read aloud.

Sloth's once esteemed, vain specimens now reach
To teach proud kindred fears each mind contrives:
The unenvisioned consequence that each
Might face in fate for living of their lives.
    But, in dilemma, all must acquiesce:
        With mouths swelled full with what they would confess.

The lone traveller stopped reading and considered not just the words, but their careful selection within each rhyme of the stanza. Poets and politicians were not so very far apart—both attempted to change the world with words.

And these words were rather quite good.

F or faith evades conceited, haughty souls
That, confident of absolution, lift
Foul hands corrupted as by blackened coals,
Who public plead and pray in furtive shrift:
    Besmirched by fault, each sin-soaked mind enflames
    To claim the life it mutilates and maims.

William flipped back to re-examine the much more modern jacket into which the vellum pages had been carefully stitched. As with most everything in life, the simplistic cover belied the complexity within:

The Works of Robert Traverner
The Year of Our Lord
1187

and carefully penned directly below:

Left To The Library Of
The University at Oxford
Best of Friends As Ever We Were
Morgan ap Seisyll
Lord of Upper Gwent

That the University at Oxford considered the poetry even worth keeping was impressive enough, William supposed. That it was bequeathed by the author's friend who just happened to be, likewise, from Gwent; well, that seemed quite the coincidence. As his horse trudged through the evening fog of early April, he turned back to finish the last stanza of the page.

>
> U p from the soil, the rank and fetid air
> Twirls slow in pungent whirls of greyish blue,
> Between the figures huddled in despair
> Whose ashen limbs the swirling fumes imbue
>   As animated, stick-like toys of death:
>   Who dance forever, ever void of breath.

"Damn!"

Perhaps it was his sudden realisation that the fog appeared to be growing more and more dense with each passing minute. Possibly, it was the stroke of coincidence once more: but William found it strange that his surroundings seemed to be mirroring whatever he happened to read aloud.

The envoy suddenly had the distinct impression that he was being watched.

If not watched; then most certainly followed. He craned his head round in both directions to check the track behind but could see no one lurking in the encroaching shadows. At first, his instinct was to blame the feeling upon the mood of the writing: the author's highly crafted descriptions of Hell were doing little to fend off the beckoning arms of the lone traveller's vivid imagination.

"Damn tales of flighty minds," he murmured to himself as he jammed the vellum binding back into his outside jacket pocket.

William ap Thomas patted his horse upon the neck and began to hum an old, familiar drinking song; his knees involuntarily goading the animal to reconsider its unhurried pace. If he wasn't careful, the Steward of the duke of York was about to find himself caught in the twilight of Raglan Wood: a situation he had personally vowed to avoid at any cost.

As the pair now trotted up the Usk Road that sliced up through the heart of Gwent and led to Raglan, William tried to rationalise away his growing sense of foreboding.

Across the abandoned vales and glens, there were untold square miles of meadows and stands of timber. The coming of the spring had signalled the heavy sap to rise and forced the forest to stir from its reluctant slumber. Distant beeches and elms gave testimony to the coming warmth by dropping the tiny unnecessary twigs that had been left over from last season's puberty. Their cracks and splintered fractures from hitting other limbs played havoc on the Steward's imagination. A light breeze playfully slapped the emaciated fingers of yews and evergreens against their neighbours' bark; causing the entire wood to sound as if its unusually bleak landscape was crawling back to life from underneath the ground.

A notion that did nothing to set his nerves at ease.

* * * * *

A mere ten miles from home, the Lord of Raglan reined his mount up the turn off to his left that led to Rhiwlas and Llanvair Kilgeddin. Glancing back toward the eastern hilltops, he could just make out the farmers lighting their lamps upon the distant ridge.

Without warning, his horse shuddered to a complete stop in the middle of the road.

Initially, William was, true to custom, far from understanding and cursed the animal while kicking it firmly in the ribs. When that failed to break his mount's attention to the distant bend, his master whipped him lightly upon the flanks to provide the beast some additional encouragement.

Still the animal refused to take another step.

Careful to wrap the reins tightly around his hand so the steed could not simply bolt away and leave him there alone, William dismounted. Deciding to take a gentler tack, he stroked the gelding's velvety muzzle while speaking softly as possible.

"Almost home," he whispered.

His mount ignored him.

"Almost home. Hey," he tried to sound as cheery as possible considering the circumstances.

"Your friends will be there eating grain in the stables. You don't want them to get all of yours, now do you?"

Glancing off to the distance, he noticed storm clouds coming up the valley behind them from the south: huge, billowed mountains of high banked indigo threatened to slash up the valley from the Severn and drench them at any moment once they managed to clamber over the crest of the nearby peak.

William decided to read one more time. Perhaps the sound of his voice might keep the horse slightly more calm. Feeling that he was being watched again, he turned to see a small set of eyes catch the feeble light. He laughed.

"It's a cat."

The man reached over the pommel and patted his horse with a firm determination to end the episode. "It's just a damn cat."

His horse had seemed to calm back down, so the steward carefully inched his way back into the saddle and gently coaxed the animal into continuing down the lane. The incessant clop of the gelding's hooves faded slightly as the annoying drizzle broke into a scattered, spattering rain and, before the light was lost altogether, William thought he would give the writing one last try.

York's ambassador took another look at the cover and, as he flipped quickly through the pages, discovered a ragged piece of parchment tucked discreetly between the pages.

The fact that the fragment had been torn from the exact yellowed vellum of the pages made it obvious that it had been deliberately included when originally bequeathed to the shelves in 1187. What had been curiously inserted had been penned by a different hand; probably Morgan ap Seisyll himself. It simply read:

ERE HE LACKING SIN LIVED

HE FLESHED THE VAST WORLD

TO NURTURE MANKIND

A benediction of sorts, he supposed; at least until he took note of the following page. There the ink had bled from the rain and transferred portions of the saying neatly in reverse. Even in the fading light, there could be no mistake at what had been spelled out on the opposite side.

W. B. Baker

ERE HE LACKING SIN LIVED
HE FLESHED THE VAST WORLD
TO NURTURE MANKIND

had become in reverse:

DEVIL NIS GNIKCAL EH ERE
DLROW TSAV EHT DEHSELF EH
DNIKNAM ERUTRUN OT

Even for William ap Thomas, this freakish message was far beyond simple happenstance. His eyes now darted back and forth as the man looked for the silhouettes of demons in every shadow. He violently kicked the poor animal in the ribs to demand more speed. On through the muffled rain, the ungainly Blue Knight of Gwent galloped toward the familiar outline of Bluet Manor.

Noticing the strange sensation of heat in the centre of his back, between his shoulder blades, he risked a hurried glance back down the lane.

What he saw there terrified the man beyond all sense of reason.

Two gigantic hounds leaped out from either side of the underbrush—almost as if each had been waiting for the exact instant he had decided to turn around. With glowing crimson eyes that seemed to burn with the coals of Hades, they immediately gave chase from the irregular hedge of broken briars and yellow gorse that lined the edges of the road.

William then beat the labouring horse without mercy in an effort to stay ahead, but the beasts managed to catch up with the gelding in only a matter of strides. Now the steed saw them as well and bolted at a pace that even surprised his master. The animal was running for his very life, and if his master happened to fall off; well, then horse would only be able to run even faster.

William ap Thomas gave up on the now useless reins and dug his fingernails through the thick mat of the horse's mane; so terrified that he slid his legs forward, wrapped his ankles around the great beast's throat, and desperately clung to the neck of the runaway horse like a dying cat.

The great black hounds never made a sound.

They were fully as large as any man; over three feet high at the shoulders and near seven feet in length. The size of good-sized calves, their tongues flipped up and down with every stride; then back and forth against thick, frothing lips of foam: almost giving the impression that each was licking its lips in greedy anticipation.

Neither looked once in William's direction.

The wraiths bolted down the muddy track; bookending the gelding so that he could neither turn nor stop: intent on herding William ap Thomas and his horse straight down the slippery artery to Hell.

Murmurs of wind that had risen from the darkness now clawed at the man's back. Swaying limbs caught in the sudden gale crackled and snapped and fell across the road. Though the horse was forced to catapult over every obstacle; the spectral hounds simply ran right through and never once broke their ghostly stride.

The faint murmur at their back exploded into an audible growl as the whipping wind began to mount even faster. Dead and rotting leaves were flung across the grooved cart path like a million decaying mice and rats—the storm appearing to hurl their bony bodies through narrow cracks between the red-hot hinges of the Gates of Hell.

Manic with fright, William ap Thomas hurtled on through the constricting throat of twilight.

Twigs from the swaying limbs whacked at his face and clothes like jointed, skeletal fingers; trying their damnedest to scrape him sideways off the saddle while the two great hairy apparitions kept pace on either side. Lightning stabbed across the last few hundred yards of the midnight chase; as if Satan himself had lit the sky for a better look at William's inevitable end. Afraid to take his eyes off the road ahead for even an instant, the man could almost swear the illuminated outlines and silhouettes of oaks along the road were moving: their grotesque arms slapping each other on the back and sides as the wind laughed on and on hysterically.

The Lord of Raglan Wood made it at last to the tower and literally threw himself from the saddle and crawled on his hands and knees toward the safety of the wall. Thunder boomed from a lightning strike not fifteen feet away; instinct forcing the man to turn and glance back down the lane at his pursuers. There, not fifty yards from the clearing gleamed four bright bloody eyes. Lungs heaving with yellowed mouths agape, they glared at the torches of Bluet Manor: their curved, bleached fangs catching glimmered reflections of the flickering torches mounted on either side of the door.

"And hello to you, too."

The head of Gareth ap Hywel popped over William ap Thomas and so caught him by surprise that the man started to strike out.

"Hey, Hey," the foreman held up his hand in mock surrender.

"Have a drink."

Completely shattered, the Steward clutched at the cup with both hands; trembling so badly that he could barely swallow. Trying to gather up the shredded strips of his composure, William made up an excuse for his appearance.

"Almost didn't get here before the thunderstorm."

"What storm?" Gareth asked quite innocently.

William spun on his feet and pointed back down the road to Raglan. "That maelstrom that blew up from the Forest..." The Lord of Raglan stopped.

The midnight sky was completely clear.

Moonlight shone down brightly from the full moon across a cloudless heaven—so clear a night that one might see the horizon miles in any direction beyond the trees. The Steward's clothes and hair were completely dry.

Plainly terrified, William pointed out the glowing red eyes of the phantom hounds that now retreated to either side of the bend of the road adjoining the ruined cottage.

"God, at least tell me that you see those eyes."

Gareth squinted and held up his hand to block out the unusually bright moonlight. From either side of the narrow track gleamed the unearthly gaze of no animal he could identify: Hellish eyes that never appeared to blink—that turned and silently made their way back through the bristling thickets that lined the narrow road.

The master mason emptied the remainder of his cup to steady his voice.

"Those...," he stammered.

"Those I see."

* * * * *

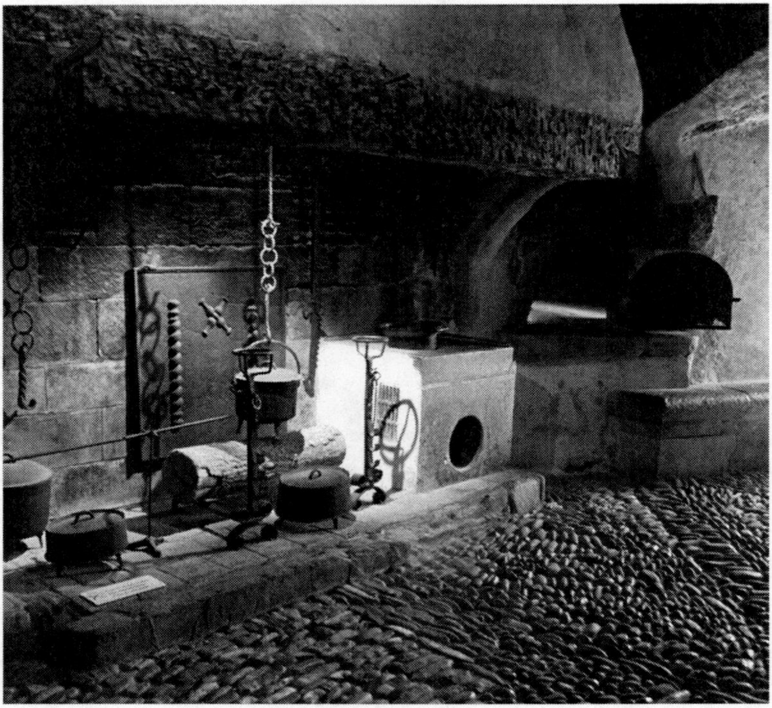

Chapter Eighteen

William ap Thomas continued on with his building scheme.

True to his original design, most of the original buildings of Bluet Manor were systematically razed to the ground; with many of their component stones finding their way into the new castle. The Steward's ultimate appointment as Sheriff of Glamorgan only provided more incentive for William the father to continue with his ever more complicated battlements.

He shrewdly abandoned any connection with the earlier Bluet Manor and adopted the name of the nearby village. Raglan or 'Ragland' as a designation or title had been around since Walter Bluet was granted the area as part of the Lordship of Usk almost two hundred years earlier. From the Welsh *rhag* 'fore' and *glan* 'bank,' the resulting 'rampart' or by some accounts 'border,' was far more conducive than retaining the family name of William's first wife's family. If he wished to indelibly scrawl his influence upon county Gwent's heritage, the first goal would be to firmly establish an association with his recent acquisition and his own name.

Successive alterations made the new Raglan Castle more of baronial mansion than an effective feudal castle; the style reflecting more of the architecture the Lord had witnessed while traipsing across France with Henry V than other construction projects across Wales and England. True to his original wish, the fortification was stately and handsome; though that objective may have had more to do with William ap Thomas' political aspirations than with any military considerations.

William's celebrated triumph was the construction of Great Tower of yellow sandstone with its six corner turrets. Deliberately situated on the parcel of land where the earlier Norman defences had been levelled, one would have to concede that even survivors from the House of Morley would have found it difficult to detract from their successor. The workmen would, upon completion, encircle the self-contained fortress with an actual functioning moat, which would not only highlight the unusual hexagonal design but echo French influence and the grandiosity of the new owner. Unlike all of the earlier castles constructed from Nottinghamshire to Berkshire, along England's somewhat irregular frontier with Wales; that of William ap Thomas at Raglan was specifically designed to withstand attack from gunpowder. Entirely independent from any other buildings to be constructed later, the Great Tower was to be surrounded by a broad, effective moat that completely complemented its impressive height of five stories and circlet crown of battlements.

Raglan was the badge of wealth that William intended to flaunt not only to his relatives and in-laws but to guests venturing to England's frontier across the Severn. The keep of the Yellow Tower at Raglan would dominate not only its finely manicured courtyards but the halls of Abergavenny and Chepstow as well: for the expansive interior would be sumptuously furnished with paintings and tapestries that displayed William ap Thomas' accomplishments and wealth. True to his original intention, long before the edifice ever saw completion, his great monument to his own affluence immediately became the favourite gossip of Monmouthshire.

Still, despite the man's rising notoriety as not only a Knight; an unusually rare achievement for any Welshman of the day, but as a local hero and Welsh nationalist who many believed might be able to wrench Gwent from the fist of England: for all that and more, William ap Thomas had changed.

The Sheriff of Glamorgan had found religion.

Well, it might be more fair to say—the semblance of religion. Under any other circumstances, this unexpected transformation might have proven of interest and great value to his previously abused family and friends. For William ap Thomas, though, it seemed that he had merely substituted addictions: the worship of drink for that of his own interpretation of religious conviction.

He refused to allow a drop of spirit in the house; nor would any be admitted who were under its persuasion. Again, on the surface, quite admirable for any who abstained from alcoholic beverages. Regrettably, he often associated his particular slant on the scriptures with a hard-nosed defiance to contrasting judgments or opinions: which meant that, now, instead of simply passing out after tirades, the man could go on soberly berating the inferior beliefs and values of guests for hours on end.

Visitors to Raglan Castle seemed to evaporate overnight.

Sad; for creed and religious convictions did more to ostracize the man from his family than simple alcoholism ever could. Worse: his new-found faith gave William the dubious posture of being right based on the mere fact that he was the Lord of his castle: which, in point of fact, he was. Terrible—that people so deeply entrenched in their own beliefs may completely miss their own family's frantic hope for help: that, without charity, a despot may truly be sharp as a tack and, regrettably, just as flat-headed.

Abuse no longer amused the man. Not when condescending, patronizing, or humiliating those around him seemed so much more gratifying. Everything in the scriptures was to be taken as entirely literal; though the same did not pertain with applications to his own life. He was unnecessarily brutal when dressing down his wife and children; a brutality that, simply because it was completely unnecessary, made it all the more vicious and cruel.

As his children aged, he neatly substituted threats with sophisticated rebukes.

When they wondered why they ought not to lie when their father did so every day whenever deception played to his advantage, he would chastise them with questionable homilies such as:

"Do as I say, not as I do."

When asked why, touting his convictions, he never seemed to be bothered to pray himself, he would offhandedly remark:

"Well, God knows how I feel."

A strange response since, whenever frustrated, William ap Thomas would still regularly and quite deliberately take the name of the Lord in vain. Behaviour that could not be easily defended to his three children was dismissed with his accustomed proverb:

"When you are as old as I am, you will see it my way."

None did much to endear him to his offspring; nor to Gwladus either: his wife quietly retreating rather than daring to escalate the situation back to the earlier years of actual physical violence. When the children's father failed to bring them presents for their birthdays or at

Christmas, their mother, having predicted and prepared for their father's obvious lack of interest, would magically produce gifts with little notes that stressed that they were from the both of their parents. Sadly, William ap Thomas had come to expect his wife to make such offerings on his behalf. Regrettably, his children resented their father for the same.

The Sheriff of Glamorgan and Lord of Raglan Castle ruled his household like his private little monarchy. Never a night went by that his family and staff did not hope for a coup and pray for insurrection.

* * * * *

William's mother had given the matter quite a lot of thought; even calling upon her friends and family for their insight and opinions. Her oldest son's latest imaginary friends were, according to everyone with whom she took into her confidence, perfectly normal. She, too, had possessed an active imagination as a child and her imaginary playmates had been a source of constant companionship when she felt her family might not have had enough time to spend with her.

Gwladus' mother, Gwenllian Verch Gwilym, had told her much the same; that as a widow in Abercrai, Traeanglas, near Brecon, Gwladus was left as a little girl to play with her own imaginary friends; though now grown to womanhood, she remembered little of the particulars.

Not being able to come round to visit, young William's grandmother gave her daughter the best advice she could: that taking the time to listen and understand her child's conversations with his make-believe friends might tell her much about what the boy was going through. Particularly with the added trauma of losing his brother Thomas so early, young William might be re-directing his sense of loss over his brother into pretend friends who could understand what he was feeling. A bit of fantasy might very well help the boy cope a little better with a rather traumatic childhood—especially since he and his father had so terrible and strained a relationship.

So, while the young mother was assuredly concerned when the boy began to talk about his imaginary puppies; what with the emotional maelstrom William had been through recently, she was certainly not surprised.

* * * * *

"Still, I'd love to buy him for what he's worth—and then sell him for what he *thinks* he's worth."

The cook and scullery maid shared a quick giggle before their mistress made it through the doorway from the dining room. From the mudroom, young William rattled the kitchen door as he fumbled with the latch.

"May my puppies come in with me for lunch?"

Gwladus ignored the cook's scoffing glance to the scullery maid and turned back to the table to pour the boy a glass of milk.

"You know your father will have a fit if he sees animals in the house," his mother's fleeting look told the staff to play along.

"That's ok," William answered from the doorway. "They're invisible."

"Mind you have them wipe their feet."

His mother fired an angry glare directly at the heavyset domestic at the fire: a fierce gaze that made it clear a cook could be quite easily replaced.

The scullery maid took the mother's side to show her support.

"I just mopped so don't let them track up the floor."

The teenage girl then turned and continued a conversation with the cook to play off the entire affair. "I saw another mouse this morning. Nearly scared me right out of my . . . ," she caught her mistress looking in her direction.

" . . . my shoes."

Young William bounced over to the far end of the long kitchen table and plopped down upon a stool. Sensing her misstep, the cook immediately attempted to regain her mistress' graces and carefully placed a heaping plate of venison stew before the boy.

Without encouragement, William dove into the meal. He had been playing outside for hours and was completely famished.

His mother stepped round toward the window to let the maid finish the floor and started to discuss the evening menu. She was expecting guests from Raglan; whom, upon assuring themselves that the master of the house was leaving again that afternoon, suddenly found their previous plans amenable to change. From the corner of her eye, she watched what the lad was doing.

Not thinking that anyone was paying any attention, William was sneaking chunks of boiled potato off his plate with his left hand and dropping them for his imaginary friends. So, too, he would eat the centre of a slice of bread and then break the crust in two and slowly lower the pieces with either hand out of sight underneath the table.

Gwladus smiled to herself.

It was nice to have her son again.

The oldest boy had kept quite to himself for months now and simply refused to talk with anyone. His mother realised he was trying to find a way to deal with losing his brother and was prepared to give him all the leeway the lad needed to deal with his grief. If playing with imaginary animals did anything to make the lad's adjustment any easier, Gwladus was more than willing to replace the entire household staff should it ultimately prove necessary. The maids would simply have to pick up underneath his chair until William outgrew his imagination.

"I have a little present for you," his mother slipped a tiny packet from inside her bodice and handed it to the boy.

Chewing faster to swallow a mouthful, William's little hands ripped through the thin paper wrapping to reveal a small silver dragon suspended from a leather thong. His eyes widened in excitement; for it was, by far, the nicest gift the lad had ever received.

"Do you like it?"

Still chewing far more than his tongue might navigate around to speak, his face clearly expressed his appreciation. Taking it carefully from his hands, Gwladus carefully tied the narrow strip of leather in a hard knot around her son's neck.

"The dragon of Cadwaladr, King of Gwynedd. One of our distant relations. Owain Glyndwr used it on his standard when I was a little girl about your age." She slid the knot around to centre it behind his neck and positioned the pendant in the middle of the boy's chest.

"There you go."

Leaning in to whisper in William's ear, his mother pulled the front of the lad's shirt back up a bit to cover the creature's head and wings with cloth.

"Don't let your father see it."

She gently cupped his face between her palms and kissed his forehead.

"He has been trying so hard to be English of late."

Scraping his spoon against the bottom of the plate to get the last of the broth, the child then tipped up his cup with both hands and guzzled down the last half of his milk. He started to wipe his mouth on his sleeve but, noticing his mother still looking in his direction, picked up the untouched cloth napkin and used it instead.

"May we go back outside and play now?"

His voice offering the semblance of manners as his feet were already headed for the door. He nearly knocked the scullery maid over as she toted the bucket of mop water to the window to pour it outside on the ground.

"Don't go too far from the road."

Gwladus shouted toward the now empty doorway as she took a dirty dish from the washing up pan and knelt down to save the maid the bother of picking up the pieces of food William had sneaked off to hide underneath his chair.

The floor was clean.

Placing the plate beside her knees, the woman glanced around the table legs; then tipped the chair back to see if the boy had somehow stuck the morsels to the bottom. Her search was cut short by a scream.

Standing in the doorway was the scullery maid. Her mop bucket held up against her bosom as a shield, the girl had jumped backwards through the doorway and had instantly faded into a most deathly shade of pale. Gwladus and the cook each picked up a broom and pan respectively and rushed over, assuming that the young girl must have stumbled across yet another mouse.

There, on the freshly mopped floor were the tracks of William's little boots; flanked on either side by the unmistakable muddy prints of two tiny sets of paws.

All three women looked down the hill to where William was now running back toward the woods as fast as his little legs could carry.

"Wait for me!"

* * * * *

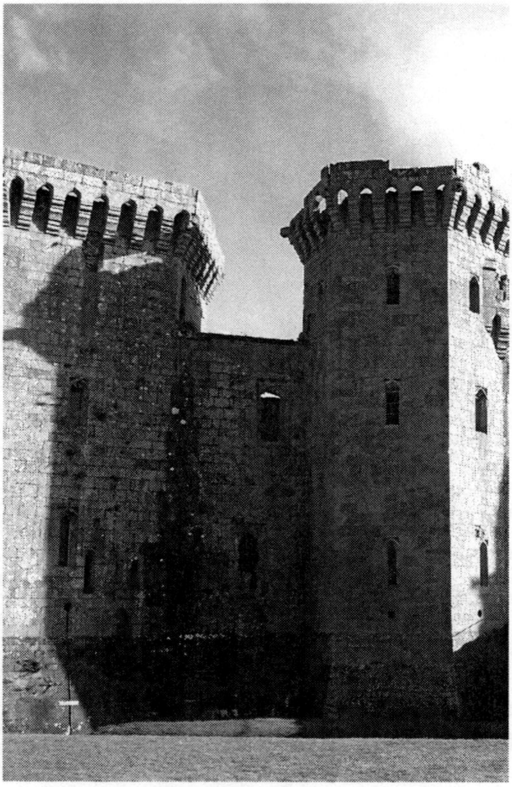

Chapter Nineteen

The itinerant workman, Charles Gardiner, suffered from the same affliction as many followers of the early Church. Not that, Heaven forbid, mother Church might, under any circumstances, be compelled by God or man to ultimately step forward and assume responsibility. Just as any parent must eventually decide when and where to wash their hands of an irreverent, wicked child and abandon them to their fate; so, too, organised religion can never be held ultimately responsible for practitioners who, after wandering off the straight and narrow track, have relished the sampled fruits of perdition and refused to be bullied or coerced from the sty or paddock each subsequently claimed as home.

Charles' errant perception that kept him from regaining the prodigal, if oftentimes unlit, path to recovery was that he misconstrued the meaning and function of penance. It was a normal mistake; one that most men and women seem to rationalise out by themselves sooner or later; with or without the intercession of a priest.

Gardiner, you see, had mistakenly presumed that self-inflicted penance might actually save his soul.

It was a conventional error made by so many who took the teachings of religion at face value and never committed to the spirit of the law or Lord. From an all too brief indoctrination as a child, he understood that Heaven waited to absolve: that, true to its own nature, the universe was compelled to exonerate any who identified their failings and performed the necessary atonement of apology. Regardless of his personal commitment to reparations, God must, according to the by-laws of His own unshakable covenant, basically be forced to acquiesce: forced to forgive and forget by His own adherence to the rules.

While not particularly ideologically sound, the perception of organised religion was, for Charles at least, practically foolproof.

Whenever the man felt a twinge of guilt or remorse for conduct or sins of omission, he simply found a nearby priest who told him how to make the feeling go away. As much as he transgressed and fornicated, those who knew him well thought that, by now, his twinges of guilt should have escalated into full-blown fits of convulsions.

Still, according to Gardiner's interpretation of Christianity, forgiveness usually involved making a donation to some local congregation and repeating a simple prayer by rote some specified number of times. It was actually a terribly small price to pay for the privilege of continuing to live life on one's own terms.

The problem with his reasoning lay in the fact that, after sobering up from a particularly forgettable episode in some strange woman's bed, he would immediately detour to a priest on his way to Raglan Castle the following day. Sacraments accepted and atonement made, Gardiner would quite honestly work at overcoming any sense of failure as a man: until, eventually, he became so terribly depressed again that he drank himself into a stupor. Which, inevitably led to the miscreant later waking up naked in another bed with a different and quite often even nastier whore.

Still, as Charles had no wife or family to provide for, he methodically divided each day's earnings between food, a room, the usual prostitute, and a tip for the priest for hastening to absolve his soul—as was the minister's duty.

All in all, Gardiner considered his hedonistic lifestyle nothing if not quite gratifying; and, with the exception of some unpleasant, unmentionable ailments and often questionable rashes and sores, a rather good bargain for the money.

W. B. Baker

* * * * *

The arrival of the campaign season meant that the weather improved enough to employ even more men: Raglan Castle's construction being a great boon to the limited local economy. That, more than any real affinity for William ap Thomas, might have accounted for the man's rocketing popularity across county Gwent. Realistically, any building project that put hundreds of otherwise unemployed men to work and flooded the surrounding villages of Monmouth and Abergavenny with English gold would have endeared most of the starving inhabitants along the river Usk and the head of the valleys to the son of the devil himself.

With the rising tide of summer, the sun crossed slightly higher over the intersecting limbs of Raglan's artificial forest each afternoon.

Scaffolding had sprung up on each of the six sides and sported dozens of workmen labouring on the inner and outer walls. Though the face and interior were beautifully and precisely fashioned of perfectly squared sandstone, the many feet of space that lay between them in the walls were simply filled with miscellaneous bits of castoff stone and rubble. An intelligent and elegant solution: in that, where no corridors or archways were called for in the plans, Gareth ap Hywel would, in basic terms, dump the odd sized and broken chunks of stone inside and then pack them down to anchor the inner and outer facades.

Which is exactly why unskilled labourers like Edward Ruddel and Charles Gardiner were absolutely necessary on the building crew. Master masons and their apprentices commanded much higher salaries and were difficult to find; while brute men with broad backs were penny a day labourers, able to earn their pay by only showing up each morning and moving about great piles of stone.

Accordingly, conversations around the site tended to reflect not only the education and aspirations of particular groups but, except for singular exceptions, strayed rarely from the cliché. While occasional exchanges compared the attributes of religion and qualities of disparate ideologies, most common were the bantered vulgar tête-à-têtes one comes to expect whenever great crowds of sweating, swearing uneducated men gather to strain under the unrelenting sun. Combine the raucous crowd with that very real and likely possibility that someone could be disfigured or maimed in an accident at any time and the lure of the construction site proved simply irresistible to Gwladus' two remaining sons.

William and Richard had actually become quite proficient at escaping the watchful eye of their governess and showing up to watch the rigmarole. Knowing enough to stay well out of the way, the boys would carefully sidle through the commotion to end up by Gareth's table. There they could see not only what was going on, but hear the wealth of profanities and curses that spewed out from sacrilegious mouths in almost every direction.

Gareth ap Hywel tried to keep the lads away as best he could, but didn't have the time or inclination to step on the toes of his employer. Particularly when William ap Thomas was, this morning, standing right next to him discussing the pattern for the battlements; but even less so when the mason caught sight of the Lady of the Manor cutting a deliberate swath through the idle company.

It didn't take a mental wizard to see the hurricane surging in toward them from the horizon. Not even a first class fool could miss the epic tornado that threatened to explode at any second across the morning's serenity.

Hoodwinked into believing that her husband had not arrived until that morning, Gareth knew better.

As did most of the crew by now, since their backsliding, inebriated employer had sat beside Charles and Edward most of the night. Exchanging lurid tales of nauseating whores and foul witticisms over frequent foamy pints of brew might be hidden a bit better from the abandoned spouse if one were to purge such pursuits out of one's system before actually returning too near home.

As it were, the fact that Gardiner had been repeating many of the dirty limericks on the line and boasting that he had heard them from the Lord of Raglan at the pub in the village only the night before: well, that made it even more likely that the stories might somehow, quite unbelievably, make it the scant fifty feet across the lawn to greet the ears of William's faithful wife. One would have had to have looked quite close to see if any trace love still lurked around her eyes. But that would have meant putting oneself within reach and range of her arms and fingernails.

"Get out of my way!"

The normally peaceable Lady of the Manor physically shoved men twice her size out of her way: splitting the morning shift like a white-hot blade through a block of wax. Gwladus swept through them like a kingfisher; her knees kicking at a long blue dress trimmed with orange: mimicking the unmistakable rapid flight of the winged predator slicing through a defenceless swarm of unwitting damselflies.

"Move out of my way, damn it!"

The raging hellcat loping on a course toward her husband through the grass appeared anything but adoring, caring, or warm. Scalding hot would have been a better description; a two-legged panther doting only on the idea of laying unchristian hands upon her cheating spouse.

Luckily, the Welsh foreman caught the full frontal charge of the man-eater coming through the ranks and stepped back just in time to avoid any affiliation and, even more likely, the chance of being mortally wounded by accident if caught upside the temple by some deadly ricochet. Which, as events would almost immediately bear out, proved to be his most sensible decision of the day.

"So you ignore your wife and children to stay out all night whoring with your friends?"

Gwladus waved her arms to include everyone within earshot: a no-nonsense opening shot across the bow that absolutely no one within shouting distance failed to miss.

Workers fled for their lives in every direction like frantic, little mice scrambling off a piece of discarded cheese.

The cat had hit the floor.

"You dirty, disgusting, son of a bitch!"

Then the slapping began. Not a single, sharp insult of a slap; rather, a lathered, layered series of open handed blows.

Much like a maligned dog that had been beaten and kicked for years, it seemed that this latest incursion had finally tipped the scales of the woman's righteous anger. With the fury of an enraged bitch defending her helpless brood, Gwladus ferch Dafydd unleashed untold years of pent-up rage. Having been up the last three nights with fevered children as they wretched and vomited endlessly from the flu, William ap Thomas could not have returned to Raglan and stepped into it at a worse time if he had set out to deliberately try.

Slapping quickly sank into closed fists, which stooped to repeated kicking, and ultimately descended into whacking the miscreant with a lucky wooden stake. Having never seen or faced such uncontrolled fury before in his life, the helpless William ap Thomas hurriedly decided to cut his losses and made a strategic, lifesaving departure. His beeline retreat for the front door might have been the only thing that saved his life.

Far from the hysterical laughter of literally hundreds of employees hooting in the distance: farther from the wayward husband's cowering flight from an unending rain of blows that forced him to cringe and shrink away in search of some refuge inside the castle walls. No. Still further, from some vantage point only God knows where, Gareth could not help but think that, wherever he was and looking down, her father, the late Sir Dafydd Gam, could not have been more proud.

* * * * *

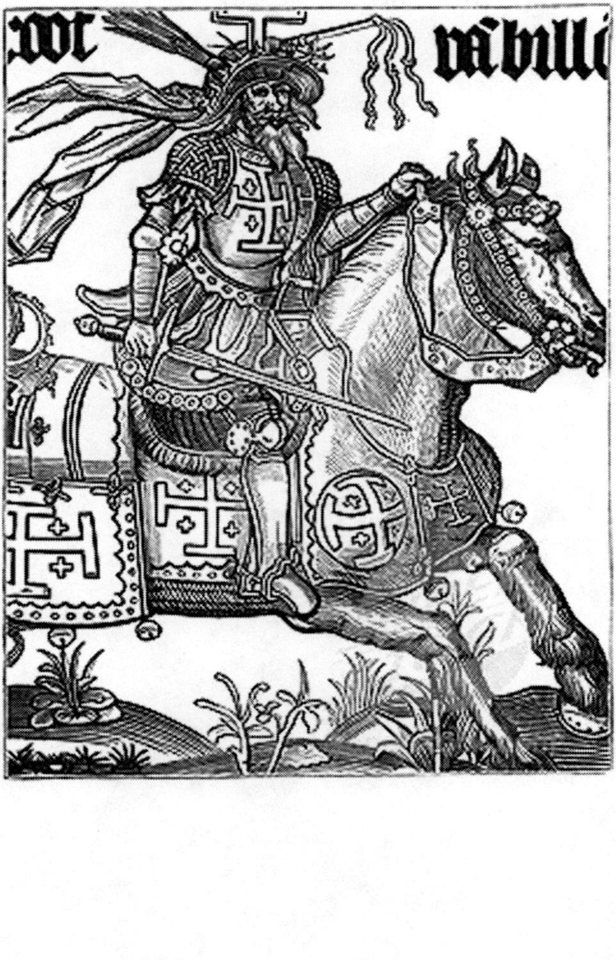

Chapter Twenty

Young William leaned back against the wall at the top of the stairs and listened from the shelter of the shadows.

Several of his father's drinking companions had come for dinner that evening and, as far as the boy supposed, appeared not to want to leave. Long after his mother, Richard, and Elizabeth had retreated from the ever loudening swell of dirty stories and profanity, the boy crept down the hallway on his hands and knees until he could clearly make out what was being said.

Recovered from his wife's indignation and relatively confident Gwladus could not hear, his father appeared to have regained his nerve and was, once again, back in rare form.

"So the knight says, Your horse wanted me to tell you that he doesn't like the new bit on his bridle. It cuts the corner of his mouth when you pull him back.

Your cow said that I should mention that it would be thoughtful for you to drop a bit more grain in the trough when you are milking her each morning.

And your sheep said . . .

The farmer held up both his hands to hush his visitor and screamed, "Don't believe a single word!

All those damn sheep are liars!"

Screams of hilarity echoed from the Great Hall below the landing; William ap Thomas' low-browed sense of humour always played particularly well to the inebriated. Though his son didn't understand exactly what was so terribly funny, he had the feeling that his father would be very upset if he knew he were listening.

The lad pulled his silver dragon out from underneath his nightshirt and tilted it back and forth to catch the reflection of the torches. The nicest gift he was apt to ever receive, young William wondered if Cadwaladr, King of Gwynedd, or Owain Glyndwr would think his father was so terribly funny. Or Jesus, for that matter.

Gwladus talked to Jesus all the time.

Sometimes, when he would come back from the woods for a drink, he could hear his mother crying and calling out his name. Young William knew that God and Jesus were supposed to listen and care, but her son had never seen either coming round. Particularly not after his father had slapped her around during one of his infrequent visits back to Raglan and his mother softly called out for help after her husband had passed out across the bed.

Without evidence, her oldest son simply assumed that she could see them; the way he could see and hear his dogs. That, the boy thought, must be why she said her prayers aloud when walking down the corridors: Jesus must have been talking with her as they slowly walked along. And, though the boy couldn't see or hear Him himself, he realised that He must be real for just that reason; and was terribly happy his mother had someone to talk to whenever she was sad.

Lately, she seemed to be sad so very often.

* * * * *

"Whip me. Beat me. But, for the love of all the Holy Hills in Heaven—Please, please stop boring me."

Fortunately for William the words did not manage to make past his tongue. His father might well have taken him up on it. Still, the boy only wished he had a farthing for every time he had to suffer through hearing the same old story time and time again. It only demonstrated how insignificant his son felt in the eyes of his father: that the man couldn't even remember that he had already told the tale to family and friends at least a hundred times.

"When I was a boy of eight or ten, I happened to dream a dream."

The prologue was always the same and, invariably, made the lad cringe inside—knowing that everyone in the room was going to have to hear about his father's premonition. Fortunately for most of them, they were only forced to hear it once or twice. His family, on the other hand, could almost repeat it themselves from memory.

"I was dressed in armour . . . beautiful, shining blue-grey armour."

It was at this point that, true to form, William ap Thomas would reach out, touch his own polished suit of steel, and wistfully interject.

"That is why, when I received my knighthood from King Henry, I had this suit made in light blue-grey as well."

His son tried to get comfortable and looked around for some distraction as the narrative droned on and on.

"I can remember it as if I dreamed it only yesterday. Riding on a majestic charger through the streets of some town I had never seen; on the brightest afternoon that ever was. Women leaned out their chamber windows and waved their handkerchiefs; men cheered and slapped my legs as I rode by myself through the centre of town."

His family waited for it.

All at once, the man's face would drop into a contorted frown of contemplation; suggesting the arrival of some thoughtful emotion each knew was not really there.

"Suddenly, I was by myself on the self-same street. The sky was grey and overcast and my horse was wading through the bodies of the slain. Blood was spurting down the gutters like a stream. Like it says in Zechariah,

> 'And they shall be as mighty men, which tread down their enemies in the mire of the streets in battle . . . '

I was that man."

Right on cue, he reached out to caress the suit of armour on the breastplate.

"I have often wondered if it was never a dream but, instead, some vision, some prophecy. God telling me of what was meant to be."

At this point, the Lord would stand there with head slightly bowed and wait for someone to comment. Much like an actor holding for applause, he froze in position until some guest felt so terribly awkward that they offered him a flattering compliment of agreement or expressed admiration of their host's keen insight.

Like trained dogs, the performance never failed to inspire approval or tribute from the captive audience. His son had to hand it to him; it was a remarkable performance of contrition and pathos for a man who had never bothered to practise penitence himself: whose tiresome moralizing about the sanctity of simple virtue was only marred by the complexities of his own life.

* * * * *

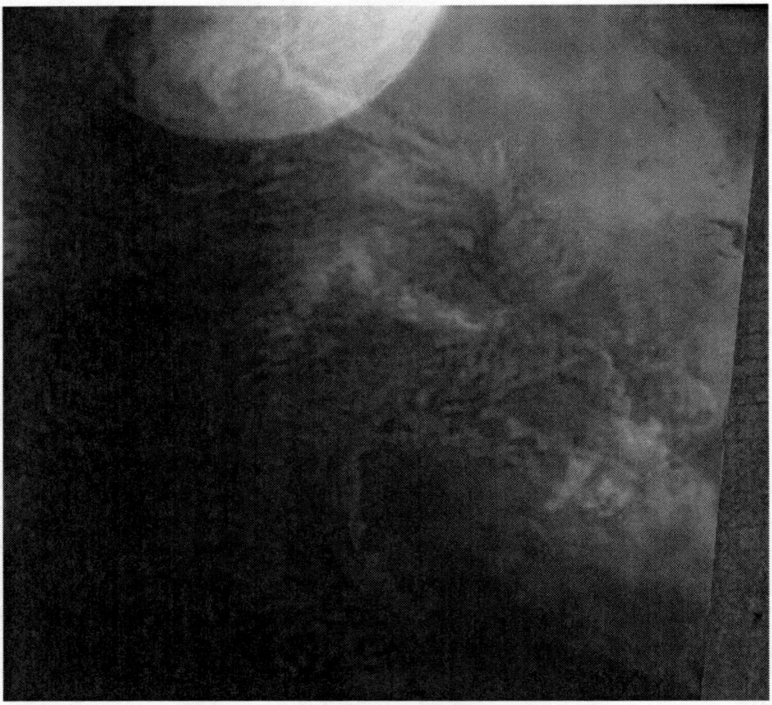

Chapter Twenty-one

"I've named the quiet one 'Tooth'."

The boy now had his mother's complete attention.

"He has a chipped one in the front. Just here." William pointed to his third tooth over on the right.

The lad's mother sat beside him as they leaned back in the grass against the rotting log. The pair had been there for near an hour watching clouds. Now that the two youngest were a bit older and could be left alone with their governess without going into hysterics, Gwladus was doing her best to spend more time with her oldest son. Watching clouds had become one of the nicest times of their day and when the rains of Wales scampered back across the hills, mother and son would sneak away and spend some time together.

"That one looks like a boat, don't you think?" Gwladus didn't want to appear too interested and put the boy on guard.

"The taller one is 'Fang'."

"Fang?"

The lad laughed a bit as he squirmed over on his side and faced her. "He really isn't taller. It's just that he tends to want to jump up more. His two front teeth are bigger than Tooth's," his excitement at talking about his friends getting the better of the boy's usually understated banter. "And the name 'Fang' just sounds really scary."

"It certainly does," his mother smiled and carefully prodded the child for a bit more information.

"Do you get to see them every day?"

William rolled back over, fumbled to find his dragon beneath his shirt and rubbed his prized possession between his thumb and forefinger as he leaned against the log to continue staring at the sky. "You can't see them at all in the daylight. Just at night. But I can always tell when they are around."

All the stories of Gwladus' childhood came flooding back from her memory. Uncles and aunts had told of spectral black dogs who haunted the glens of the Brecons and Forest of Dean; hounds with glowing red eyes that stood seven feet tall on their back legs and were supposed to be portents of evil or death. Much like legends of dragons, fairies, or lights moving through the sky at night; she had simply taken them as tales to keep her from roaming off alone in the forest. All fairy-tales were simply yarns of curmudgeoned old men, she supposed; that is, until one happens to chance across them face-to-face.

Young William lay in the patch of sun and closed his eyes to take a short nap. Napping was the last thing on his mother's mind.

Her father told her once that he had seen hellhounds up in the Brecon Mountains: that they had appeared from nowhere in the middle of the lane and blocked his path. His voice had cracked a bit even after years since seeing them; telling his little girl that they were only visible when the lightning storm passing overhead happened to hurl a particularly bright bolt across the night sky.

Familiar with most of the old Welsh legends, Dafydd Gam had pulled her up on his knee and explained that the black dogs were the hounds of Annwn, god of the underworld and death. As the son of Llywelyn ap Hywel Fychan and intimately familiar with the castle of Einon Sais at Pen-pont on the river Usk, on stormy nights he would tell how some of his aunts and uncles believed that the ghost hounds haunted the graveyards of murderers; others held that they were spirits sent to protect the helpless or innocent:

some that they walked the moonlit fields in search of souls to drag to Hell. The gwylligi, or Dog of Darkness, was widely reported to have been seen in the glens just north of Abergavenny and had been rumoured to range up the length of the Rhymney Valley for centuries.

Gwladus' first husband, Sir Roger Vaughan, had first told her stories of the yeth hound in Devon when on their honeymoon; how a headless dog seen there was supposed to be the soul of an unbaptised baby that wandered through the forest wailing for its mother. Then, there was the legend of St. Peter Port, where a unscrupulous bailiff tried to frame a local farmer with theft in an attempt to steal his land. After the officer of the court was executed by hanging, the sound of dragging chains had been heard ever since the incident back in 1320: how those who glanced out their windows regularly witnessed a huge black, shaggy hound wandering aimlessly back and forth along the lane.

When her new husband realised how truly terrified she was, the bridegroom made a point to explain that his father, Roger Vaughan of Bredwardine, told him stories as a boy of the Black Dogs helping farmers herd their animals, how they were said to protect children, and occasionally watch over lost travellers on dark, lonely roads.

The caveat really didn't help all that much.

For every tale of benevolence, there were at least fifty to sixty of outright horror. Shape-shifting demons in the form of dogs were said to haunt the grounds of Peel Castle on the Isle of Man ever since its construction by the Vikings in the eleventh century, while the appearance of Mauthe

Dooge or Black Dog of Manx was reported to foretell the death of anyone who ever saw it clearly. In Hertfordshire, a red-eyed hound was whispered to haunt the middle of the road in the village of Tring: precisely where the gallows used to stand.

Now that the legend had apparently come round to touch their lives, Gwladus genuinely hoped the tales of her first husband were true. Perhaps, for the innocent, the barghest or Cwn Annwn might go out of their way to guard the guiltless from harm. It was a bit of a stretch for the woman's faith, but much better than making allowances for the alternatives.

Noticing that her son had now awakened from his nap, she lovingly brushed the hair back out of his eyes and leaned in to softly pose another question.

"If you can't see them in the sunlight, how do you know when your friends are coming by to play?"

"I can hear them laughing."

Without missing a beat, the boy had started in on the game of finding shapes in the clouds again. Suddenly excited, the lad pointed off toward the east and the Forest of Dean. Stabbing at the sky with his finger, William couldn't hide his enthusiasm.

"That one there looks just like my puppies."

"That one?" She tried to follow his arm by laying her face against his sleeve.

"No, that one right there."

He raised his hand a bit to the left and stabbed at the tumbling puff of white that suddenly silhouetted against the early moon.

There was no need to strain or focus.

The flawless portrait of a ferocious wolfhound stepped from the nebulous fluff of swirling clouds. A great snarling beast made entirely of mist and haze, the outline of its great gaping maw and snapping jaws seemed to gnaw its way out of the approaching rainclouds. Disturbed both by the apparition in the clouds and that her son seemed to instantly recognise the spectre that soared against the drifting haze, Gwladus composed her sense of dread and tried to pass the vision off with as much restraint as her growing terror might let her.

"You're right." She whispered to hide her cracking voice. "It does look a bit like a dog."

Mother and son sat in silence for a moment and watched as the southerly wind from down the Wye folded the outline and edges of the ghastly likeness into themselves. Within seconds, the bank of clouds had dissolved back into billowing towers of churning ivory.

"Do your puppies get along with everyone?" Gwladus knew she was taking a big risk but was trying to get the boy back on subject.

"They like nice people."

"What about the bad people?"

William thought about it for a second before answering.

"They chase bad people down and steal their breath away."

"Oh."

The conversation had gone about as far as his mother dared to press.

"Want to go look for sycamore balls? We could colour them and hang them in the window of your room."

"They would look terrific hanging from the curtain."

William took her hand and led his mother back through the bushes toward the gravelled lane. Just as they reached the road, the boy stopped and added nonchalantly.

"But sometimes they rip off people's faces."

Without missing a step, the lad began to drag his stunned mother to the shade of the nearby sycamore. Involuntarily, Gwladus glanced over her shoulder to the west to see if they were being followed.

The fact that she couldn't see anything standing in the shadows did not ease her mind in the least.

* * * * *

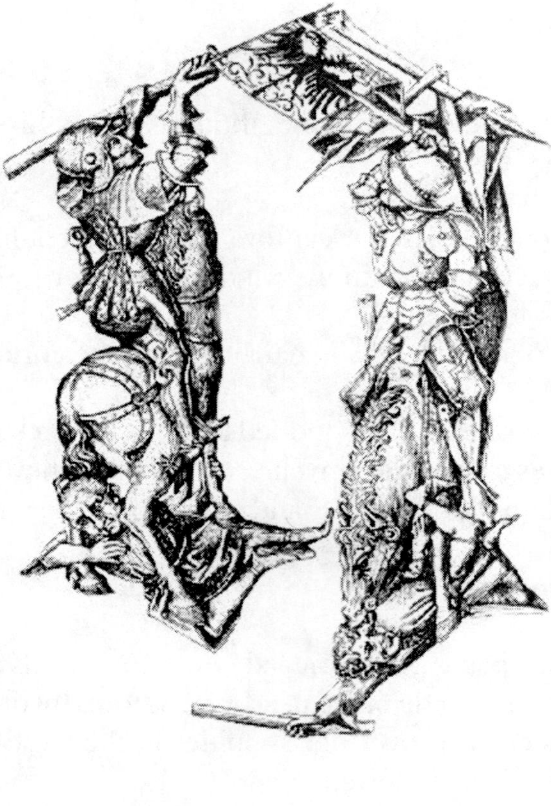

Chapter Twenty-two

April's morning sun was peeking over the distant hills, slowly drawing down the shadows like darkened coverlets across a rumpled bed. Dawn framed the silhouettes of grumbling workmen stumbling up the grade against the retreating gloom.

Creatures of the twilight rustled back through the underbrush to bury themselves amidst the grass and leaves until the inevitable evening, while squirrels and deer hesitantly ventured out from their hiding places to face the coming day. Small yellow blooms of biting stonecrop opened their blossoms to dry the dew while thousands of daffodils took turns to stab their pointed heads up across the fields. It was a typically remarkable morning of the month, when serenity baulked back from the clumsy footsteps of invading humankind.

Edward Ruddel and Charles Gardiner had made the same mistake of so many Englishmen that ventured west across the Severn: they expected familiarity.

Many of the villages were typical of those that lay sprinkled across York, Sussex, and Hertfordshire; in that the cottages were quaint by London standards and the streets were only wide enough to accommodate one ox cart at a time. So, more than a few who decided to trek into Monmouthshire fully expected to simply disappear into anonymity.

Trudging through the hills of Wales as an Englishman during the early fifteenth century was very kin to stamping north to wander through the highlands of Scotland: venturing very far from the larger towns might prove to be one's last serious mistake. London's claim to be the head of the realm did not carry any weight once one passed Chester on the road to Edinburgh; any more than one might expect to be welcomed with open arms in Gwynedd or Dyfed. The Hundred Year's War was only a passing distraction to Ireland, Scotland, and Wales: their common hatred of the English traced back for centuries. Relations were pockmarked further by explorers and entrepreneurs who typically estimated their neighbours to be inferior: that anyone not English by birth must, by process of elimination, be menial or second-rate. A fine claim when made within the safety of your own living room—a somewhat dodgy assertion when made standing upon the lawn of one's ancient enemy.

Gardiner had the bad habit of binge drinking whenever presented with the opportunity. Rather generously proportioned, he would inevitably drink until he reached the point of becoming sick, then deliberately pick fights with the locals or anyone else from the castle workmen whom he thought might give him a challenge. More often than not, he had his ass handed to him by the sturdy and all too accommodating Welsh masons, but one had to admire his perseverance. Having most of his front teeth knocked out over the years didn't really slow the man down at all.

Picking fights with the Welsh in their own neighbourhood was tantamount to fighting hornets. Unable to really assess his chances while drunk, Charles erringly assumed that, once stung, the finest solution would be to follow the single hornet back to its nest; then hit the nest repeatedly with a big stick until everyone inside realised that it was unwise to tangle with him. The results were, expectedly, always the same: and, not surprisingly, a endless source of free amusement for his friend.

Edward Ruddel was, by exclusion, Charles' best and only mate.

Even after several hours of imbibing, Edward knew to leave well enough alone; but took great delight in provoking his drinking companion into challenging anyone and everyone to fight. He would taunt Gardiner into making some lurid comment about their mothers, wives, or girlfriends and then quickly get out of the way before blows began to rain in from everywhere. Win or lose, Ruddel would make sure his friend made it back to their shared single room to sleep it off and have him back to work on the walls of Raglan Castle the next morning: a testament to the man's loyalty, if not to his character.

* * * * *

Meals were not the most celebrated of occasions. Rather, they became, over time, just another opportunity for William ap Thomas to reassert his inflated delusions of authority. The tragic thing was, everyone in attendance could clearly see through the man's thinly veiled attempts at coercion.

Gwladus kept her mouth shut and took whatever derogatory comments her husband had to offer with saintly patience. True to her convictions, their mother never let the children see any conflict between their parents: not to say that she did not occasionally let loose with indignation when the children were out of earshot and sight. Still, the dinner table was hardly the place to bare grievances one could never hope to resolve during the other twenty-three hours of the day.

In self-defence, the children learned to eat as quickly as they could and get away from the dining table.

Put simply, this was one of the very few times they ever saw their absentee father; and the less time they had to spend with him, the better. So, they sat there—the entire family; listening to the Lord of Raglan ramble on and on about subjects, incidents, and opinions no one but him actually cared about enough to counter.

The boy was not even sure what it was that set him off.

It might have been the off-handed derogatory comment about his mother's father, Dafydd Gam. Talking evil and taking cheap shots at the dead when they were no longer around to defend themselves seemed more than a bit cowardly. Young William was terribly certain, at least from what he had been told of his late grandfather, that William ap Thomas would have had his kneecaps broken or face punched in if Sir Dafydd Gam had only still been alive.

Perhaps it was the sweeping generalisation about the white people being better than the other races and how the Bible made that perfectly clear. Expounding the possible political virtues of slavery to offspring who were little better than slaves themselves seemed a bit callous and unkind.

It might have been the unjustified remark about the workmen. Having spent a small fortune and a great deal of his wife's inheritance on the construction of the great Yellow Tower of Raglan Castle, William, despite the fact that it wasn't really even his own money, regularly made insulting comments about Gareth ap Hywel and the crew. The fact that he was Welsh and from the exact same stock seemed to somehow escape the man: particularly when it came to his new best friend—his second wife's seeming inexhaustible supply of funds.

After sitting through virtually the identical diatribe each and every time his father chose to come around to bless them with a visit, his eldest son carefully chewed his bread and came to a rather astute conclusion. Of all the endless one sided conversations round the dinner table, perhaps it was the derogatory comments about his own Welsh family and neighbours that set his boy off the most.

"I don't care what anyone says, any woman who has more than four or five children is no better than a sow."

Despite the fact that no one else at the table appeared to be listening to the man's ranting, his oldest boy had just about reached his limit. Most of the poor who tilled the fields and tended the flocks had large families; and needed to, in order to work the land. Particularly when anyone who could not pay their debts could so easily have their land and inheritance stripped away from them by corrupt magistrates and judges. William ap Thomas knew that as well. He was simply trying to bolster his sense of self-importance; attempting to distance himself from his own heritage and blend in with his cronies in the English aristocracy.

"Perhaps if they were paid a fair price for their goods and toil, they might be able to afford to live without so many mouths."

No one at the table could believe that young William would have dared to speak up at the table: least of all the lad himself. The words had only cleared his tongue before he wished he could have sucked them back down his throat.

His father seemed to have been waiting for someone to speak up for years. All the colour drained from the man's face as he angrily defended the sovereignty of his table.

"Are you arguing with me, boy?"

The child shot a glance at Gwladus who, for the moment, seemed completely powerless to help him. The other two children were not about to get involved: Richard quickly bowed his head down into his vegetables; while Elizabeth snatched her cup and immediately filled her mouth with milk.

Noticing that his oldest son still had some meat on his plate, his father came at him again.

"What do you mean, fat boy?"

All there knew young William was anything but fat; his father resorting to any insult or abuse necessary to put the child back in his place. The boy realised that he had put himself in mortal danger, but a sudden inspiration cropped into his mind.

"Well . . . ," he stammered; giving his father a false sense of superiority before whacking the legs of his argument completely out from under him.

"You said that any woman who had more than five children was a sow."

"That's right. And?"

William ap Thomas was beginning to close in for the proverbial kill when his namesake snapped the trap.

"But your Lord, Richard, the duke of York . . ."

"What?" His father's voice almost raised up to a shout.

"His great-grandfather was King Edward III . . . and he and his wife had thirteen children."

The Lord of Raglan had not seen his son's manoeuvring in time to cover himself and now lay out completely vulnerable at the table.

"So you are saying that King Edward was married to a sow?" Before his father could squirm away, William plunged in another knife. "And that the duke of York's grandfather, Edmund of Langley, was, in turn, the son of a sow?"

The boy asked the question with all the naïveté he could muster, knowing full well that his argument left his father twisting in the wind.

The entire room went deathly quiet.

Gwladus, his brother, and sister realised that, for the first time ever, William ap Thomas had been put in his place. And by his own child. At his own table.

The servants standing around the room appreciated the gravity of the moment as well; for the Lord of Raglan could not say anything that would not, sooner or later, reach the ears of his Liege and employer. Likewise, he could do absolutely nothing with regard to retribution or punishment that would not surely do the same.

He had, with almost surgical precision, been outmanoeuvred and neatly neutered by a ten-year-old boy.

"You . . . eat your peas." His father stabbed at him impotently across the table with his spoon.

It was at that moment that young William realised a most important truth: that he understood and appreciated the power of words and intellect over brittle brawn. The child had, after years of desperate searching, found a chink in his father's armour. For the first time in his life, the boy had hit upon a weapon with which he could defend himself and his family against his tyrant of a father.

He would learn to wield it quickly and quite well: this wonderful new weapon of words.

* * * * *

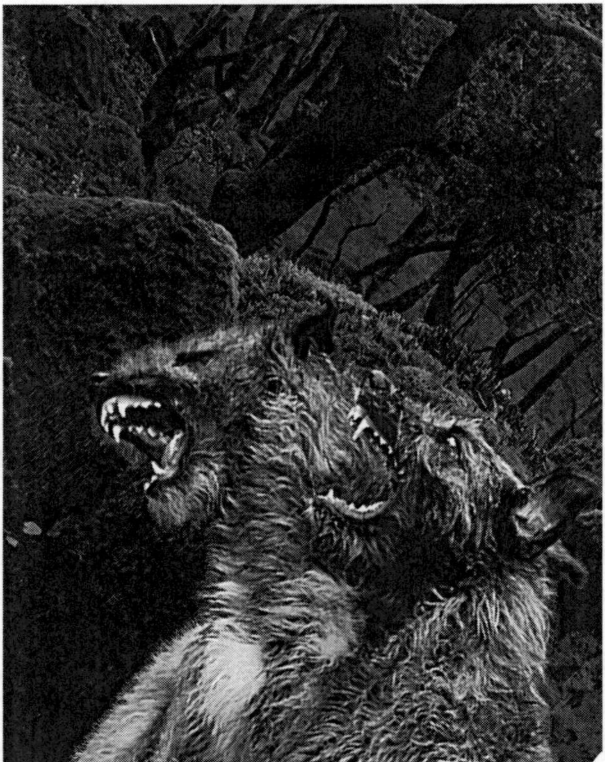

Chapter Twenty-three

It was after a particularly suicidal skirmish on a sweltering evening with his fellow labourers in the pub that Charles broke from his friend's restraint and stormed out alone across the fields.

Relatively hammered himself, Ruddel not only had no idea where Gardiner could be heading, but absolutely no intention of following him to Hell and back while he waited for the man to sober up. After a few attempts to shout him back, Edward gave up and stumbled back along the lane alone.

Ruddel distinctly heard the sound of Charles crashing into someone's trellis. He recalled that some of the local girls were leaning against it when the pair had passed by minutes earlier. Certainly not going to miss out on the chance to thoroughly embarrass his drinking companion, Edward turned round and cupped his hands to megaphone his voice.

"See that he pays you up front!

Remembering that at least one or two of the latest prostitutes were French, he translated as best he could and once more delivered the warning at the top of his voice.

"Voir qu'il vous paie avant!"

Terribly amused with himself, the only slightly less stable inebriant leaned against a timely tree to steady himself for a moment before braving the uphill grade.

Startled like a rat that suddenly spies a terrier, he froze motionless with a breath half caught in his throat.

Standing not more than seven feet away stood the largest black wolfhound Edward had ever seen.

Even in the moonlight, the creature loomed like a giant. It must have been a full forty inches tall at the shoulders; with the muscular neck and massive head towering on up to almost let the monster stare him straight in the face. Had it not been for the wiry, shaggy coat and especially bushy eyebrows and hair on the creature's chin, Ruddel might well have mistaken it for a pony.

This, to the man's regret, was plainly no pony.

The creature's massive muzzle tapered out and sniffed at the midnight traveller; with its ears flattened up and back as if the beast were contemplating a lunge. Its deep and heaving chest panted slowly in and out as if it had been running for some time to track him down; the massive round paws obviously soaked from cantering about through the undergrowth. The mouth dropped opened menacingly and puffed out great gulps of foggy breath even on this particularly warm night: its lips slowly drew back against hot pink gums and bared the largest set of fangs Ruddel had ever seen. They gleamed in yellowed ivory against the moonlight; great curved sabres that well might have severed a grown man's thigh with a single snap.

What petrified Edward's shoulder to the sapling was not the demonic snarl that resonated from the barrelled chest. No, what horrified him to the point of collapse were the beast's glowing scarlet eyes.

Riveted now only an arm's length away were twin, bloody pools of fire. Unblinking. As large, he supposed, as those of a cow; they seemed to glow in waves of crimson from a hateful fire lodged somewhere deep within its brain. Inhuman; yes, but not animal either. Bestial in the most demonic sense.

Just as Ruddel caught a whiff of the creature's unconsecrated breath, another set of eyes seemed to materialise from a vagrant billow of fog only a few feet further away. Even more menacing, if that could even be possible, a mauling nip from the second apparition distracted the first and allowed the poor man a chance to pull scant inches back. Now completely sober, Edward stood as silent witness to a fierce and furious rage that nothing living might ever hope to survive.

Fiendishly brutal.

A monstrously violent attack that literally hurled both beasts into the air, the force of their combat threw them backwards into the rocks and undergrowth. Massive claws swiped down and flailed the moss from boulders in great, thick strips; while fantastic fangs slashed through the swaying foliage and sent leaves and lichen quivering to the forest floor. Bellows and grunts roared out as one would be savagely knocked from its feet, only to be returned with equal rage as the advantage shifted back again.

Though both had been deep charcoal grey if not completely black and virtually invisible in the darkness, their colour began to change dramatically as each became the more enraged. Fury appeared to drain the crimson from their eyes; dispersing a white-hot wrath underneath each shaggy coat that enveloped and bathed the spectres' bodies with a radiance that sprang from underneath the hide. Seething rage had triggered a supernatural transformation: the wraiths now illuminating the stones and trunks of trees with a vaporous amber glow.

Beyond belief, Edward began to note that, while the skirts of Raglan Wood were being systematically ripped apart, not one drop of blood was spent by either hound.

Not a single hair was ripped out from either hide, no tooth fractured in half or broken off, no ear ripped through, nor gleaming eye put out. It was as if the apparitions shuddered through the trembling thorns and limbs: totally impervious to any injury themselves. Then, without hint or signal, the demonic beasts suddenly stopped the contest; standing side by side and muzzling each other as though nothing had ever happened.

Ruddel was so shaken up that he was not at all certain that it had.

From down the lane came the high pitched sound of a woman's laughter. Both creatures pricked up their ears and turned to stare down the track past Edward. Then, without a sound, the massive canines bolted straight past the man as if he simply wasn't there: their crimson eyes disappearing round the distant bend of the lonely track.

Without waiting to see if they might happen to come across his friend, the Welshman launched himself over the stony hedgerow and sprinted off like a flash of lightning through the field toward Raglan Castle.

The poor bastard was on his own.

* * * * *

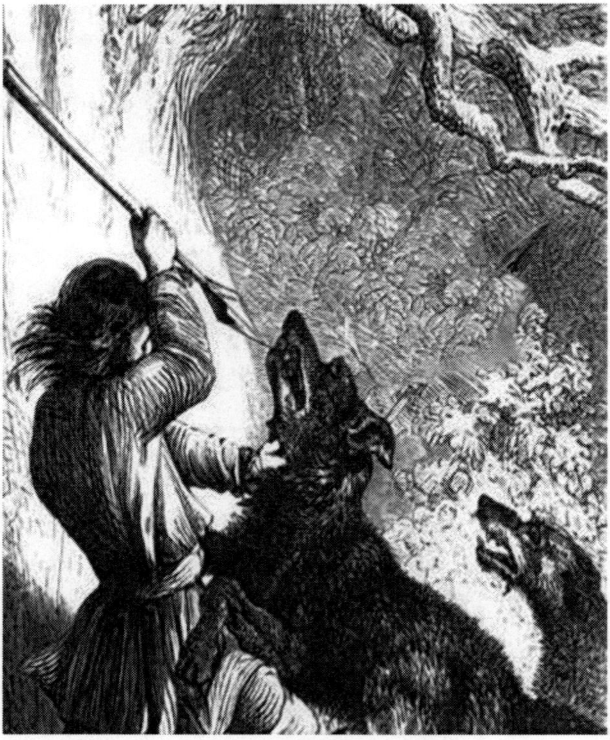

# Chapter Twenty-four

Events in the summer of 1441 were to desecrate young William's realm. Even years afterward, he would recall how his childhood was an unfortunate casualty of consequences: victim of an unlikely series of incidents and unrelated occurrences that violated his perception of the world.

In early June, word reached Raglan of the despicable death of Joan of Arc. Despicable in that the whole of Europe recognised her execution had been entirely political:

contemptible in that the Church allowed itself to be browbeaten into capitulating with powers of state.

After being raped while in prison, she was tied securely to a pillar in the Vieux-Marche in Rouen under the shadow of the great cathedral and burned alive in the presence of the clergy.

Once her screams and cries for help were engulfed by the blaze, the English soldiers left in charge raked back the coals to fully expose her charred body so that no one could later claim the maid had somehow escaped alive. Then, to prevent any collection of religious relics by the hundreds of zealots and onlookers, her charred remains were then burned two more times to reduce everything to ash. Only when the clerics were entirely convinced that absolutely nothing might be salvaged to be revered did the officers of the court command the street to be swept, completely scraped, and the powdered residue be cast into the nearby river Seine. Even her executioner, one Geoffrey Therage, considered the execution particularly savage and commented afterward to his friends that he greatly feared to be damned by God for his participation.

As he well might.

The account permanently soiled the boy William's opinion of the Church. His mother had tried to teach him right from wrong; to overlook the glaring fallibilities of his father and try to see some vestige of good in everyone. She had almost convinced him when announcements came up from Bristol that the Portuguese had brought back men from Africa to sell as slaves in Europe.

Sailors were ferrying Nubians across the sea by the thousands: purchased from rival tribesmen for alcohol, glass, bits of iron, and jewellery. Having suffered from his own share of beatings and abuse, William could only wonder how any survived the lengthy trip to be sold across the channel on the continent: how horrible the Hell they were now expected to exchange for their lives. There seemed no charity or Christian compassion in selling men like animals; even less in smiling priests who allowed such deeds to happen right under the fleshy jowls of the Church.

The novelty of kidnapping and forced slavery had come right to the lad's front door; a fact he was to discover for himself one bright July morning in the year of our Lord 1441.

Unbeknownst to Gwladus, William ap Thomas had made arrangements for his son to be sent to Eton: actually carried away kicking and screaming would probably have been a bit more accurate.

Not that Eton in itself was undesirable.

The King's College of Our Lady of Eton beside Windsor had been founded only months before by King Henry VI. Located about a mile north of Windsor Castle, Eton was conceived as a charity school to provide free education to poor boys who might not otherwise receive an education. An independent boarding school for boys aged thirteen to eighteen, at seventeen, young William had just made the cut.

King Henry VI was far more enthralled with the idea than many of the original students. He granted Eton a large number of endowments, huge tracts of land, and valuable relics such as a piece of timber attributed as being part of the True Cross and a fragment said to be splinters of Christ's Crown of Thorns. That said, most of the boys consigned to its halls by their fathers were not at all impressed.

It might have had something to do with the corporal punishment.

Based on Winchester College, founded in 1382 by William of Wykeham, Bishop of Winchester and High Chancellor of England, Henry even appropriated half the scholars and headmaster from Winchester to staff his charity school for boys. To instil the proper sense of gratitude and subservience, Eton became instantly renowned for beating its students into submission. Each and every Friday, with the singular exception of Good Friday, boys were lined up and disciplined one by one for any indiscretions committed during the week.

Though some lads cried and spent their nights conspiring on how to get even with their tormenters, William resigned himself to accept his punishments as inevitable. For the son of William ap Thomas, it only meant that someone new was now brandishing the belt.

His appreciation for being unceremoniously uprooted from Raglan and thrown into a world of poor and indigent strangers became eminently clear once the lad learned that half of the scholars had been, likewise, abducted from the rolls of Winchester: that and the fact that all the boys were to be educated at the King's personal expense.

William ap Thomas had found another way to exploit his questionable affiliations and political contacts. Though far from poor or deserving, his increasingly independent son had been neatly removed from the troublesome influence of his mother—and his thirty-seven-year-old father did not even have to pay a penny for the timely disposal.

* * * * *

Work on the Great Tower of castle Raglan had become a second job for many of the men: their primary interest in showing up at all being merely to make enough money to offset their nightly gambling debts, intake of alcohol, or obsession with the local whores. For Gardiner, at least, the nightly conquest of women had apparently become the man's sole purpose in life.

He certainly showed an aptitude for it.

Seducing the fairer sex appeared to be his forte; though, considering the overall nature and regularity of his conquests, seduction seemed to really have very little to do with it. Truthfully, any woman he had could be had by any other man for exactly the same price: and they often were. This only reinforced Gardiner's philosophy of life: that, if one were prepared to lower one's standards low enough—a man could have sex all the time—and one would be hard pressed to find anyone who had lower standards than Charles Gardiner. He would venture forth to conquer any challenge, regardless of its, or in this case her, degree of difficulty: and, to be brutally frank, the majority of the prostitutes the man bedded were, in point of fact, no real challenge at all.

That said, even he was more than a bit surprised at the beauty that almost reluctantly conceded to spend her valuable earning time with him one evening in late July.

Most of the ladies, to the great disappointment of men who actually managed to catch them in the light, were relatively as attractive as the desperate men willing to pay for their company. Which, as it turned out most of the time, placed them well below the average woman one might come across during the day. Still, good looks, though not the main currency of harlots and whores, certainly had a profound effect on their innate resale value.

Flirting more than most, Charles had immediately been taken with the young girl's innocence. Contrary to popular opinion, vamps often come across as more trashy than sincere and the appearance of virtue and corruptibility are often more alluring and sexier than experience and confidence. Gardiner took the young woman's flirting as a sign of her inexperience at the game; playing along in a mock game of foreplay that only kept his interest piqued as they navigated the moonlit lane.

"We could climb the fence," she offered. "It seems silly to spend the entire evening looking for an opening."

The game had apparently begun.

Slipping his arm around her waist, Charles glanced further down the lane and scanned the hedge for any sign of a gate. "I think you're right. We're just going to have to force our way through."

His teenage companion had started out by stating that she was trying to get back to castle Raglan: a manoeuvre that Gardiner immediately took as a ploy to get the two of them alone.

"Any passageway through is going to be incredibly tight, but I'm willing to give it a go if you are."

The buxom teenager stepped up into the thicket and tried to sidestep through. Right behind her, Charles pushed firmly against her back and bottom to keep her from falling backwards onto the road. The girl's skirt, caught by the hem, began to ride up her thighs. As she kept trying to poke her right arm through the tangle, the flexible sprouts of gorse kept springing back up as she wriggled back and forth against the hedge.

"I've never worked so hard to get something between my legs," she giggled.

Aroused, Charles deftly spun the petite girl around and pushed her back into the flowering gorse. He closed in for a kiss when her whimpering protests caught the man entirely by surprise.

"What's going on here?"

The booming baritone of Gareth ap Hywel resonated through the stillness like a drum.

"Oh, hello Daddy."

"CRYSTIN?"

The three froze motionless under a waning crescent moon.

"Daddy?"

Gardiner loosed his lecherous grasp and could not fail to notice that the burly Welshman brandished a hefty knotted club.

Stepping carefully out of the thicket, pulling her skirt back down, and crossing over to her father, the girl took his arm and gave the stout mason a light kiss on the cheek.

"I was just coming back from town to see you," she answered innocently, "when this nice man offered to walk part the way with me."

The two men stared at each other without expression.

Gareth knew exactly what kind of man Gardiner was; while Charles now realised that the girl was not guilty of any double entendre, but truly was as innocent as she had originally appeared.

After an uncomfortable minute of silence, the suspicious father decided to give both the benefit of the doubt and took his prized earthly possession by the shoulder.

"I'll walk with you the rest of the way myself."

He shot Charles a threatening glance just in case the man had been entertaining impure thoughts and escorted his cherished virgin up the lane.

Watching until the pair had come to the sheepcote and turned to head across the field, Gardiner then took the biggest breath of his life and let out an audible sigh. Two minutes more and he might well be dead right now; the front of his skull caved completely in by an angry father whom no one would dare to blame. In that moment, the letch considered himself the luckiest man in Raglan.

But Raglan was almost a mile away and the man's next moment would prove to be anything but lucky.

* * * * *

If the Hounds of Hell were supposed to be confined to ancient pathways, lonely crossroads, and places of execution; then the lane that ran past the ruins of the Morley's caretaker's cottage and on up to castle Raglan would, at first glance, seem to fit none of the criterion.

If, on the other hand, the spectral beasts were condemned to wander the lonely lanes; reincarnations of the condemned or of those who had sold their souls to the devil for aid or profit during their lives; then the wraiths of Raglan Wood only appeared to display the first attribute. However, it seemed that no one ever considered that the monstrous apparitions might simply be what they appeared: the ghosts of loyal wolfhounds that had been summarily murdered in an attempt to thwart some ancient, silly superstition; whose poor bodies had been entombed within the walls of Bluet Manor: who, now that their ancient crypt had been dismantled and defiled, were finally loosed to exact some justice from the hand of cruel man.

In any case, such reflections really made little difference in the end.

Whether mysterious demon hounds, the souls of human beings, or apparitions of dogs in their own right; what really mattered most and mortified Charles Gardiner at the moment were the pair standing directly in front of him upon the Raglan road.

No stranger to the legends, the man had dismissed the warnings of his friend Edward as the ravings of an intoxicated imagination. There, in the moonlight, alone and now most regrettably sober, Charles stood face to face with the apparitions: whatever the hell they were.

Calf-sized, the pair of coal black hounds made utterly no sound as they crossed the rutted track, stepped up to him, and started sniffing at his skin. So tall that each had to drop its head to get a whiff of his hands, in tandem they abandoned poking at his chest with hairy muzzles and settled directly in his face to smell his breath.

Charles thought it strange that, seeing the man could not hold his breath forever, the hounds did not smell like animals at all. Actually, the creatures gave off an odour that forced him to squint his eyes. Smelling, at best, of rotting flesh and probably closer to a recently defiled grave; the black hounds rammed their wiry muzzles up to mash his upper lip right below his nose. From the reaction when he exhaled, the shaggy creatures did not appreciate the scent of Gardiner any better.

Three whores stumbled through the doorway of the nearby pub. A failing farmhouse that had seized upon the influx of workers and women to make a tidy sum from the sudden increase in population, the owner leaned out the front door and shouted down the steps.

"You little minxes come back any time."

The painted women stopped their preening and giggled betwixt themselves.

The landlord phrased his next comment with slightly less volume; so the customers still inside could not hope to hear. "And don't worry if it's been a slow day," the balding man whispered in a voice that carried rather far against the calm, "I'm sure we can always work something out."

"You randy little bastard!"

The tallest of the three flirtingly threw the praise back over her shoulder as another blew the middle-aged farmer a kiss. The third clutched the top of her bodice and pulled it down with her right hand to expose the top half of her breast: giving the landlord something to think about after they had gone.

The tallest turned and caught sight of the monstrous hounds; which had Gardiner pinned against the adjacent stone wall that bordered the road and led away to the now abandoned barn. She screamed out of instinct as much of terror, instantly drawing the attention of the other girls and landlord to the spectral hounds.

Fits of screams instantly raped the dead of night as all three of the prostitutes scooted back up the steps and shoved their way inside. Instantly tempted for a second to slam the door shut to protect himself and leave them to their fate; the landlord quickly decided to fight back the impulse to thrust the whores back out of the night.

The young women's screams drew the attention of the black beasts away from Charles and, in that instant between their screams of terror and the slamming of the door, Gardiner made a break for it over the wall.

He hurled himself over the rocky obstacle with the surprising grace of someone half his age and size; actually somehow managing to land on his feet before taking off along the bend to keep the barrier between himself and the apparitions.

Recognising that the whores were now safely barricaded inside with the light, the Hounds of Annwn instantly spun round on their haunches and took down the lane after their prey. A good sixty to seventy feet ahead by now, Charles dared a glance to see if the dogs of darkness had decided to give chase.

What the man saw nearly turned his heart to stone.

Rather than running along the opposite side of the barrier, the shadowy apparition simply stepped straight through the two foot thick rock wall. While the obstruction seemed to force each to consciously press its great weight through the mortar, the broad obstacle of stone only slowed the beasts down for a second or two. Suddenly, the things were directly behind him and coming up at quite a clip.

Running for his life, the man detected that their colour had lightened drastically from the instant each had introduced himself only moments earlier. They began to glow as if sprinkled with powdered phosphorous: their black coats dialling up from the dark, dingy grey each had been to almost amber-brown. It seemed that each had caught fire from the inside as they bolted better than greyhounds and, like a frantic rabbit, ran him down.

Crossing the lines of comprehension, the paired apparitions flickered in and out of sight between the broken patches of moonlight. Foliage that shrouded out the moon made them appear all the brighter; while each stride that took them back into the light made each seem to disappear. The noise of the creatures' panting became all the more high pitched with their increase in speed; becoming so shrill and intermittent that their breathless gasps began to sound very much like the laughter of a child.

Laughing death.

The shadows of the Cu Sith or Capelthwaite quickly closed in upon the fleeing man. His only chance was to hurriedly clear the fence, reverse his course, and hope that the fiends continued to track along the wall. To do so, however, meant doing something within the next twenty feet. After that, the stone fence made a sharp break to the left and would not provide any cover upon the open pasture until it reached the sheepcote of castle Raglan. Just before the crook of the field, Charles rounded the corner and was out of sight of the transparent shadows for only a matter of seconds. He dove head-first through the hedgerow: just clearing the top row of stones with the tips of his toes.

Not wasting a second, Gardiner rolled to his feet and bolted back up the track in the opposite direction: back in the direction of the public house and its contingent of still-screaming girls. After almost a full minute, he saw no swooning shadows doing the same and presumed his strategy might have worked as he intended.

The out-of-breath mason collapsed against the ancient rock wall, trying to catch his breath without ever taking his eyes off the road.

Just then, the drooling muzzle of one of the massive hounds bled through the solid stone not three feet away: passing through the dense barrier of rock as a wave of mist might waft through an open door. The great beast's salivating maw snapped right toward his nearest leg and seized Gardiner by the back of his right calf. Congealing from the vaporous haze only where the ghostly silhouette actually touched his clothing, the rest of the apparition's body continued to exit the field straight through the wall as ghastly fangs sank effortlessly into his flesh.

Screaming in terror, a hair's breadth from insanity, Charles tried to drag his right leg free and witnessed the second hound clamber atop the barricade only a few feet further up the track. Breaking through from the thicket of thorns in the darkness, its rear claws ground a barrage of sparks from the stones as the goliath rushed to drag its weight up from the opposite side.

Stark and unspeakable horror swept over the man. Faced with the prospect of a gruesome death; of being dragged screeching and screaming into the tall reeds only to be throttled to death and mutilated: Gardiner ignored the blinding pain and ripped his lower leg free from the vice-like grip of the apparition's gory jaws. Fangs like sabres sliced the muscle in half; leaving the back of Charles' leg carved into bleeding shreds.

He bolted down the lane as best he could under the colourless light of the sickle moon.

The reprobate only made it six or seven steps before the second beast impaled him from behind. Caught in mid-stride, a massive toe-nailed paw swiped through his coat and crushed the fugitive's spine. He collapsed head-first into the ditch and skidded into a crumpled heap, now completely helpless and unable to get away. Cold dread took hold of Gardiner's hysterical expression as two great salivating jaws closed down upon his face from either side and swallowed the poor man's panicked screams.

Thank God, the decapitated thing that gurgled crimson froth as it crawled along the ditch through its own blood did not live for very long.

His companions found his body the next morning.

Covered with great puncture wounds and mutilated beyond recognition, the corpse had been ripped nearly in half: bearing all the signs of having been butchered by a demon. The dead man's face had been bitten off completely: leaving jagged ribbons of ragged flesh that reached back in finger-width strips all but to his ears.

Stretched out next to the ruins of the abandoned caretaker's cottage, shocked constables were forced to identify the mutilated remains of Charles Gardiner by his clothing.

* * * * *

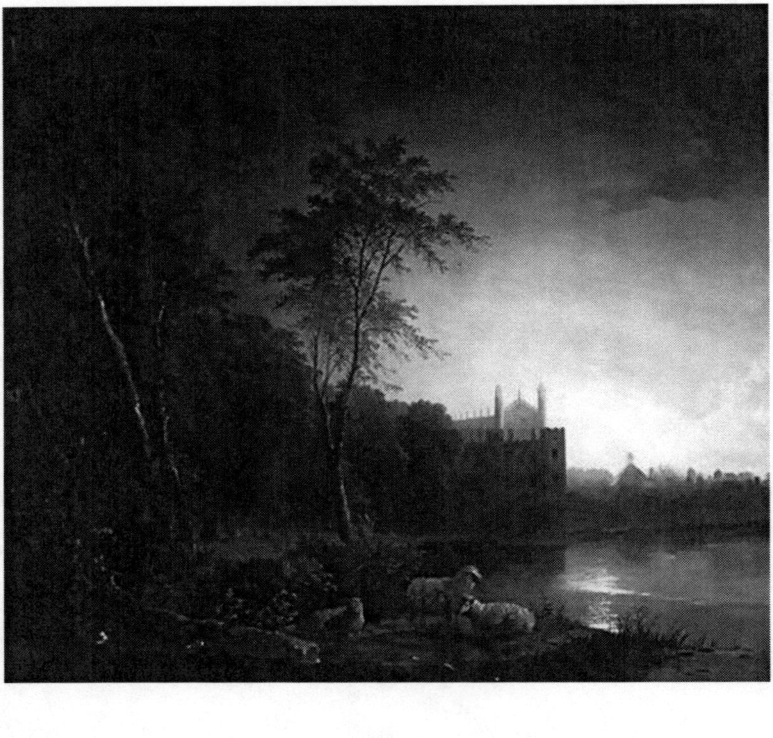

Chapter

Twenty-five

The North York Moors and Yorkshire Dales had both, in turn, presented Windsor with one of their finest sons in Robert Aynsley. A fitting donation to The King's College of Our Lady of Eton was their robust and resilient groundskeeper. Fitting in that Aynsley's home might well boast the greenest fields in all of England; ironic as well, given that it was almost impossible for most of the scholars and instructors to decipher his incredibly thick Dales dialect.

Even after years spent in southern England, Robert's deep and gruff accent made it almost impossible to understand what the man was saying. The son of William ap Thomas, being from southeast Wales, had a great advantage in picking apart the drawn out vowels, diphthongs, and swallowing of consonants. Upon learning that their country cousin could communicate much easier with the caretaker, William was often summoned to translate Aynsley's challenging pronunciation into a form of English the staff at Eton might better understand.

"Spent orl mornin clippin back t' tendrils o' ivy fra t' ya'," Robert spoke slowly to William. "Na, wor 'eadin daahn ta weed t' cabbages 'n onions afowa takin uz lunch."

The provost, Henry Sever, for all his education, was struggling to follow the conversation.

"He says he spent most of this morning trimming the ivy and was going to weed the garden before lunchtime." William paraphrased a bit to make the old groundskeeper appear a bit easier to understand.

"Can you ask him what he intends to do about the lawn?"

The provost's secretary was more than a bit officious in his tone: something Aynsley picked up on immediately. The boy put out the question.

"Well, 'ell. ah don't kna," Robert wrapped his calloused hands tightly around the handle of his hoe. "Ah 'ed planned ta wang abaht six sheep art theear pa acre, bur if 'a' dunt suit theur, why don't theur gerr daahn on thy 'ands 'n knees 'n chew it daahn yursen!"

William had no need to interpret the old man's irritation. Trying to keep the peace, the lad simply paraphrased once more.

"He said he's going to put some sheep on it to graze it down."

Satisfied, Henry Sever and his personal secretary nodded to Robert as if the Yorkshireman were deaf, then smiled and made their way back to the main building.

Watching the pair exit through the wet grass, the straight-talking groundskeeper took William by the shoulder and gave him some heartfelt advice.

"Listen. Doa wha' theur li'. Bur I'd advise theur ta stay clear o' those 'aughty Englishmen. Thee couldn't finn' thea arse wi' both 'ands int' dark."

Both stood and watched the instructors scoot back to the seclusion of their rooms. Though a bit coarse and rough, the caretaker might well have had a point.

* * * * *

Eton's original Foundation Charter had provided for the accommodation of six choristers; to be led and instructed by a choirmaster hired by the College specifically to provide inspirational music. Though it was initially difficult to inspire much interest, when construction of the College Chapel began in 1441 a few more students and staff began to show some enthusiasm.

Initially, direction of the sextet was delegated to one John Meissel; an unenviable post since Henry VI's expectations were so high from the outset. Still, blessed with absolute or perfect pitch, John was able to name and reproduce any tone without reference to an instrument. This proved invaluable when musical manuscripts were prohibitively expensive and even rare amongst the church institutions. The simple chant of unison voices was giving way to polyphony or harmony; with different voices assigned consonant intervals of perfect fifths, octaves and, later, perfect fourths. Though sometimes accompanied with wooden flute, recorder, or lutes, the fledgling choir at Eton tended to rely on a cappella selections where no instruments were required; regularly bringing their choirmaster's God-given talents into play.

That said, the son of William ap Thomas and reluctant scholar at Eton could not carry a tune with both hands and a basket. Still, that handicap did nothing to dissuade the young man from being terribly impressed with music and anyone who could reproduce it at their whim. Reading schools or free periods would often find young William within earshot of the choristers.

It was while at Eton that young William all too rudely discovered that the Welsh moniker of 'ap' immediately segregated him from the other boys. The other scholars were from the home counties and fields of England and sported typical surnames like Bardeslay, Gybson, Radclyffe, or Warmemouth. Branded as an outsider before ever given the opportunity to fit in or distinguish himself, the son of William ap Thomas, whose full name was William ap William, quickly attempted to tone down his Welsh accent and adopted the surname of Herbert. Not completely convinced of the family tradition that he was supposed to have been descended from Herbert the Chamberlain, who many believed was the bastard son of Henry I, William assumed the surname for the simplest of reasons.

He could spell it. That and the fact that the surname sounded incredibly English.

For all the misfortune of being completely tone-deaf, Meissel took a liking to the gangly youth and went out of his way to help the lad acclimate. The newly self-christened Herbert, so very far from home and often desolate, took some comfort in the fact that a stranger actually seemed concerned about his well-being: coming to confide in John when life at Eton seemed close to unbearable.

For a Welsh teenager abandoned on the pitch of Windsor, those occasions seemed to come round with amazing regularity. It was John Meissel's random feats of kindness and often anonymous maverick acts of heroism that kept William ap Thomas' son from losing hope.

It was on just such one of those instances that William waited for the boy's choir to finish practise and approached Meissel to vent about one of the particularly cruel and demanding history instructors.

"After serious thought, I can say I honestly hate the man."

William was at that razor edge of passion that lay between tears and uncontrolled rage. "Kelsey deliberately picks on me to try to make me mad; then laughs about it right in front of me with the other students."

John pursed his lips and bowed his head. Mindful of the lad's dilemma and his age, the choirmaster took a moment and then tipped his head back, glanced toward heaven, and let out a shattered sigh.

"I myself was forced to give up hating people years ago. I might have been too lazy, but it was just so damn exhausting."

William pulled back a bit from the crumbling ledge of emotion.

"Someone would do something that would make me want to pound their head and that would make the blood throb so hard against my temples that I would very nearly get a headache. Rather than simply beat them into the ground; I would try to be Christian about it and walk away before sensing I needed to actually offer them the other cheek."

Young Herbert knew exactly what the choirmaster meant.

"But, then, I would calm down eventually and forget about wanting to strangle them. Until I saw the person again. Then, I would have to remember why or what that particular person did to make me mad; work myself back up from a standing start into being angry, and then wind my emotion and stress back taut enough to hate them all over again. After some years, I learned my lesson and realised that my hating someone did nothing to affect them at all. They either didn't know or simply didn't care and I was wasting all that time and energy on having to keep my hatred going all alone."

William hadn't expected Meissel's comeback and could not hide his reaction.

"Anger just eats your insides away over time. You only hurt yourself, really." His much older friend turned to look straight at the excitable teenager. "And, besides, I have to deal with that bastard Kelsey every day myself. Trust me, the pretentious git isn't even worth the effort."

Herbert sniggered a bit to himself. John was probably right. Once he stopped to really think about it, hatred did seem to be a terrific waste of his time and enthusiasm.

"When it comes to people like Joseph Kelsey, I try my very best to forgive and forget. Forgive them; since my Lord asks me to: then forget that their opinion matters. Keep rubbing a man like that out of your attention and concern and, pretty soon, any influence he might have had on your life will be nothing more than a smudge."

William had to agree; taking no notice of his persecutor was far better than the alternative.

"I want you to listen to this," John retrieved some papers from his pocket. "Tell me what you think."

For Honour is urchin: motherless child
Who, forgotten, wanders through darkened world;
And Glory, its shadowless mate, who wild
Colours men's faces when 'neath banner furled.
For both reprehend with epithet hurled;
    To leave him amazed, who held to his grave:
    That both were worth life: they proved him a knave.

Unprincely heritage bequeathed to woe,
Cloistered courage noble honour offends;
Not judging on mercy granted to foe,
But for transgressions forgiven by friend.
Lessons ill-tempered in memory bend:
    For passion befriended fans hot dim coals,
    As justice untended burns up men's souls.

For men are men, no better and no worse
Than any who have tread this field before;
And, for whom, life's brief underserved curse
Endowed each one the linen shroud each wore.
Each life must go, as each has gone before;
    Yet, pity those who, as our foe or friend,
    Vain lived their lives as if they'd never been.

William was stunned. He wasn't entirely sure if it was the words or the way Meissel read them but, either way, the feelings that they created in the boy's mind were unlike any he had ever felt.

"Did you write that?"

John smiled.

"Way over my head, I'm afraid. They were written by a man named Warin from Llanhennock in Wales, back in 1315." He paused. "Each and every time I read them I think of Glastonbury, back home in Somerset; and how I might be wasting my entire life here without even realising it."

They sat there in silence for a moment; both lost in their thoughts.

As though struck with a sudden inspiration, his friend tried to change the subject. "You know, it's none of my business," John waited for the boy to tell him yea or nay, "but I've noticed that you don't hang out with the other lads and try to track down the girls."

He deliberately let the comment hang there in the air. If Herbert wanted to answer, then he would know the subject wasn't entirely out of bounds.

Slightly embarrassed, William stuttered and hemmed and hawed a bit as he attempted to explain.

"Well, most of the girls my age are too flighty and come across as conniving and devious. They all seem to be scheming all the time: always on the lookout for a bigger, better deal. And the older ones that visit Windsor from Marlborough, Marlow, and Middlesex either seem two-faced, completely false-hearted, or way too experienced to have any virtue left."

"I know what you mean." Meissel signalled his understanding with a nod.

"What I'm waiting for, I suppose," William rolled his eyes up to conjure up the perfect female in his mind, "is a girl who is loyal, straightforward, and sincere: you know—a lonely, beautiful, petite little virgin."

John laid his hand on the young man's shoulder as if to break the disappointing news.

"Son, there are no *lonely* beautiful little virgins."

Both shared a snigger. Then, hearing the distant laughter of a bevy of young women from the direction of the river, his older friend came up with what appeared to be a great suggestion.

"Let's go watch the girls come across the bridge down on the High Street," he elbowed William in the ribs.

"The wind usually kicks up a bit off the Thames this time of the afternoon."

Though the lad was pretty sure Meissel had given up gawking and ogling for a little glimpse of leg quite a few years ago, he appreciated the older man's enthusiasm on his behalf.

Having taken even more interest in girls since arriving at Windsor, young William Herbert cinched up his trousers, tucked in his shirt as he raked his hair over with his fingers, and glanced down toward the Thames.

"Why not."

* * * * *

Der selig hainrich süsze coſtentz geborn am bodner ſee
Nam die ewig wyſſhait zům gmahel gaiſtlicher ee
Sein gespons tet in den namen verwanden
Amandus hieſz ſy in nennen in allen landen
Sein leben wz er in irm dienſt vergeren
Des fröet ſich vlen die ſein grab vnd hailtů halt in ere̅

Chapter Twenty-six

"I don't care." James was not going to let it go.

"Even if he was the lowest form of life, we're not leaving until someone says a few kind words over him."

The five men looked at each other as they stood in the morning rain, each waiting for one of the others to step forward and pronounce some form of benediction. Problem was, each knew Gardiner far too well to have much compassion or consideration for the man. Not a single member of the dead man's family had even bothered to make the short trek from his home in Llandenny, and that was less than three short miles away. Which was, one might suppose, a relatively fair indictment of Charles Gardiner's life. Still, custom should be observed; whether from the heart or not.

James turned to Edward, wondering if he might ultimately regret bothering to ask, but forcing out the words.

"For God's sake," the most pious amongst them tried to get some kind of reaction. "He was your best friend. Surely you can think of two or three kind words to say."

Edward stood there for a moment, clearly not having wanted to become any more involved than absolutely necessary. Finally, the burden of their stares became too heavy for him to ignore.

"Well, shit."

Reluctantly, Ruddel stepped up to the edge of the muddy mound of earth: close enough to make his point but far enough away to avoid having his legs spattered too badly by the mud.

"Here lies the late and lamented Charles Gardiner," he paused, "My friend."

From the expressions of his companions, each of them fully expected more. Ruddel rolled his bottom lip between his teeth and gave the matter a bit more thought.

"Who will always be our guiding light down the road of life that we must now travel upon without him."

The four other men were stunned. Which was nothing compared to what they felt when the usually bumbling and thoroughly blundering Edward continued on.

> "Through Death, the work of each man's life is weighed.
> Through God, the thoughts hidden in his heart made plain.
> A Finer Friend than any in this World have made
> And True: Until our Souls may chance to meet again."

The uncouth and often foul-mouthed workmen stood there in the now heavy shower, with the rain sheeting off their hats; wondering if the good-for-nothing reprobate they all had known actually deserved so fine a benediction.

* * * * *

Progress on the Great Yellow Tower of castle Raglan had slowed to a proverbial crawl.

In point of fact, it was entirely to be expected: what with Edward Ruddel's nightmarish account of his encounter with the hostile Hounds from Hell upon the Raglan road; and then the discovery of the mutilated body of Charles Gardiner lying disembowelled in the ditch between the ruins of the old Bluet Manor and the town. Much as when a pin-sized hole appears in a levee or earthen dam. One breach suddenly leads to another, then more and more; until, suddenly one is overwhelmed with fissures and the entire structure fails. Once the workmen actually started talking amongst each other about the recent events, others dared to set aside their caution and relate their experiences as well.

Come to find out, at least a quarter of all the workforce employed at castle Raglan had either seen or heard things they simply could not explain: incidents each had decided to keep to themselves for fear of living with ridicule.

Ridicule now seemed far less a concern than living.

When Gareth ap Hywel climbed up the ladder midmorning to inspect the progress of the tamping between the inner and outer walls, he spied a group of five men off who had obviously moved off together by themselves. Still manipulating the piles of irregular sized stones with their long iron rods and flattened pry bars, the drudgery of wedging and compacting the smaller rocks and debris was progressing despite their laboured conversation. One of the older bearded men was carefully re-wrapping a blister on his palm while he spoke.

"I was sitting by the well," he pointed through the castle curtain wall as if it wasn't there, "and saw a set of bright, glowing red eyes not more than fifteen feet away. The beast behind them had the body of the largest wolfhound I have ever seen, the shaggy black hair dripping with water even though it hadn't rained that day. The beast turned around without ever noticing me sitting there, took four or five strides toward the edge of the road and sank straight into the ground."

What normally would have past for fanciful bar talk took on new importance with the recent goings on at Raglan Wood.

"Aye, James," the tamper across from him stopped for a moment to pull the top of his left boot up a little higher to keep the tumbling stones from rubbing against his leg.

"I used to be convinced that my mother told me stories to keep me from bringing home every stray dog that we boys found around our farm. Until, one day when we were in Amlwch, up north of Holyhead in Gwynedd; my father, younger brother, and I came across a huge dark grey hound with bright red eyes. Even though the light was not all that great, all three of us will swear to this day that the creature was floating at least two feet off the ground."

Gareth was about to say something when the youngest of the group actually stopped tamping and sat down, leaning back against the inclined bank of river gravel and filler stones.

"My grandfather says that they are the Cŵn Annwn, the ghost hounds of Annwn or Gwynn ap Nudd, lord of the dead. He told me and my sister that they have wandered Wales for the past three thousand years—that the Dogs of Annwn were the servants of Epona and Rhiannon; the ancient gods."

James spoke up again after tying the rag off around his palm in a knot with his teeth. "I used to believe the same as Ian there; that stories of a devil dog would definitely keep your children out of the forest and that that was about all there was to it. Like my father used to say: extraordinary claims require equally extraordinary evidence."

The senior member of their crew paused for an instant to nod at the boy and motioned for him to get back to his feet and start tamping again.

"My grandmother told me that some of her neighbours had been slaughtered by the English back in the Glyndwr Rising of 1405. They had tried to retreat through the river Usk and into the forest of Monkswood toward Mynydd Pwll Melyn, but were caught out in the open and butchered alive. Buried beside the road in shallow graves, she says that every night since then a great dark hound appears at midnight at that very spot on the road to Basingwerk. It runs straight toward the crossroads dragging a huge length of chain behind it and disappears right into thin air. Hard evidence or not, nothing would ever get me to go down to that crossroads after dark."

"Whew Wee."

Edward stomped tamping to wipe his forehead with a dirty rag yanked from his back pocket. Down between the inner and outer shell walls, very little breeze made it inside unless one happened to stand right next to the framed windows.

"Damn. It's hotter than a nanny goat in a pepper patch."

The tampers simultaneously stopped packing the rubble and stared at Edward; who continued mopping his brow.

"What?"

Overhead, Gareth just shook his head and started off to check on another crew. Waiting around to ask, in this particular instance, would have been a serious mistake.

Edward's laboured explanation would only have proved even more painful.

* * * * *

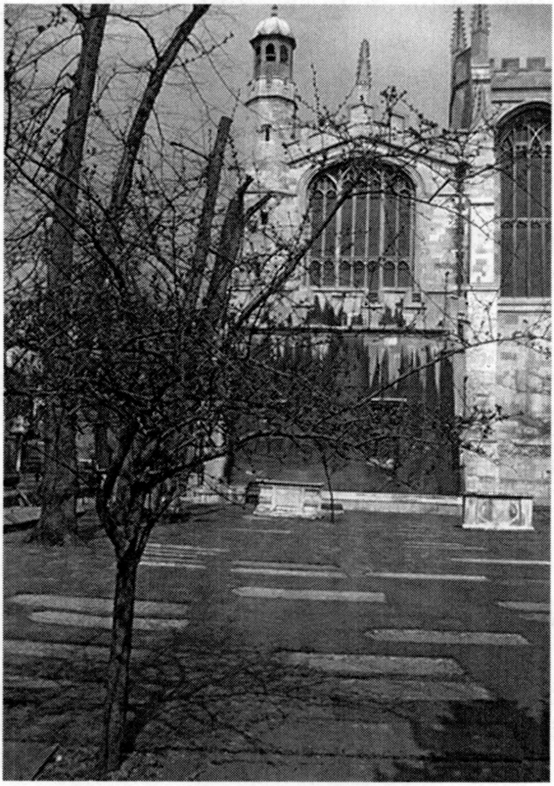

Chapter Twenty-seven

William Herbert at long last understood why people sometimes decide to kill themselves.

His entire life, he had been told how suicide was terrible—the cowards' way out; suicide might be the one unforgivable sin. The clergy said so anyway; in that, once committed, a person never had the opportunity to ask God for forgiveness for ending his or her life before staring Him straight in the face.

And, there were, no doubt, far preferable ways to die.

To pass away of old age; surrounded by loving family who all came round to show how terribly they would miss you. To die as Thomas his brother had: to be in full run; only to trip and crash through the Pearly Gates without warning—to not even realise you were dead until you were sliding past Saint Peter and already halfway across God's breakfast table.

But, there could be no more horrible way to die than that of John Meissel.

The choirmaster had been taken by a mysterious ailment; an unknown malady which no doctor seemed to be able to explain away or cure; which, over the course of weeks, made it practically impossible for John to continue to do the work he loved. He would suddenly be struck with blinding pain while in the midst of ordinary duties; only to double over and be unable to function for hours.

Quickly replaced and ushered out the doors of Eton with hardly more than a 'we'll miss you terribly' and 'don't let the door hit you on the ass on your way out,' the entire situation was particularly overwhelming for young William Herbert. To watch as his dear friend was supplanted by someone who suffered from the inexcusable malady of passionless employment: possessing apparently absolutely no inspiration whatsoever. It must have been sheer torture for John to watch helplessly from the pews as everything the musician had worked for his entire life was methodically dismantled and indiscriminately discarded.

More than simply not to be missed or appreciated— ultimately not even to be remembered.

William, with his experience, might well have understood better than anyone how his mentor felt. To wake up each and every day for the rest of one's life and know that absolutely no one cared . . . not about his feelings, his failing health and pain, and even less his contribution. To die so lonely a death as from meaninglessness.

That must be the most horrible death of all.

Knowing that when you finally died, no one would ever miss you. That your absence would never be felt; nor even noticed by obnoxious colleagues who had abandoned and eagerly ignored you so easily all those years ago. To wake up from dreams that only seemed to repeat and magnify one's sense of abandonment: crying through repeated nightmares; only to wake and face the remorse of endless, indifferent days crying just the same.

Yes, William thought to himself. God must surely understand.

How such a disappointing death as emptiness must be terribly agonising for someone who actually cared about his fellow man. For there is no understanding in meaninglessness: of an existence suddenly void of worth and purpose. One can excuse pain, sickness, or disability; one can allow for stupidity or folly that merely allots one as idiot. Several seem to be perfectly acceptable reasons for wanting to leave one's life behind.

But to be forgotten long before life gave you the opportunity to walk away: to fade into nothingness before one's very eyes—to be suddenly faced with the realisation that the world would never notice what you might have tried to accomplish, what you actually managed to do, or even care enough to miss you when you're gone.

If there is a Hell on earth, then that must be.

To know forevermore and not be known: to exist without any use or reason for existence. How excruciating a survival—how agonizing a death that must be. God would surely understand. Killing oneself seemed far less miserable than living alone within the anonymity of men and one's unforgiving, unrelenting memories.

William Herbert stood alone at the choirmaster's grave.

Lying on the east side of the chapel he had loved so dearly, the lad could think of no finer resting place for John Meissel. The lad unfolded the homily he had carefully copied from John's favourite poetry and read just loud enough for his departed friend to hear.

To God, that tales of victory were true;
That honour, 'neath a pale moon, squarely stood.
Alas, the light of night makes yellow, blue;
And often blurs the line twixt bad and good.
In truth, truth seldom shines as bright it should:
    Devils oft' masquerade as Sons of Light,
    And God's soft voice is oft' unheard at night.

The Wraiths of Raglan Wood

Man fails to see the sky in muddied brook
And aimless hacks a path through forest green;
To give a world much less than in life took,
With signs from God around him seldom seen.
"Tis sad to say, but so all men have been:
    These are the fools who fight for fields of clay,
    To die and be forgot at end of day.

Like dowagers, wild mares with tangled manes
Roam o'er the heath and browse where blood once ran
And valiant fell to die in evening shade;
With deeds forgot, who bravely fought for land:
As all men die, to lie beneath the sand.
    How fickle the world, that poets now lie
        On soft, blood-stained fields, where heroes once died.

John Meissel had passed away alone that silent night in February. Within the peals of Eton's chapel bell; so close, indeed, he would have heard the choristers singing: had they only been allowed to practise any longer at that hour. The former choirmaster did not take his life with poison, not with knife or sword, or even hangman's knot.

Nothing so ostentatious or grandiose.

John Meissel died simply because he had decided not live with the pain of living any longer.

And that, upon reflection, seemed to young William Herbert by far the most meaningless of all.

* * * * *

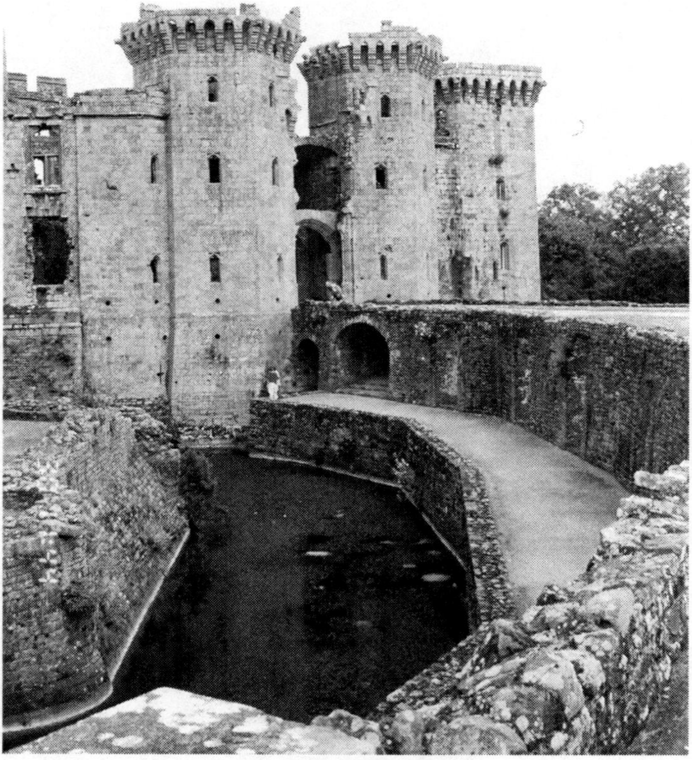

Chapter Twenty-eight

Terrified workmen were beginning to abandon the Gwent construction site in droves.

The apparitions now seemed to appear most every other night and, while a disproportionate number of people were found mangled and mauled, no one could really be sure whether the ones that simply went missing had been taken by the beasts or merely deserted in fear of their lives. Running away was, one might have supposed, the simplest way to have dealt with the labourers' inability to cope with something well beyond their comprehension.

Though Gareth tried to recruit more workmen from as far away as Shrewsbury and Wroxeter in Shropshire, replacements for the already migrant labour force were proving even more difficult to find. Plus, there was the problem of supervising the masons on such a complicated floor plan. If the foreman of the crews left for any period of time, work ground to an almost immediate standstill whenever anyone questioned the schematic drawings or the intended order of completion of the sandstone tower's component parts.

Though William ap Thomas' regular business trips kept him from being underfoot most of the time, Gareth was beginning to feel the pressure of completing the project on time and within budget.

Nearby villages were full of rumours and superstitious yarns that, despite being based on fact, did nothing to help retention. To make matters worse, the end of the building season was rapidly approaching and the weather would all too soon be far too wet and cold to continue on the convoluted hexagonal design.

Gareth was sitting with his head in his hands; staring at the plans for a few moments and then looking up to try to determine exactly where they were and how far the construction ought to have progressed. It wasn't looking all that promising, even before Edward Ruddel walked over to the table to try to cheer him up. The uninvited intruder made himself overly obvious as he stared at the drawings over Gareth's shoulder.

"I saw you and James down here rumping early this morning."

Suddenly the supervisor's headache seemed far less critical.

"Rumping?"

Gareth ap Hywel suddenly pictured a worse case scenario in his mind and, even worse, the prospect of Edward spreading such a negative rumour amongst the crew.

"Rumping?" The old man tried for an explanation that, hopefully, was far better than the one ricocheting around in his imagination.

"You know, rumping and roughhousing. When you were pretending to fight each other with those stakes of wood and that wicker basket top," Ruddel explained.

Gareth had to think about it for a second before he understood.

"ROMPING."

Gareth leaned in to drive the correction firmly into Edward's brain.

"You mean *romping*. Pretending to fight in a boisterous or playful way. Rumping would mean something far, far different."

"Such as what?"

Edward appeared to be truly clueless to the whole concept of buggery and homosexuality; and his supervisor had neither the time nor intention of explaining the sensitive matter in an appropriate manner so the simple man might understand.

His headache now back with a furious vengeance, Gareth simply held up a hand to signify that the subject was closed. The older man pulled a small leather bag from his inside pocket and tapped approximately a spoonful of white powder into the bottom of his cup.

"What's that?"

Of all the men at Raglan, who spent their incredibly long days hammering, chipping, carrying, mortaring, or tamping; Gareth honestly felt that he tried harder than most to humour Edward Ruddel. Still, as he squinted his eyes from the already blinding sun, the mason knew this was going to be a particularly rough day.

"Willow."

"What?"

"Willow."

"Sorry?"

"WILLOW."

Gareth barked a bit too loudly; which only made his temples pound all the more. He poured some water in the bottom of the cup and sluiced it around to dissolve the particles. Craning his neck as far as possible in both directions, the foreman tried to stretch out the cramping muscles a bit and then, with one final swirl, took the bitter mixture down in a single shot.

His face left no doubt as to the taste.

"You know, willow for a headache . . . ," The old man tried to make an innuendo without having to spell it out. He could see, however, that there would be no shortcut when it came to Edward.

"You know, the old kitchen rhyme—

> Boiled willow bark is for one's head
> Horehound spares heaving in bed
> Mugwort with Valerian Root down swelling gets
> Goats' Rue and Feverfew both stop the sweats
> And cuts and nicks will heal quite good
> If you but bath in cold Wormwood

Didn't you learn that from you grandmother as a child?"

Now Edward looked confused and even more bewildered.

Gareth gave up and went back to the drawings. He started making notes, scratching some figures out with his right hand. After a few minutes with Edward continuing to stare at him from over his shoulder, he resigned himself for another round.

"What?" The supervisor asked with as much compassion as he could presently find in his heart.

"If you can't beat them, then join them," Edward quipped. "Then beat them . . . they'll never see it coming."

Listening to Ruddel was proving to be nothing short of exhausting.

"Please, not this morning," Gareth pleaded. "I'm running out of ideas here and have an absolute killer of a headache."

Now writing with his left hand, Edward noticed the difference right away. "I thought you were right-handed?"

The Welshman closed his eyes and sat there for a moment; trying to consciously will the pounding behind his eyes into submission. "I can write with either hand. Have done all my life."

"What's that called?" Edward was a buzzing mosquito that simply wouldn't fly away.

Gareth slowly tipped his head and drove his chin toward his chest in an attempt to stretch the muscles at the base of his skull. "Ambidextrous."

"Sorry?"

"Am-bi-dex-trous." His foreman repeated the word in syllables as he massaged the back of his neck with his fingers. "It means you can write or throw with either hand."

Ruddel took another bite from what had to be the loudest apple in all of Britain and chewed it noisily a few times.

"I'd give my right arm to be ambidextrous."

Gareth collapsed on top of the drawings—beginning to earnestly pray for death. "Please! PLEASE, for the love of God. Just go away!"

The spectator took a big bite from his apple and crunched deafeningly with an open mouth.

"You know, it's really more ambivalence than apathy."

Knowing that Edward's fractured logic and apparent lack of common sense often made him appear thicker than a whale omelette, his long-suffering supervisor was honestly afraid to ask what he meant. The mason pretended to be dead, hoping that Edward would just have mercy and leave him alone to die in peace. True to form, Ruddel never gave him the chance, but continued to express his opinion.

"You see, the men are not lethargic, lazy, or even bored. There is no lack of interest or concern in finishing on time."

Fighting through the migraine headache, Gareth slowly rose from the dead, took a deep breath, and allowed the man from Abergavenny to go on.

"What you are fighting is ambivalence between the different crews, my friend." Ruddel took another bite from the now half-eaten apple in his hand. "There is a conflict and uncertainty about whose elements or sections should be priority. It is this opposition of attitudes and emotions that are resulting in a dispute between the groups and that controversy is slowing down the overall completion."

Smiling broadly, Edward took a rather large bite from the other side of the crispy fruit and chomped on it nonchalantly.

Gareth was truly astounded.

He had to give it to his fellow Welshman: he could not have expressed it any better himself. The flow of thought was clear, concise, and remarkably insightful; three attributes he would never have given Ruddel credit for possessing, let alone of actually being able to articulate.

"You're right," the master mason conceded with gratitude. "Now all we have to do is inspire the men to work together and not against each other."

"Want me to have a quick word?" Edward proposed.

Normally, this would have been Gareth ap Hywel's worst nightmare but, based on the man's incredibly eloquent assessment and his migraine, he motioned for Ruddel to step up make his point.

Edward put two fingers in his mouth and whistled to get everyone's attention. He then stepped over Gareth and stood on the bench next to where their foreman was sitting and began.

"All right, men." He cleared his throat.

"This is where and what separates the men from the men who only wished they were men before they stop to think about it: who are really only boys pretending to be the men they might want the men they know to be. Now, if we all pull together like we would each like the other to pull, then we won't have any problem knowing which men among us should be pulled for first, and that might be a lot easier to see once we all begin to pull."

He paused to swallow a bit of apple peel.

" . . . as men."

Gareth ap Hywel's mouth fell open on its own accord.

Utter silence resonated across the open field.

From far in the back one could hear a single, "What the Hell?"

Edward smiled broadly down at Gareth and slapped him on the back as if he had just solved all his problems. He then picked up the remainder of his apple and strolled away, oblivious to the everyone's stunned reaction.

Without the slightest idea of what the man had said, the crews began to quarrel between themselves all over again.

Gareth turned back to stare at the plans, drove his index fingers as hard as he could into his temples, and repositioned his head between his hands. The poor man's migraine headache was sharply, and not surprisingly, even more unbearable.

* * * * *

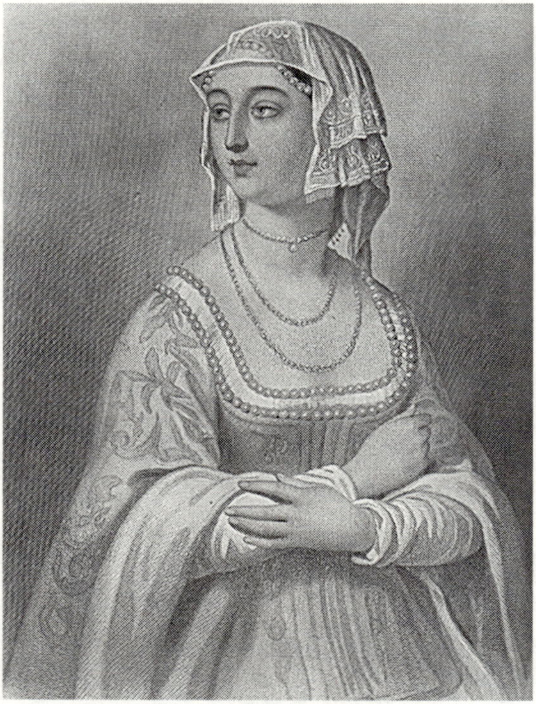

Chapter Twenty-nine

William Herbert was thoroughly convinced he was dying.

It wasn't any sudden loss of weight or even feeling ill: more a feeling that Time had noticed him and would very soon, without his even realising, transform him into an old man. Other than studying at Eton, he had absolutely nothing to show for his life; excluding being the son of a well-known politician and heir to a small castle in Gwent he had not even seen completed.

Loneliness appeared to be his only friend now that John Meissel had passed away.

William wondered if his late friend had felt it too: that sense that one was simply passing through life as a wanderer on a pilgrimage: daily questioning what the purpose of it all might be. Sitting upon the lawn, he flipped open to his favourite passages from The Siege at Caerphilly, Meissel's favourite work of Warin of Llanhennock. He had carefully copied the entire folio from the library at Eton; though some of the stanzas seemed to reach out to him more than others.

Lately the words, though written almost two hundred years earlier, seemed to capture the young man's growing sense of futility.

What satire that men faint for stride of rock;
Whose quarried kin might grace a village pool,
And daily drip with scent of perfumed lock
'Midst blossomed boughs within a garden cool;
Yet defaced kin doth monarch prove a fool
    By breaking fiery-forged steel at hilt,
    To lie baptized by blood of valiant spilt.

What irony that mothers contemplate
The fate of sons whom Glory marched away;
To venom other mothers' sons with hate
Whom they had never met, nor heard one say

One rankered deed about before that day.
    Yet then, as now, from all antiquity:
    The thorn that pricks each mother's son, pricks thee.

F or souls must know, kind sirs and ladies near,
Each step you take, this castle wall around,
In morning dew, for those forgotten here,
Writes epitaph in grass that covers ground.
As noiseless wings do soft same wall surround:
    So soft, no ear may hear their ancient song,
    They soundless talk with those who walk along.

Y et, ken: no sweep may sever hollow tread,
As limpid time provides thin, windowed door;
That ambulated gaits of hallowed dead
Articulate of deeds done late before
Our time; and souls wait near the crystal shore:
    To cyclic turn and mould transparent time,
    Perchance lives past at last entwine with thine.

There was something almost magical about words.

They moved the heart; uncovered some faint emotion that well might have been hiding under discarded memories. These words in particular. It wasn't the rhyme, not even the rhythm: there was something that made these stanzas strike a chord in William's soul. He supposed it might have been the same with the music of the choir and John

Meissel: some memory of God that life had, over the years, driven into hiding or straightforward forgetfulness. Young Herbert pulled out a second scrap of paper and stared at the scrawl.

For time remembers not so much as name,
And even less, the character of man.
One only trusts that justice truly reigns
Before the Builder of the Wind; whom with mere sand
In His palm, did blow across the prone and lonely land,
    The high mountains to raze with holy breath:
    Who holds the Light, for all who fall in death.

Few are those souls who pause on heights of life
To understand: Time by no plan proceeds,
But marches new each morning to life's fife
And none can do but follow where it leads.
    Fewer perceive: Only through struggle we,
    Past gold, past gain: attain Nobility.

Suddenly the boy missed Wales terribly.

* * * * *

"**W**hy not?"

Gwladus was not letting her husband off this morning without a pretty good defence.

Sensing the same, William ap Thomas delivered his response with as much contempt as he could muster.

"I'm far too busy spending the money I married you for."

With that bombshell, the Steward of the Duke of York spun around and casually strolled outside to find his horse. It was fortunate for him that the children were still fast asleep. When a liveried messenger arrived to request his immediate presence at Windsor Castle, there would be absolutely no excuse for tardiness. A fact that William ap Thomas knew all too well.

The last survivors of the Regency Council of King Henry VI had suddenly found themselves very nearly knee-deep in a steaming pile of pony loaf.

With the coronation of Charles VII Valois as King of France on 17 July, 1429, the eight-year-old Henry was immediately crowned King of England at Westminster Abbey on 6 November of that same year. This was to set up his further coronation as King of France on 16

December, 1431 at Notre Dame Cathedral in Paris. Still, even until 1437, upon reaching his fifteenth birthday, the young King Henry was only granted limited authority over the monarchy by the Regency Council.

The hornets' nest that was British politics ultimately fell from the branch when Henry's mother died in 1437 and the prince was finally declared of age. To the dismay of many of his governors and mentors, the peaceful, pious, even some would say timid, Henry VI almost immediately permitted the court at Windsor to be dominated by a few noble favourites: who, predictably, vehemently disagreed on the question of the ongoing war in France.

Not surprisingly, the young monarch ultimately favoured the strategy of peace with their longstanding enemy. Which meant that, despite the protests of Richard, duke of York, Henry of England decided not to continue funding the conflict. Having been proposing peace negotiations for some time, Cardinal Beaufort and William de la Pole, the earl of Suffolk, convinced Henry that the most straightforward path to ending the struggle would be a marriage to the niece of the Valois King Charles VII's wife, one Margaret of Anjou. Rumours had even managed to reach London of the fifteen-year-old girl's striking beauty, which made the idea of an impending engagement even more appealing to the post-pubescent twenty-three-year-old Henry VI.

All this had unfolded in a relatively short period of months and caused no small amount of anxiety for the duke of York. As a result, Richard had sent liveried messengers to ride straight to Wales; to comb the tracks of Gwent and Monmouth for William ap Thomas and, once found, deliver him straight back to London immediately for emergency deliberations on how best to save the monarchy.

Which made it virtually impossible to live with the Steward of the duke of York.

It was one thing to tout yourself as indispensable: it was entirely another to be tracked down and personally delivered to Parliament on the Thames. William's opinion of himself was so inflated and grand, it was a wonder he managed to get his head through the tower doorway. His wife's opinion of the man leaving her to, yet again, deal with the ongoing problems of finishing construction of the Great Tower of Raglan Castle was, curiously, not quite so grand.

At this point in their marriage and relationship it would be fair to say that, had she the opportunity, Gwladus would have happily traded William ap Thomas for a pet monkey.

And would have felt to have the better end of the bargain.

* * * * *

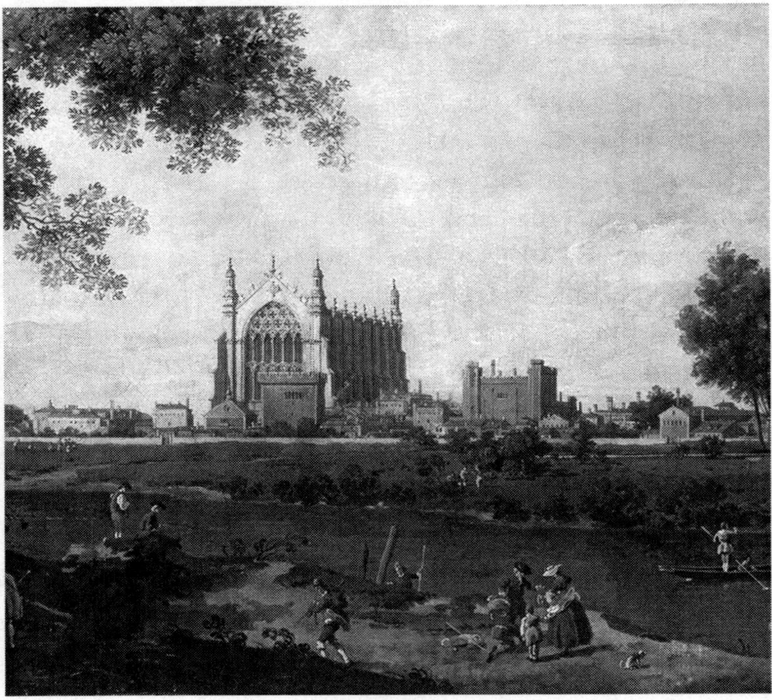

Chapter Thirty

Months joined hands and rolled over upon themselves to build a barrier of years at King's College of Our Lady of Eton. For all the homesick boys who had been sequestered there in various halls, none took his forced confinement quite so seriously as William ap Thomas Herbert. Perhaps no lad amongst its rolls had nearly half the incentive.

Long walks to the castle gardens outside the grounds of Windsor did little or nothing to ease Herbert's melancholy.

What a shame that people tend not to pay attention when listening becomes a chore; that they immediately assume that someone conventional may be more credible than another with whom they cannot immediately identify. There was much wisdom hiding in the mind of Eton's groundskeeper—far more than his educated employers might ever care to concede. Truth be told, William Herbert learned more about the world, men, and God from Robert Aynsley than from any of his studies.

The weathered caretaker kept right on talking as he clipped back the barricade of coarse English laurel. What had obviously seemed a capital idea only a few years before had turned into an absolute nightmare for the person responsible for its care. Laurel was very likely the poorest choice for a well manicured hedge, in that it seemed to almost spring out of the ground in all directions; forcing Aynsley to spend an inordinate amount of time whacking it back into some semblance of submission.

"Damn pest, dis 'edge. Why couldn't thee av planted summa' eur bit mor tam. It dun't even look good; wha' wi' its great, ragged leaves."

Attempting to lend a hand on a quiet Saturday afternoon, William was forced to agree. The hedge of laurel around the chapel seemed, in hindsight, to have been an utterly ridiculous idea.

Robert tried to take the manicure in stride and returned to the point he had been trying to make about God.

"When theur gi'o'a 'n think abaht it, theear are only two prayers 'a' ivva cross t' lips o' men. Thank the, Lurd or God 'elp uz. Reet?"

The young Herbert tried to think of all the prayers he had ever uttered or heard in church. The grizzled man had a point. Every prayer he had ever heard was one of either praise or desperation. William acknowledged his agreement with a nod.

"When life seems terrible or not worth livin, we assume 'a' God 'as someha forgotten wee or, even wahrse, 'a' t' Creytor simply isn't theear."

The boy kept snipping the rampant fronds with his knife and struggled to translate in his mind.

"If t' Bible is reet, 'a' God nivva slumbers nor sleeps; 'a' God allus keeps His promises; 'a' God is love: then t' upshot o' everythin is: God will nivva, ivva abandon wee. When we feel 'e does, we meight be just searchin for Him int' rong place or int' rong way. When men search for God i' heaven, thee need ta realize 'a' God is reet 'eear wi' wee."

Robert pointed to William with his shears.

"If theur are 'eear, then by God, thy God is 'eear. So, when theur think thy ship is sinkin, kna 'a' God is reet ont' boa' wi' theur. He will gerr theur thru—often i' eur way completely different fra thy expectations."

Sensing that the boy was struggling with ideas was well as dialect, Aynsley gave William some time to mull it over.

The teenager kept clipping the front of the bush into a vertical line. He had never thought of God that way before—or men either.

Perhaps the groundskeeper was right; that the problem lay with men's perception of their Creator more than anything else. If He promised never to abandon men to the world, then when He seemed absent or far away; it might just be that one had forgotten where to look. When things looked the bleakest, the Lord said He would get His children through all tribulations: just not exactly as one might have hoped.

God might, in fact, be using the world to save men from it.

That was quite a revelation.

* * * * *

Not only was he hundreds of miles from his home and family but, with the recent replacement of John Meissel, Joseph Kelsey and his cronies had taken the opportunity to redouble their torment of the boy from Wales.

The history instructor now actively lay in wait for William to pass by; then would pretend to initiate conversations with his confederates that the boy could not help but overhear. Far worse than simply casting aspersions at his lineage and genealogy, Kelsey took particular enjoyment at dismissing the quality of the boy's grandfather, Sir Dafydd Gam. Mocking laughter at his inelegant death at Agincourt led to mimicry and hateful comments that could be construed as nothing but contemptuous.

"Couldn't even fend off a Frenchman."

Joseph whispered behind his palm; not to disguise his comment, but to direct it intentionally to the teenager's ears.

The instructor ridiculed young William Herbert for the most petty and small-minded of reasons. The boy was Welsh. In the minds of many students and faculty at Eton, that gave him absolutely no entitlement to share the King's benevolence and even less the college's privilege.

In an effort to cope, William Herbert had taken to daily walks alone down along the northern bank of the river Thames. Convinced that no one might see or hear, he pulled the paper from his pocket and read aloud to himself.

F or justice is a hot, two-edged sword.
Whose haft may glow as brightly as its blade;
To wield it long, a man may ill afford:
Its white-hot hilt demands a tithe be paid;
And from its bearer equal justice weighed.
    Its glowing scabbard then is wisely left
      With Him who deftly man from earth hath cleft.

Alone along the path that paralleled the bank, the boy tried to put his life into perspective.

While life at Eton was far from idyllic, at least his absence from castle Raglan meant that his father could not use him as a target for his frustration. That might be rather difficult now anyway, as the boy had sprouted like a weed over the past two years. Now fully five feet eleven inches tall and nearly one hundred seventy-five pounds, William towered over the classmates who had been his size upon arriving at school. While they now averaged a good six inches shorter than the boy from Wales, it was the fact that he outweighed most by a good two stones or nearly thirty pounds.

That growing disparity in size was, more than likely, the only reason he had not run away years ago. William's advantage in height and weight made it impractical for any of the boys to take him on one-on-one and ill advisable for Kelsey to push his taunting persecution to the point of blows.

So, young Herbert took to wandering the track down by the river at sunset.

He would close his eyes and pretend that he was back on the Raglan road; holding out his arms as he slowly strolled along and pretending that his dogs were there beside him in the English twilight. More than once, he actually thought he could hear them breathing and feel his fingers glide through their thick matted hair.

Imagination may often prove more real than our unwitting desperation may ever care to admit. So, too, one's power of invention might turn out to be far more valid than our conscious minds may ever choose to consider.

A proposition that young William Herbert would soon have to cope with face-to-face.

* * * * *

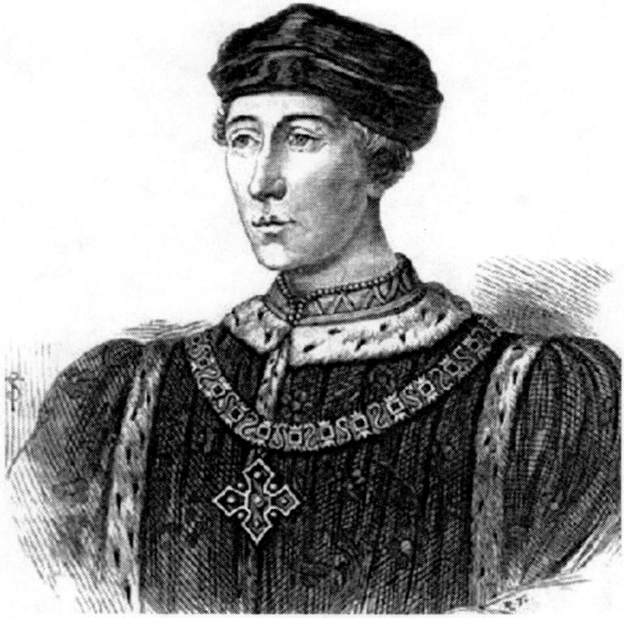

Chapter Thirty-one

Over the objections of Humphrey, duke of Gloucester and Richard, duke of York, the twenty-three year old King Henry VI had personally dispatched William de la Pole, earl of Suffolk, off to France. His one objective: negotiate with King Charles VII for the hand of his niece, the fifteen-year-old, pubescent, Margaret of Anjou.

Well into the virgin's prime as quality breeding stock, the scrupulous king of France had deliberately kept her sequestered away from the attentions of men—saving the young maiden for just such an occasion.

Who said there weren't any lonely, beautiful little virgins left to be had?

Of course, living under the constant separation and subsequent isolation from anyone her own age made the royal offering to peace quite anxious to escape: even if it meant being traded to an English king. Margaret had long accepted the proposition of being marketed to another kingdom in Europe as an unavoidable destiny. Such was the fate of any girl born into the ruling bloodline.

While she had some serious misgivings about England and, in particular, a King almost twice her age: she praised the Lord that her better than average looks had kept her from being bustled off to a situation that could have actually been quite worse. There were more than a few old, lecherous monarchs scattered across Europe who would have paid her uncle quite handsomely to bed her themselves.

King Charles VII recognised this as well and wagered quite well on his long-term investment.

In return for his wife's niece, the king of France insisted that any man lucky enough to have her would not receive the customary dowry. Indeed, if Henry really wanted her that badly, then England would have to relinquish the territories of Anjou and Maine as part of the bargain. Small wonder Richard Plantagenet, duke of York, had argued alongside Humphrey, duke of Gloucester, to simply continue the Hundred Years War.

Populating the king's bedroom with an attractive little virgin was going to cost England and the monarchy an arm and a leg.

With the blessings of Cardinal Beaufort, the envoy of King Henry VI, William de la Pole, earl of Suffolk, agreed to dispense with the 20,000 livres dowry and foot the bill for a court ceremony. Suffolk made the concessions upon the advice of Beaufort, since Margaret of Anjou was the daughter of penniless René of Anjou and had no money of his own to pay for the wedding.

To make everything legal and non-negotiable, the stipulations were set forth in the self-styled Treaty of Tours. Realising that the concessions by England would be adamantly opposed by members of Parliament, the crown simply kept the conditions of the marriage secret and the marriage went ahead in 1445. All things considered, it was a rather poor deal for England in the long run; being that Margaret was only distantly related to King Charles VII of France, by marriage and not by blood.

To say that Richard Plantagenet took the conditions of the contract badly would have been an understatement.

The Treaty of Tours only worsened the political discord of Henry's court and would later, according to some historians, actually help instigate the Wars of the Roses. Pitting the houses of Lancaster and York against each other for decades, the civil war would ultimately bestow the monarchy to the forces of the earl of Richmond, one Welsh-born, Henry Tudor.

A beautiful little virgin for Windsor's boudoir would prove to be unbelievably expensive.

* * * * *

The sky, it seemed, had become the unwilling battleground between Science and the Sublime.

"Foul neet."

Joseph Kelsey was caught off guard by the whispered voice from the nearby shadows. Apparently, finding Kelsey out roaming the grounds at midnight had much the same effect on Eton's conscientious caretaker. The coming thunderstorm was flashing its undoubted intent across the heavens: forewarning all still awake of its coming wrath.

Lightning and its noisy mistress, Thunder, simultaneously split the atmosphere: forcing both men to instinctively duck back under the feeble protection of a gabled arch that marked the edge of the walkway. Neither laboured under the delusion that the already rotting arbour above their heads offered any real protection. The swaying awning of slate was doing all it could simply to remain upright in the wind. Still, at least for the moment, it was better than standing in the rain.

What had been only a light drizzle minutes earlier instantly became a torrent. Curtains of rain came down in sheets from dark, menacing clouds that seemed to race up the valley as though summoned by a spell. Lower clouds from the west now boiled up into the waiting megaliths of white that sprang toward them from the south. It was a beautiful display: one of those rare storms where whole sections of the sky seemed to battle with the encroaching charcoal-grey. A mesmerizing scene of muted purple, blue, and green exploding skyward as light intensified through the twirling mass and stabbed back at the moon.

Several bolts struck out and seemed to span the sky; tearing ragged lines through the slate-grey pool of clouds that continued to hang underneath the chaotic tempest. In the quiet that followed, Robert Aynsley made his observation.

"Just t' soarts o' neet, ah fancy, 'a' demons await—to try 'n steal fra God t' souls o' men."

Fast moving storm clouds from the west closed over Eton like the fingers of a glove; not only pronouncing the end of moonlight, but seeming to agree with the groundskeeper's suggestion.

Strange, how two completely different personalities may sometimes be pressed into unlikely companionship by forces entirely out of their control. Even more remarkable that both men sensed an ominous presence in the air; though Kelsey was not about to admit it to a member of the staff.

"You must have some menial duties that desperately need attending." Joseph's choice of adjectives and tone quite clearly conveyed that he did not intend to fraternise.

"I kna eur gentleman o' thy importance wouldn't care ta be seen wi' . . ."

"Bugger off."

Joseph pulled his collar up until his coat covered his ears and sauntered off defiantly into the brunt of the downpour. The man was nothing if not forthright; even if it meant being bad-mannered and disrespectful.

Aynsley watched Eton's pretentious professor of history disappear into the force of the sudden deluge. Taking off his cap and deeply bowing at the waist in a correspondingly pompous exaggeration, Robert smiled and delivered a parting descriptor; certain he would not to be overheard above the rain.

"Dumbass."

* * * * *

It might just be true: that, possibly, every rumour begins at the intersection of two completely unrelated goals.

Springing from the fertile mixture of two entirely impartial ideas, stories that start out life as factual and real may all too suddenly be convoluted into the tittle-tattle of juicy gossip once more than one storyteller joins the telling. If so, then there were certainly enough narrators the next morning to see that any obligation to the truth was quickly erased.

Lying on the north bank of the Thames and connected with Windsor solely by a single bridge, Eton lay almost twenty-two miles from London. As a matter of fact, the only reason the village came into being at all was the necessity of keeping that lonely bridge in good repair. Windsor had learned its lesson with the Spitelbrigge, or Beggar's Bridge that previously connected Upton and Eton across Chalvey Ditch. Keeping the thoroughfare from the north open all the way to London meant, by means of exclusion, maintaining the Eton bridge.

The establishment of King's College of Our Lady of Eton, with its provost, ten priests, four clerks, six choristers and scholars meant that the tiny village north of the Thames saw a sudden influx of artisans and labourers. Normally, this would have been a great financial windfall: except for the veritable horde of pilgrims streaming into Eton in response to the papal bulls of 1441 and 1442. Under these letters patent by the Pope, indulgences were granted to those who visited the church of Eton at the feast of the Assumption.

It was early morning after the storm, on the day of the Feast of Assumption, that the body of Joseph Kelsey was discovered on the lawn outside the chapel.

Morning services were cancelled while the local authorities investigated the suspicious death of one of Eton's own. What had enticed the instructor to leave the sheltered confines of his room and venture out into the thunderstorm baffled everyone: as did the way he died. No marks were found upon the body; no telltale sign of how the man might have met his end.

The position of the body gave the impression that the man simply breathed his last lungful of air and then just dropped in a heap upon the ground.

Almost as if the very hand of God had reached through the clouds, seized him by the throat, and stolen his breath away.

* * * * *

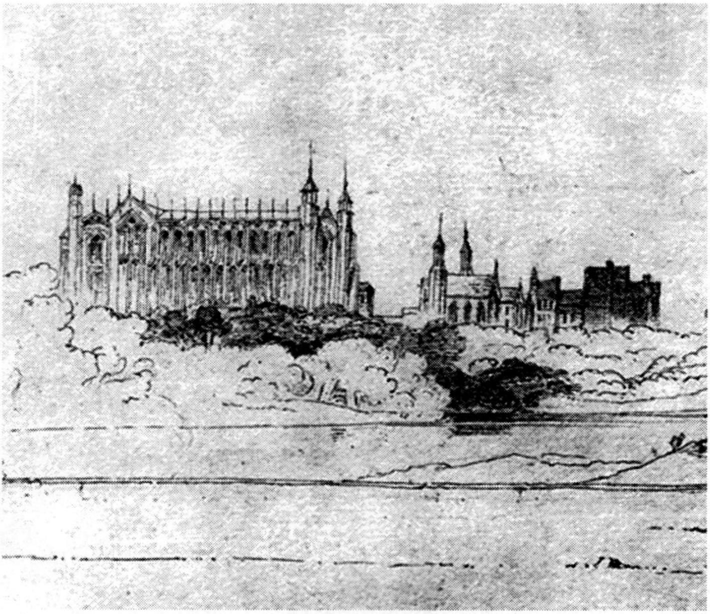

Chapter Thirty-two

Letters from Raglan and his mother were few and far between.

Not surprisingly, William's younger brother, under the guise of spending more time with his cousins, had wisely abandoned Raglan to live at his uncle's home outside Abergavenny as soon as he turned fifteen. Elizabeth was now courting Sir Henry Stradling of St. Donat's Castle; which overlooked the Bristol Channel from the village of St. Donat's near Llantwit Major, just west of Cardiff. A clever girl, her consequent engagement not only neatly removed her from the turmoil of Raglan but provided a physical deterrent to any retribution of her father. Sir Henry Stradling was not a man to be trifled with—particularly when it came to matters of the heart. Any interference from Elizabeth's father would have been personally dealt with long before reinforcements could ever hope to arrive from Parliament or England.

Now feeling more alone than ever since being ostracized to Windsor, William Herbert began to neglect his studies and spend hour upon hour walking by himself and staring at the currents of the river Thames. There, amidst the almost unearthly silence, the setting sun would frame the lad's silhouette against the coming gloom. As usual, he would close his eyes and pretend that he was back walking along the Raglan road.

Deliberately stopping along the track, he extended his hands down by his sides and shuddered as a chill ran up his spine. Eyes closed and listening to his own breath, he pretended that his faithful pups bookended him on either side against the night: against whatever grief or terror the future might yet hold. Frozen there against the twilight, William sensed something of the eternal; the flash of conception of an epiphany—a fleeting sense of what eternity must be. Then, all too suddenly and sadly, it was gone: like a falling star that desolately plummeted down to hide behind a waiting blanket of clouds.

As the boy imagined stroking the matted heads of his faithful hounds, for the first time in years, he actually considered going home.

The Wraiths of Raglan Wood

* * * * *

A direct consequence of the intrigue at Windsor Castle was that the duke of York was seldom seen at home. As a result, his Steward was not either. While this did nothing to endear William ap Thomas to his wife and in-laws, the man's absence was actually deeply appreciated by Gareth ap Hywel.

The Great Tower of Raglan was, after years of alteration and constant modifications, nearing completion. No small feat considering that the Lord of Raglan appeared to want to get his fingers into almost every aspect of the construction; and the fact that virtually none of the workmen initially hired on had stayed to see it through.

Even now, years later, the legends of the Hounds from Hell that haunted Raglan Wood discouraged more than a few from hanging round the edge of the Forest of Dean for more than a month or two. Occasional manifestations of the apparitions and the rare disappearance of labourers only seemed to fuel the fires of superstition.

For all that, Gareth ap Hywel had seen the project to its end.

To make the transporting and lifting of tonnes of stone imminently more practical, the excavation of most of the moat had been delayed until the final components of the battlements were set in place. Remarkably, some of the stones from the massive ditch actually made it to the top of the tamped fill between the ten foot thick walls. In keeping with William ap Thomas' original instruction that it be 'stately and handsome,' each of the six sides were an impressive thirty-two feet wide and a soaring five stories tall. Constructed of symmetrical, squared yellow sandstone; the master mason's attention to detail was clearly evident from the finished product.

The moat actually complimented the castle quite well; in that it was thirty feet across and supplied by a clear running stream, making the tower itself only accessible by way of the single bridge. Though more in keeping with the design of French castles than of any seen elsewhere in England, Scotland, or Wales; the edifice at Raglan was truly a remarkable piece of engineering.

For all that, William ap Thomas had stopped by for the first time in over a month and was standing atop the battlements criticising the way the standards had been arranged.

The Lord of Raglan Castle did not know the meaning of the word 'quit.'

Renounce—certainly;
Suspend—absolutely;
Desert—undoubtedly;
Abandon—yes, to be sure;
Resign—oh, without a doubt;
Surrender—why, at most any day or time;

but 'quit:' Definitely not.

He was meticulous and anal retentive to the last. Why, that thoroughly annoying trait was what made the man a perfect Steward.

His temperament and aptitude for fussiness made William ap Thomas a complete and utter dogsbody.

*****

Robert Aynsley caught sight of the young William Herbert coming around the hedge and nodded that he might be amenable for some company. Actually, the groundskeeper had been waiting for an opportunity to talk with him privately for several days. Aynsley continued to whet the long, curved single-edged blade of his scythe with a sharpening stone.

"Legends seh 'a' t' goddesses Rhiannon 'n Epona 'ood sometimes visit men int' disguise o' animals."

The boy was just about to sit down when the bizarre comment caught him completely off-guard. He plopped down on a somewhat unreliable stool and leaned back carefully to prop himself against the wall. Robert continued working on bringing back the edge and went on almost as if he were talking to himself.

"Aye, ah av often wondered abaht 'a' missen. Wha' betta way ta wanda unawares amongst mankin' than as an animal?"

"I suppose," William didn't really know how to respond or where Aynsley was going with this whole idea.

"How betta, ah av often thowt, ta wanda unawares 'n judge mankin' thru t' eyes, int' disguise, o' animals? Men shun 'em, use 'em, 'n often cruelly abuse them: wha' betta touchstone than animals ta weigh t' characta o' man?"

Still not entirely sure what the old caretaker was up to, William decided to scrap his suspicions and play along.

"Well," the boy honestly gave the concept his best consideration, "it does seem logical that if God or gods manufactured the world, someone somewhere must have concerns about man's stewardship."

"Aye . . ."

Aynsley twisted the bent wood handle of the garden implement so that the blade lay right between his knees. Sliding the stone down the length of the metal blade quite cautiously, it was obvious that the man was waiting for him to make another leap of inspiration.

"So . . . ," young William drawled to give himself a bit more time to think.

"So, maybe the animals have always known the mysteries of the universe. Maybe . . . ," William paused once more to better line up the assertion within his mind. "Maybe, while other creatures cannot help but comprehend the mind of God; there are very few people who ever catch a glimpse of Him, and fewer still that recognise Him when they do."

"Or 'em." Robert suggested.

"Or Them." William conceded.

Eton's groundskeeper stopped his sharpening and laid the scythe flat against his thighs. Wiping his hands against his grimy pockets, he leaned forward as if to share a secret.

"Ah saw theur wi' thy dogs tutheur day."

The casual remark knocked William off balance on the already tipped stool and dropped him to his backside upon the floor. No one had ever seen his pups but him. He had no answer for the Yorkshireman.

Robert calmly flipped the scythe over and started grinding off the grass caked on the other side.

"Theur wor cuttin across t' grass just theear," the old man pointed with his nose, "'an twoa great wolfhounds wor trottin along wi' theur on eitha side."

William held his breath.

"Wha' struk uz as strange," Aynsley kept talking as if there were nothing unusual at all about what he was saying, "Wor 'a' ah could see reet thru t' great beasts."

"As if thee wor apparitions made o' smoke."

The boy had no response; at least nothing that he thought would make any sense.

Sensing the same, Robert smiled and held up the blade to get a better look at its edge against the morning sun.

"Strange, t' tricks thy eyes plai on theur. Especially when theur start ta gra old."

After a few minutes of complete silence, William excused himself and started back to his room.

Perhaps it had come time for the heir of Raglan Castle to finally leave Eton.

* * * * *

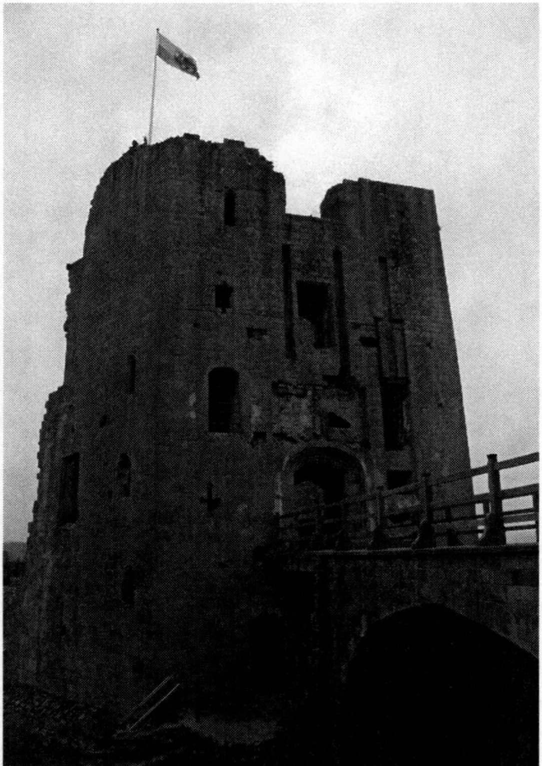

Chapter Thirty-three

William Herbert hit the gates of Raglan Castle wholly prepared for a full-frontal assault.

Vivid recollections of how horrible his father had been to him as a child had played back every day for the better part of three years. Without a doubt, memories of being on the losing side of those confrontations had contributed greatly to the young man's interest in sport. He had deliberately pushed himself harder for the past few years at Eton; trying to prime his body for whatever challenge his father might present. William was stripped of all body fat: lean, taut, and completely confident that, should the need arise, he could beat the man who had bullied him within less than an inch of his life. So, when William ap Thomas answered the door, his son squared his stance and prepared himself to start the conversation with his best right cross. All precautions that now appeared to have been a colossal waste of time.

Actually, he had to strain to recognise the man at all.

The Lord of Raglan had changed dramatically in three short years. A sedentary lifestyle had amplified his stomach into a pot belly; with his belt now slung low over bony, narrow hips to accommodate the girth. To be sure, his father's stomach was the only portion of the tyrant's body that had appeared to prosper in William's absence.

The duke of York's Steward had shrunken to about half the man he had been only thirty-six months earlier. Shoulders and arms appeared to have no meat on them at all; the bones protruding clearly, even from underneath the clothes. His face was gaunt; the temples and facial hair far greyer than his son would even give credit to the years. Even the Lord of Raglan's height was entirely all wrong. The top of the man's head now barely came up to his son's chin: the sum presenting William Herbert with no threat or intimidation whatsoever.

Then, it hit him.

While his father had silently slipped into an unrecognisable hulk at the early age of forty-four, his son had, quite the opposite, sprung upward like a sapling. The twenty-two-year-old's powerful shoulders and arms seemed to nearly fill the doorframe and, due to his height, William had to actually tip his head forward to clear the lintel.

The look upon the old man's face said it all.

He, too, had expected to greet his son at the door and was surprised to find a full-grown man. The bull of a male that met him in the doorway must have outweighed William ap Thomas by at least seventy pounds. Arms like oaken beams rippled with perspiration and were held aloft by a massive, muscled chest that cleft the shirt that covered it into distinct sweat-stained quarters. A flat, tight stomach led down to thick and powerful thighs: making the man who met him at the door one of the most intimidating figures the envoy of the duke of York had ever encountered.

Both stood there in an uncomfortable silence.

The rules of the game had completely reversed: a contest that both men, simultaneously, suddenly considered not even worth the effort to pursue.

How fickle the arm of Fate: to rob each of their contempt without giving either the opportunity to utter a single word.

* * * * *

"In my dream, I was dressed in armour . . . beautiful, shining blue-grey armour."

"Bollocks," the son thought to himself. Just when he had almost been able to smudge and blur the edges of his revulsion. The prized shell of steel that had stood in the hallway for decades now seemed to symbolize everything he hated about his father. It stood there, rigid and lifeless, taunting him like a monster from his past.

True to form, William ap Thomas reached out and stroked the brightly polished, hammered casing and replayed the dreaded anecdotes one more time.

"That is why, when I received my knighthood from King Henry, I had this suit made in blue-grey steel as well."

His son examined the breastplate and helmet closely; realising that, without its stand, the metal ensemble suddenly seemed quite terribly small. As a boy, the accoutrements of war had seemed so overwhelming and titanic. Now they seemed altogether conquerable. Having heard this exact same tale for most likely a thousand times, William yet again looked around for some distraction from the droning narrative.

"I can remember it as if I dreamed it only yesterday. Riding on a majestic charger through the streets of some town I had never seen; on the brightest afternoon that ever was. Women leaned out their chamber windows and waved their handkerchiefs; men cheered and slapped my legs as I rode by myself through the centre of town."

William waited for the inevitable conclusion: which, to his great surprise, never came.

His father's face dropped down into the exact same contorted frown of contemplation he remembered, only to raise back up unexpectedly as the weathered man tapped the breastplate with his index finger to strike the sound of tin.

"Never even put the damn thing on."

* * * * *

Gwladus came running down the stairs; almost tripping over the hem of her dress. Equally surprised at how much her son had grown, the woman's face beamed with far more adoration than William might have hoped. Lurking at the corners of his mother's eyes, however, misery and melancholy could not be masked by Gwladus' real delight at seeing her boy again. Excitement is a poor disguise for depression and despair: suffering and sadness rarely concealed for very long by simple surprise. In that instant, William Herbert's indignation at her treatment swelled from mere empathy to resentment; his mother exemplifying somehow his father's negligence and betrayal. The sorrow indelibly etched within the woman's eyes congealed the bitterness and loathing of her son's heart into palatable contempt for William ap Thomas.

"My son."

That was all his mother had to say: two words that, without argument, said it all.

The young man lifted her up off the ground with a mighty hug and swung her around in a circle like a doll. She, too, seemed so much smaller than he remembered before Eton: as if living with the Lord of Raglan had drained her very life away.

Herbert turned to glare at his father across the room.

The toxic taste of remorse, hostility, and shame in his mouth confirmed that William Herbert had, indeed, finally come home.

* * * * *

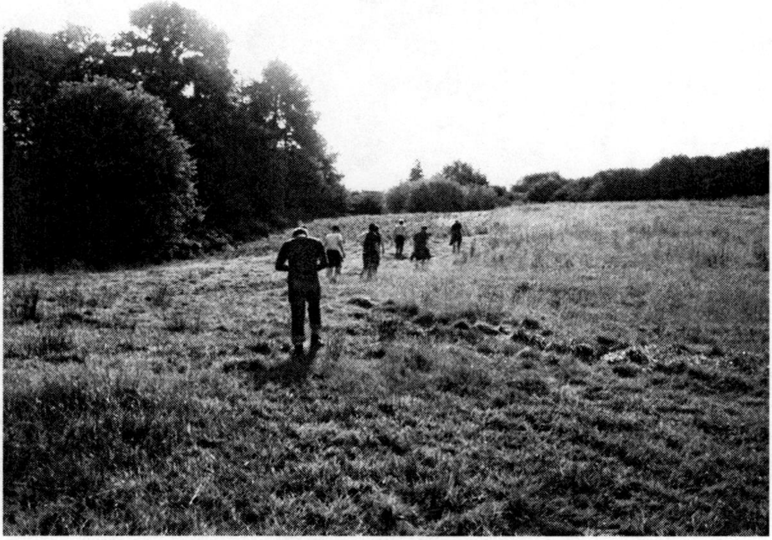

Chapter Thirty-Four

King Henry VI of England married the bartered fifteen-year-old Margaret of Anjou in 1445.

Despite the conditions of the Treaty of Tours, Henry realised that returning Maine and Anjou to Charles and France was tremendously unpopular across England and tried to back out of the stipulations that had bought the beautiful little virgin Margaret for his wedding bed.

Richard Plantagenet, 3rd Duke of York might well have been right to voice his opposition to the union but, at the end of his five-year appointment in France, he never had the opportunity to gloat. Though he saw no reason to believe that his reappointment would not be approved, much to the man's surprise, he was unexpectedly confirmed as Lieutenant of Ireland—a post that might not be so unexpected; seeing that Richard was also earl of Ulster and owned considerable estates in Ireland. To Henry's credit, the ten year appointment quite conveniently extricated the duke of York from his associations with the English in Normandy who opposed the king's policies with France; as well as removing Richard from his power base in Wales.

Shrewd manoeuvring on the part of the House of Lancaster: which, as it turned out, could not have better suited the political aspirations of William ap Thomas.

The duke's Welsh envoy now spent the bulk of his time in nearby London. On the face of it, that would have been the most prudent decision—one ratified by the many bureaucrats with whom he frittered away most of his days; except for the fact that he was married with three children back in Wales. Interestingly enough, his family thought his presence at Windsor a magnificent idea. Though now grown, their father's absence from Raglan meant a life of jubilation for Gwladus and the servants: freed from the fear of William ap Thomas stopping round unexpectedly and thoroughly ruining a perfectly good day.

The Sheriff of Glamorgan was staring straight down the cannon barrel of his own incompetence as a father.

Standing at the kitchen window staring out at an unexpectedly late March snow, the weather had forced William ap Thomas to delay his scheduled trek to Hereford. This meant the work on the battlements atop the tower had to be postponed and the crews would be working upstairs on the fifth floor all morning. The blinding snow had forced him to wait until the worst was over before wrapping a blanket around him and hitting the saddle, which would not have been that much of an inconvenience if he had not had another hellacious fight with Gwladus the evening prior.

His breath had fogged the panes and spoiled his view of the courtyard, so he stepped to his right and came face to face with his own reflection. The man in the glass seemed so much older than he expected. Worn out, he supposed, by the duties at Raglan as a father more than any undertaken for the duke of York.

He just did not understand. Being the fifth son of Thomas ap Gwilym, he had survived far worse treatment from his father and four older brothers than his own children would ever endure. His father was the kind of man who could knock one of his children across the room with a strategically timed backhand, then sit the boy up on his lap and tell him he loved him five minutes later. If it worked for his father then, surely the same should work for his children. After all, he hadn't turned out all that bad.

He blamed Gwladus. It had to be all her mollycoddling when he was out earning enough money to keep the woman in the style to which she had grown accustomed.

Just let him try to stay at home and do nothing but play with three children all day and see what would happen.

In the heat of last night's argument, the bitch had actually suggested that he never talked about anything but himself. For that, she received a good slap across the face; which pretty much ended their conversation for the evening. Still, to be fair, he had spent the last half-hour trying to think through the four or five conversations they had had over the past six months. After serious consideration, he recognized what she had been trying to do.

Yes, he did talk about the useless paperwork and recordkeeping he was forced to turn in each month; but that was part of his responsibilities as Steward. The annoying people that he had to deal with on a daily basis were just as bad and would drive anyone to the point of frustration. And, yes, he did find it annoying when people just didn't listen to him; but, if he was paying them, then they should just shut the hell up and do exactly what he told them.

What had forced the argument to blows was when his wife had the audacity to propose that he had risen to the level of his own incompetence.

That was just silly.

The ungrateful woman had actually suggested that he had simply done what he had always done in every position he had ever held; that the promotions had given him more and more responsibility and challenges until he finally reached the point where he didn't know how to cope with the pressure and obligations and just blamed everyone around him. That was what drove him over the line: the fact that he was somehow responsible for all the dunces, idiots, and incompetents he had to deal with on a daily basis.

He should never have married a woman like Gwladus. This was what happened when men let a woman learn how to read. They get the idea that, just because they have been introduced to intelligence, they somehow might be able to understand the intricacies of how the world actually operates. For that, he blamed her father, Dafydd Gam. Keeping women barefoot and pregnant in the kitchen was the only way men could truly keep women happy. It was just a shame women couldn't see the truth of the situation themselves.

The snow had finally stopped.

"Thank God." He muttered under his breath. The twenty-two workmen banging around upstairs, when combined with the squeals of the housemaids tittering in the pantry, was about to drive him insane.

Snow or no snow, it was time to get back out on the road.

* * * * *

Queues of men lined up in front of the pay tables for the very last time. Edward Ruddel took his customary place as the very last man in line. Most would have tried to save what they could throughout the years rather than simply exchanging their wages every night for alcohol and whores. Since each realised that this was to be their last pay day at Abergavenny, there were men fanning out into the brush-line higgledy-piggledy to collect what they had managed to squirrel away in secret hiding places amidst the trees.

It had long been an unwritten arrangement amongst the workmen: that no one violated the stores and holdings of any other man. Those who had not abided by the code of the masons had been ousted from their midst relatively quickly—given a sound public beating from their peers and quickly relieved of any and all monies found upon their person. It was the crews' way of not only making certain that each man's worldly goods and fortune remained his own; but also of publicly reminding each and every labourer that theft would simply not be tolerated. The practice had worked remarkably well, with the few thieves who could not refrain from stealing from their fellows made an example to those who were still weighing the odds of being caught.

Retrieving small leather purses and folded pieces of vellum out of hollow logs, from under rocks, or scattered holes in the ground; the last shift of Raglan either made their way straight into the village for one last bit of revelry or started down the road in disorganized squadrons of ragged, grubby men. With the village as their centre, hundreds of unskilled labourers spread out in all directions like the ripples of a pond.

All except Edward Ruddel.

The poor soul had absolutely nowhere to go. A vagrant who had simply wandered in from nowhere years earlier, Edward had stayed for the work and the company. He had no serious skills, but had needed none amidst so large a company—being taken under the wing of first Charles Gardiner and, after Charles' death, then Gareth ap Hywel. Having been paid for the last time, Ruddel simply stood there at the table, not entirely sure of how to walk away or really where to go.

The paymasters all turned in their records to Gareth at the head table and then headed home themselves; leaving Edward and the master mason alone on the south lawn of the Great Tower. His former overseer could clearly see the man's dilemma.

Edward Ruddel was by no means a village idiot.

He did not suffer from some congenital mental deficiency. Nor had he fallen into a state of chronic dementia that would have defined him as an imbecile. Strangely enough, Edward's problem was neither one of intermittent periods of lucidity and sanity that might have instantly labelled the man a lunatic. No, it was something entirely different. Though simple, Ruddel was rather extraordinary and altogether rare—he was an inherently decent man.

He was honest to a fault; loyal beyond all calculation and trustworthy, dependable, and consistent. While not one to set out upon his own initiative and certainly not the man to ever leave to lead a crew; Ruddel was most likely the hardest worker Gareth ap Hywel had ever seen. The kind of man whose life simply needed continual direction:

whose common sense would often wander off and leave the man alone.

Gareth had been scratching his dog under the table; trying to keep the animal interested until the last of the men were paid. He rose, looped the crude leash of rope around his wrist, came around the table and sat down next to where Edward was standing.

"So, what do you think?"

Ruddel stepped over and sat down himself; watching the stream of men slowly disappear over the distant hills.

"I was just thinking," Edward clinked the coins in his right hand over and over with the fingers of his left. "That when those men get back home, there will be no celebrations, no congratulations, no 'job well done,' and more than likely nothing for them to do until the next job comes round."

Gareth swivelled his neck to catch glimpses of the crew as they straggled north along the Monmouth Road that would take them straight to Hereford.

"You're probably right."

Ruddel looked up at the great yellow sandstone citadel that had been the sum and total of their lives for so many years.

"But their lives have been changed forever. They have been part of that," he pointed up to the towering sandstone battlements. "Part of something truly significant that will outlive us all," he paused to take it in. "It may well stand for a thousand years. People will live, love, struggle, and die within its walls generations after we have all crumbled back to dust. That makes it truly significant."

Gareth stared up at the ramparts of the Yellow Tower and began to see Edward's point.

"And playing a part in the building of something significant, even in the smallest way, changes a man."

Gareth had underestimated his former employee yet again.

Collecting himself and dropping the coins into his pocket, Edward stood back up and dusted off his trousers with both hands.

"So, where are you going now?"

Still wrestling the head of his terrier between his hands, Gareth nodded toward the northwest and Abergavenny. "Suppose I'll head back to the wife, though after being gone so long, she's likely waiting for me with a hefty stick."

He smiled.

"It'll be like hiking down the road to bang loudly upon the gates of Hell—and wondering just who or what might actually step up to meet you at the gates."

Edward stared down the now empty track.

"Been on the road to Hell most of my life."

Gareth stood and removed the leash to let the dog run free.

"Why don't you come along? He paused for a moment. "Hell was never somewhere I thought of venturing alone."

Ruddel smirked at the couched invitation. Then, without warning, he ran over to the nearest bend of the moat's retaining wall and kicked loose a corner stone. Pulling out two hefty bags of coins, he then tapped the piece back into position with his toe.

No small fortune, Gareth was now convinced Edward must have hardly spent a penny over the years.

"Bloody Hell!"

Ruddel threw the silver into his bag and joined Gareth as the terrier ran on ahead along the track.

"Precisely," Ruddel cinched tight the leather thong and matched Gareth's stride.

"I've heard the path to Hell can be a very thirsty road."

* * * * *

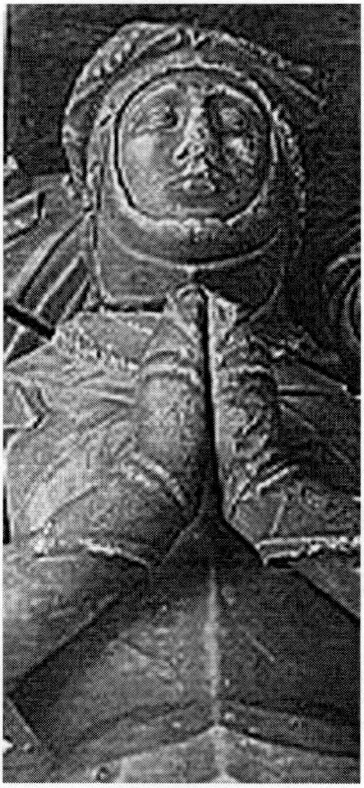

Chapter Thirty-five

Father and son never talked at all about the past.

The elder William simply assumed that his son had come to understand what and why he had done as he had; the younger took Meissel's advice and, in the simplest of terms, just decided not to waste the energy. The end result being that both took the other simply for men and little else. A heritage of parental ambivalence had provided the heir with nothing more than a frugal inheritance of apathy: which was tragic when one considered what might well have been between them; and equally fortunate when taking into account how very little each might have actually taken away. Such is the tragedy of fathers and sons, one might suppose: that neither ever feels adequate appreciation. So, rather than even bother to contest who might have been right or wrong, both decided to cut their losses and simply walk away.

"Nothing makes any difference."

Years of servitude had made William ap Thomas quite cynical. The man had dropped round to see him and his mother on one of those rare occasions when his duties brought him by; and, though father and son had absolutely nothing in common, they stood side by side and took turns skimming pebbles across the moat. It was probably the only thing they had ever willingly done together.

The Steward of the duke of York was off to London for the third time that month and, in a rare moment of candour and reflection, weighed his performance as a father.

"Call me a bastard."

"Say I'm a worthless Son of a Bitch." He paused. "I deserve it."

He raised his chin and tipped back his head to specify the tower. "Tear it down. Knock out the walls. Hell, paint it red; turn it into a brothel and piss on it every day. Or convert the whole damn thing into a church or monastery. It's yours. It's all I have to give you and, for that I'm truly sorry." The old man seemed genuinely upset as he continued, "That all I have to leave you when I'm gone is a worthless pile of stones."

William Herbert did not know exactly how to react. And he did not trust the man he knew as father enough to believe him, even if he wanted to.

"Still," His absentee parent summed up the conversation and the premise of his life, "I suppose you can build any dream—given enough money, time, and stone. And, there's the irony of life right there, my boy. The last of the three you'd ever think to run out first or cherish most is time."

It was the closest William ap Thomas had ever come to offering his son an apology.

He died in London three days later. At the age of forty-five. Alone in a cold, dark room.

The remains of Sir William ap Thomas were brought back to Wales and buried in the Benedictine Priory Church of St. Mary in Abergavenny in the county Gwent. Bards and poets of the day had misspoken; for William ap Thomas had let them down by failing to free Wales from the yoke of England. Still, they came to pay their respects along with everyone else in Monmouthshire. Despite the number of dignitaries, the glowing eulogies from contemporaries who hailed him as a hero for Wales, the burgeoning crowds that ultimately came round to view and touch his effigy: no one in his family mourned the man's passing.

Not a single tear was shed.

As his oldest son stood beside his mother at the funeral, William Herbert wondered if that might be the single, searing indictment of his father's entire existence: that, at the end of the day, no one who really knew him cared whether William ap Thomas lived or died.

In the end, he died as he had lived—utterly alone.

The absentee landlord of an impressive fortified tower the bastard had never time nor inclination to occupy.

* * * * *

Pink wildflowers popped up all along the moat's apron wall; creating a dramatic contrast to the blues and greens of the still water against the reflection of the yellow sandstone of the great Yellow Tower of Gwent.

The late Lord of Raglan's oldest son strolled down from the gate and wandered over across the open lawn to the edge of the forest. At his feet lay the rotting remains of the massive trunk that had tripped his father's horse and led to his brother's death. Herbert kicked at the pithy residue that had managed to survive these fifteen years. It was on this very spot that he had dangled his bare feet off the end; where his imaginary friends had played with him for hours without end: where the lad had hidden in the undergrowth from the horrors of his world.

William wasn't even all that sure what he was looking for. After hundreds of his father's colleagues and associates had paraded up to him and his mother to tell yet again how great a man his father was and how very much he would be missed by everyone who knew him, the new heir simply couldn't take it any more. No matter where he turned in his own house, there was someone standing there with a drink in one hand and an empty platitude in the other.

It had become a petting zoo.

He felt terrible about ducking out, but just had to get away from all the feigned condolences; from the sham of professed commiserations and poorly simulated pity. After a lifetime of battle with his father, William was now the sole survivor of a conflict he had never asked for: left to struggle on by himself for some resolution which the young man now knew he would never find.

Death ends a life but, quite selfishly, never gives solutions: withholds answers and dispenses only outcomes.

He had wanted to come back home to confront his father; perhaps even wishing for a chance or excuse to beat the bastard into the ground with his own bare hands. Now, the young man would be satisfied with some simple resolution to the uninspired skirmish taking place between his heart and head. William Herbert was now convinced that, with his father's cowardly withdrawal by way of the grave, the lifelong quarrel could now never be settled: the game never be won.

For life, it now seemed, clearly was nothing but a game; where each man and woman was merely born and introduced to the world in order to rise to the opposition. Not to win, not to determine who was better—but for the chance at discovering a meaning for it all before Death unilaterally blew the whistle and called the game on count of rain.

William realised the truth, at last.

Underhanded Death would never reveal how much time was ever left in the contest. That and, regardless of how blue the sky might sometimes seem, it will always rain.

* * * * *

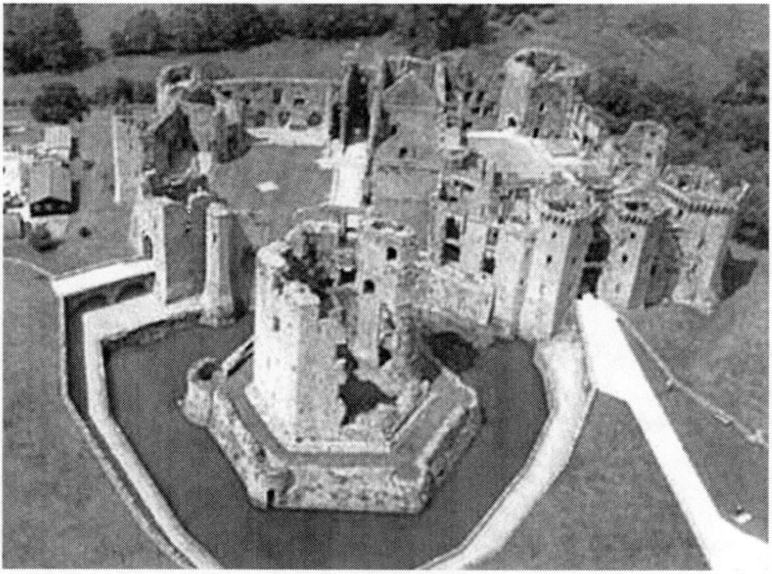

Chapter Thirty-six

Perhaps it was the blood of the warrior William Herbert inherited from his grandfather, Sir Dafydd Gam. It might have been the politics of his father, William ap Thomas, the Blue Knight of Gwent. Then again, he might simply have wanted to see the world as so many young men are want to do.

Whatever the reason, loyalty to king and country or simple wanderlust, the heir of Raglan left the estate of his mother in Wales and joined the forces of Henry VI to serve in the ranks against France.

Some who knew him well believed that the young man was simply looking for an avenue to release a lifetime of pent-up aggression and anger. What with the brewing jealousy between rival factions in England it was, in any case, far easier to distinguish one's enemies upon the field of battle: where good and evil were set against each other in simple, finite terms that everyone could understand.

Knighted himself, he left the sandstone walls of the great Yellow Tower of Gwent to cross the channel with the forces of his countryman, the duke of Somerset. Though fortune found him taken prisoner in Normandy at Formigny in April 1450, he was soon released and opted to return to England to pursue a career as a statesman. Politicians tended to have longer lives: contending more often with knives in their backs rather than swords thrust in their faces.

Raglan proved to be far less of a sanctuary than he had hoped; for his beloved mother, Gwladus died not long after his return, in 1454.

Like chalk and cheese, the funeral of Dafydd's daughter seemed to rip the heart out of county Gwent; where the death of her husband had barely seemed to turn a tear. So beloved had the matriarch of Raglan grown to be, that stories spread all the way to Windsor and London: how three thousand nobles, knights, and crowds of weeping peasantry followed her body through the streets to the Herbert Chapel of St. Mary's Priory Church for her funeral. In his elegy for Gwladus ferch Dafydd, the renowned Welsh poet, Lewys Glyn Cothi, echoed the grief and bereavement of thousands of the woman's admirers when he referred to the gentle mother of William Herbert as *Y seren o Efenni* or "the Star of Abergavenny."

Raglan Castle was not to remain serene and silent for very long.

Spurred on, perhaps, by an even greater appreciation of his mortality, the grandson of Dafydd Gam dedicated himself to extending and enlarging the castle of his father. William Herbert started the new construction almost immediately and, deliberately seeking out the men who had fashioned the hexagonal Great Tower, the son of William ap Thomas made a point to put his old friend Gareth ap Hywel in complete authority over the improvements. The aging master mason even managed to bring Edward Ruddel back to regale the long, hot afternoons.

"Don't tell me, let me guess . . . Stately and Handsome?"

Gareth stepped up to shake the hand of the boy who had grown to knighthood before his very eyes.

William burst out laughing and slapped the mason upon the shoulder.

"Nothing so pretentious." He turned to face the Great Tower with Gareth at his side, then shoved a great roll of plans into the old man's middle from his left.

Both men stood in front of the bridge that spanned the moat to the extensive grounds that led to Raglan Wood.

"I want it to be spectacular. Impressive. Powerful and forceful."

Gareth looked at William with second thoughts.

"You know. Kickass."

The old man grinned and turned back to stare up at the sandstone battlements.

"Now, kickass I can do."

* * * * *

My Lord, the simplest truth may miss man's groans
When he, in conquest of mere piece of land,
Forgets he fights above his father's bones,
And only briefly in the sun may stand.
Despite the gains of life, his finite hand
    May only once caress the timeless stone,
        That stands forever, top the Dark Unknown.

The poetry of Warin of Llanhennock had made a lasting impression upon the new master of Raglan Castle.

Under Gareth ap Hywel's constant supervision, the tonnes of imported sandstone became a veritable palace; unmatched by any building in the county. The master mason then added a palatial double-courtyard mansion and a double drawbridge. A great gatehouse was constructed next to the Yellow Tower, with a pitched stone court and elaborate fountain court featuring a series of formal state apartments for William Herbert and his household.

Kickass, indeed. Gwent had never seen its like.

In conjunction with the ongoing construction of succeeding structures, William Herbert's power and influence grew as well. He became one of the closest advisors to King Edward IV, who made him Baron Herbert of Raglan, Chepstow, and Gower. The boy from Wales was made Privy Councillor, then Chief Justice and Chamberlain of South Wales and, in 1462, was made a Knight of the Garter. In 1467, Sir William Herbert was made Chief Justice of North Wales and Constable of Carmarthen and Cardigan; and in 1468, 1st Earl of Pembroke: one of the first members of the Welsh gentry to ever enter the ranks of English peerage.

For all his accomplishment and sumptuous improvements at Raglan, William Herbert rose to far greater prominence that his father ever dreamed; becoming one of the most influential men in Wales and certainly one of the wealthiest. He had learned two very important lessons from his father. First, that given enough money, time, and stone, one might indeed build any dream. Second and more importantly, the last one of the three a man should ever waste was time.

The earl of Pembroke tried to reside at Raglan Castle as much as possible. Something about his childhood seemed to resonate amidst the Forest of Dean. Every evening, he would take his constitutional out across the drawbridge and down the lane toward the village.

Similarly, Gareth ap Hywel and Edward Ruddel timed their twilight stroll in accordance with that of their Lord. Each night at the same time, they stood in the shadows of the Yellow Tower and watched William Herbert casually stroll along the track. Next to the ruins of the ancient caretaker's cottage, regular as the moon, the shadows of two giant wolfhounds stepped out from the underbrush and joined him on either side.

Their glowing crimson eyes marked Sir William Herbert's progress down the tranquil moonlit lane.

* * * * *

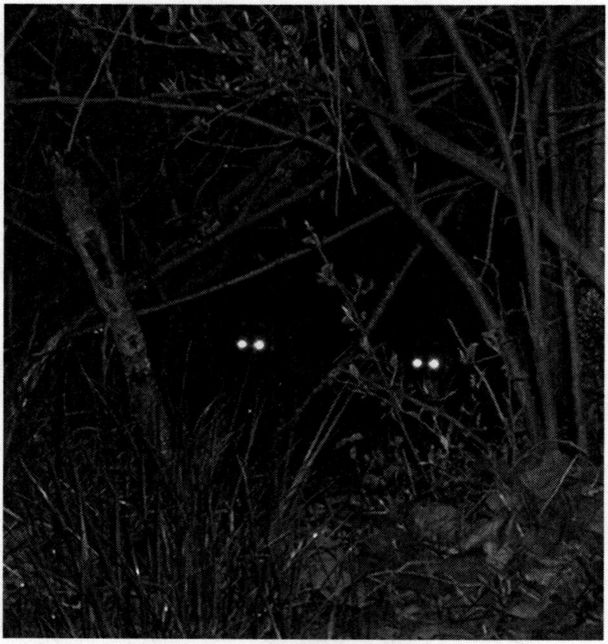

Epilogue

R esolution.

Life was and will ever be rooted in its meaning and shaped by its perception. Through dogged willpower and toughness. In determination and decision. In worth and cost. For two radically different men who had journeyed through their lives; with difficult setbacks early, and impressive victories late: there remained one challenge and one final chance for vindication. For celebration or for sadness.

William Herbert finally realised what his father had been talking about when he had said that nothing really made any difference: what genuinely mattered was to find some resolution he could hold on to until it came round his time to die.

William ap Thomas never gave his son the chance to love his father—Death, equally, never gave William Herbert the opportunity to hate the man as much as he probably deserved. Perhaps his father had known something that last afternoon they had spoken; when he had said that last thing a man ever thinks he'll run out of first or learn to cherish most is Time.

After years of struggling for an answer to a riddle he couldn't even pretend to understand, William Herbert ultimately came to a conclusion. It was weak and feeble; hell, it was downright pathetic. But, for the time being, it was the best resolution his mind could contrive.

The eldest son of Raglan Castle ultimately concluded that both of them had, in some measure, been wrong.

His father never got the point that children will always judge their parents by their actions, not by the reliability of their advice. While Herbert himself determined that, regardless of what everyone thought of his father, it didn't really matter who his father was: what ultimately mattered was how his son chose to remember him.

That realisation, at least for the present, would simply have to do.

THE WRAITHS OF RAGLAN WOOD

* * * * *

In 1455, a young English nobleman by the name of Tudor married a young girl named Margaret Beaufort.

Though only twelve years old, she was already of marriageable age and by her thirteenth birthday, she was already a widow. Only a few months later, Margaret became a teenage mother when her son, Henry, was born on 28 January, 1457 at Pembroke Castle in Wales.

Fatherless and with a mother who was little more than a child herself, young Henry Tudor was entrusted to his paternal uncle, Jasper.

Though tragic and, at first glance, a bit beside the point, this all becomes quite relevant to English history when one remembers that Margaret Beaufort was a descendant of King Edward III through his son, John of Gaunt, and his third wife, Katherine Swynford. Not in a position to take on the responsibility entirely by himself, Jasper Tudor was considering where and with whom to entrust his nephew and his upbringing. He immediately thought of the castle of Sir William Herbert at Raglan.

So, in 1462, the young Henry Tudor, Lord of Richmond, was placed in the custody of Sir William Herbert, earl of Pembroke. This afforded Jasper Tudor the opportunity to campaign for a return to the English throne for the House of Lancaster.

Actually, William Herbert and the boy Henry Tudor had much in common; far more than their lineage and inheritance might convey at first glance. Both were deprived of really knowing their fathers, Henry by untimely death— William by elected abstinence. Each were doted upon by their young mothers, as became immediately evident to Gareth ap Hywel as he continued to daily supervise the hundreds of workmen that were transforming Raglan Castle into the finest palace in Monmouthshire.

The boy Henry had never been given the chance to meet the father that had died only months before his birth. Perhaps that was what touched Gareth most; that he had several fine sons and a flock of grandchildren himself and poor Henry, being a sickly child with no real family around other than his mother, was forced to spend most days at Raglan playing by himself.

It was on a clear evening in May when Gareth was finishing the final inspection of the arched bridge.

The six arched turrets with their battlements had all been meticulously fashioned of square stone and the out-wall had not been completed to the Welshman's scrupulous standards. Rather than be accused of producing shoddy work and knowing that every piece of the project would be scrutinized for possibly hundreds of years, Gareth had supervised the modifications himself. In the gathering twilight, the old man was checking to make certain the mortared corners were perfectly square.

For the first time since the mason arrived at Gwent almost twenty years earlier, there actually seemed to be peace in Raglan Wood. The old man's mind flashed to something he had heard at chapel as a boy.

> 'And I will make with them a covenant of peace, and will cause the evil beast to cease out of the land: and they shall dwell safely in the wilderness, and sleep in the woods.'

He stood there watching the sun drop below the trees and wondered why it had taken so very long.

God was in His heaven, no doubt listening to the tales of Dafydd Gam and thousands of men like him who had buffed away the soot of a thousand years of sadness with their lives.

With sunset came the realization that it was time to finally head home to his own family; that Raglan Wood had ultimately found the peace it had been hunting all along.

A yip of excitement caught the old man's ears and he turned in time to see the small boy bolt up the lane from the forest and scoot across the lawn like a scalded cat. Clambering across the drawbridge at full speed, little Henry Tudor crashed squarely into the stocky Welshman as he stepped around the rail.

"Hold on there, my boy."

The mason used his well-practiced grandfather's voice to try and calm the child. "And where might you be going in such a hellfire hurry?"

The little Lord of Richmond clutched at his chest and sucked in several heavy breaths of air.

"I'm going to the kitchen to get some scraps." He pointed down the lane to where the stones of the ruin still lay amidst the grass.

"I just found two puppies down by the caretaker's cottage."

Gareth straightened up and stared down the road to see four crimson eyes staring straight back at him from atop the tumbled stones that stood above the underbrush.

With trembling hands, Henry pushed the future king of England toward the heavy castle door.

"Dear God," he whispered to himself as he stood there alone and stared into the night.

"The bastards have come back."

* * * * *

DÉNOUEMENT

Richard, 3rd Duke of York went on to lead the opposition against the House of Lancaster in the War of the Roses. On 30 December, 1459, he and his force left Sandal Castle and were annihilated at the Battle of Wakefield.

Richard was killed in the battle and would later be buried at Pontefract, but his head was put on a pike by the victorious Lancastrian armies and displayed over Micklegate Bar at York. He died; never suspecting that his son Edward would become king of England only a few months later. Edward IV ultimately took the throne after a decisive victory over the Lancastrians at the Battle of Towton. He, in turn, died in 1483 and York's youngest son succeeded him as King Richard III.

Young Henry Tudor rose to fame with his defeat of Richard III at the Battle of Bosworth Field and, claiming the throne as Henry VII in 1485, established the Tudor dynasty. He later married Elizabeth of York, the daughter of Edward IV, and was peaceably succeeded by his son, King Henry VIII, after a reign of almost twenty-three years.

Sir William Herbert and his younger brother, Richard, were caught up in the War of the Roses as well. When a rebellion broke out in 1469, Herbert, then Earl of Pembroke, raised an army of Welshmen to face their advance from the north. Both he and Richard were ordered to join a detachment of archers under the command of the earl of Devonshire, one Humphrey Stafford, and meet the rebels at Banbury in Northumberland. Almost immediately after camping at Hedgecote, Stafford and William Herbert were involved in a serious quarrel and the earl of Devonshire simply roused his force and led them away from the field. Though the Battle of Edgecote Moor on 26 July saw desperate fighting between the forces of York and Lancaster, both William Herbert and his younger brother were taken prisoner and beheaded. The body of William, earl of Pembroke was buried in Tintern Abbey, his brother, Sir Richard, in Abergavenny Church.

As for the youngest child of Sir William ap Thomas and Gwladus ferch Dafydd, their daughter Elizabeth Herbert, her story is best divulged as such:

The Wraiths of Raglan Wood

Sir William ap Thomas
The Blue Knight of Gwent
Born 1401 whose daughter was

Elsbeth ferch William (Herbert)
Born 1427
whose son was

Sir Thomas Stradling
(Lady Diana Spencer's 11th Great Grandfather)
Born 1454
whose son was

Sir Edward Stradling
Born 1474
whose daughter was

Catherine Stradling
Born 1512
whose son was

Sir John Palmer
Born 1544
whose son was

William Palmer
Born 1587
whose daughter was

Sarah Palmer
Born 1609
whose son was

Moses Rowley
Born 1632
whose son was

John Rowley
Born 1667
whose daughter was

Sarah Rowley
whose daughter was

Margery Lunsford
Born 1703
whose son was

Robert Traywick
Born 1729
whose son was

George Traywick
Born 1768
whose daughter was

Esther Traywick
Born 1794
whose daughter was

Mary Ann Taylor
whose daughter was

Rachael Ann Jackson
Born 1861
whose son was

George Kanion Colwell
whose daughter was

Annie Bell Colwell
Born 1915
whose daughter was

Alvada Dale Sanders
Born 1936
Whose Son . . .

Wrote This Book

* * * * *

CASTLES CITED IN THE TEXT

Any attempt to list the each and every castle across Britain, as I have stated before in previous publications, would be quite comparable to reducing the London A to Z into one easy to carry laminated card. A great idea: at least until you reach the nine hundredth and realise not only that you haven't even reached half-way, but that no pocket in the world can accommodate the thickness—no matter how tightly you try to fold it.

Some critics may challenge the notion of so much material being presented to the reader regarding the history of individual fortifications and their tenure of ownership to various houses. That would be a mistake. It is only by realising the inherent state of conflict during the period, the scale of investment by the owners, and the importance of these castles to the subsequent development of the region, that modern readers can truly judge their impact on history.

When considering the many castles across Wales and England that might be historically relevant to this particular novel, the author faced an even greater challenge than in previous attempts. Over 1,400 castles in England and 641 castles throughout Wales, if simply named and briefly described, would leave little room between the covers for a story.

As a result, what follows should be regarded as an extremely condensed list of only the specific fortifications alluded to within the text; and, only then, during the years specific to the narrative. To do any more would involve producing an addendum with enough cross-references to challenge the King James Bible.

Perfectionists might find this decision a bit flippant. But then, very few of them have actually sat down and tried to organise such an overwhelming compilation. Most readers merely want enough details to grasp the political environment of Britain and fortresses of the novel anyway; so this abbreviated overview should more than suffice for anyone not compiling a dissertation of their own.

* * * * *

Special appreciation for historical information and research is extended to:

CADW
Welsh Historic Monuments

This organisation conserves, protects, and presents the built heritage of Wales and undertakes the Secretary of State's statutory responsibilities for securing all ancient monuments for the future, for grant-aiding rescue archaeology work, and for offering grants to owners of historic buildings.

* * * * *

Abergavenny Castle

Located in Abergavenny, market town of Monmouthshire in south east Wales.

One of the earliest Norman castles in Wales, the 1081 castle was sited above the River Usk, overlooking the river valley and the union of the River Gavenny with the River Usk on a site that would have been naturally defensible. With steep slopes down to the river on three sides, the remaining side was where the town proper sprang up; incorporating the earlier Roman fort and settlement.

The castle has Norman origins, though the early motte was recorded as being built by Hamelin de Balun as the first Baron Bergavenny; by command of William the Conqueror in 1075. In 1233 AD the castle was sacked by Richard Marshal, 3rd Earl of Pembroke, during his alliance with the Welsh leader, Llywelyn the Great.

Arnallt Castle

Located approximately four miles south-east from Abergavenny, in Monmouthshire—south east Wales.

Less of a timber castle than a relatively heavily fortified manor house, it stood on the east bank of the winding River Usk. For generations, the home of the Chieftains of Upper Gwent. Burned to the ground by Norman troops from Abergavenny under the command of William de Braose (The Ogre of Abergavenny), in 1175; while the residence of Seisyll ap Dyfnwal. de Braose had murdered Seisyll and other Welsh Chieftains after inviting them to Christmas dinner.

Married to Gwladus ferch Gruffydd, The Lord of Gwent Uwchcoed or Upper Gwent, Seisyll was the brother-in-law of Rhys ap Gruffydd, the Lord Rhys, King of Deheubarth.

W. B. BAKER

Arundel Castle

Located: West Sussex, on the river Arun.

Home of the Dukes of Norfolk for over 600 years, Arundel Castle dates from the reign of Edward the Confessor (r. 1042-1066) and was completed by Roger de Montgomery, who became the first to hold the earldom of Arundel by the graces of William the Conqueror.

From the 11th century, the castle has served as a hereditary home to several families and is currently the principal seat of the Duke of Norfolk. Arundel Castle was built in 1068 during the reign of William the Conqueror. After Roger de Montgomery, Arundel Castle and the earldom have passed through generations almost directly since 1138, with only the occasional reversion to the crown and other nobles for a brief time. In 1176, William d'Aubigny died and Arundel Castle then reverted to Henry II, who spent a vast amount of capital re-structuring the building. When Henry died, the castle remained in the possession of Richard I ("the Lionheart"), who offered it to the Aubigny family under William III, count de Sussex. The last in the male line was Hugh Aubigny, who died young in 1243, but when his sister Isabel married John FitzAlan of Clun, the castle and earldom returned to him.

Basingwerk Castle

Also known as Holywell Castle and Bryn-y-Castell.

Located: One mile south of the Dee estuary, approximately half-way between Chester and Rhuddlan.

An earthwork castle, more than likely erected by Norman forces in the early twelfth century within the walls of an even earlier Saxon fortress. Basingwerk Castle overlooks the Holy Well of St Winefride and is thought to have been constructed to protect the lucrative Pilgrim trade attracted to the site. The castle changed hands several times during the territorial struggles that took place between Welsh princes and Norman rulers, before being eclipsed by larger stone castles that proved far more formidable against attack. The motte and bailey castle itself was destroyed during the reign of King Stephen, but was rebuilt by Henry II.

Following an invasion by England, Owain Gwynedd attacked and captured Basingwerk in 1166 and it remained in the hands of the Welsh until burned to the ground by Ranulf III, Earl of Chester. Ranulf then had the castle rebuilt to protect pilgrims to the Well Church, but it was taken again by Welsh forces led by Llywelyn ap Iorwerth. By 1280 the castle was obsolete due to Edward I's construction of a larger stone castle at Flint.

Bowes Castle

Located: In the village of Bowes in County Durham, England. (Formerly North Riding of Yorkshire)

Originally in the corner of the Lavatrae fort (an old Roman fort that guarded the Stainforth Pass) on the Roman road through Stainmore in the Pennine Mountains. Around 1136, Alan, Count of Brittany and Earl of Richmond, started construction in the north-west corner of the ruin. With the death of Alan's son, Earl Conan the Little, ownership of Bowes Castle eventually passed to the Crown.

Between the years of 1171 and 1174, England's King Henry II built a massive stone keep; despite an attack from the north in 1173 under King William I of Scotland—where it was substantially damaged and basically was completely rebuilt in 1187.

In about 1216, enemies of King John again laid siege to the castle. England's forces held and Bowes Castle remained intact until a regional feud between the Earl of Richmond and Henry Fitzhugh in 1322.

The battlements fell into ruin, with only portions of the keep of Henry II remaining intact.

Bramber Castle

Located: In the village of Bramber, West Sussex overlooking the River Adur.

William De Braose constructed this Norman motte-and-bailey castle along with a church around 1070. Except for a period of confiscation during the reign of King John, Bramber Castle remained in the ownership of the De Braose family for almost 250 years; until the family line ultimately died out in 1324. During the period of the Norman invasion, the coastline would most likely extended much further inland with high tide bringing the water line very near the castle walls.

Very little survives of the structure, with hardly more known of Bramber Castle's history. Records kept during the Civil War only mention a 'skirmish' in the village around 1642. Only the ruins of the gatehouse remain to suggest the imposing nature of this castle.

Bronllys Castle

Located: Bronllys, the county town of Powys, Wales.

A motte and bailey fortress standing just outside of Talgarth, Bronllys Castle was founded in or soon after 1144. The district was granted to Walter de Clifford by Roger Fitzmiles, 2nd Earl of Hereford. In 1165, the round tower on the motte caught fire and a stone tumbling from the battlements killed Earl Roger's last surviving brother, Mahel de Hereford. September 1233 saw a force of over 200 men with Walter III de Clifford defending the castle against his father-in-law Llywelyn ab Iorwerth. The castle passed from the Cliffords to the Giffards and eventually the de Bohun Earls of Hereford.

Bronllys Castle was additionally fortified against Owain Glyndwr during his rebellion in the early 1400's, but by 1521 it was categorised as 'beyond repair.'

Caerleon Castle

Located: Caerleon (Welsh: Caerllion) a village on the River Usk in the northern outskirts of the city of Newport, Wales.

Built on the site of a Roman legion fortress or Castra (headquarters for Legio II Augusta from about 75 to 300 AD) and an earlier Iron Age hill fort. The name *Caerleon* is derived from the Welsh for "fortress of the legion"; the Romans themselves named it Isca. A Norman-style motte and bailey castle was erected outside the eastern corner of the old Roman fort, more than likely by the then Welsh Lord of Caerleon, Caradog ap Gruffydd.

Caerleon was an important market and port and presumably became a borough by 1171. Both castle and borough were seized by William Marshal in 1217 and the castle was rebuilt in stone. The remains of many of the old Roman buildings stood until this time and were demolished for their building materials.

Geoffrey of Monmouth established Caerleon as one of the most important cities in Britain in his *Historia Regum Britanniæ*. He attributed a long glorious history from its founding by King Belinus: then making it the location of a metropolitan see, an Archbishopric superior to either Canterbury and York under Saint Dubricius. He was followed by St David, who then transferred the archbishopric to St David's Cathedral.

This builds up to its use by Geoffrey as a Court for King Arthur.

Caerleon is one of the sites most often connected with King Arthur's capital later called Camelot. Although there was no Camelot mentioned in the early Arthurian traditions, these same Arthurian authors contend that Arthur's capital was in Caerleon.

Caerphilly Castle

Located: Caerphilly, (Welsh: Castell Caerffili) approximately twelve miles north of Cardiff, Wales in county borough Caerphilly between Glamorgan and Monmouthshire.

Caerphilly Castle one of the largest Castles in the United Kingdom, built in 1268-1271 by the Anglo-Norman lord, Gilbert de Clare. In 1266 Gilbert de Clare had taken Gruffydd ap Rhys prisoner and started construction of Caerphilly Castle in 1268. Llywelyn ein Llyw olaf completely destroyed the castle in 1270 and, after appealing to Henry III and the Archbishop of York, construction resumed in 1271.

One of Henry III's most powerful and ambitious barons, Gilbert de Clare, lord of Glamorgan, built this, the second largest castle after Windsor. Concentric, with two curtain walls and a pair of moats that extend some thirty acres and form a defensive lake, the west mound was extended south to create a dam across the Nant Gledwr stream, leading to the formation of a large defensive lake south of the main castle. The dam was fortified on both sides and had a gatehouse to the south which received the access road. The central island is the site of the main structure of the castle, which consists of a retaining wall, middle ward with gatehouses located to the west and east, and a secure inner ward with additional gatehouses and circular towers.

In the final phase of construction, the dam was extended to form another lake to the north of the moat and bank, and a further moat and bank to the west, while an outer gatehouse and outwork in the middle of the dam gave access to the west, leading to the village of Caerphilly proper.

Unlike many other 13th-century Welsh castles, Caerphilly was not built by Edward I in his attack on the Welsh clans, but by Gilbert de Clare, as a response to a ongoing dispute with Llywelyn the Last.

The castle enjoyed a relatively peaceful period for approximately a century, but was assaulted in 1294 during the revolt of Madog ap Llywelyn. In 1316, Llywelyn Bren actually succeeded in breaching the outer curtain wall; with the forces of Owain Glyndwr capturing Caerphilly Castle in 1403.

Though some maintenance was undertaken by subsequent owners, Richard Beauchamp, Richard Neville, and Jasper Tudor; the castle fell into disrepair by the beginning of the sixteenth century.

Cardiff Castle

Located: Cardiff, capital of Wales (Welsh: Castell Caerdydd) in county Cardiff, South Glamorgan.

The Norman keep was built c. 1091 by Robert Fiszhamon, lord of Gloucester, on a high motte on the site of a Roman *castra*, first uncovered during the third Marquess of Bute's building campaign. After the failed attempt of Robert Curthose, duke of Normandy, William the Conqueror's eldest son, to take England from Henry I, Robert of Normandy was imprisoned within the walls of Cardiff Castle until his death in 1134. The castle was an important stronghold of Marcher Lords, through the de Clare and le Despenser dynasties, the Beauchamps, Earls of Warwick, and came to Richard of York through his marriage into the Neville family, and then to the Herbert family, Earls of Pembroke.

During the eighteenth century the castle became the property of John Stuart, 3rd Earl of Bute.

W. B. BAKER

Chepstow Castle

Located: Chepstow, county Monmouthshire. (Welsh: *Cas-gwent*) Overlooking the river Wye, Chepstow is the oldest surviving stone fortification in Britain.

Built under the instruction of Norman Lord William fitz Osbern, Earl of Hereford, from 1067, and was the southernmost of a chain of castles built along the English-Welsh border in the Welsh Marches.

The speed with which William the Conqueror committed to the creation of a castle at Chepstow was testament to its strategic importance. There is no evidence for a settlement there of any size before the Norman invasion of Wales. However, it was an important crossing point on the River Wye, a major artery of communications inland to Monmouth and Hereford.

Welsh kingdoms in the area were independent of the English Crown and castle Chepstow helped suppress the Welsh from attacking Gloucestershire along the Severn shore towards Gloucester. The castle and the associated Marcher lordship were generally known as Striguil until the late 14th century, and as Chepstow thereafter. Further fortifications were added by William Marshal, Earl of Pembroke, starting in the 1190s. Marshal extended and modernised the castle, drawing on his knowledge of warfare gained in France and the Crusades.

In 1270, the castle was inherited by Roger Bigod, 5th Earl of Norfolk. The castle was visited by King Edward I in 1284, at the end of his triumphal tour through Wales.

From the 14th century, and in particular the end of the wars between England and Wales in the early 15th century, its defensive importance saw a marked decline. In 1312, it passed into the control of Thomas de Brotherton, Earl of Norfolk, and later his daughter Margaret. Though garrisoned in response to the 1403 rebellion of Owain Glyndwr with twenty men-at-arms and sixty archers, its great size, limited strategic importance, geographical location and the size of its garrison all probably contributed to Glyndwr's forces avoiding attacking it.

In 1468, the castle was part of the estates granted by the Earl of Norfolk to William Herbert, Earl of Pembroke in exchange for lands in the east of England. In 1508, it passed to Sir Charles Somerset, later the Earl of Worcester, who remodelled the buildings extensively as private accommodation. From the 16th century, after the abolition of the Marcher lords' autonomous powers by King Henry VIII through the Laws in Wales Acts of 1535 and 1542, and Chepstow's incorporation as part of the new county of Monmouthshire, the castle became more designed for occupation as a great house.

Conisbrough Castle

Located: Conisbrough, South Yorkshire, England.

Conisbrough Castle was, more than likely, built by Hamelin Plantagenet on the site of an earlier Norman castle and passed to the Warrene family. Prominent and wealthy, the Warenne family also held Sandal Castle near Wakefield, Reigate Castle in Surrey, and Lewes Castle in Sussex.

The name Conisbrough itself is believed to be a derivation of the Anglo-Saxon *Cyningesburh*—meaning 'the defended *burh* of the King', implying that the area once belonged to one of the Anglo-Saxon kings, prior to the Battle of Hastings.

At the time of the Norman Conquest the manor of Conisbrough was held by King Harold, who died from wounds received upon the field.

The Yorkshire lands ceded to The Crown on the death of John de Warenne, 8th Earl of Surrey, as he died without an heir in 1347.

Dinefwr Castle

Located: Near Llandeilo in Carmarthenshire, Wales; Dinefwr Castle overlooks the River Tywi (Towey).

Standing upon a ridge on the northern bank of the Tywi, with a steep drop of several hundred feet down to the river, Dinefwr was the chief seat of the kingdom of Deheubarth.

According to legend, a castle was first constructed on this site by Rhodri the Great. Dinefwr later became the chief seat of Rhodri's grandson Hywel Dda, the first ruler of Deheubarth and later king of most of Wales. Rhys ap Gruffydd, ruler of Deheubarth from 1155 to 1197 is thought to have rebuilt the castle. Rhys ap Gruffydd also built the castle at Carreg Cennen, only four miles to the south.

Upon the death of Rhys ap Gruffydd, Dinefwr Castle passed to his son Rhys Gryg. Llywelyn the Great of Gwynedd was now extending his influence to this area, and Rhys, finding himself unable to defend Dinefwr, dismantled the castle rather than give it over to Llywelyn. Not to be denied, Llywelyn had it restored and held it until his death in 1240.

Dingestow Castle

(Welsh: *Llanddingad*)

Located: Three miles south of Monmouth and approximately the same distance north-east of Raglan in the village of Dingestow in Monmouthshire, south-east Wales.

Once the site of a Norman motte and bailey castle, Ranulph de Poer, the Sheriff of Herefordshire, started to build a stone castle at Dingestow. With a sheer drop to the river on one side and a dry gorge on the other, the banks of the earthen and timber hill fort made it quite easy to defend. Perfectly situated to secure the Raglan corridor into south Wales, any fortification at Dingestow could quite easily protect access across the river Trothy.

The stone structure began by Ranulph de Poer was destroyed by Rhys ap Gruffydd, the Lord Rhys, King of Deheubarth in 1182.

Dover Castle

Located: Dover in Kent, on the channel coast of England.

Begun in 1066, but largely a product of Henry II's expansion in 1170, it was during his reign that Dover Castle actually began to take recognisable shape. The inner and outer baileys and the great Keep belong to this period. When Louis VIII of France crossed the channel and attempted to take the English, he actually had limited success in breaching the walls of Dover but was unable ultimately to take the castle. The vulnerable north gate that had been cracked open during the siege was converted into an underground forward-defence complex and new gates built into the outer curtain wall on the western and eastern sides.

During the 13th century, King John ordered the building of underground tunnels connected to sallyports in order to surprise any attacking troops. After being abandoned for more than a century after the Napoleonic wars, tunnels under Dover Castle were later used as a military command centre during WWII.

Fotheringhay Castle

Located: Fotheringhay, civil parish of Northampton, England. The castle lies six kilometres (four miles) north east of Oundle and sixteen kilometres (ten miles) west of Peterborough.

Fotheringhay is most noted for being the site of Fotheringhay (or Fotheringay) Castle; razed to the ground in 1627. There is nothing left of the castle to be seen today other than the motte on which it was built overlooking the River Nene.

As the home of the great Yorkist line the village was, for a considerable part of the 15th and 16th centuries, of national standing. The death of Richard III at Bosworth Field altered its history irrevocably. The first written mention of a settlement here was in 1060, and the Domesday Book lists the site as 'Fodringeia'. John Leland wrote this as 'Foderingeye' or "Fodering inclosure", referring to the section of the forest that is segregated for the purpose of producing hay. During the medieval period the village was variously mentioned as Foderingey, Foderinghay, Forderinghay, and Fotheringhaye.

Access to the village was formerly via a ford of the Nene adjacent to the former castle site. The first bridge built was ordered by Elizabeth I in 1573. The present bridge was built by George Portwood of Stamford in 1722 under the orders of the Earl of Nottingham, then proprietor of the estate.[1]

During the Middle Ages, it hosted a weekly market, held between at least the start of the fourteenth century and around the mid-fifteenth century, and was also the site of an annual fair beginning on the eve of <u>the feast of St Michael</u>. The lordship of the town and the castle passed through many hands through the years. From the Earl of Newport, the lordship passed to Sir George Savile, Marquis of Halifax, and thence to his son, William Savile, the second Marquis, who died without issue. The manor and castle were then sold by his father-in-law, Daniel, Earl of Nottingham, to Edgeley Hewer, who died without issue on Nov. 6, 1728, when it passed to Hewer's heirs, the Blackborne family.

After the manor came into the possession of <u>Edward III</u> he passed it to his son <u>Edmund of Langley, 1st Duke of York</u>, founder of the Yorkist line. The castle then became the home of the <u>Dukes of York</u>. <u>Richard III</u> was born there in 1452, and his father, <u>Richard Plantagenet, 3rd Duke of York</u> was re-buried at the nearby church in 1476. His wife, <u>Cecily Neville</u>, Duchess of York, was interred in a tomb opposite. Fotheringhay is also where <u>Mary, Queen of Scots</u> was tried and <u>beheaded</u> in 1587, and her body lay there for some months before burial. It later fell into such disrepair that it had to be pulled down, and the stones were all taken to be used in other local buildings.

W. B. Baker

Grosmont Castle

Located: Grosmont, county town of Monmouthshire, Wales. Approximately eight miles northeast of Abergavenny; between Hereford, Abergavenny, and Monmouth.

Grosmont Castle, now in ruins, would have been founded after the time of William FitzOsbern, 1st Earl of Hereford. Earl William was killed within twelve months, with his son, Roger de Breteuil, 2nd Earl of Hereford, being stripped of his lands by the crown in 1075. The land on which Grosmont castle was built then passed either under the control of the de Ballun family of Abergavenny or the de Lacys of Weobley, Ludlow and Longtown. Marcher Lord Pain FitzJohn acquired Grosmont during the reign of King Henry I and converted it into the seat of his lordship.

The early hall at Grosmont was most probably built within forty years either side of 1110. Both the first Earls of Hereford and Pain FitzJohn had great financial resources and ruled Gwent at a time when the stable rule of the Normans in Wales seemed inevitable. Grosmont Hall is certainly not a fortress. It was built as the administrative centre of a barony with both comfort and administration in mind.

Rebellion erupted across Wales in 1134 and in July 1137, Pain Fitz John was killed. Immediately before his untimely death, Pain had granted all his honour of Grosmont to King Stephen in exchange for the province of

Archenfield. With the rebellion of 1139, Brien FitzCount of Abergavenny took Grosmont Castle from the King and in 1142 granted it by charter to Walter of Hereford. When Walter was killed around 1160 fighting in the Holy Land, Henry II regained possession and the castle remained a royal fortress for the next forty years and in 1201 was granted to Hubert de Burgh 'for his maintenance' during the conflicts of the period.

After the death of King John in 1216, Hubert regained his castles in the Welsh Marches in 1219. It was Hubert who was responsible for turning the administrative castle of Grosmont into a fortress. In 1233 the castle witnessed the rout of Henry III's army by rebel Welsh and English forces, which included Earl Hubert de Burgh. In the aftermath Hubert was again granted Grosmont and held it until his final fall from grace in 1239.

In 1267 King Henry III granted the castle to his second son Edmund Crouchback, 1st Earl of Lancaster, who undertook the conversion of the fortress into one of the Earl's main residences. He demolished one of Hubert Burgh's D-shaped towers and built accommodation over it and raised the height and extended the south-west tower to make it into a five-storeyed great tower similar to that of Raglan.

Kenilworth Castle

Located: Kenilworth, Warwickshire, England. Historically, within the Forest of Arden.

The current ruin of Kenilworth is of Norman origin; consisting of a great square stone tower built by Geoffrey de Clinton in about 1125. Henry II took control of the castle during the Revolt of 1173-1174, bestowing the Clinton family another castle in the county of Buckinghamshire in compensation.

Work immediately commenced to enhance the defensive qualities of Kenilworth, which continued to the reign of Henry III and converted the castle into, quite arguably, one of the strongest in the Midlands. With walls twenty feet thick, a great man-made lake was created to defend three sides of the castle. Extending over 100 acres, it was no small investment, but the barrier kept siege engines out of range of the castle's walls.

Kenilworth Castle was regularly used for tournaments throughout the medieval period, as being one of the only five such licensed venues throughout England.

Knaresborough Castle

Located: Knaresborough, county of North Yorkshire. Overlooking the river Nidd.

Situated at the top of a large cliff, with a commanding view of the River Nidd and the Forest of Knaresborough, the castle ruins do not convey its important role in the development of the English nation. For most of its history, Knaresborough Castle has been in royal control, and it has retained this long tradition to the present day.

It is now in the possession of the Crown, as part of the Queen's inheritance of the Duchy of Lancaster.

Very little is known about the early history of Knaresborough, and origins of the castle are equally obscure. The first reference to the town is from 1086 in the Domesday Book, and although much of 'Chednaresburg' was in the possession of the King, there is no mention of the castle. The earliest castle at Knaresborough was established after the Norman conquest, predating the standing fourteenth century remains by nearly 200 years. In 1170, when Hugh de Moreville held the castle, he and his followers took refuge there after they had murdered Thomas a Beckett in Canterbury.

King John maintained Knaresborough Castle as one of his administrative strongholds in the North and is reputed to have spent more money on the castles at Knaresborough and Scarborough than on any others in the country.

Knaresborough repaid his patronage, and was held for the Crown during the Baron's Revolt in 1215-16.

In the early 14th century King Edward I began a programme of modernisation at Knaresborough Castle, and made repairs. When Edward of Caernarvon succeeded his father Edward I to become King of England, the country lost a strong ruler to a weaker man, who was influenced by unpopular favourites. Piers Gaveston was the first of these men to gain Edward's favour, and in 1307, Edward II granted the Honour and Castle of Knaresborough to Gaveston. In reality the estate remained in the King's control, and a substantial amount of money from the royal purse was spent on the Castle.

Edward II's reign was marked by continuing internal friction amongst powerful factions, and ever increasing raids by the Scots into northern England. This general unrest led to rebellion and on 5 October in 1317, Knaresborough Castle was seized by supporters of the Earl of Lancaster, and held against the King. The Constable spent £55 to mount an attack to retake his own castle, and used a siege engine to breach the curtain wall and recapture it three months later. In 1318 the raiding Scots penetrated as far south as Knaresborough.

In 1331, Edward III's wife Queen Philippa received the Honour and Castle of Knaresborough as part of her marriage settlement.

It may have been memories from his childhood spent in Knaresborough that encouraged John of Gaunt, in 1372, to give up his properties in Richmond for the Honour and

Castle of Knaresborough and the Honour of Tickhill. As Duke of Lancaster, John of Gaunt had a large inheritance including many castles of great importance. Knaresborough from that time onwards was joined to these estates and belonged to the Duchy of Lancaster.

Upon John of Gaunt's death in 1399, King Richard II confiscated the Lancastrian estates as the property of the Crown, disinheriting Henry Bolingbroke, John of Gaunt's son and heir. Henry returned to claim his inheritance, landing at Ravenspur, and travelling to receive support from his Castles at Pickering, Knaresborough and Pontefract This confrontation eventually led to the downfall of King Richard II, who was deposed and imprisoned. Henry Bolingbroke's ascendance to the throne as King Henry IV brought the lands of the Duchy of Lancaster directly under the control of the Crown, and Knaresborough was a royal castle once again.

It remained directly in control of the Crown throughout this period, except from 1422 to 1437 when it formed part of Queen Catherine's dower, when her husband King Henry V died.

W. B. Baker

Lewes Castle

Located: Lewes, county of East Sussex. Originally known as Bray Castle. Overlooking the river Ouse on the edge of the South Downs.

William the Conqueror returned to Normandy in 1067, and made grants of land, including the town of Lewes, to one of his lords and his brother-in-law, William de Warenne. In 1075 the King appointed Warenne joint Chief Justiciar, and soon after that he became the first Earl of Surrey.

Lewes Castle was built in 1087 and William de Warenne and his descendants also had estates and built castles in Reigate, Surrey and in Yorkshire at Sandal Castle and Conisbrough Castle. When the last of the Warennes, John, the 8th Earl died without issue in 1347, his title passed to his nephew Richard Fitzalan who was also Earl of Arundel. As there was no legitimate heir upon his death in 1347, Lewes Castle became untenanted, and passed into the hands of the earls of Arundel.

The first fortification on the site was a wooden keep, later converted to stone. Lewes Castle is unusual for a motte and bailey construction in that it has two mottes. It is one of only two such remaining in the country.

Monmouth Castle

Located: Monmouth, county seat of Monmouthshire in south east Wales. Overlooking the river Monnow, it stands close to the centre of the town.

Once an important border castle, it stood until the English Civil War when it was damaged and changed hands three times before suffering the indignity of slighting to prevent it being fortified again. After partial collapse in 1647, the site was reused and built over by Castle House.

It was built by William Fitz Osbern, 1st Earl of Hereford, the castle builder, in around 1067 to 1071 and shares some similarities with Chepstow Castle, another of Fitz Osbern's designs further south on the river Wye in Monmouthshire.

Initially Monmouth was simply a fairly typical border castle presided over by a Marcher Lord and similar in style and status to its neighbours Grosmont Castle, Skenfrith Castle, White Castle (Wales) or Abergavenny Castle.

In 1267 Monmouth Castle passed into the hands of Edmund Crouchback, Earl of Lancaster and son of King Henry III of England, who redeveloped the castle and expanded it as his main residence in the area. It was also improved by Henry of Grosmont, 1st Duke of Lancaster.

The castle was a favourite residence of Henry Bolingbroke, later King as Henry IV. It was here that in 1387 the future King Henry V of England was born, to Bolingbroke's first wife Mary de Bohun.

The turmoil and conflict in Wales during the ten years of the Owain Glyndwr rebellion did not directly affect Monmouth Castle as it was a stronghold of the region and lesser targets presented themselves more readily to essentially a guerrilla army. However other local towns, settlements and castles were directly attacked with Grosmont and Abergavenny being razed and Crickhowell Castle and Newport Castle successfully attacked.

It is one of the few British castles in continuous military occupancy.

Newport Castle

Located: Newport in county Monmouthshire. (Welsh: Castell Newydd) Name comes from reference to 'old' castle at nearby Caerleon or older castle on Stow Hill.

Newport Castle was built between 1327 and 1386 by Hugh de Audley, 1st Earl of Gloucester, or his son-in-law Ralph, Earl of Stafford as one of their castles. It replaced the earlier bailey castle on Stow Hill, which had been destroyed in conflict. The newer castle, while possessing a strong structure, was never needed for military purposes. It was sacked by the forces of Owain Glyndwr during the early 1400s and never really recovered. In the early fifteenth century the castle was occupied by Humphrey Stafford, the first Duke of Buckingham. After Humphrey Stafford had left the castle, it became abandoned.

Newport Castle had an active life of just 200 years and was only rarely involved in political situations. It served more as an administrative base for the Lordship of Wentloog.

Now that the castle has been neglected for so long, the east side is the only part of the castle to survive.

Orford Castle

Located: Approximately twelve miles northeast of Ipswich in the village of Orford, Suffolk, England.

Built between 1165 and 1173 by Henry II of England. In a region controlled by the Bigod family, heirs to the title of Earl of Norfolk and owners of Framlingham Castle, Hugh Bigod, 1st Earl of Norfolk, dissented against the Crown.

In 1177, Henry the Young King, Henry II's oldest child, rebelled against his father and the 1st Earl of Norfolk supported the son over the king. This predictably led to the garrison of Orford Castle by soldiers of the Crown and, with the eventual collapse of the rebellion, also led to the confiscation of Bigod's Framlingham Castle by Henry II.

Orford Castle was captured by Prince Louis of France, who invaded England in 1216 at the gracious invitation of English barons disenchanted with the king. The River Alde eventually silted up to a point that shipping could no longer be viable and the castle was eventually sold.

Pontefract Castle

Located: Pontefract, county of West Yorkshire. Site of demise of Richard II of England.

The castle was first constructed in approximately 1070 by Ilbert de Lacy on land which had been granted to him by William the Conqueror as a reward for his support during the Norman conquests. There is, however, evidence of earlier occupation of the site. Initially the castle was a wooden structure, but this was replaced with stone over time.

Robert de Lacy failed to support Henry I of England during his power struggle with his brother and confiscated the castle from the family during the 1100s. The de Lacys lived in the castle until the early 14th century. It was under the tenure of the de Lacys that the magnificent donjon was built.

In 1311 the castle passed by marriage to the estates of the House of Lancaster. Thomas, Earl of Lancaster was beheaded outside the castle walls six days after his defeat at the Battle of Boroughbridge, a sentence placed on him by King Edward II himself in the great hall. This resulted in the earl becoming a martyr with his tomb at Pontefract Priory becoming a shrine. Later John of Gaunt, a son of Edward III of England, as Duke of Lancaster was so fond of the castle that he made it his personal residence, spending vast amounts of money improving it.

Richard II of England was probably murdered within the castle walls, in the Gascoigne Tower.

William Shakespeare's play Richard III mentions this incident:

Pomfret, Pomfret! O thou bloody prison,
Fatal and ominous to noble peers!
Within the guilty closure of thy walls
Richard the second here was hack'd to death;
And, for more slander to thy dismal seat,
We give thee up our guiltless blood to drink.

In 1536, Pontefract Castle was handed over to the leaders of the Pilgrimage of Grace, a Catholic rebellion from northern England against the rule of King Henry VIII. The castle's guardian, Lord Darcy, was later executed for this alleged "surrender," which the King viewed as an act of treason.

Pontefract Castle has a long and tumultuous history, having being besieged three times, witnessed the alleged murder of a king and being the last fortress to hold for King Charles during the English Civil War.

The town of Pontefract was an important settlement during medieval times, being situated close to the Great North Road from London to Edinburgh. A timber fortress was constructed on the site of the present stone castle, shortly after the Norman Conquest of 1066. A stone castle was constructed by the de Lacy family, early in the thirteenth century and its seven towered design and high aspect ensured that it dominated the town and surrounding area.

The de Lacys were a prominent Yorkshire family, and in the late twelfth century, one of the family, John de Lacy, married the Countess of Lincoln, after which the de Lacys became known as the Earls of Lincoln.

In 1322, Thomas Earl of Lancaster, who had married Alice, the daughter of the last Earl of Lincoln, opposed King Edward II and was tried for treason at Pontefract Castle and executed on a nearby hill.

John of Gaunt, son of Edward III, became custodian of the castle in 1361 and sheltered in the castle during the Peasant's Revolt, when he was at risk during the uprising. Pontefract was one of the Black Prince's favourite residences and he spent large amounts of money improving the buildings.

During the late Middle Ages, Pontefract Castle, as one of the most important castles in the North of England, acted many times as a royal prison, most notably for King Richard II, who was allegedly murdered there. King James of Scotland and Charles, Duc D'Orleans were also imprisoned here and the Lancastrian armies used the castle as a base from which to set out to the Battle of Wakefield, during the Wars of the Roses.

Raglan Castle

Located: North of the village of Raglan, county Monmouthshire. (Welsh: Castell Rhaglan).

Its origins lie in the 12th century but the ruins visible today date from the 15th century and later. The peak of the power and splendour of the castle was attained in the 15th century and 16th century, as the Marches fortress of the great family of Herbert.

The castle was the boyhood home of Henry Tudor, later King Henry VII, who was placed in the custody of William Herbert during the War of the Roses.

Raglan castle is undoubtedly the finest late medieval fortress-palace in Britain. A lavish proclamation of the success of an entrepreneurial Welsh family, it was begun, probably on the site of a small Norman castle, during the 1430's by Sir William ap Thomas.

His still more successful son William Lord Herbert, Yorkist viceroy in Wales during the War of the Roses, added a palatial double courtyard mansion, luxurious within but defended by a formidable gatehouse and many towered walls. Like his father, he imitated fashionable French building styles and employed expert masons whose trademarks can still be seen on Raglan's finely dressed sandstone walls.

Reigate Castle

Located: Reigate, county of Surrey. Approximately twenty-two miles south of London; four miles west of Bletchingly Castle and five miles east of Betchworth Castle.

Reigate Castle is a late 11th century earthwork ring-motte and bailey fortress, founded by William de Warenne. In the 12th century, the earls of Surrey founded the stone castle, which was strengthened in the late 14th century. The site was ruinous by 1441 and after being occupied in the Civil War, the fortifications were slighted in 1648.

King William I granted the land around Reigate to one of his supporters, William de Warenne, who was created Earl of Surrey in 1088. It is believed that his son, William de Warenne, 2nd Earl of Surrey, ordered Reigate Castle be built.

In 1216 the castle was briefly taken by Louis the French Dauphin. In 1347 the castle became the property of Fitzalan, Earl of Arundel. From 1397 it was owned by a number of Lords of the Manor of Reigate, including the influential Howard family.

None of the original castle buildings have survived, with the exception of the Barons' Cave.

W. B. Baker

Rochester Castle

Located: East bank of the River Medway, in Rochester, Kent.

Rochester Castle is one of the best-preserved castles of its kind in the UK. There has been a castle on the site since the Roman occupation (c AD43), though it is the central keep of 1127 and the Norman castle which can be seen today. The Norman period commenced with the victory of William of Normandy at the Battle of Hastings; thereafter appointing his half brother Odo, Bishop of Bayeux, as Earl of Kent. Rochester's first Norman castle was probably of the earlier motte and bailey type on Boley Hill.

Henry I granted the custody of the castle to the Archbishop of Canterbury, William de Corbeil. It was he who started the construction of the great stone keep in 1127, much of which survives to this day. At 113 feet high with walls of ragstone as thick as 12 feet, Rochester Castle remains the tallest and certainly one of the finest Norman keeps in the whole of England and has dominated the city of Rochester for 800 years.

Sandal Castle

Located: Edge of city of Wakefield. County of West Yorkshire, England. Overlooks the river Calder.

Sandal began as a motte castle of the 12th century, consisting of a motte about 45 ft high with its own ditch opposite a horseshoe-shaped bailey. It has been suggested that Sandal Castle passed from royal ownership to William de Warrenne the second earl of Surrey between 1106 and 1121.

After 1200, the castle was converted to stone, with the building continuing to about 1280. With the death of the 3rd earl in 1150, the property passed to his daughter. She married Hamelin Plantagenet, natural half brother of Henry II, who became the earl in right of his wife. Hamelin was the builder of Conisborough Castle around 1180-90 and it was Hamelin who began the stone conversion at Sandal.

It is unclear whether or not Sandal remained in this family's hands until the line lapsed with the death of John de Warrenne in 1347, at which time the family's Yorkshire estates passed back to the king, Edward III, as in 1317 King Edward II granted the manor of Sandal to Lord d'Amory as a reward for his services at the Battle of Bannockburn. From 1353, Sandal was held by Edmund of Langley, Duke of York, 5th son of York, and his successors. Sandal was one of the chief residences of Richard, Duke of York.

Edward in turn granted Sandal and other northern holdings of the Warennes to his fifth son Edmund of Langley who was six years old at the time. Alongside his more vigorous elder brother John of Gaunt (who built up a Yorkshire base with Pontefract Castle and Knaresborough Castle), Edmund grew his estates more gradually, over time being granted Wark Castle near Coldstream in the Scottish Borders, and in 1377 Fotheringhay Castle in Northamptonshire, and for the next 75 years the family seems to have spent little time at Sandal, leaving it to the management of constables or stewards. In 1385 Edmund was made Duke of York as a reward for his support for his nephew, Richard II of England.

In December, 1460, the Duke and his son Edmund, Earl of Rutland, were killed in a skirmish against Lancastrians near Wakefield and the castle passed to the Duke's eldest son Edward, who had become Edward IV after the Battle of Towton. Sandal was also one of the two headquarters of the Council of the North, beginning in 1484. Richard III spent some time at Sandal Castle, though in 1558 it was transferred to the Duchy of Lancaster. Eight years later Elizabeth I granted it to several private owners, who could not afford to maintain it.

By 1592, the castle was a ruin.

Skenfrith Castle

Located: Skenfrith, (Welsh: Ynysgynwraidd) on the banks of the river Nonnow. Five miles north of Monmouth, Wales in county Gwent.

The first defences were built shortly after the Norman Conquest of 1066, although the remains of the castle that stand today date from the early thirteenth century.

Grouped with Grosmont Castle and White Castle, Skenfrith is one of the "Three Castles" or Trilateral Castles built in the Monnow Valley as part of the Norman conquest of South Wales. The Three Castles are customarily grouped together for the reason that, during most of their history, they were held under the control of a single lord.

There is little evidence of building activity at any of the castles until the late twelfth century, when they were fortified by Ralph of Grosmont, a royal official who supervised building work for the king in Hereford. The castles were then completely overhauled by Hubert de Burgh, who was granted lordship of the Three Castles in 1201 by King John. Although control of the Three Castles was briefly granted to William de Braose in 1205, when Hubert was a prisoner of Philip Augustus of France, de Braose quickly fell out of favour and, by 1207, the King had systematically forced him into financial ruin. Hubert de Burgh returned to power and was appointed Justiciar in 1215.

After Hubert de Burgh, the Three Castles were held in royal hands, and in 1254 Henry III granted them to his eldest son, the future Edward I. In the 1260's, the southern March was threatened by the Welsh Prince Llewelyn ap Gruffudd, who annexed the lordship of Brecon, and attacked Abergavenny. Although Llewelyn's attack on Abergavenny actually failed, the Treaty of Montgomery in 1267 recognized his southern conquests, and he was considered a significant threat.

1267 saw the Three Castles being granted to Edward's younger brother Edmund, Earl of Lancaster. Although the Welsh threat was soon subdued with the death of Llywelyn in 1282, the Three Castles were used as residences and centres for local authority. Skenfrith passed down through the earls of Lancaster until the death of Henry of Grosmont, Duke of Lancaster, whose daughter Blanche married John of Gaunt, son of Edward III. John and Blanche's son, Henry of Bolingbroke, deposed Richard II in 1399 and became King Henry IV, at which time the Three Castles also became royal possessions once more.

Although the Three Castles briefly saw action during the rebellion of Owain Glyndwr in 1404-05, they never again played a major role in military affairs. Henry VI carried out repairs to White Castle and Skenfrith Castle in the mid fifteenth century, but by 1538, Skenfrith was abandoned.

Usk Castle

Located: Usk, central county of Monmouthshire, south east Wales.

Usk castle and town was probably laid out and established in 1120, after some of the other Norman settlements and castles of the region, such as Monmouth Castle and Abergavenny Castle. However, the site had a history of previous military, strategic, and local significance, for it was here that the Romans had established their early Legionary fortress before relocating it south to Caerleon.

Usk is first mentioned in 1138 in the context of it being captured by the Welsh. It passed back into Norman hands, only to be captured by the Welsh again in 1174, as was Abergavenny, when turmoil again developed into open conflict in this area of the Welsh Marches.

The Normans had to control and subjugate the region, and brought in Marcher Lord Richard Fitz Gilbert de Clare who sought to strengthen the castle's defences against Welsh attack, but he was ambushed and killed north of Abergavenny in 1136. The Welsh duly captured Usk castle again in 1184.

William Marshal was the next Marcher Lord to strengthen Usk castle. However, his conflict with King Henry III of England brought the Normans new headaches.

Gilbert de Clare, 8th Earl of Hertford, another holder of Usk castle, was killed at the Battle of Bannockburn when the English crown's focus was on defeating the Scots, and the castle was untroubled until the early 15th century.

The rebellion of Owain Glyndwr, between 1400 and 1405, brought significant conflict to the area once again, and the Welsh forces of Owain Glyndwr attacked Usk town in 1402. The Battle of Pwll Melyn was fought nearby, and the region only stabilised under the efforts of local Welsh warrior and ally of King Henry IV of England and Monmouth-born Henry V, Dafydd Gam.

After the rebellion, the castle passed to the hands of the Duchy of Lancaster, and, with stability restored, the castle needed no further redevelopment and refortification, and was allowed to gradually decay.

Wallingford Castle

Located: Wallingford, county of Oxfordshire, adjacent to the River Thames.

Wallingford Castle was built between 1067 and 1071 by Robert D'Oyly on orders from William the Conqueror. It was strengthened by Brien FitzCount before the wars between Empress Matilda and King Stephen.

The castle was subsequently faced with three separate sieges and during the third siege of Wallingford Castle in 1152, the king's men took both the bridge and the town proper and besieged the castle for an entire year before Matilda's son, Henry, the Duke of Normandy, finally arrived to relieve the garrison. King Stephen moved to personally lead troops against Wallingford, but terms were ultimately agreed and combatants withdrew from the field. It was this meeting which eventually led to the signing of the Treaty of Wallingford and ended the Civil War, as Henry (later King Henry II) was accepted as Stephen's heir.

King John added further to the castle, and Richard, 1st Earl of Cornwall spent substantial sums on it during the 13th century. Prince Richard, Earl of Cornwall held the castle for much of Henry III (his brother) and spent vast sums on improvements.

Wark Castle

Located: Wark on Tyne in Northumberland.

Probably built by the Earl of Northumberland, Walter Espec with permission of King Henry I of England in 1139. A new castle replaced the original in 1165.

Sometimes referred to as the castle of 'Carham'. The site originally featured an unusual six sided construction, with a keep which was five storeys high in places, "in each of which there were five great murder holes, shot with great vaults of stone except one stage which is of timber, so that great bombards can be shot from each of them" (1517).

A curtain wall encircling this keep curved around and down to connect with the bailey courtyard walls. This barrier itself was divided into two distinct sections to permit defenders of the garrison to progressively retreat if the gatehouse was to eventually be taken during a siege. The gatehouse opened near the river Tweed—as the river was fordable at that point and, for additional defence, a great trench extended from the river up past the gatehouse.

By all accounts, the castle was a relatively unimpressive building with regard to aesthetics but it was an extremely functional castle: given its location on the border and being under constant threat from the Scots. Though considered by many historians as a minor castle when compared to the much more substantial Norham Castle, Wark Castle still had a strong influence on the overall defence of the border with Scotland.

Wark Castle had been attacked by King David I of Scots on three separate occasions in during 1126, being taken and controlled by the Scots for a brief period. It was then besieged again, unsuccessfully, in 1138 while the Scottish descended from the north and quite nearly destroyed most of Northumberland. It was again besieged in 1139, when the English used it as a central command centre for retaliatory attacks into Scotland. Ultimately, the English soldiers garrisoned in Wark consented to offer their surrender.

With a turbulent history, Wark Castle was rebuilt again by King Henry II in 1157, but had been destroyed yet again in 1216.

All that currently remains is a rather large mound of earth; a farm now occupying the original site.

W. B. BAKER

Warwick Castle

Located: Warwick, county town of Warwickshire.

Sitting on a cliff overlooking a curve in the River Avon, Warwick Castle was built by William the Conqueror in 1068. The river, which runs below the castle on the east side, has eroded the rock the castle stands upon, forming a cliff; which provided natural defences.

Its strategic location made it vital to the safeguard of the Midlands against threats of rebellion and from 1088 the castle traditionally was held by the Earl of Warwick and served as an icon of his authority. Henry de Beaumont was proclaimed the first Earl of Warwick only months after the Battle of Hastings and founded the Church of All Saints on the castle grounds.

Since construction in the 11th century, the castle has undergone many obvious structural changes; most noteworthy being the addition of residential buildings and formidable towers. Though originally raised as a wooden motte-and-bailey stronghold, it was rebuilt in stone during the 12th century and the façade was refortified during the Hundred Years War.

Taken by Henry of Anjou in 1153 and later by Henry II, King of England, the structure was rebuilt during the reign of Henry II and featured a new layout with the buildings against the curtain walls. The castle is surrounded by a dry moat on the northern side where there is no protection from the river or the old motte. There was originally a drawbridge over the moat in the north east and in the centre of the north west wall is a gateway with Clarence and Bears towers on either side; this is a 15th century addition to the fortifications of the castle. The residential buildings line the eastern side of the castle, facing the River Avon and include the great hall, the library, bedrooms, and the chapel.

Throughout the barons' rebellion of 1173-74, the Earl of Warwick continued to remain loyal to King Henry II, and the castle and all lands associated with the earldom were passed down to subsequent heir of the Beaumont family until 1242

With regard to its cost of construction and status, Warwick has often been compared with Windsor Castle.

Windsor Castle

Located: Atop a 100 foot cliff overlooking the River Thames in Windsor, Berkshire, England.

Windsor Castle is the largest inhabited castle in the world and the oldest in continuous occupation. The enormous castle was begun by William the Conqueror and added to by just about every Monarch since over the centuries, most notably by Edward III in 1349. Edward's efforts made Windsor Castle the single largest crown building project of the entire Middle Ages.

While Henry I replaced the wooden structure with a shell keep of stone, using stone quarried at Totternhoe in Bedfordshire, Henry II rebuilt the defences and added a second bailey in 1175. Henry III contributed some minor building but the next major builder was Edward III. Later monarchs added to the complex of buildings now recognised as Windsor castle. Henry VIII built the great entry gate which continues to bear his name and the last major building took place under George IV; when the tower was raised—to make it the highest of any castle tower throughout England. From that time, Windsor has stood as one of the principle residences of the British monarch.

The castle withstood two sieges during the early medieval period. When Prince John attempted to take the throne in 1194 when his brother Richard I was out of the country, nobles who remained loyal to the king tried and failed to wrest control of the Windsor away from John. Later, when John was legitimately made king, Windsor was unsuccessfully besieged again by the nobles—as part of the hostilities which ultimately culminated in the signing of the Magna Carta.

Of particular mention is St. George's Chapel, perhaps the most beautiful example of medieval church architecture throughout the whole of England. Official home of the Order of the Garter, St George's Chapel was begun in 1475 by Edward IV, and only finished 50 years later. Within its chambers are the tombs of 10 monarchs, including Edward IV, Charles I, George V and Queen Mary, George VI, Henry VIII, and his favourite wife, Jane Seymour.

Immediately behind St George's Chapel is the entrance to the Albert Memorial, constructed by Queen Victoria in memory of her husband and consort, Prince Albert: though Albert himself is actually buried in the Frogmore Mausoleum within the grounds of Windsor Great Park.

* * * * *

Selected Bibliography And Contributors

There are quite literally thousands of excellent reference volumes available for further research; though, sadly, many of the contemporary editions merely echo previously established information. After three years of research and wading through copious articles, volumes, and opinions, the author would like to recommend the following research materials.

This assortment represents an eclectic illustration of publications and articles that are currently available throughout the United Kingdom and are presented here in alphabetical order.

Agrarian History of England and Wales, The; E. J. T. Collins, Joan Thirsk, Stuart Piggott, H.P.R Finberg, H. E. Hallam, G. E. Mingay, Edward Miller; CUP Archive; 2000.

Bosworth Field and the Wars of the Roses; Rowse, A.L. Wordsworth Military Library; 1966.

Brut y Tywysogion; Jones, Thomas; Caerdydd; 1953.

Brut y Tywysogyon : Peniarth MS 20; Jones, Thomas (ed.). Caerdydd: Gwasg Prifysgol Cymru; 1941.

Brut y Tywysogyon : The Chronicle of the Princes: Red Book of Hergest version; Jones, Thomas (ed.); Cardiff; 1955.

Buildings of Wales: Monmouthshire, The; Newman, J; Penguin Publishing; 2000.

Burke's Peerage "A Genealogical History of the Dormant, Abeyant, Forfeited and Extinct Peerages of the British Empire"; Burke, Bernard (Sir); 1883.

Continuation of Brut y Tywysogion in Peniarth 20' in T. Jones & E. B. Fryde (eds), Essays and Poems, The; G. & T. M. Charles Edwards; Aberystwyth; 1994.

Dark and Dastardly Dartmoor; Barber, Sally and Barber, Chips; Obelisk Publications; 1988.

Early Glamorgan: Glamorgan County History [vol 2]; edited by Hubert N. Savory; 1984.

End of the House of Lancaster, The; Storey, Robin; Sutton Publishing; 1986.

Fairy Faith in Celtic Countries, The; Evans-Wentz; Citadel Press; 1966.

Folklore of Cornwall; Deane, Tony and Shaw, Tony; Tempus Publishing; 2003.

Folklore of Guernsey; de Garis, Marie; The Guernsey Press; 1986.

'Forest of Dean: Bounds of the forest', A History of the County of Gloucester: Volume 5; Bledisloe Hundred, St. Briavels Hundred, The Forest of Dean; 1996.

From Wakefield to Towton; Haigh, Philip; Pen and Sword Books; 2002.

Glamorgan and Gwent: A Guide to Ancient and Historic Cymru; Whittle, Elizabeth; 1992.

Gwent County History—Volume 2: The Age of the Marcher Lords, c. 1070-1536; Griffiths, R. A., Hopkins, T. and Howell, R.; University of Wales Press; Cardiff; 2008.

Haunted London; Clark, James; Tempus Publishing; 2007.

Haunted Places of Bedfordshire & Buckinghamshire; Matthews, Rupert; Countryside Books; 2004.

Haunted Places of Surrey; Janaway, John; Countryside Books; 2005.

Haunted Winchester; Feldwick, Matthew; Tempus Publishing; 2007.

Historical Tour of Monmouthshire; Coxe, William; 1801.

International Dictionary of University Histories; Devine, Mary; Routledge Publishers; 1998.

Lancashire Dictionary of Dialect, Tradition and Folklore, The; Crosby, Alan; Smith Settle; 2000.

Lancashire Magic & Mystery; Fields, Kenneth; Sigma Leisure; 1998.

Lore of the Land: A Guide to England's Legends, The; Westwood, Jennifer and Simpson, Jacqueline; Penguin Publishing; 2005.

Magna Charta Sureties 1215 (additions by Walter Lee Sheppard Jr,) 5th Edition; Weis, Frederick Lewis; Genealogical Publishing Co., Inc.; 1955.

Mystery Animals of Britain and Ireland; McEwan, Graham J.; Robert Hale Ltd; 1986.

Mythology of Dogs: Canine Legend, The; Hausmen, Gerald and Loretta; St. Martin's Press; 1997.

Oxford Companion to British History, The; "Eton College." Cannon, John; Oxford University Press; 2002.

Oxford Dictionary of English Folklore; Simpson, Jacqueline and Roud, Steve; Oxford University Press; 2003.

Phantom Black Dogs; Trubshaw, Robert Nigel (ed); Heart of Albion Press; 2005.

Phenomena: a book of wonders; Michell, John F. and Rickard, Robert J. M.; Thames Hudson Ltd; 1977.

Queens, Bones and Bastards; Hilliam, David; Sutton Publishing; 2000.

Surrey Ghosts Old and New; Stewart, Frances D.; AMCD; 1990.

The Mabinogion; Gantz, Jeffrey (trans); Penguin Classics; 1976.

The Middle Ages: Glamorgan County History [vol 3]; edited by T. B. Pugh; 1971.

Wars of the Roses, The; Goodman, Anthony; Routledge & Kegan; 1990.

Welsh Chronicles, The; Lloyd, J. E.; Humphrey Milford; London; 1928.

Welsh Ghostly Encounters, Gwasg Carreg Gwalch; Pugh, Jane; 1990.

Y Bibyl Ynghymraec, sef cyfieithiad Cymraeg Canol o'r 'Promptuarium Bibliae.' Jones, Thomas (ed.); Caerdydd; 1940.